ANTE UP!

Chautona Havig

ISBN: 1534766111

ISBN 13: 978-1534766112

Chautona Havig lives in a small, remote town in California's Mojave Desert with her husband and eight of her nine children. When not writing, she enjoys paper crafting, sewing, and looking forward to home education retirement

Fonts: Times New Roman, Alex Brush, Eterea Pro
Cover photos: krooogle/istockphoto, JZuch/istockphoto, digitalskillet/istockphoto
Cover Art: Chautona Havig
Edited by: Haug Editing

Connect with Me Online:
Twitter: https://twitter.com/Chautona
Facebook: https://www.facebook.com/pages/justhewriteescape
My blog: http://chautona.com/blog/
Instagram: http://instagram.com/ChautonaHavig
My newsletter (sign up for news of FREE eBook offers):
http://chautona.com/chautona/newsletter

Fiction/Christian/Contemporary

Dedication

~To Angela~

Because without your but, there'd be no colon in this story.

~To Joy~

Thank you for the reminder to enjoy each day with your children. You're right. And so is Libby. ☺

Hymns in *Ante Up!*

Chapter 1: Shall We Gather at the River?
I Will Call Upon the Lord
Are You Washed in the Blood?

Chapter 2: Softly and Tenderly Jesus is Calling

Chapter 3: Holy, Holy, Holy
It Is Well with My Soul

Chapter 4: Haven of Rest

Chapter 5: Trust and Obey

Chapter 6: Face to Face
Whiter than Snow

Chapter 7: Master the Tempest is Raging
There's a Great Day Coming
Leaning on the Everlasting Arms

Chapter 8: Abide with Me

Chapter 9: I'll Fly Away

Chapter 10: Send the Light

Chapter 11: Count Your Blessings
Tell It to Jesus

Chapter 12: Peace, Perfect Peace

Chapter 13: I Gave My Life to Thee

Cast of Characters

Aggie Sullivan: Age twenty-six: wife of Luke, aunt and now mother to the children.

Luke Sullivan: Aggie's husband and best friend.

Vannie (Vanora) Stuart: Age: sixteen

Laird Stuart: Age: fourteen and a half

Ellie (Elspeth) Stuart: Age: turns 12 in this book and twin to Tavish.

Tavish Stuart: Age: turns twelve in this book and twin to Ellie.

Kenzie (MacKenzie) Stuart: Age: nine

Lorna Stuart: Almost seven and twin to Cari.

Cari (Cairistonia) Stuart: almost seven and twin to Lorna.

Ian Stuart: Age: four—youngest of the Stuart children.

Ronnie Sullivan: Age: Almost three and Aggie and Luke's first child.

Ron (Ronald) Milliken: Aggie and Allie's father and the children's maternal grandfather.

Olivia (Libby) Sullivan: Luke's mother, a widow and a Titus 2 mentor for Aggie.

Tina Warden: Aggie's best friend.

Zeke (Ezekiel) Sullivan: Luke's uncle and mentor.

Martha Sullivan: Zeke's wife and Luke's aunt.

Mrs. Dyke: Elderly woman across the street.

William Markenson: Deputy Sheriff, dear friend, and Tina's boyfriend

Ellene Tuttle: Neighbor.

Geraldine Stuart: Mother of Douglas and paternal grandmother of the children.

Douglas Stuart Sr.: Husband of Geraldine and paternal grandfather of the children.

Chad and Willow Tesdall: Luke's cousin and his wife—"Aunt and Uncle" to the children. They live on a farm fifteen miles away. The events immediately preceding this book take place in their series, *Past Forward,* in volume six.

Christopher and Marianne Tesdall: Luke's aunt and uncle. Marianne is Olivia's sister.

In Previous Books...

It's been a while since Aggie and clan graced the pages of one of my books, so I thought I'd add a little recap.

Ready or Not: Aggie Milliken, twenty-two and fresh out of college, inherits her sister's eight children after a freak blood mix up at the hospital following a car accident. With no real experience with children, and a grandmother-in-law who acts determined to ruin hers and the children's lives, Aggie moves the family out of their Rockland home to a fixer-upper in the small town of Brant's Corners sixty miles away.

Grieving children, inexperience, and a house under constant renovation combine with Murphy's Law to ensure that Aggie feels like a failure at every turn. Her parents live two hours away, and a heart condition keeps her mother from being much help.

New friends in Brant's Corners become Aggie's lifeline, along with her p-mail (prayers), hymns, and late-night chats on messenger with her best friend, Tina.

Summer winds down, the house is finished, and she's figured out that local deputy William Markenson makes a great friend and ally, but a horrible date. In fact, dating is the last thing she ever wants to think about again. Meanwhile, Luke Sullivan, her ever-present handyman, and his mother Libby, help keep her sane as decision after decision pummel her.

The book ends with her family settled, William's strange behavior regarding the house explained, and a housewarming party that warms her heart as well.

For Keeps: Chicken pox derails back to school plans and the grandmother-in-law has ramped up her efforts to gain custody of the children. Aggie decides that homeschooling might just solve her educational problems (because it's easier to teach eight kids yourself than to send them off for most of the day, right?) In the midst of all of this, she informs William that she's not interested in pursuing a relationship just as Luke finally admits his feelings for her. They begin a "purposeful friendship" that he hopes will end in more.

William, instead, begins a tentative relationship with Tina that shows promise.

Her world is turned a bit upside down once more as Aggie learns she doesn't *have* to keep the children after all. Her sister, along with all the financial provisions one could hope for, also arranged for an "out" — in case the burden was too much. Aggie has to decide if she'll keep her life as it is or return to the one she'd originally planned. Of course, she is too invested in her little family to give them up now.

Here We Come: Aggie and Luke become engaged and the whole family is awash in wedding plans, interrupted schooling, and Christmas! Then one of the children goes missing, and it looks like the grandmother is responsible. New lessons in faith and trust pummel Aggie and Luke as they fight to find their child and wind down to the wedding. Their honeymoon is the first break Aggie has had in over a year, and I suspect she needed it. I know I would have!

Past Forward Volume 6: Luke's cousin lives on Walden Farm with his wife Willow, twin sons (almost 2) and infant daughter. When Aggie and clan return home from a visit to her parents' in early November, nearly four years after their marriage, they find doors open, pipes burst, and a house that reeks of animals and mess. So, all eight of the nieces and nephews, Luke, pregnant

Aggie, and their nearly three-year-old son, move in with Chad and Willow while Luke works night and day to repair damage that, at first, appeared to be just a door that didn't get shut on the way out of town. Further investigation shows that vandals are the culprits, and the oldest girl blames herself. While at the farm, another of the children, Tavish, in a desperate need for quiet, climbs a tree overlooking a thin, ice-covered pond, to read a book. He falls in and has to walk back in frigid temperatures while soaked. Hypothermia sets in and he barely escapes pneumonia, but his health has been compromised. The family returns to their repaired home that, while not the beautiful place it was, is functional now, and the family is eager to be *home!*

There you have it. I hope these memory triggers help as you take on *Ante Up!* It's almost four years later (from the end of *Here We Come,* anyway) and a lot has happened!

Shall We Gather in the Kitchen?

Chapter One

Monday, November 24th

Through the now bare branches of the great oaks that filled the front yard, the house stood stalwart, resolute, but welcoming as the vehicular monstrosity otherwise known as a fifteen passenger van pulled into the semi-circular drive. The moment the gear shift rested in park, doors opened and a motley assortment of legs and feet—bodies attached but lagging—tumbled from the van and screeches of delight filled the air. Aggie Sullivan turned toward her husband and eyed him with wry amusement. "There goes the neighborhood."

Luke's crinkled eyes showed his smile before his lips caught up to him. "You know it's been much too boring around here. The neighbors will probably threaten to lock us in skunk-infested, flooded basements if we don't promise never to leave again."

"*Previously* skunk-infested, flooded basements. You assured me that everything is back to normal-ish!" A glance around her prompted a sigh of contentment. "It's been almost a *month.*" Even as she spoke, Aggie grabbed her purse and pushed open the van door.

Though Luke raced around the front of the vehicle to help her, Aggie had the door shut before he could reach her side. "I would—"

13

"Have helped. I know." Aggie slid one hand up his chest and hooked it around his neck. "That's why I love you #2394."

With a wink and a smile, Aggie turned and waddled up the front steps. She made it inside and halfway through the living room before it occurred to her that something was amiss. A quick glance around her showed a perfectly clean living room—one with new throw pillows and a couple of smaller things missing, but she'd expected that. *If vandals had to destroy furniture, did it have to be one of my favorite pieces? Couldn't they have thought I liked the chair by the front door?*

A glance around showed Tavish gone. *He needs to go rest. And take another antibiotic.* Her eyes rose to heaven. *Is it wrong to forbid your nephew from reading in trees in winter? Or maybe, just forbid him from reading in trees overhanging ponds?*

She opened her mouth to call him downstairs when her eyes widened and voice strangled.

"Mibs? Wha—"

"That's it! That's what's wrong!" She whirled—much like a Weeble toy—to face him. "Do you hear it?"

With the infinite patience that characterized the man who had spent the past two weeks cleaning and repairing the mess left by unknown kids while they visited family up north, Luke listened and shook his head. "Sorry, I don't hear anything."

"And that doesn't bother you?"

He didn't hesitate—didn't stop moving. In a wide arc, he jogged back through the living room and upstairs. Aggie, on the other hand, put out visions of shell-shocked children who saw the loss that came with their recent vandalism issues, not to mention the drama that would follow, and forced her aching hips to carry her into the kitchen for a glass of water. *First water, then we get back on track. We've lost a month! First the trip to Mom and Dad's, and then two weeks while he fixed this mess. Thanksgiving is almost here, Christmas will follow, then the baby. I don't have time to "dilly-dally" around, as Libby would say.*

Tears formed as she rounded the corner and stared at what had been her dream kitchen. The custom cabinets, formed to look like various pieces of furniture tied together with a counter top, now sported a spray painted message, complete with dripping letters. The words—not repeatable.

14

In a move so automatic that she almost didn't realize she'd done it, Aggie pulled her cellphone and the family cell from her purse and set them on the charging docs inside one of the cabinet doors. *I thought he fixed everything.* Her eyes took in the words once more. *Obviously not.* She opened the door and remembered the soaked and destroyed food he'd had to toss. The door shut with more force than she'd intended. *Still, he could —*

"Um, Mibs — ?"

She didn't even turn to face him. "Why didn't you tell me?" In the unfamiliar silence that shrouded the Sullivan-Stuart home, Aggie received the answer she wanted to hear least. All it took was Luke making a single swipe on the paint and seeing a hint of white across his finger to realize what he hadn't said. She swallowed the lump forming in her throat before stating the obvious. "This is fresh. And that's why everyone's quiet. There's more."

"I called William."

"How bad is it?" The words formed and and she spoke them before she could stop herself. "Wait. Just tell me if we have to leave again."

His arms stole around her waist as he pulled her close. "Nope. It's not that bad. Mostly Vannie's room, a scratch in the stairwell, and this."

"Vannie — why *her?*" she turned in his arms and *attempted* to rest her head on his chest, but the "baby bump" that had turned into Half Dome made it awkward and a little uncomfortable. "Side hug. How did I forget that?"

With a quick kiss, Luke pulled away and began removing the doors from the cabinets. "Gotta get these down before the kids come down."

"Is it better to try to get that off while it's still kind of wet?"

Aggie watched as Luke pulled every other door down as quickly as he could. She opened her mouth to ask why, when the reason showed itself in an illegible message. "Smart thinking. I'll go get, what, paint remover?"

"Thinner… and a putty knife. Gloves." She hadn't made it to the doorway before he added. "Maybe a couple balls of steel wool."

The state of the basement took hurt and disappointment and

morphed them into white-hot fury. "You nasty little—" Aggie bit back words that fell a little close to the nasty line themselves. "Hooligans! This was where my children *played*, dreamed, *lived* in the winter months. Now what are they supposed to do? How can anyone be so cruel?"

With every turn, something else assaulted her heart. Swings—gone. Area rugs—gone. Flooring—ruined. Boxes stored—gone. "I don't even want to think about what was in those. Lord, *please* let me have finished putting the keepsakes in totes."

The locked cupboard—new lock on it—looked definitely worse for wear. She turned to go ask for the key and found Vannie on the stairs. "Aunt Aggie?"

"Yeah?"

"I'm sorry. This is my fault—I know it. I shouldn't have gotten mad about a couple of punks making fun of me. I'm supposed to be the one who's almost an adult."

She could have said many things, but the misery in the girl's voice and eyes told her it wasn't the time for lectures. "Vannie, I don't care what you said or did. These kids knew what they did was wrong. *They* made the choice to break the law. You didn't *make* them do this."

"But I was wrong, too."

Well, if you want to talk about it now, so be it. Aggie asked her to go get the new key to the lock and kneaded the small of her back with her fists as she waited for Vannie to return. Not until she had the key in hand did she decide how to handle the situation. With her back turned and as she fiddled with the lock overhead, Aggie tried to explain. "Look, you were wrong. But you aren't responsible for their actions. It's like when a man walks through Rockland's Crypt at midnight wearing gold chains and a Rolex. He did *not* make anyone mug him. Those people are responsible for *their* actions. He's only responsible for ignoring good sense and putting himself in a bad situation."

"But he shouldn't have to avoid—"

"No he shouldn't, but because he knows it isn't safe, he's responsible for *his* stupidity. He's just not responsible for the others' illegal actions. Do you see the correlation?" Aggie pulled paint thinner from the cupboard and locked it again. "Where's the

putty knife?"

As they talked, Vannie rummaged for the rest of the necessary items without even asking why they were already beginning repairs. *I hope this doesn't mean she thinks they're for stuff upstairs. Ugh.*

"Let's get this back up to Luke. Then you can show me what they did upstairs."

"We can't do anything yet. Mr. Markenson is here taking pictures for his report." Vannie sighed. "At least there wasn't much *to* do in there. They just sliced my duvet and wrote on the walls."

"Well, that's something anyway. They sure got the kitchen, though.

Vannie apologized again—and again. "He's going to go talk to the kids' parents. We can't prove they did it. We *need* to do that, but I don't know how!"

Something in Vannie's tone raised alarm bells in Aggie's heart, but she couldn't decide why before Luke's voice called down to them. "Mibs, William needs to speak to you."

Halfway up the stairs, Vannie asked, "Do you think he'll still call you 'Mibs' when you are so old you've lost *all* of your marbles?"

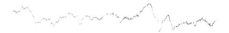

From the corner of the kitchen, almost out of sight, Vannie listened as Aggie described walking into the room and seeing her cupboards defaced. "If you want to know what it said, you'll have to have Luke arrange the doors for you—nasty, nasty."

It might not be my fault they did it, but they wouldn't have if I had kept my mouth shut. William's voice pulled her out of her thoughts, but the sinking feeling in her heart didn't leave as easily.

"Well, we still haven't proven it's them, but it does look like it. You're the only vandalism call in three months, and the one before that was Mr. Kopinski complaining that hooligans were assaulting him and his property with rocks."

Luke guessed first and correctly—the former a surprise, the latter not so much. "Marilyn Ferguson's boys playing golf again?"

"Yep. It sounds like it *has* to be Vannie's little punks, but that's easier said than proven." William gave her a reassuring smile. "We'll make a report, but I don't think we need a full crime scene sweep. We have enough on the other one to nail them if we find any proof. But we need more than, 'I want your kid's fingerprints because I think they vandalized a house,' before I can expect parents to cooperate. If it were *my* kid, I'd say no, even if I knew there was zero doubt that my kid did it."

Vannie slipped around behind the kitchen and through the back of the house to the stairs. As much as she didn't want to look at the remnants of what had once been an oasis in the midst of chaos, she also wanted a second look before Mr. Markenson wandered through her room again. The curtains Luke had found for her on eBay had been replaced with simple sheers and a promise to help her find new ones that she liked. The walls had words spray-painted on them—words she didn't want the little ones to see. An uncovered duvet lay spread across her bed, ripped through the middle with what had to have been a pocket knife. *At least I can sew that.* Her Bible. Vannie choked at the empty spot next to her bed. *If I'd only taken it with me. I just wanted to use Mommy's old one.*

A voice in the doorway startled her. "Are you okay, Vannie? Is anything missing?"

"You mean, other than the room I left? I don't know what they did in here the first time, but it had to be bad. I don't recognize this place." She turned to the officer standing there, tears welling up in her heart, and begged him to help her understand. "Why would anyone *do* this, Mr. Markenson? So I got mad and said some things I shouldn't have. How is this fair?"

Before William Markenson could respond, a red-headed blur streaked through the door and flung her arms around William's waist. "Hi! You're here. Did you see what they did to Vannie's room? You'll find them, won't you?"

"I'll do my best," William assured her.

But Vannie recognized his tone—the one that he reserved only for Kenzie. *Does he know he does that? Does Uncle Luke?* The question felt ridiculous the moment she mentally asked it. Of course, Luke did. The man was one of the most observant people she'd ever met. She'd even learned a bit about becoming *more* observant by watching him. *I guess I really want to know if he minds.*

18

He loves us so much. It would hurt me if my niece loved a cop more than me.

"Vannie?"

She jerked from her reverie and tried not to look vacant as she met William's gaze. "Hmm?"

"I asked if you had most of your clothes with you on your trip."

In a bit of a daze, Vannie crossed to her closet, took a deep, cleansing breath, and opened the door. Her heart sank at the empty clothes hangers. With no bureau in the room, Vannie could only imagine what had happened to them. "They got them all?"

"Luke said yeah. Some of the stuff he washed and hung up while he was working got ruined this go-round. He pulled them out so you wouldn't have to see them, but if you were counting on them for the next week or three, you're out of luck."

Tears sprang to her eyes. Her best winter clothes—her dress coat—gone. "I'll have to go into Rockland. Wonder if Aunt Aggie or Uncle Luke is the best to ask on that one."

"I could talk to them for you," William began.

But Vannie shot down that idea. "If I want them to think I'm mature enough to handle the drive in the city by myself, then I should probably at least ask myself. Maybe if I take Laird with me. The whole buddy system thing. They forget we're too old—"

The expression in William's eyes cut her off. He asked Kenzie to go make him a cup of cocoa and waited until he heard her halfway down the steps before he stepped a bit closer and murmured, "I know being a cop makes me a bit more paranoid than the average dad, but it's my opinion that a buddy system in the city is good for people of all ages. Your chances of being accosted drop exponentially *just* by being with someone—anyone."

"Yeah, I suppose." She glanced back at the empty closet. "Hmm, I'll have to do something fast. I just brought the bare minimum to Grandma's so it wouldn't take up too much space in the van. There's not enough to fill a whole load, and of course, they're all dirty now. I thought I'd wash with Ellie when I got home." Vannie gave him a sheepish look. "Hanging your underwear in your uncle's hallway is kind of weird."

"I can understand that."

She wandered from the room, leaving William standing there—alone. His eyes swept the barrenness that replaced what had been a mini-retreat for Vannie, and a sigh escaped. His hand reached for his phone before he realized he'd done it. His finger swiped across the screen and tapped send before he could talk himself out of it.

VANNIE NEEDS CLOTHES AND BASIC ROOM FURNITURE. ALL SHE HAS IS A BED AND RANDOM LINENS SCAVENGED FROM THE REST OF THE HOUSE. WHAT DO I BUY HER?

Tina's reply hit his phone before he made it halfway down the stairs.

SHE'S A TEEN. GET HER A GIFT CARD. SHE'LL WANT TO PICK IT OUT HERSELF. I LOVE YOU FOR THINKING OF IT.

I love you, too. We've got to decide what to do about us *before Aggie kills me for hurting her best friend. Then again....* William swallowed hard. *It's not like I* want *to hurt you.*

Grocery shopping—instant priority. They had nothing fresh in the house, and most of her pantry had been raided. Aggie only *hoped* that the kids had taken the food and used it. She suspected worse. A glance at Luke as he worked to free her cabinet doors of graffiti nixed the idea of asking. *You know the answer—deep down, you know it. Why make him confirm what he hopes you won't discover?*

"I'm going to head in to the store. We can't even eat dinner without groceries. Who should I put on Ronnie duty?" Before Luke could even look up, Aggie shook her head. "Nope. I'll take him and Ian. Then you're free to shamelessly use the kids as slave labor."

Luke's smile answered before he could formulate a response. "I'll be sure to hang them in the dungeon by their toenails or something equally horrific."

A streak of red hair and denim flew through from the back of the kitchen. "Aunt Aggie, can I take Laird into Rockland to do some shopping? Mr. Markenson says I have *no* clothes. And he's right. There's only what I had at Aunt Willow's—all dirty, of course." In the two seconds Aggie had to try to formulate a response, Vannie added three promises. "I'll take Laird, I'll call every hour, if you like, and if the weather gets icky, we'll come right back."

"You did great until the last one, Vannie." Luke winked at Aggie before smiling at Vannie's chagrin. "The correct response to bad weather is, 'We'll drive straight to Uncle Christopher and Aunt Marianne's if the weather gets bad.'"

"Yeah! That. Or better yet, we'll call and see which you want us to do, depending on where the weather is coming from!"

Her gut said *"Not on your life."* But Luke's encouraging expression hinted that she might need to stretch her comfort zone. "Are you sure you wouldn't find anything in Brunswick?" The question drowned out the intended caveat, "If you promise to be home by dinner."

"Well, we looked a couple of months ago. I just didn't want to waste time, but I could try. Maybe there's new stuff for Christmas."

Aggie heard it—that strained tone that hinted Vannie was *trying* to be agreeable and respectful and finding it difficult. *Don't exasperate her. She's not a child anymore.* Her slow nod elicited a squeal from Vannie that did its best to puncture her eardrum. "You can go, *but*—"

"Yeah?"

Oh, the delight that comes with making your teens nervous! Aggie couldn't help but hesitate a bit longer—make the girl sweat a bit. Then the reminder of inadequate clean clothing stopped that torture before it tortured the rest of the family. "You have to keep your eye—and preferably the phone—out for cute stuff for the baby. If this *is* a girl, I want to have something delightfully feminine to put on her right away. I haven't had the baby girl thing, and man... at Willow's."

"I know, right? Definitely!" She reached inside the pantry and retrieved a cellphone. "Oh, yeah. I guess I do have to take the family cell if I'm going to call every hour."

"You don't have to call. Just zip a text or photo every now and then. That's sufficient."

Vannie squealed again—this one decidedly less painful, but just as joyous—and raced off to convince Laird that he needed to wander the Rockland malls with her. Aggie watched her retreating form for a moment and sighed. "How much you want to bet he holds out until she promises to take him to Sonic or something?"

"Not taking that bet unless losing is something I want."

Aggie stepped closer, whispered something, and turned to go. She hadn't made it to the doorway before Luke says, "I'll go all in on that one."

Thought you might.

Three carts, two boys, and one *very* pregnant woman inched their way through the supermarket. An elderly woman smiled at her as Aggie dumped eight cans of Italian diced tomatoes into her cart. The comment—inevitable. In fact, Aggie might have done a countdown from three if her eternal optimism hadn't suggested that it might not happen if she didn't provide that introduction.

"My, you have your hands full, don't you?"

"Better full than empty." The words formed and released with the precision of an expert archer. She almost winced as she heard how… *piercing* they sounded. "Even on long, hard days like today."

It worked. The woman's startled expression relaxed and morphed into a smile. "I remember those. I had four *under* four at one time. But those kids have such close relationships now. It makes those hard days worth it."

"That's what I remind myself." The memory of Laird and Vannie laughing and joking on their way to the car prompted a careless response—one she knew better than to risk on less-frazzled days. "I'm already seeing it with the older kids."

Had she been the swearing sort, Aggie had little doubt she would have resisted. The woman's eyes widened and narrowed just as quickly. "Older kids?"

To avoid eye contact, Aggie snagged half a dozen cans of *Mexican* diced tomatoes as well. "Ian has several older siblings—teens. I am surprised at how much I enjoy teens."

Ian, who had never mastered consistency in calling Aggie "Aunt," tugged at her sleeve. "Mama, can I get hominy? We could have it for breakfast."

Without another word to the woman, Aggie turned around and went in search of the request. "Of course. We haven't had that in a while. Now, what about applesauce? It's not as good as Aunt Willow's but...."

All through the store, she kept a running dialogue with both boys, determined not to give anyone else the opportunity to tempt her to share too much information in a moment of mental weakness. Both of her carts also filled much too quickly for her comfort, and Aggie knew if she didn't limit herself, she'd never get everything to the van. Ian's cart held the lighter things—toilet paper, confectioner's sugar, cereal. "Okay, boys. We'll just grab some apples and be on our way."

"But we got applesauce."

"That's right! Good enough for me!" Aggie pushed her first cart into the shortest line she could find and struggled to help Ronnie out of his seat. "You're too big for these things. Getting in is one thing, but getting out...." She frowned. "No, you just stay there until we get to the car."

A man passing heard and offered to help. Her appreciation rose and promptly fizzled the moment his helpfulness switched to flirtation. "I can't stand to see a pretty lady struggling."

Ronnie glared at him. "She's *my* pretty mommy." Ian inched his way closer.

"I can see that. Is she having a little brother or sister for you?"

Aggie relaxed a smidge. *Overreacting, much? The guy just is really friendly.*

"Whatever God gives us. I want a girl. Because she had a boy last time." Ian glanced her way. "Is that a sin?"

She almost couldn't prevent a snicker as the guy backed away with a look of abject panic in his eyes. "Well, you guys help your mama there. She needs all the help she can get."

On a roll, Ian pointed out that she had all the help she needed with the Lord. "It is my Bible verse. 'I can do all things through Christ who gives me strength.' Philippians... four...." He glanced at Aggie with a sheepish look of chagrin. "You *said* the book and chapter count most."

By the time Aggie finished reassuring her little nephew that book and chapter would always help you find verses, but the verse is important too, her would-be rescuer had disappeared. "Okay when we get up there, you can help put stuff on the belt." Aggie moved to Ronnie's side. "But you'll have to stay in the cart."

"I wanna help!"

"That's how you *can* help. By staying put."

"Can we have a candy bar — to share?" The offer of sharing, tacked on at the end of the request, hinted that Ian knew the answer before he asked it.

"Nope."

The questions began. Was it because candy was bad for their teeth? Because they'd become hyper? Because the other kids didn't get any? Because she didn't want a mess? By the time they reached the conveyor belt, Aggie had answered every one she'd intended to and a dozen more for good measure.

"Then why?"

"Sometimes," Aggie said as she transferred her groceries from the cart, "the answer is no because that is sufficient. You don't always get a reason. Sometimes you just have to accept that no is no."

The woman behind the register scowled at Aggie and voiced her unrequested opinion. "Children don't learn to understand their world if we don't explain why. I thought he gave you excellent reasons."

"He did." Patience — she begged for it, pleaded for it. Not a drop surfaced. "However, none of those were the reason. This time the reason was simply because I said no." She smiled down at Ian before sliding her favorite flavored coffee creamer on the belt beside the jar of peanut butter Ian had plunked down. She turned back to the woman and forced herself to ask, "Having a nice day?"

"You'll learn, when you have a few more years of parenting under your belt, that children need better answers than, 'Because I said so.' When they get to be teens — "

"They usually get the answer, yes. But that's because my teens have already learned that once in a while I won't tell them why and they need to accept that." Aggie took a slow, cleansing breath and asked again, "Are you having a nice day? Sure is busy

24

in here. Wish I didn't have to shop the week of Thanksgiving, but with no food in the house—kind of imperative, you know?"

On she rambled, never giving the woman a chance to answer the question she'd put forth. She saved Ronnie from two nose dives, fumbled for her debit card and finally grabbed a credit card. "Ian, can you remind me to ask Luke where my debit card is?"

"You gave it to Vannie—for the store, remember?" Ian did the knock-kneed shuffle as he whispered in tones only loud enough for *half* the store. "I need to *goooo*."

"Oh, brother. I should have known better. Okay." She kneaded her back and swiped her card. "You have to hold it until we get these carts out of the line."

"I can go by myself. The boys bathroom is right in there. *Please*…."

Oh, how she hated age four—just on the edge of too old for the ladies room but not as well. "You go in, count how many people are in there, and come tell me."

Ian dashed off, and Ronnie begged to go, too. "I gotta—"

"You can wait." *If for no other reason than I had the forethought to put a pull-up on you!*

"But!"

"Do not argue with me, young man. You *will* wait until the groceries are in the carts again. Now *sit down!*" Her heart screamed the words at the top of her lungs, her voice managed only to whisper them at decibels close to Ian's "whispers."

Ian dashed to her side and declared the restrooms empty. "I even looked under—but not all the way. That's gross."

"Go ahead." *And please make it!*

The checker tore the receipt from the printer and passed it to Aggie, along with a dozen or two coupons that would do little more than add to the guilt of a woman who couldn't manage to remember she *possessed* them, much less remembered to take them on her shopping trips. As she wrestled the carts to the other side of the exit aisle, Aggie tallied up the money she'd throw away when she tossed the coupons. "Six dollars. Better than most." She reached for Ronnie. "C'mon, little man. Let's do this thing."

But before she could lead her son through the door clearly marked "Women," Aggie turned back and stood outside the men's room door. "There wasn't anyone in there when he went in, and no one has gone in since. So...." She counted to ten. Twenty. Thirty. A glance around her showed no men making a beeline for the door. Aggie cracked it open a little and called out for Ian. "Are you done?"

A man's voice answered her. "Um, if you're here to clean, can you give me a minute?"

Ian screamed. The voice shouted. Pants half hanging around his knees, Ian rushed for the door, leaving a trail of urine in his wake. Aggie groaned. "Sorry, sir. My son thought this restroom was empty."

"I looked! I did! Even under the stalls!"

Without another thought to the words the man spoke, Aggie blocked the view from curious onlookers and pulled Ian's pants up for him. She hustled both boys into the ladies' room and demanded they go. "All the way. Both of you. Then we have to find a mop or something for Ian to clean up his mess — preferably *before* that man gets out of there and slips on it."

"Sorry. I just got scared when this voice —"

"I know, I know." And in that moment, what had been mortifying, horrifying, and an assault to her comfort zone exploded from her in a fit of giggles. "Oh, wait'll Luke hears about *this*."

Vannie's latest text — the fourth in as many hours — assured her they were on their way home. I HOPE YOU LIKE WHAT I GOT. THERE WASN'T MUCH I LIKED.

That either means you bought stuff you know I won't *like, or you bought stuff you* don't *like. Ugh.*

Two boys, four hands, six pumps of soap, a mile of paper toweling, and a blast of hot air from a hand dryer later, Aggie finally made her way to her carts and stopped a passing bagger. "I need a mop. My son made a bit of a mess in the men's room."

"I'll get one of the guys to do it."

"But —"

Despite her protest, the girl shook her head. "It's an insurance thing. We can't let you do it. But thanks for offering — even just for telling us. You wouldn't believe how many people don't."

"Well, then can I get your help? I can't get all this out there

26

by myself."

"Sure!"

Twenty-minutes. It took a full twenty-minutes to unload all three carts, return them to the corral, and climb up into a van that every day felt more like a mountain to scale and less like a vehicle. Once seated, she sagged against the steering wheel and fought the urge to fall asleep. A kick to the back of her seat, and the squeeze of her uterus jerked her out of semi-somnolence.

"Okay! Who wants fries for on the way home?" As she spoke, Aggie started the van and inched forward into the parking row ahead of her. *Never back out with a van the size of some apartments when you can pull forward, I always say.*

With the kind of exuberance that produced enough noise for half her kids, Ian and Ronnie squealed their agreement. "This is why the lady is wrong!" In the rear view mirror, Ian sat with arms folded over his chest. "Because you like to do nice things when we listen and don't argue."

"And most of the time, I just like to do nice things because you're nice little people." Of course, by the time Aggie sat in a line behind six other cars, the genius idea of French fries fizzled. She shoved the van into park and crossed her ankles. Her uterus protested. The boys sang devotional songs at the tops of their lungs.

Even still, all would have been well—or so she liked to think—but Ronnie belted out a line from "I Will Call upon the Lord," and all hope for bladder containment dissolved. "So shall I be saved from anemones!"

"Note to self," Aggie muttered under her breath as she jerked the car into gear again and inched forward to pay for fries that she no longer wanted to purchase. "No more *Finding Nemo* for the boys. Anemones. Seriously."

The moment she pulled into the drive, her bladder kicked into overdrive and demanded relief—preferably ten minutes earlier. Aggie climbed down and willed it to hold for another hundred feet. Like a recalcitrant toddler, it refused.

Vannie and Laird pulled up behind the van and parked. They bolted from the car and rushed to help. Had she not been looking straight at them, ready to insist they get the boys inside for her, she would have missed a silent order for Laird to keep his opinion to himself. *I recognize that anywhere. She bought "iffy" clothes. Great.*

At the door, Luke met her with jacket in hand and a smile. "That took a while. Sorry."

"Me, too. Gotta get in and change. My bladder is no longer lined with iron, and your *son* is going to be saved from anemones. He's got some pretty fishy theology." With that, Aggie took both flights of stairs up to her bedroom—kicking every part of her *except* her bladder for not making a pit-stop on the way. Her uterus protested again—why, she couldn't even imagine. "On principle, I suppose."

A voice outside the door—Vannie's. "Um... what?"

"Sorry. I just brought up what I bought for you to give your okay on. But there's one little problem."

Her uterus squeezed, and the baby kicked in protest. *I'm with you, little one. No more squeezing today. I'm too tired.* She washed her hands and opened the door with more than a little trepidation. "And that is?"

"I can't take it back. But we can use it for something else if you want."

"You bought clothes—" Aggie swallowed rising irritation and gripped her midsection as it protested with her. "That you can't *return?!*" *Well, you did okay until the last word. Not terrible.*

Vannie pulled several piles of fabric from the bag. "I bought fabric." Her eyes filled with frustrated tears as she burst into a ramble of explanations that included words like immodest, expensive, and boring. "I swear, Aunt Aggie. Laird will back me up. There was nothing decent that wasn't too blah even for an Amish girl in WITSEC."

"Then your plan is to wear... saris?" Aggie stared at the fabrics, hoping they didn't mean what she suspected they did.

"I thought I'd spend the next week making new clothes—like Alexa's."

Her objection deflated with those last two words. "You want retro clothes? Historical? Like the long dresses—"

"Not those. Just the twenties through the early sixties. We talked about it at church last week." Stars filled Vannie's eyes as she recalled the conversation. "Can you believe I stood around church and discussed *fashion* with *the* Alexa Hartfield?! It was so

cool. But she said those were the eras I seemed to like best. She said probably mid-forties to late fifties, so I bought patterns."

Her hands dug into one of the bags and pulled out a stack of patterns. "I thought these...." Without looking to see if Aggie reached for them, Vannie shoved the patterns into Aggie's arms and dug through a bag from Nordstrom. "I bought four sweaters to wear with skirts and four uniform tops."

Vannie pulled a luscious crepe from another bag and spread it out on the bed. "I thought for Christmas and church — something from the twenties?"

The idea made Aggie want to crawl into bed and not come out again for the final eight weeks of pregnancy. *You have school work to do. We're so behind! And the mess!* To hide her facial features, Aggie turned to her bureau and retrieved clean underwear, a fresh bra, and a t-shirt. Her favorite jersey skirt was still in her suitcase, but she extricated it with some finagling. As she inched her way toward the bathroom, Aggie tried to make her words sound positive, encouraging, *not* dismayed. "As long as you can work quickly enough to stay clean and not let it interfere too much with your other responsibilities."

"Really? I was afraid I'd blown my savings on something I'd have to give to Miss Hartfield — Ms. Freidan — what *do* we call her?"

"I think she prefers Alexa." Aggie winced as she said it. *Allie, forgive me. But it's just as rude to demand a kid use "miss" or "missus" when someone doesn't like it, as it is to use a first name without being asked.*

"Now," Aggie said with a wave of her clean clothes. "I have damp underwear, thanks to your cousin. Go ask him to sing 'I Will Call upon the Lord' for you."

Aggie's eyes took in her shower as the bathroom door closed behind her. *It's a total waste, but....* A softly sung hymn breathed through trembling lips as Aggie divested herself of her clothing and turned on the hot water. By the time she stepped into the steaming spray, her voice had grown strong, loud, confident. *"...are you washed...?"*

Loudly and Ornerily
Children are Squalling

Chapter Two

Tuesday, November 25th

The book snapped shut with a finality that should have meant the end of the story, but for Vannie, it signified only the end of the day's reading. A small part of her ached to read "just one more chapter," but pins, scissors, pattern paper, and fabric called her name from the library. She left it on the bed, grateful it hadn't been destroyed with the rest of the books in her room, and grabbed a cardigan on her way out again.

As she passed Laird and Tavish's room, she smiled at Laird's usual study stance — seated at his desk, head in his hands, eyes not six inches from the book, as if that would somehow imprint the information into his brain. "Maybe if you got glasses…."

Worked every time. The mere mention of glasses sent him upright and reaching for a pencil. "Just resting my eyes."

That's what Daddy used to say when he dozed in the chair. A familiar ache squeezed her throat, but tears that once would have filled her eyes stayed hidden. They waited now — waited for things she couldn't predict. The way a man on the street walked, a florist's bouquet in a movie, the way Aggie held a baby with her cheek pressed against its head. *Just like Mommy.*

Those thoughts filled her mind as she rushed down the stairs and into the library. All eagerness for her project fizzled at the sight of yards of fabric strung up all over the room into tents — impressive ones for such little guys, if she were willing to admit it. "What are you *doing?*!"

Ian's head popped out from beneath a dark, mossy green length of jersey. "We made a tent city — like the book! Isn't it cool?"

"It's a nightmare! This is my *wardrobe* you're messing with." At the sight of one corner knotted around the tops of a chair, Vannie lost what little self-control she'd managed to display. "That's it. Get out here, both of you!"

Ian scrambled out, looking around the room with a mixture of fear and pride. "We should have asked."

"You think?! Ron*nie*. Get. Out. Of. There!"

A ripple wafted through the turquoise she'd purchased for a "Jackie-O" suit. "But I don't *want* to. I'm having fun. Go 'way, Vannie. You're mean!"

"I'll drag you out, young man. You are not going to destroy my clothes before I have a chance to wear them. Now get *out!*"

With one hand hooked under her belly — did mothers honestly think it would keep babies in place? — Aggie appeared. "What's going on? I can hear you across the house!"

"Look what they did to my fabric!"

She would have sworn that her aunt gripped her belly harder, but Aggie acted normal enough. "She's right, boys. You had no business using her fabric like this without permission. When you asked to make a tent, you said *nothing* about that."

Why did you say they could if you knew I was going to be — ?

"And, frankly, I should have told you to do it in the guest room, anyway. She's going to be sewing in here for days. Just help her fold up this mess and then go play somewhere else." Aggie sank into a chair and propped herself up with hands on her knees. "Sorry, Vannie. I think I get more absentminded every day."

"That's fine. Can I just clean it up for them? It's more work — " Even before she finished, Vannie knew the answer. She grabbed one end of the turquoise, untied a corner, and shook it. "C'mon, Ronnie. Get the other end."

Only Aggie's continued presence kept Vannie from snapping as harshly and loudly as temptation dictated. The boys, in their

31

exuberance, kept jerking the fabric from her hands until even Aggie scolded and sent them from the room. "Well, it seemed like a good idea. Sorry." A sharp intake of breath followed by a wince — Aggie stood and shuffled from the room.

"Aunt Aggie?" It took every bit of selflessness she could muster, but Vannie waited until her aunt's eyes met hers and added, "Why don't you go lie down for a bit? I'll get lunch and work on this while the boys are resting."

"Thanks, but I've got it." At the library door, Aggie turned back. "You've always been a treasure, Vannie, but I have to say, lately, I don't know what I would have done without you."

Her heart swelled with gratitude and pride. *Appreciation makes sacrifice hurt less.* Modesty, regardless of how unnatural it felt, required she return the compliment. "You give so much to and for us. I couldn't hope to be as self-sacrificing as you are. But it means a lot that you said it." And then something wonderful happened. As the words left her lips, Vannie felt genuine appreciation in her heart. *I wonder if that's that thing Uncle Luke is always talking about. "Doing the right thing, even when you don't feel like it, develops the habit of right doing. When your heart is in tune with the Lord's Word, doing the wrong thing becomes painful, and those right habits help with that. It's a beautiful catch-22."*

"Vannie?"

"Hmm...?"

Aggie stepped a bit closer, her eyes searching the girl's face. "Are you okay? I asked if you needed help with anything."

The idea of Aggie hovering, wanting to read every inch of a pattern before cutting the first piece, rereading again before cutting the fabric — the pain was almost physical. "I've got it, Aunt Aggie. Just call me if you need me. I'm going to start with a simple circle skirt. It'll be perfect for church tomorrow night."

With wide eyes, Aggie waddled from the room, calling for all wayward laundry to be sent down the chutes pronto. Vannie stared at the wads of fabric and sighed as she turned to go. She met Aggie in the mud room and leaned in, hanging onto the doorjambs as she spoke. "Um, can I send mine down? I don't have enough of anything for a small load." A new thought hit her before Aggie could answer. "I should have bought underwear yesterday. I wasn't thinking!"

"Go get your clothes, and then order what you need. By the time we got into town and out again, expedited shipping would be worth every penny. Just grab my card from my purse and go for it."

"I can—"

Aggie turned and wagged a finger at her. "Vannie, you spent your money on clothes that weren't your responsibility to replace. I didn't reimburse you for that yet, but I can at least buy you a new coat and some underwear. You'll *have* to go get some new shoes on Monday, though. I don't think your current shoe wardrobe will cut it."

The full weight of the expense that the vandalism had caused slowly pressed on her with every step upstairs. *And it might be my fault. Hundreds—maybe thousands of dollars because I couldn't keep my mouth shut over a few little punks yapping about my clothes.*

Resting on the couch—she'd done it more in the past twenty-four hours than she had in a month. But the boys were actually sleeping, she could thank a genius scavenger hunt concocted by Laird for that, and the other kids had gone downstairs to try to reassemble the swings and slide for the little guys to use when they awoke. *I need to get those rubber mat squares ordered. Obnoxious kids. What made them think of cutting the locking pieces apart? That's just wasteful, but Luke's right. They'll end up sliding around, and someone will get hurt.* The truth hit hard—embarrassingly hard. *Probably me.*

The basement door creaked open. It hadn't creaked *before* burst pipes and massive amounts of damage. Irritation welled up in her, but it dissolved as she watched a weary-looking Tavish drag himself from the basement to the little closet under the stairs, where he often spent hours reading or working on small projects. The door closed with a soft "whoosh" and all was quiet once more.

Sleep stole in on thoughts and plans and covered them until she succumbed to afternoon dreams of babies sliding about on pink and blue fluffy clouds. Something in her subconscious mind protested at the thought, but the delightful picture overrode any objections. She watched storks fly past with empty bundles, but babies giggled and slid away until one flew into the air and disappeared. The others giggled, tumbled and crawled back to higher clouds for another slide down again.

The dream morphed into her wandering through dense fog. She heard someone calling her name—Luke. It had to be Luke. No one else called her "Mibs." A soft brush of a hand on her face, warm breath on her cheek, someone lacing her fingers in his. "Mibs?"

Aggie's eyes flew open. "Hmm?"

"Sorry to wake you, but the insurance guy needs those pictures, and I don't know what happened to the folder."

As her focus adjusted, she saw a middle-aged man smiling at her. "Sorry to bother you, but I thought you might want that check sooner than later."

It took the full length of time for her to extricate herself from the couch before she could remember what the pictures were and why an insurance adjuster might need them. "Oh, they're in my purse. I remember. I thought I'd drop them off at the office later."

"Well, I came to see the new stuff and pick those up for you."

Her eyes widened and dismay filled her. "The doors! Luke, we just—"

"I got pictures while you were in the basement. It's good." Luke nudged her toward the stairs. "Why not go take a real nap?"

But the clock chimed four-thirty just as she stepped forward. "What?! I've been asleep for three hours? Where are Ronnie and Ian?"

"Laird took them out to the tree house. They're playing it's a ship on icy seas or something like that. Ellie rode to town to get them some jerky—for authenticity, of course."

"Lorna and Cari?" The question—unnecessary. They'd be up with the boys, of course. "Crew?"

Luke's grin told her what he'd say next. "I hear Cari's planning a mutiny. I overheard her tell Lorna, 'I've always wanted to try that.'"

"She tries it with us almost weekly."

The insurance adjuster forgotten, Aggie laughed. "Hey, it

used to be daily."

"Hourly," Luke countered.

From within the library, Vannie's voice reached them. "And sometimes every other minute! When you think of how far they've come...."

My sister might not think I totally failed them. Now if I can do as much for my ornery little hellion....

Bed forgotten, Aggie shuffled toward the library. The draped fabric shelves and tables had given way to piles of virgin and cut fabrics. A skirt hung from a hanger over the curtain rod — finished, other than the slightly raveled hem. "Wow! Look at that. I love that plaid! How did I miss that?"

"Isn't it awesome? Washable wool! Crazy expensive, but warm and no dry cleaning." Vannie ran a hand down one side. "I want to hem it now, but it'll just be a mess if I do."

"Why — oh. Right. Bias cut, right?"

"Yep." She eyed the skirt with a suspicious eye — one Aggie recognized. Before Aggie could comment, Vannie threatened the garment with a low growl. "And if you *dare* to be one of those fabrics that stretches indefinitely, I'm going to cry."

Aggie fingered a lightweight, khaki twill and tried to imagine what it would be. "I give up. What'll you make from it?"

The early twentieth century suit jacket and skirt looked a bit much, but Vannie pulled out olive trimmings — braid, piping, buttons — and an image formed in her mind as she listened. "So, kind of a conceptualization of what a female army uniform would have looked like if she'd been a ranking officer?"

"Yeah! That's a great way of putting it. I mean, it's totally not authentic, but I want it to feel like it could be. I wouldn't wear the jacket around the house, of course, but it would be nice to have for going to the store or whatever."

Despite Vannie's words, Aggie knew, without a doubt, that the girl would wear the jacket every time — at least that year. *If she didn't like people making fun of her clothes before, what's she going to do with these?* The question formed on her lips, but Vannie had already begun pinning another circle skirt. *And really, what's the difference? Kids'll mock anything but jeans and a t-shirt, or a skirt that gives your knees frostbite.*

She'd never manage not to mention something — offer some

35

sort of warning. Instead, Aggie reiterated her willingness to help and waddled down the hall to the bathroom. As she made her way back through the living room, a half-strangled cough under the stairs sent her to check on Tavish. The door creaked a bit as she tugged it open. Tavish lay on the foam mattress that took up most of the space, sound asleep. Musty, dank—the little closet smelled of mildew and stale water. A stain down one wall hinted that the bathroom above might have leaked through the walls and into the room.

"Luke? Can you come here?" Tavish stirred, but the musty scent that assaulted her nostrils killed any guilt she might have felt about waking him. When he didn't fully waken, she shook him, and this time they both coughed. "Tavish, c'mon. You need to get out of here."

Luke rounded the corner and stared as she coaxed the boy out. "What's up?"

"I think there's still some mildew or something in here. Could this mattress have gotten wet again?"

Her husband turned a chartreuse-tinged gray. "Oh, man. I forgot all about this. I didn't do more than blast a fan in there overnight for a couple of nights. I don't even think I checked to see if that mattress got dry."

As if to punctuate the trouble, Tavish barked out a long, hacking cough. Aggie pushed him toward the stairs. "Go take a shower. Get out of those clothes. We'll get your space cleaned out today."

"I'll do it, Mibs. You shouldn't be breathing—"

Anger—unfamiliar and icky—filled her. Without a glance Luke's way, Aggie followed Tavish up the steps. "And neither should the kid still recovering from hypothermia. His lungs are already compromised."

"I'm sorry."

Her heart softened for a moment at the genuine pain she heard in Luke's tone, but another cough from Tavish and the sluggish way he dragged himself up the stairs froze it solid again. "Yeah. So am I."

Standing alone in the living room, Luke stared up the stairs until he could no longer see his wife's swollen ankles. *What just happened there, Lord?*

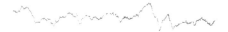

The disgusting spatter of grime and grease in the microwave kicked in premature nesting urges. So, while Luke corralled the youngest children into bed, checked on Tavish's cough again, and let Laird and Vannie pour out their souls—well, in Vannie's case, anyway—Aggie ordered her phone to dial her mother's number and attacked the appliance with a cloud of chemicals guaranteed to give her asthma. "Aggie? What's that sound?"

"That's the sound of bronchial protest combined with squeaking glass and plastic." Aggie couldn't restrain a grin at her mother's chuckle. "How's my favorite mother feeling today?"

"Better not let Libby hear that. You'll crush her."

"She'd crush me if I said it any other way!" Aggie beamed at the beautifully clean door and, turning to one side and on unbalanced tip-toes, dove into the cavernous recesses of the microwave itself.

"Very true. Did you start school up again today?"

Her sigh probably answered for her. "Sorta. I got them going, anyway. It's just, there's so much. The school room is still not quite up to par, Vannie needs to make all new clothes—like she has time—and Ellie has fallen in love with chemistry. She tried the old vinegar and baking soda thing. No biggie, right?"

"Yeeeessss?"

"Well, then she got the semi-not-so-brilliant idea of seeing what happened with other chemicals. I came into the kitchen just in time to stop her from pouring ammonia into a mixture of bleach and vinegar."

Martha Milliken's cry of dismay brought Aggie's father to the phone. "What happened?"

As Aggie rinsed the rag in the sink, Martha brought her husband up to speed. The left side of the microwave beckoned just as her father asked, "Did her lungs survive?"

"Hers did, but I'm not sure about mine. The toilet *has* to be clean, though. I held my breath and emptied the jar down the toilet."

"Why not the kitchen sink?" Martha's confusion rang out into the room.

With eyes closed, lingering fumes of 409 filling her nostrils and burning her lungs, Aggie tried to explain the inexplicable. "Because a pregnant woman doesn't have to make sense. She just has to survive nine months of oxygen-deprivation to the brain."

"Martha, it's scary how quickly she came up with that—especially pregnant."

"Dad!" Aggie's laughter drowned out any further attempt at a protest, but she kept scrubbing until the rest of the microwave sparkled. "You know...." Her musing interrupted some story her mother told of a follow up visit with her surgeon. "I think we should be grateful one of those little creeps didn't put a fork in the microwave and destroy the magnavox tube."

A snicker in the doorway told her she'd gotten it wrong. Again. She turned, prepared for Luke's amused smirk and found Tavish standing there. "Hey, buddy, what is it?"

"Magnetron tube."

"Thanks, but I meant what do you need?" Her heart sank as she heard the wheeze in his lungs. "Chest hurt?"

Tavish just nodded. Pain-filled eyes told her it was much worse than he'd ever admit. "I just can't cough enough to make it stop. Coughing *hurts* and doesn't do any good."

"Can you breathe?"

The boy nodded. "It just hurts."

Aggie stepped a bit closer to her phone. "Mom? Take him in or give him the night?"

"He says he can breathe. I'd give him some Ibuprofen and see if the lack of pain lets him breathe better tonight. Not getting good breaths can make it worse, so I'd start there."

The relief in Tavish's eyes told her he'd held off coming to her out of dread of going in. "As long as Tavish promises to tell me the *truth* about how he feels in the morning...."

A flush crept up the boy's neck as he nodded. "Sorry, Aunt Aggie. I just hate the questions and the constant beeping of those machines. It makes me want to throw them out the window."

Interesting reason not to like doctors. As she passed Tavish a tablet and poured him a drink of water, Aggie listened to his conversation with her parents. *I think they have a better relationship with Mom and Dad now that Allie and Doug are gone. I wonder why. The GIL?* The moment the children's paternal grandmother came to mind, Aggie had no doubt of it being the cause. *Probably couldn't risk too much, or she'd complain.*

Her mother's voice ripped her from her thoughts. "Aggie?"

"Sorry, what'd I miss? Lost in thought there."

"I was about to have Tavish do CPR to restore some of that oxygen deprivation you mentioned."

With a smile and a hug, Aggie sent Tavish back to bed, silently demanding he wake her if he felt worse. The boy nodded and called out goodnight to his grandparents. "Hope you're feeling better, Grandma."

"I do. Much better. Love you, Tavish." The boy hadn't made it around the corner before Martha continued. "Dad's here, glaring at me because I haven't told you yet."

"Told me about what?" She inched toward the wall separating the kitchen from the dining room and peered. Tavish stood there. In a moment of fortuitous eyebrow hair-to-star alignment, or some other ridiculous explanation, Aggie's right eyebrow rose just when she willed it to. The boy scuttled off toward the stairs.

"—surgery they always thought might be beneficial? Well, the surgeon says while he was in there with the camera, he took a peek, and he's confident that he can do it with excellent results. But...."

Aggie's budding excitement wilted again. "What? You're not strong enough?"

"No. I have to decide and agree before my birthday. With every year of age it becomes riskier, and he thinks once I flip over sixty-five we'll have a harder time getting approval since it's still considered somewhat experimental."

"They've been talking about it for fifteen years! How can that be experimental?" Luke entered and gave her a curious but concerned look. "Mom, Luke's here. He's confused, too."

From the way his lips tightened, Aggie realized she'd misread him. "He's obviously not confused about that. It'll bug him until one of us calls, so I'm just putting it out there now."

A sense of satisfaction washed over her at the sight of the wounded expression on his face. Shame followed on its heels. *Since when do you* enjoy *getting in a dig at your husband? Seriously?*

Aggie grabbed her washcloth, rinsed it out, and she started

in on the stove as Martha explained the new procedure that replaced the old one. "—less risk and a shorter recovery time. Most of the time it's not a full 'crack open the chest' surgery. Mine could be, though. They have to do some more tests, but...."

"You'll do it, right?" Luke pulled the cloth from her hand and tried to nudge her toward the living room, but Aggie snatched it back. "I can manage to wipe down a *stove*. If you want to be useful, how about bleaching Tavish's cubby? Maybe then he won't be on the verge of a *hospital* visit tomorrow."

"Mibs...."

She turned away and attacked the stove—all memories of her mother's phone presence forgotten. "Just go deal with it or I will."

"Aggie!"

Heat flooded her cheeks. She glared at Luke until he turned and left the room. Conscience urged her to follow—to apologize. But her mother's scolding voice stripped all penitence from her. "Mom, I don't want to get into it."

"Did you hear how you spoke to him? If anyone spoke to a dog that way, you'd let them have it."

"He left a moldy, mildewy mattress in Tavish's space! The boy was *sleeping* on it."

The silence—more chastening than any rebuke she'd ever received—filled the room. Aggie tried twice to explain—to defend. Both times failed. Instead she just whispered a ragged, "Mom?"

"You know what's right, Agathena."

Fine. Bring out the full name. Make me feel five again. Do you have any idea how mortifying it was to hear that when my friends were over? Do you know how many times one of them got mad at me and shared it with the rest of the class? Oh, about one every year!!! *College was the best thing ever. Far away from anyone who knew it.*

"Mom!"

"If you forgot something important—something you'd feel horrible about once you remembered—like paying a bill or saying 'I love you' to a beloved daughter the night she died—" Martha's voice choked. "Wouldn't you want to be forgiven for what was a genuine oversight rather than a slight?"

Tears poured down her face—silent tears of grief and shame.

40

"Oh, Mom...."

"Go, Aggie. Apologize now before the breach widens. I love you."

"I love you too, Mom." Aggie's voice caught as she tapped the screen to end the call. *And now I know why you always make sure to say, "I love you."*

She docked her phone on the charger and snapped off the kitchen light. Despite half-expecting to find Luke on the other side of the wall, the downstairs remained empty. Aggie wandered through, picking up, closing doors and vents, and locking all outside entries. With the house buttoned down for the night, she climbed the stairs, each one feeling taller and harder than the last.

Only the small lamp by the door illuminated their room. Luke lay curled close to his side with his back to the middle of the bed. Aggie choked back an unexpected sob and crept into the bathroom to change into PJs and brush her teeth. A fresh pair of sleep pants and billowy t-shirt hung on the door—a testimony to her husband's ability to heap those fiery coals while trying to bless her.

Aggie dressed, scrubbed her face and teeth, and hurried to bed. Never had Luke gone to bed without saying goodnight, without kissing her goodnight, without trying to resolve any conflicts. But there he lay, back to her, not even shifting as she pulled the covers over her and snuggled up to him.

"Luke?"

"Hmm?"

"I'm sorry."

Never would she have imagined that he wouldn't turn and speak to her. Instead, he murmured. "Me, too. I love you. Night."

A minute passed—two. Five. His regular breathing hinted at sleep. All Aggie wanted to do was go somewhere and cry—somewhere he couldn't hear her. Somewhere the kids couldn't hear and go wake him.

As quietly and with as little disturbance as she could manage, Aggie slid from the bed and crept from the room. A contraction forced her to pause halfway to the second floor, but she kept going. The bathroom called to her by the time she reached the first floor. *Probably best that I got up anyway, then. Couldn't have avoided it.*

The scent of fresh paint still permeated the guest room as she entered it. Aggie opened the heater vent again, cracked the window, and slid under the covers. Hot tears slid down her cheeks as the rest of her body shivered in an ineffective attempt at warmth. A swath of dim light cut across the room as the door opened and a silhouette filled the doorway.

Luke.

Without a word, he shut the door, climbed in beside her, pulled her close and held her. After nearly four years of marriage, she should have known his silence at a time like that meant prayer, but not until he whispered her name did Aggie realize why he hadn't spoken.

"I shouldn't have gone to bed. I thought— Well, it doesn't matter what I thought."

"Maybe it does." Aggie blinked at her own words. Delay tactics? Curiosity? Unexpected moment of insight? She couldn't decide.

Luke drew her head onto his chest and murmured an explanation. "I just thought you needed sleep. You sounded exhausted. I thought maybe we'd both be clearer-minded in the morning."

"Because you don't understand why I'd act like you deliberately didn't clean that out?"

His chest rumbled with the vibrations of a low chuckle. "I did wonder."

"Mom let me have it."

"She shouldn't have—"

But Aggie couldn't let him say it. She knew the temptation to revel in justifying her actions. "No. She was right. I know you better than that. You got this whole place fixed in *two* weeks. His cubby isn't prime living space. I should have thought to tell him to ask if it was ready. I just didn't think."

Long into the night, their quiet murmurs filled the least inhabited room of the house. At one point, Luke suggested going back up to their room, but before either of them stirred, both drifted into that wonderful slumber that comes with a mind and heart clear and refreshed by forgiveness.

MOLDY, MOLDY, MOLDY

Chapter Three

Wednesday, November 26th

As hard as he tried not to, Luke found himself banging around as he wrestled a musty mattress from its moorings. His face mask slipped as he dragged it through the house, down the steps, and shoved it over the tailgate of his truck. Dark clouds threatened rain, or worse, snow. The chances of him making it to Brunswick to have the mattress recycled *before* the rain began... slim. The dump would have to do.

The toilet flushed just as he stepped back in the door, and Luke grinned at the sight of his sleep-drunk wife stumbling back out of the downstairs bath and into the guest room once more. The door shut with finality that hinted she wasn't anywhere near ready to awaken. "Lord, thank you for her. I love that woman."

Luke managed to empty the rest of the closet fully-masked. A bleach solution removed the spots of mold and mildew along the edges of the baseboards and the floor. He scrubbed, stepped outside for fresh air, replaced his mask for a new one, and scrubbed again. After three passes, he washed down the walls with TSP and went to retrieve a can of primer. Tavish met him at the top of the stairs.

"Do you know where Aunt Aggie is? Her bed's empty, the

van's here, but I can't find her."

"She's asleep in the guest room." The moment the words left his lips, Luke groaned inside and ordered himself to be more careful with what he shared.

"Oh." Tavish looked at him with an odd expression. "Is that the dog house?"

A snicker escaped before Luke could stop himself. "If it is, we're both in trouble because I slept there, too—long story, but all is well."

"What're you doing?"

"Just getting ready to fix your space." Luke remembered when he had to sit to meet Tavish's eyes without looking down at the boy. Now Tavish stood almost as tall as he was. "Sorry about that, son. You can't know how bad I feel."

A slow nod. A smile. A wracking cough that hurt to hear. "That's why she's down here."

"She thought I was mad at her. I was giving her space. Silly misunderstanding. We fixed it." Why he felt obligated to explain a private, marital issue to a twelve-year-old, Luke would never be able to explain. "Why do you need Aggie?"

"She made me promise to tell her if it was worse. It was." Pleading eyes tore at Luke's heart as he continued. "But it's better after that cough—really. You don't have to wake her up, do you?"

Indecision wracked him. The trust of a boy he considered a son or the trust of his wife. In a sense, it was a no-brainer. Wife wins every time. But the abject misery on Tavish's face, combined with the confidence that the boy didn't exaggerate made the decision harder than he'd expected. "Compromise," he offered at last. "We won't wake her, but we will tell her that you were going to until you coughed and felt better."

Tavish sagged in relief. "Thanks."

"Why don't you go take a shower? Get it as steamy in there as you can."

He waited for some sort of joke about them not allowing steamy situations in their home, but it wouldn't come. Tavish wouldn't. Laird, on the other hand....

Tavish made it halfway up the stairs before he called back down again. "Uncle Luke?"

"Yeah?"

"Waiting is okay if I can breathe, right?"

The uncertainty in the boy's tone nearly sent Luke down the hall to wake Aggie right then. "Difficult to breathe or relatively normal?"

"Closer to normal than hard."

Relief washed over him. "Then you should be good. How about I call Mom and ask her?"

Whatever Tavish mumbled, Luke took as agreement. So, instead of taping off the floor and cutting in corners, Luke stepped into the library and tapped his mother's number. The chill in the room sent shivers through him as he waited for her to answer. Guilt kicked him in the gut as he heard her sleepy voice.

"Everything okay, son?"

"I think so. Sorry to wake you, but Mibs had a hard night, and I've got a question that maybe shouldn't wait."

His mind saw the scene as if he stood in the doorway. Libby grabbed the other pillow, stacked it with her usual one, and propped herself against the headboard. She reached for glasses, took a sip of water, and adjusted the blankets—all while trying to soothe his heart. "I'm sure everything is fine. Now tell me about it."

"Tavish says Aggie made him promise to tell her if his lungs got worse. He woke up and came downstairs to find her. Couldn't. Then he had a big coughing fit." A lump swelled in his throat at the memory. "It was bad, Ma. Bad. But he looked and sounded better after it, and he says he feels better now."

"Might just have been a bunch of congestion that formed while he slept. You breathe shallower when you're asleep. Makes it hard to fill those lungs with air, so they fill with gunk. I think."

His mother's words soothed and reassured just as they had when he was six and he'd gotten the wind knocked out of him falling out of a tree. "That's what I thought." He took a deep breath and confessed his decision. "I told Tavish to take a shower—since he's better. It just seemed like a good compromise." Water came on upstairs. "I thought it might loosen up more for him."

"Listen to his coughs, but yes. That sounds correct." The Sullivan silence—exaggerated on Luke's part, for sure, but characteristic of many in the family—it hung in the air between their houses. "Luke?"

"Yeah?"

"Are you sure you don't want me to come over and do Thanksgiving tomorrow? I can. I don't mind."

A decision lay before him—one he'd rather *not* make. Luke considered a dozen options, reconsidered half of them, and narrowed it down to just one. "Um, I think it would hurt Mrs. Dyke's feelings if you did that, but I'm sure she'd love another guest if you'd rather come here than go to Corinne's."

"It is Corinne's turn, but I know she wanted all of you, too."

"I know, but we've been gone so much. A chance to stay home and just be together was too hard to pass up."

Just as Luke decided to end the call, Libby spoke again. "Son, if either of you have any doubts about Tavish's lungs, you call Corinne. She's gotten pretty good at diagnosing just by hearing it with Rodney's issues."

"I'll do that. Thanks, Mom. I love you."

She'd stuffed down irritation—with Luke, Tavish, *and* herself—and had come out on the other side with a more rational response. But now, with Luke working happily in the little closet, likely growing high on paint fumes, and the children scattered about doing schoolwork and playing, Aggie risked what little sanity she'd managed to salvage and dialed Corinne before Mrs. Dyke could knock on the door and create chaos. Her sister-in-law picked up on the first ring.

"Been waiting for your call. Ma said you'd be calling hours ago!"

"Well, I slept in. Been having stupid Braxton-Hicks contractions already. The midwife comes on Monday, and I'm determined to find out what I can do to slow 'em down. It's hard to get anything done with your hands gripping your stomach like it's the safety bar on a roller coaster ride!"

Corinne's laughter relaxed her. If the woman wasn't demanding to hear more about Tavish already, maybe things were okay. "The mental picture—good one. So where's my boy? I want to hear him breathe. And if you tell anyone I listen to young men's heavy breathing over the phone, I'll deny it."

"*Your* boy?"

She heard the telltale squeak of Corinne's kitchen door that led to the garage. It protested and then all went silent. "Any of your kids listening in?"

"No…."

Corinne cleared her throat, coughed, and cleared it again. "Look, I'll deny it, too, if any kid asks me. The Lord'll have to forgive me for it. Maybe Paul was wrong about the grace abounding thing. Maybe we should. Who knows? But I'm not admitting this to my little brother's kids."

"Admitting what?"

"I've got a soft spot for Tavish, okay? I mean, I don't 'do' favorites any more than the next Sullivan, but if I did…."

So many things made sense with those few words. Aggie ran through a dozen or more scenarios in the space of seconds. "I should have figured that out." Maybe she shouldn't have asked — probably shouldn't have — but Aggie did. "Um, why Tavish?"

"He's so like Luke was. He doesn't get into as much *trouble.* That, your Ronnie got. But the quiet, introspective, out of the blue thoughtfulness — that's Luke all over. I just love seeing brother in a kid that doesn't share a bit of his genes. That's just the kind of cool that only comes from the Lord."

"I can't imagine Ronnie *ever* getting the quiet side — *ever*. I suppose we should both be glad."

Corinne's laugh lasted only long enough for her to remember to ask to hear Tavish's lungs. "Can you bring him over?"

"I thought you said over the phone?" Aggie glanced at the time on her phone. It would take at least an hour for her to drive to Corinne's, get a 'diagnosis' and drive back — assuming Corinne didn't send them to the clinic. Awfully close call for lunch.

"Just joking there. I doubt I can hear enough through the phone. Oh, and make him wear a t-shirt so I can really listen. If I have any difficulty guessing, I'll unwrap my Christmas present."

She could only imagine. "The one you decided you wanted, bought six months ago, and wrapped last week?"

"Bought it two months ago, thank-you-very-much." But

Corinne couldn't keep the excitement from her tone. "Stethoscope. Cost me a fortune, but worth it. Rodney...." In an attempt to cut the call shorter, Aggie suggested after lunch, but Corinne protested. "If Mom said to call, I suspect you shouldn't wait."

"It's just that it'll delay lunch, then naps....."

This Corinne pounced on and held fast. "Oh, no. You have *two* teenagers in that house and *two* tweens. You have Luke home today, right?"

"Well...."

"You get your butt over here and bring Tavish with you." A moment of silence followed. "I stand corrected. One tween—or nearly so—by the time I steal him."

Knowing Tavish would prefer his aunt to a clinic full of nosy nurses and an overworked doctor, Aggie agreed and disconnected the call. She made her way to the stairs, saw Luke's backside sticking out the door, and realized Tavish wouldn't be in there. *Not today.* "Luke?"

"Yeah?"

"I need to take Tavish to see Corinne. It's either more serious than we thought, or she's determined to see at least some of us on Thanksgiving—use any excuse she can."

He crawled out, a paint brush in hand and grinned at her. With a glance around to be sure they weren't overheard, he leaned forward and murmured, "She's just extra fond of him—reminds her of me."

Aggie's jaw gaped as she stared into his twinkling eyes. *Does everyone know this stuff but me?*

Tavish burst through the door, nebulizer mask over his face, calling, "Are you my mummy?"

A glance in the library showed it empty, save a pile of scraps, another of cut pieces, and another of pieces waiting to be cut. Aggie shrugged at the confused look on his face until a burst of laughter erupted from the kitchen. "I think you'll find your audience in there."

"I will probably sound like Rory MacKenzie, but man, that

just kills a line — repeating it."

"They don't know it's a repeat, though. That makes it different." She nudged him forward. "Go get your jokes out. We've got to get this thing up and going now."

What made her think of it at that moment, no one could have guessed. But Aggie whipped out her phone and set an alert for writing out her home birthing plan for her midwife appointment on Monday. "One more thing — done. Sorta."

Cari rushed up to her and squeezed her belly until the baby kicked in protest. "It kicked me! The baby kicked me!"

"I think it's her way of saying, "Be gentle."

"She should be a boy. Ronnie wants a brother. He needs one — to play with."

"Because he couldn't play with a sister?" Aggie cupped the little girl's chin in her hand and shook her head. "If the Lord gives us a girl, that'll be wonderful, too."

A call from the kitchen sent Cari scampering off again. *She's so like her littler self — even now. Strange how alike and dissimilar people can become.*

Luke's voice in her ear sent her phone flying and then skittering across the floor. "Oh, sorry. I thought you saw me. You looked right at me."

"I did? Weird."

Squeals of laughter stole his attention for a moment. He grinned. "I take it the gas mask, so to speak, is proof that the boy needs a bit more attention?"

"Corinne didn't even get to unwrap her Christmas present to listen to his lungs. She stepped close, heard a wheeze, asked him something about what it felt like — it's an elephant kneeling on his chest, if you are curious — and ordered me off to the clinic — in *Fairbury.* She said it was faster and they'd have the machine for him to take home. So we went. You should have a couple of texts on your phone."

Luke patted his pockets and frowned. "I had it when I called Mom...."

"I'm not buying you another phone. If you lose this one, the replacement is your Christmas present." As she threatened him, Aggie called up his contact and tapped the screen. She typed out the words, FIND ME, and hit send. From within a pile of painting supplies, Matt Smith's voice announced, "You've got a text message. Text messages are cool."

While Luke retrieved his phone, Aggie suggested that perhaps the family's recent fixation with all things Doctor Who might have hit the overkill mark. "I even hear the 'find me' text with that evil woman's voice. 'Feed me!'"

Luke looked up from the phone, clearly discouraged. "Bronchitis? Did the doctor say if the mold or mildew aggravated it?"

"He said it could, but the cause was definitely the plunge into Willow's icy pond and then walking home in freezing weather. The kid should have needed a week in a hospital. We did good." Though she spoke to Luke, Aggie meant the words to reassure herself more than anything.

"Good. Oh, and you might as well get mad at me now." Luke reached to brush a wisp of hair from her face and paused. "I gave the kids the rest of the week off. Mrs. Dyke asked for cooking help, and I doubted they'd get much done on Friday anyway, so…."

Deciding which irritated her more, the decision to thwart her plans to get the children back on track for school or that she'd made him skittish enough not to want to touch her when she was irritated — difficult and awkward in the moment. Aggie took his hand, held it, and pressed it to her cheek. "I need reminders sometimes that this isn't all on me. You can make these decisions, too." Every part of her heart screamed, "Hypocrite," but she kept talking. "Thank you for just doing it. If we'd talked, I wouldn't have agreed. And you're probably right."

He's totally right, and you know it. And you don't like it — not one bit. That is the longest string of nonsense you've ever assembled. What a joke.

But the pressure of Luke's hand on her face, the featherweight touch of one finger to move her hair from her cheek, the brush of his lips that returned again. Lingered. Drew her into an intimate moment shared only in their minds and hearts. All angst melted as Luke murmured, "You know I love you, right?"

"I know. Still can't believe it some days, but I always know."

He'd kiss her again. Aggie saw it in the graze of his eyes on

50

her lips, the pressure of his hand on her waist, the smile that formed as he leaned closer. She melted into him and stiffened as a screech from the kitchen and a cry for "Uncle Luke" disrupted the moment. His eyes said it all. A perfect blend of, "Not again" and "Catch you later."

Lorna flew through the living room and stopped short at the sight of Aggie. "*Your son* just ruined Mrs. Dyke's pie! It's all broken!"

With one hand sliding under her belly, Aggie inched away from Luke. "Apparently, I need to deal with *my son*."

They found Ronnie in the kitchen, being stared down by Winnie Dyke. The older woman didn't flinch, didn't blink. Ronnie just smirked. Any remorse the boy *might* have felt had dissolved in the showdown the older woman had innocently created. Aggie, on the other hand, refused to engage. "Apologize now, Ronald Stephen Sullivan."

"I'm sorry."

He didn't sound sorry. Furthermore, the way he rocked on his toes hinted at what she'd begun calling "silent sass." She waited for Mrs. Dyke to melt. *Three, two, one….*

"Oh, honey. I know you didn't mean to."

The smirk. It gave him away. She'd seen it on Luke's face enough times when he had played some little practical joke. "I'm afraid he did mean to, Mrs. Dyke. Now, he's going to get a dishcloth and scrub up all the flour on the floor while you let me fix this crust."

"Why, I really don't think—"

"You had sons…." Aggie held the older woman's gaze until she sighed and nodded.

Mrs. Dyke turned to Ronnie and interjected a bit of sternness into her tone. "I'm going to inspect that floor, little Ronnie. It better be spotless."

Thank you, Lord, for people who support you in child rearing instead of thwart you at every turn.

"Can I go work on my outfit, Aunt Aggie? I'm down to a zipper and a couple of buttonholes. Even the hem is done—so cute! I could wear it to church tonight, if…." Vannie's eyes pleaded for more than permission to work on an outfit. Aggie saw it in the way she inched away from a pile of washed and quartered potatoes.

"Sure. Show me what you're doing and then I'll be back to do that crust."

Mrs. Dyke tried to protest. "Aggie, I—"

"Please. I need to do this. You're already doing so much. Let me fix my child's vandalism of your artwork."

Lorna's voice stopped her at the doorway. "What artwork, Aunt Aggie? I thought Ellie did the art around here."

"Well…." Aggie slipped her hand into Lorna's and led the child from the room as she followed Vannie through the house to the library. Seeing Luke working in Tavish's cubby, she paused and murmured, "You might give your son a bit of a scolding for making more work for others. It always comes better from you."

"Not penitent?"

She shrugged. "Sure doesn't act like it. I can't always tell with him, though. But it never hurts." Luke backed out of the closet, ready to go, but Aggie stopped him. "Not yet. I'll kick you when I go in. It'll make more impact if I'm actually working when you come in."

"Good point." Luke smiled over at Vannie. "Finally got to look at that dress. That is amazing. You should send a picture of you in it to Chad. He could show Alexa Hartfield next time he saw her. She'd like that."

"Oh! I will! I wondered how I could show her."

Scraps littered the library floor, and threads created cobwebs all over every surface. Vannie, usually a neat little seamstress, ignored them and rushed to show Aggie her dress. Chocolate lightweight suiting created a crisp bodice that still allowed for a flowing, flared skirt. "I would never have thought to use that fabric for a dress. It's perfect. And those buttons—how'd you find such perfectly matched buttons? That satiny stuff just really gives it a bit of dressy without being too much. Wow. I want one." She held the dress up to her and stretched it across her belly. "Well, maybe two."

"Is that 'dressing for two'?"

"Yep." Her eyes followed the square neckline with its unexpected collar. "Was that your idea or did the pattern have it?"

Vannie dug out the pattern jacket and tapped the front. "See.

It's authentic. That's why I did the sateen there, too. To match the buttons." She laid the sleeve over her arm. "I keep wanting to add a touch of it at the wrists, but it's not on the pattern. Too much?"

"What about French cuffs? I mean, they look like that collar, almost, you know?" Something Vannie said finally clicked. "Wait, this does match the buttons… and that belt! It has a buckle! Wha—"

"I just used a belt kit and covered the buttons. I cheated on the buttons, though. I cut a piece of batting to cover them to make them softer."

She'd long known Vannie's skills were far above her age, but Aggie stared at the belt in utter amazement. "Wait, you *made* that? A *belt?*"

"Don't sound too impressed. I ruined four before I got it right. That stupid suiting frays like you wouldn't believe. I finally got smart and fray-checked it." She reached into a bag and pulled out several boxes. "And I have more to return. I bought ten—just in case." Vannie ducked her head. "Gotta say, I'm glad I did. I really thought I'd only use one or two."

Several times, she'd been tempted to suggest a career in fashion design or even just a job working for some place like the Boho Boutique in Rockland, but Aggie had also resisted leading the girl too strongly in any direction. Now she spoke without reservation. "You know, I've often wondered if you'd go into fashion design or dressmaking of some kind. But now I wonder if you shouldn't work with that company Alexa Hartfield owns. Because this is seriously amazing."

Ellie stepped in and interrupted. "Isn't it? It's not *me* of course. I don't know what 'me' is, exactly, but I wish I could find something like that—something that *is* me." She gave the dress one last lingering look before turning to Aggie. "Sorry, but Ronnie refuses to clean anymore. And he's only made a couple of swipes at the floor. If he'd even *tried*…."

"Coming." Aggie gave Vannie one last smile. "You did great. Really."

As she strolled across the house, Aggie's voice slowly filled the rooms. "*…eeever my lot….*" The sight of Ronnie spinning in a streak of flour choked the next words, but she finished strong. "*…with my soooul.*"

Ronnie grinned. Aggie frowned. "You get that dishcloth and eradicate every speck of white from that floor, *now!*"

"What's daditate?"

In a desperate attempt not to scream out her frustration, Aggie chomped down on her inner lip until she drew blood. Eyes closed, patience nearly gone, she pointed in the general direction of the mess. "Floor. Clean. Now."

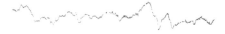

Being late for church does have its advantages. The thought nearly found its way to her vocal cords before she could repress it. She scootched to the edge of her seat and gripped the pew in front of her for support as she tried to rise on overtaxed legs. "Mom's doing much better, and we did get the house habitable again. Well, Luke and the older kids did."

"I heard about Tavish's accident. He's not here, is he?"

"I made him stay home. He needed another breathing treatment, and the cold air seems to set him off." Aggie hoisted herself up and inched her way to the aisle. Once standing, the ache in her legs seemed to dissipate—the opposite of what she'd have expected. "But, he'll be fine, the doctor says."

The woman's hand slid over Aggie's belly without even hinting for permission first. Aggie gritted her teeth and tried not to feel like a Buddha in a Chinese restaurant. "You're getting huge! When are you due again? Last time I saw you, I didn't think you looked very pregnant, but…."

"Eight weeks or so to go." Aggie grinned. "And you saw me a month ago. You start getting bigger once you pass that six to seven month mark—or I did with Ronnie."

Myra Vaughn, the minister's wife, stepped up and gave her a hug. "Sorry to hear about your troubles. You're feeling well?" She turned to the other woman and offered a hug as well. "How's your arthritis today, Sandy?"

"Not too bad."

Before Sandy could start in on her aches and frustrations, Myra turned back to Aggie, winked, and asked about their Thanksgiving plans. "Are you going to family or…?"

"We're staying home. Mrs. Dyke is cooking for me so I can rest. Apparently, I need to rest." Aggie gave an exaggerated roll of her eyes. "As if Ronnie and Cari will let me do such a radical thing!"

"Well, I don't know how you do it." Myra turned and elbowed Sandy. "Do you? I mean, when she had Ronnie, she was in here with the whole crew two days later as if it was nothing. Now look at her!"

A seed of pride germinated in her heart and sprouted a leaf. *Well, I tried. I don't want to be one of those women who treats pregnancy and birth like she's some kind of invalid. Ugh.*

"I remember my mother giving me grief for coming back to church in two weeks. Why, when she had me, they stayed home for six weeks!" Sandy shook her head. "I mean, I always thought Mother's method a bit extreme, but I can't help but wonder if Aggie isn't a bit, too—just in the other direction."

"Well, if she can't handle it, I'm sure she won't do it. Aggie has a good head on her shoulders." She nudged Aggie. "Did you find out if it's a boy or a girl?"

"Still not cooperating, but both technicians and the doctor are guessing girl—citing 'lack of parts' and heart rate as clues."

"I thought the heart rate thing was a myth." Sandy gave her a suspicious look—one that clearly said, "I think you're messing with us."

Aggie shrugged. "I think they're basing the *guess* on the fact that it's different from Ronnie's, *and* in the general 'range' of girls, *and* the fact that they don't see parts. They're not saying it's accurate."

"Right. It's a contributing factor to a guess." Myra led her out into the aisle. "I forgot. There's someone I want you to meet. We have a new family from Brunswick who started coming about three weeks or so ago—the Wares."

A couple talking to Mac and Savannah MacKenzie looked up at the sound of their name and the women's approach. "Mrs. Vaughn. Good evening." The man gave Aggie a happy smile. "You must be Mrs. Sullivan? I met your husband."

"Where is Luke? He disappeared almost the minute the closing prayer ended." Aggie peered around the corner to the vestibule but didn't see him.

The man's wife—Mrs. Ware, Aggie presumed—gave her a reassuring smile. "He had a little one in tow—first to the bathroom and then outside. Perhaps there was an accident?"

"Probably trying to avoid an accident in behavior choices. Run some of Ronnie's mischief out before bedtime." Aggie tried to adjust her words. "Sharing" about her son's need for continual training still counted as gossip in her book. "We've had a long day."

"You have a lovely family. I met Ellie, Kenzie, and…." The woman's eyes sought Myra for confirmation. "What was the one little girl's name—the twin?"

Myra shrugged. "I can never tell which is which. Either Cari or Lorna."

"Lorna!" Mrs. Ware nodded with exaggerated emphasis. "I remember noting that her name didn't end in 'ee.'"

Mr. Ware called her "Mrs. Sullivan" once more, and Aggie shook her head in protest. "Sorry, I don't care if children call me missus. I'm proud of being Luke's wife, but I can't handle people my age and older doing it. It makes me feel pretentious or something. I'm Aggie."

The man held out his hand. "Gregory Ware." Gregory slipped his other arm around his wife and added, "This is my wife, Wanda."

Wanda shivered as the door opened and a young boy of about eight burst through it. "Mom, they're playing hide and seek. Mr.….." His forehead furrowed until he saw Aggie. "Her husband is supervising. Can we play?"

"You *may*, yes."

"Sorry. Thanks!" Without even turning around, the boy backed back out of the church and disappeared into the night.

A shake of the head and an exaggerated sigh—Gregory shrugged and "introduced" his now absent son. "That's Isaiah. Josiah is around here somewhere, too…." Even as he spoke, the man's eyes swept the room, looking for his son among the clusters of people chatting.

"I think he went outside with some of the young people." Wanda's expression could have meant anything from complete approval to abject disgust at her son's behavior.

Not knowing how to respond, Aggie just gave a strained

smile and suggested that perhaps it was time to get her crew home. "It's already been a long day...." Inwardly, she groaned. *Pretty sure you already said that.*

From her perch in the front seat, Vannie watched as the children played, but when three boys circled Kenzie, her radar pinged mercilessly until she wrapped her coat tighter around her and stepped from the van. The wind carried their voices away from where Luke stood and right to her ears. "Stupid kids — think you're better than everyone. You look like freaks!"

A warning light clicked on in her spirit, but Vannie pulled the wire and strode forward, steam billowing from her nose and mouth that made her look even angrier than she felt. She reached Kenzie's side in no time, but not before Rory MacKenzie put himself between Kenzie and the trio of obnoxious boys.

With one finger, he pushed his glasses up his nose and stared down the group. "Just leave her *alone*."

Spunky little thing. He's lucky we're at church, or he'd be sporting a face full of dirt right now.

The kids ignored her as Vannie inched closer to Rory. The oldest boy — an overgrown kid of about twelve — shoved Rory and sneered at him. "Look at the little nerd — sticking up for his *girlfriend*." He peered around Rory's shoulder and laughed at Kenzie's evident embarrassment. "You know, if you marry him you'll have the stupidest name ever — Kenzie MacKenzie. He'll have to become a Sullivan."

"Stuart." Kenzie's single word dropped in the night air with the lack of emotion that even unsettled Vannie when she heard it.

"Huh?"

Kenzie stepped out from behind Rory and smiled at him before turning to the others. "My name is *Stuart*. And my aunt says talking about marriage when you're nine is pretty stupid."

"Well your *aunt* is stupid. She got stuck with all of you, didn't she?"

Vannie had heard enough. The other two must have been watching her, because they backed away a step or two. "Listen you stu — foolish." She could almost hear Aggie's reprimand

57

before the word made its way into the boys consciousness. "Whatever. Leave my little sister and her friends *alone*. Just go away and leave. Them. Alone. Got it?"

The boy didn't back down. His sneer repeated itself with an extra flourish. "Or *what?*"

Saying, "I'll tell" wouldn't do anything, and she knew it. Threatening bodily harm to a kid younger than her would likely get her bawled out by every adult in her life—and half the kids. But something in the kid's face confirmed a suspicion she'd had and the words flew from her mouth before she could consider the wisdom of it. "Vandalism is a *crime*, you little—" Oh, how she ached to let a few unsavory terms fly. Sure, they'd still be too sanitized to make much impact on a kid like him, but if it got back to Luke and Aggie that she'd called names....

"Yeah? I heard you got some at your place. Wish I'd have been home. I might have gotten in on the fun."

Kenzie sniffled—a sound that could mean anything from ready to cry from the attempted repression of fury or the cold blast of air that hit them and stung their noses. Rory turned to look and nodded. "We should go inside."

Duh. Takes a nine-year-old to think of the easiest way out of this mess. But the satisfaction on the boy's face kept her from agreeing fully. "Go ahead. It's almost time to go anyway. Maybe Aunt Aggie needs something." She turned back to the snickering oaf before her and reiterated her demands. "Leave my siblings alone. If you don't like us. Fine. We don't care. But picking on a little girl just because you think her *outfit* is stupid isn't exactly proof of your superior intelligence. Now get out of here before I decide I don't care how much trouble I get in for smacking a few of your heads together."

Surprise, delight, utter amazement—they filled her as the boys shuffled off. Pride welled up inside and warmed her against the next blast of wind, but the realization that they received no satisfaction in tormenting someone who wouldn't be tormented, and therefore, left to find someone else to annoy, sucked the warmth from her. *Lord, will I ever learn?*

She made it halfway to the van before a voice called out. "Nicely handled."

A glance over her shoulder showed an unfamiliar boy

leaning against an equally unfamiliar sedan. "Um... thank you?"

He shoved himself away from the vehicle and crossed the parking lot to her side. "I'm Josiah Ware. You must be one of the Sullivans."

"Stuart, but yeah. Aggie's my aunt." Just as he began to speak, Vannie realized she hadn't introduced herself. "I'm Vannie."

"I think Mrs. Vaughn said you're the oldest?" Josiah's laughter filled the night air, ringing out even over the squeals of some of the hiders and the seeker. "I'm not stalking your family. Mrs. Vaughn introduced us to everyone—every week, in fact—and every week she said, 'Oh, but the Sullivans aren't here.' Then we got a run down on about half of you. But she always started with, 'Vannie. Such a wonderful help to her aunt.'"

She couldn't help it. No matter how much Vannie wanted to let compliments roll off her, she clutched at each one and held it close. Still, she did manage to assume some modesty as she shrugged. "I think she's being nice. People think all teenagers have to be self-centered, demanding brats, so if someone acts even the slightest bit human, they assume you're amazing or something."

Josiah watched her as she spoke, his eyes seeming to pierce through her façade and see the real her beneath it. But his words and his tone belied the disapproval she expected to hear. "Want to go inside and talk? My parents wouldn't appreciate me standing out here in the dark with a girl."

Come to think of it, Luke might have something to say about it. I don't even want to think about what Mr. Markenson would say. As if summoned by her thoughts, William's cruiser pulled into the parking lot. "Um... sure."

They turned, faced another blast of wind, and with unspoken agreement, dashed for the church doors. Once in the vestibule, Vannie unbuttoned her coat and hung it on a hook. The puffy ski jacket looked ridiculous with her retro dress, and the incongruity of it smarted. *I have to find a new coat or make one. Alexa Hartfield would never approve.*

"Nice dress. Classic."

Vannie smoothed the skirt with an absentminded swipe of her hand and lowered herself onto the bench beneath the coat rack. "Thanks. All my clothes were ruined by the stupid kid—I mean, the *vandals* that thought destroying property was a good way to spend their free time." She flicked a finger at her jacket. "I don't have a decent coat to wear with it yet." Even as she spoke, Vannie ordered herself to be quiet. *He doesn't want to hear about your wardrobe woes. He's a guy. Ask about football or something.*

"Well, anyway, it's nice."

She'd planned to ask about when they'd moved to the area or what school he went to, but seeing the genuine admiration in his eyes and hearing the compliment once more—the question dissipated. Somehow, she managed to croak out a simple, "Thanks."

Maven of Mess

Chapter Four

Friday, November 28th

The gallon milk jug slipped from Cari's hand and sent a wave of white spray all over the cabinets and a river flowing across the floor. Aggie stood there, hands gripping the counter top and eyes closed, praying for the strength to say anything that wouldn't devastate the child any further. "Anyone know what we did with the honey?"

"Huh?" When she opened her eyes, Tavish stood there, a blank expression masking any hope of coherent thought.

"Well, if we can add honey to it, we could just rename the kitchen Canaan."

"Uncle Luuuuuke!" Lorna stared at her wide-eyed—almost looking terrified—and screamed it again. "Uncle Luke! Hurry!"

Feet thundered down the stairs with such vim and vigor that Aggie couldn't help but giggle. "He sounds like twenty kids." In one of those moments—common enough in many pregnancies—in which seemingly innocent words become uproariously funny, Aggie dissolved into an uncontrollable fit of giggles.

And that's when Luke arrived. He took one look at the scene, his wife shaking and with tears pouring down her face, and wrapped his arms around her. "It's just milk, Mibs. You know we'll never hear the end of you crying over spilled milk."

Aggie only laughed harder. She gripped her belly with both arms, wincing and fighting back a scream as pain like a hot knife severing a ligament ripped through her. "Ooohhh...."

"If you tell me you're in labor, I'm going to spank you."

She nearly kicked him in an attempt to shut him up before the pain grew worse. Instead, she sank to the floor, gripped her belly tighter and howled even louder. Ever helpful, Laird walked into the room and asked, "What's so funny?"

Those words wiped the look of concern from Luke's face and replaced it with suspicion. He turned to Ellie, who worked ineffectively to eradicate the Borden River from the kitchen and asked the obvious question. "Laughing or crying?"

"Laughing." She gave Laird a smirk and added, "She was asking for honey to go with our flowing milk, and then Uncle Luke said something about not crying and...."

Everyone in the kitchen erupted in uproarious laughter — right up to the moment where Ronnie rushed to tackle his father's legs. One foot slipped, the other flew up in the air after it, and he landed on his back in the middle of the milk puddle. A resounding, *crack*, followed by the boy's piercing screams filled the room. Aggie only laughed harder.

Lorna stormed from the room, indignant at the callous display of cruelty toward the poor kid.

At that point, Aggie laughed until she couldn't determine if the dampness on her skirt was caused by milk or other, more nefarious causes. The baby's sudden kick to her bladder answered for her. She tried to talk — to ask for help — but Murphy's Law induced hysteria made it impossible to do more than laugh and gasp, " — ba — bathroom."

Vannie wandered into the kitchen just as Luke helped Aggie up and to the doorway. "Do I want to ask?"

"Please. Don't." Aggie gasped. "I just. Stopped. Laughing."

As her eyes took in the scene before her, the girl shrugged. "Only Sullivan-Stuarts would laugh at spilled milk instead of crying over it."

Laughter erupted around her, and Aggie bolted toward the bathroom, one arm supporting her belly, the other gripping furniture as she passed. "My bladder hates you!"

"Can you get the stuff Uncle Luke wants while I get the milk and bread?"

Laird waved a twenty-dollar-bill over his head as he took off toward the hardware store. "Will do."

"I'll meet you at the Pizza Palace!"

He felt her presence long before the girl spoke. "Wish you'd meet *me* at the Pizza Palace sometime."

"Hi, Kendra." As much as he tried not to show any interest, his lack of enthusiasm sounded rude, even to himself. He cleared his throat.

"Did you have fun on Thanksgiving? My mom is still bummed that you didn't come to our house."

I doubt it. More like you were bummed. She just saved cooking for an army. Luke's familiar response blurted out before he could stop himself. "We're not a visit. We're an invasion." He pulled open the door to the hardware store and a whiff of dust, machine oil, and the faintest trace of pipe tobacco filled his nostrils. *Best smelling place in town — next to the pizza place, of course.* Kendra still stood there looking a bit wounded. Laird gave her a weak smile. "But I know Aunt Aggie appreciated the invitation. We don't get many — that invasion thing."

"Maybe you should accept more. People think you're just stuck up." To his dismay, she followed him inside and added, "*I* know you're not, of course. You're just shy."

Freaked out is more like it. Can't you leave me alone?

The attention — flattering. He'd never pretend it wasn't. But each trip into town, each group game after church, every opportunity that presented itself, Kendra or one of her "besties" would try to corner him. *"They like you, Laird. That's a compliment."* Vannie's oft-repeated words did little to reassure him.

"So, what are you getting in here?"

"Uncle Luke needs some sandpaper and another can of WD-40."

To his relief, her phone buzzed. Laird skirted the row, made a beeline for the row of sandpaper options. *Medium grit... medium... medium... there!* On a mission, he bolted around the aisles until he found oil and lubricants, grabbed the dual pack, and raced to the long counter that separated the front from a million bins of nuts, bolts, and nails. Cole Thanes stepped up, reached for the receipt book, and fumbled in his shirt pocket for a pen. Laird glanced around him, waiting for Kendra to pounce.

"Hey there, Laird. Luke got you runnin' errands? Kendra your girlfriend now?"

"No!" Laird's face flamed. *Too loud. She'll hear you. That's just rude.* He gave the items a gentle shove and said, "This is it for today." He slapped the twenty on the counter and gave the man a desperate, pleading look and added, "I'm kind of in a hurry."

Again, Laird felt her presence before Kendra said anything. "He's getting pizza with his *sister*." The girl leaned back against the counter, elbows propped up on it, and gave him a frighteningly flirtatious smile. "Now what guy does that?"

Words failed him. Laird nearly exploded with the repressed desire to run, scream, *demand* his receipt. But Cole Thanes just wrote each word in his slow, precise, all-caps style, added it mentally, calculated the tax—mentally—and then confirmed it with a calculator. *Can't you just do one or the other? Why don't you have a register? Get people out of here faster?*

The answer to that—obvious. The man *wanted* people to linger and talk. *And you usually like to. He's a cool guy.* That thought prompted him to try another tack. "I'm just in a hurry. I know Uncle Luke needs this stuff, and Cari spilled all the milk this morning, so Vannie's getting that. But Aunt Aggie said we could get breadsticks and soda."

"I *love* the Pizza Palace's breadsticks. They're the *best*."

Cole Thanes gave Kendra a *look* and asked if she'd see if his wife was coming. She started to argue, frowned, and then grinned. Laird groaned and didn't manage to keep all of it silent. The moment she stepped through the door, with a cold blast of air assaulting him, Cole leaned over the counter, arms folded and propped against it. "She likes you."

"Ya think?"

"Not interested? She's a nice girl—sweet. Pretty."

Laird gave the twenty on the counter a pointed look and shrugged. "Yeah, and Uncle Luke says playing around with relationships when they can't go anywhere is a great way for people to get hurt or to hurt others. I'm stayin' out of it."

"You've got some strange folks there, Laird. I'm not saying what he says isn't true, but kids've had crushes for centuries. Can't see that it hurt the world too much."

Another cold blast of air hit his legs as Kendra swept back into the store again. "Don't see her."

Cole grabbed the bill, made change, and counted it back to him—old style. "Need a sack?"

"Nope. It'll just end up in the landfill." He shoved the bills and coins in one pocket, grabbed his purchases, and nearly bolted from the building. "Thanks, Mr. Thanes. Bye, Kendra."

Her voice reached his ears just before the door slammed shut behind him. "See you around...."

She's coming to the Pizza Palace. I just know it.

"Hey!" Vannie's voice startled him from his thoughts. "What took you so long?"

"Mr. Thane was chatty. And Kendra Vassili was flirty." He glanced over his shoulder and groaned aloud as he saw her light up. "Great. Now she thinks I was watching for her or something. Bet she comes into the palace and everything."

They dumped their purchases in the backseat of the car and made their way across the street to the Pizza Palace. Vannie must have noticed how jittery he'd become, because as she got in line, she murmured, "We can take the breadsticks to go—eat at the park or something...."

Kendra sidled up to them before Laird had a chance to answer. "Hi, Vannie! Did Laird tell you how we missed you guys yesterday?"

"No, sorry. We were talking about other things."

Their turn came before Laird or Kendra could reply, but when Vannie started to say she wanted the order "to go," he couldn't let her do it. "Let's just eat here. It's too cold for the park today."

"Oh, good! I'll get some, too! And Lizzie is coming in. She's mailing Christmas cards for her mom at the post office."

That is early.... Even Grandmother would say, "It's premature to do anything Christmas related before the first of December. So common."

They filled their own glasses, retrieved napkins, slid into a booth, and waited. Vannie's apologetic expression soothed a bit,

65

but when her eyes widened in dismay and her voice dropped, he panicked. "What?"

"I should have sat beside you! She's going to—"

Sure enough, Kendra bounced over with a glass that should have been empty with the exuberance of her stride and slid in beside him. "Hey, are you guys going on the Soul-Slopes trip?"

When he couldn't speak, Vannie shook her head and tried to divert the conversation. "No.... I thought about it, but I just spent a fortune on clothes. I just don't want to spend the money. Laird said he didn't want to go."

"You really should—both of you. Who can put a price on telling others about Jesus? I mean, you *have* to have clothes. I get that. But you also need to invest in the souls of others."

"And it has nothing to do with spending a weekend skiing," Laird muttered as he took a sip of his drink.

Kendra bumped his shoulder with hers and giggled. "Well, of *course* it does. I mean, that's kind of the point, right? Show how Christians can have fun, too?" Something in her voice, her stance—something changed. Kendra whipped her head back to Vannie. "Oh! Your *clothes.* I didn't think of that. Won't your aunt let you wear ski pants just for a weekend?"

"I'm sure she would." When Kendra sniffed, Vannie went into explanation mode—something no one had managed to cure her of yet. Laird glared at her, but Vannie kept going. "Mommy would have, so I don't see why Aunt Aggie wouldn't. But it's not that. I just don't want to spend the money."

Again, Kendra presumed to know too much. "You know, they have a scholarship program if it's too expensive. I heard Dad tell Marcus that if we didn't need ours, we could send it to one of the other churches. I could call...." She pulled out her phone.

"It isn't about the money. Aunt Aggie would pay for it if I asked—I think. I just don't *want* to spend the money." Vannie's eyes lit up. "Hi, Lizzie!"

If the smirk on Vannie's lips meant anything, Lizzie was *not* happy to find Kendra seated beside him. Laird watched as Lizzie Leyton slid into the seat beside Vannie and wondered how two girls who looked so opposite could be such good friends and be so exactly alike. She cocked her head and stared at him for a moment.

"You got a haircut." When he nodded, she actually reached across the table and fingered the front before sighing. "You know, you should let this grow a bit. If it swept across your forehead like Duncan Channing...."

Kendra leaned around him, her face near enough that he could feel her breath on his neck, and nodded. "She's right. You'd be totes *cute!*" She ducked her head and sank back into the seat. "Not that you aren't already, but—I mean—"

In a desperate ploy to change the subject, Laird asked Lizzie about the ski trip. "Are you doing the Soul-Slopes thing?"

"Yes! Are you coming? We'll have a *blast*. Want to take me to the banquet? My sister—"

"They aren't coming." Kendra leveled an inscrutable look on Vannie and added, "She says it's because they don't want to spend the money, but I think she's worried about skiing in her skirts. She'd freeze."

Lizzie picked up the baton and ran with the idea. "Hasn't your family had enough of the whole dresses thing? I mean, after the break-in at your house...."

"What does that have to do with anything?" Laird glared at Vannie, but his sister ignored him. "They're vandals—criminals. How will me wearing ski pants, or even *jeans*, prevent that?"

"Well, I heard they were just getting back at you for being all uppity about your clothes being more godly than everyone else's."

Vannie blanched—her face the most unattractive shade of gray-green-white. "Wha...?"

You knew it. You talked.... Laird sighed. *And you didn't really believe it—or rather, didn't want to.*

"Well, Drew was bragging how he got you back for getting all up in his face about how you guys are more godly because you don't wear immodest clothes."

Before Vannie could speak, much to Laird's relief, their breadsticks arrived. She just stared at them. Laird kicked her. "Looks good."

"Yeah." Vannie pulled out the family phone. "I'm calling Mr. Markenson."

Kendra's eyes widened. "The cop? Why?"

"Because. If you know a crime has been committed, it's the

law. You have to report it. You said Drew bragged — "

"But you can't go telling the stupid deputy! Drew will come after us next. And my mom just got a new kitchen!"

But Vannie nearly shoved Lizzy from the booth in her quest for justice. "I'm calling. He would kill me if I didn't."

Left alone, Laird inched his way to the corner of the booth, put his knee up between him and Kendra, and grabbed a breadstick. When the girls gave him a dual panicked look of, "Do something!" he just shrugged. "You really thought it was smart to tell *my* sister that you knew who did this? That it was *her* fault? Nothing sends her into fix-it mode faster than something like that."

"He just bragged that he got you back. He didn't say *how*. For all I know, he told someone that you were gone!" Kendra tried to lean close, but Laird's knee blocked her. "*Please*. Stop her."

Lizzy jumped up. "Yeah. Like now. She's yelling at Drew!"

A glance out the window sent a cold shiver down Laird's spine. "Let me out of here."

"I—"

He didn't wait. With the skills of a kid who had once been a restaurant escape artist, Laird slid under the booth and crab-walked around their legs and into the aisle. "Eat the breadsticks if you want 'em."

"Laird…."

But he didn't wait. Laird bolted from the restaurant. *First time I've ever wished I had my own phone.*

Stretched out on the couch, her laptop perched precariously on her ever-expanding belly, Aggie typed out her dream birth. A hush, reminiscent of a fresh, heavy snowfall, blanketed the house as the younger children napped or enjoyed a quiet hour with books. Tavish had holed up in the guest room while his retreat received a complete makeover, and Laird and Vannie had gone to town on errands. Even Luke, in an attempt to give her just a bit of peace and quiet, had jumped in his truck and gone to Brunswick to make a list of work to do on his latest acquisition — one that had been languishing for weeks now.

"Painless." Aggie smirked as she typed the word and deleted it again. Then again, it was supposed to be a "dream birth." She typed again. *I will focus on my breathing and relaxing until I don't notice the pain.* With a nod, she smiled. "At least it's more realistic."

A jab to her ribs, as often happened, produced an instant craving—this time for coffee. "I swear, that rib has a craving button on it or something." She gave her belly an affectionate whap, and muttered, "Child, this better not be prophetic—like you're going to be able to 'push my buttons' or something."

The kitchen still startled her every time she walked into it. Doorless cupboards stared back at her, taunting her with the reminder that someone had been in her home, had *defaced* it with vile words. She punched the button on her coffee maker and reached into the mug cupboard for her favorite mug. It wasn't there. A glance in the dishwasher showed it surprisingly empty. "Well someone did her job without being told. Way to go, Cari!"

But a cursory sweep of the room showed no sign of the mug. She shuffled through the cupboard and realized that several were missing—all the special ones that the kids had given her, Luke, or each other. Their monogram mugs—gone. Her "Best Aunt Ever" mug. Gone. But the one she wanted most—the one with "Mibs" in a loopy script—that one hurt the most. "Lord, I don't know how much more I can take. First, our wedding photo this morning, now this? What *else* did they destroy that I haven't found?"

The boring mugs that came with their dish set would have to do. She mixed the cup and carried it into the living room, but before she could retrieve a coaster—and discover that there weren't any anymore—Aggie watched as Laird and Vannie pulled into the drive, followed by William. "Oh, no. What'd they do?"

Aggie rushed for a salad plate to serve as a saucer and bolted to the door. Vannie met her on the steps, eyes red from crying. "It's all my fault! The stupid kids! They did it because I got fed up with them teasing us about our clothes. I can't believe they really did *all* that stuff just because I got mad!"

The words made total sense—context, not so much. Aggie glanced at Laird and back again. "What does this have to do with William following you home?"

Laird shrugged. "She pulled a Vannie."

Heartsick, Aggie led the girl inside, pointed to the couch, and closed the door behind Laird. "Talk fast before William gets in here," she hissed. "Are either of you in trouble?"

"No." Laird stared after his sister for a moment, dropped his voice into a low whisper, and tried to explain. "She just confronted Drew Flintman after hearing that he bragged about getting back at her for going off on him."

Okay… great. Lord, help here? Please? I'm out of my element. Shocker, I know. Help. Okay?

A knock preceded William's entrance. "Hey, Aggie." His eyes dropped to her belly. "Feelin' okay?"

"I was until about thirty seconds ago." Aggie kneaded her back with her fists as she waddled back to her spot on the couch.

They all sat there, unspeaking, for the better part of a couple of minutes. William held his hat in hand, spinning it on a couple of fingers every few seconds. Laird's eyes darted from person to person as if trying to place bets on who would speak first. Vannie just stared at Aggie's coffee and looked ready to bawl if anyone spoke a word. And Aggie prayed. It seemed as though there wasn't anything else *to* do until she heard more, and asking Vannie right then seemed unwise.

"Aunt Aggie, why are you using a plate for a coaster?"

Just thinking about it cut deep, but Aggie chose honesty. "The coasters are gone. I assumed ruined."

"Why are you using that little mug? You hate thos—oh." Her eyes widened. "How many are gone?" When Aggie didn't answer, Vannie jumped up and strode to the kitchen. Her cry of, "Oh, no!" dug a deeper hole in Aggie's heart. "Why didn't I keep my mouth shut?!"

Aggie tried to wrestle herself out of the corner of the couch, but William stood. "Let me get it. She's right. She shouldn't have antagonized them, but this wasn't her fault. They chose to do wrong, and she needs to embrace that as well." He winked. "Something I know I've told her recently, and I suspect you have, too."

Aggie filed an SOS through her usual "p-mail" account and reached for her coffee. *Might as well drink it while it's hot. I may need it.*

A low rumbling reached them from the kitchen, but Aggie couldn't make out William's words. She gave Laird a pointed look. The boy shrugged his shoulders. But at the disappointment she couldn't hide, he jumped up and moved through the dining room. Her conscience screamed at her to call him back, but Aggie smothered it with another sip of coffee and a promise to apologize later.

He slid into the seat beside her a moment later. In a whisper Vannie could probably hear, Laird gave her the Twitter version. "He told her she shouldn't antagonize people—like he said he would, you know?"

Aggie nodded. "Okay. Good."

"And he told her that she did the right thing calling. Destruction of property isn't a valid response to people irritating you. And he said something else...." Laird glanced over his shoulder. "He said that they probably didn't *mean* to make it as bad as it was. The pipes and stuff. That was just because they were stupid and didn't close the doors. He hopes he can prove who did it so the parents can help cover the costs—like the electric bill—insurance won't cover it forever.."

Her heart sank into her stomach where her uterus kneaded it until it was numb. *I didn't even think about that. The utility bills are going to be crazy! Noooo....*

When her uterus squeezed again, her bladder protested. Aggie fought her way out of the couch and rushed for the bathroom. *Lord, this is only baby number two. I have the bladder of a woman who has given birth a dozen times right now! Help!*

Too late. She diverted and raced up the stairs. By the time she reached her room, she barely had time to grab a fresh pair of underwear and close the bathroom door behind her before her bladder refused to hold anymore. "Lord! A little help, here?"

Raised voices greeted her by the time she changed, washed up, and hurried back downstairs. Vannie, Laird, Tavish, and Ellie all stood in a semi-circle in the living room, arguing. William just stood to one side, arms folded over his chest, but not doing anything about it. Aggie opened her mouth to put a stop to it, but he shook his head. She raised her eyebrows. He shook again.

"—has to be Drew. Vannie let him have it that day, and he bragged about it," Ellie insisted.

71

Tavish shook his head the entire time she spoke. "He's always bragging about stuff like that, and we know most of it isn't possible. I think he's just trying to create a reputation for being a bad kid—feeding off others' stuff, you know? He wouldn't know that our mugs are important to us. Why would he do that? That's just not like him. The cabinets—that's him. Ruining Vannie's clothes, maybe." Tavish looked over at William. "Right?"

"Makes sense."

"But no one else—"

"What about that guy at the park the day you took the little kids." Laird's eyes went wide even as he spoke. A hushed, "Sorry," hinted that they had conspired *not* to share this story.

Vannie glanced over her shoulder at Aggie and glared at Laird. "Thanks a lot. And I don't think just because I told some guy I didn't want to go out with him, he'd ruin the house. I think Ellie's right."

"Who was that, Vannie?" William held his phone in his hand, and Aggie suspected he'd recorded the entire conversation.

"That new guy—the one everyone says to stay away from. Troy something. I just said no thanks. He left."

"After calling you a few choice words." Laird shrugged at her growl. "Might as well tell the whole thing now. I already blew it."

William inched toward the door. "I'll look into it. Anyone else who might have *anything* against your family?" The kids shook their heads. He turned to Aggie. "Anyone didn't get to buy a house or…."

Aggie shrugged and moved to the couch. Once she'd lowered herself into it, she spoke. "I just don't know. I can't think of anyone. Maybe it's not even us. Maybe we were just convenient because we weren't home and whoever it was just wanted to be—"

"No, Aunt Aggie. It has to be someone I made mad. Why else were *just* my clothes ruined?"

"Why weren't they ruined the first time, then?" Ellie turned to William for support. "It doesn't make sense. It seems to me like the vandals came back when they found a way to make it look like someone else did it."

A new argument erupted. Aggie closed her eyes and

mentally counted to two, but before she could get to three, William spoke. "Arguing about it isn't going to solve anything. Talking...." He winked at Ellie. "Talking does. If you think of anything, let me know. But don't stress out Aggie just because you want to prove your theories. She's got enough on her plate."

She should have gotten up and walked him to the door. She should have thanked him for coming—for helping. Aggie knew it all, but instead she sat on the couch, arms wrapped around her belly, and prayed for the contractions to stop. *Lord, isn't it a bit cruel for me to have to deal with these stupid Braxton-Hicks things this early? Can't it wait another month?*

CRUSHED AND No WAY

Chapter Five

The sounds of weeping in the library reached Luke as he backed out of Tavish's hideaway. After twenty-four hours of emotional outbursts, Luke's sympathy had worn precariously thin. He rinsed his hands, glanced up the stairs to ensure Aggie wasn't on her way down, and sauntered into the library. "Vannie?"

She flicked tears from her eyes and rubbed her nose across the back of her hand. Luke tried not to wince. With an impatient shove of the fabric stretched out before her, Vannie then watched as it slid off the table and pooled onto the floor. "And you can just stay there."

"Something wrong?"

"I forgot that I needed to do the brown dress in this fabric."

Luke's eyes swung from the fabric on the floor to the pattern jacket on the table — decidedly *not* the one she'd used for her brown dress — and up to her face. "I don't think I understand. That's not the brown dress pattern."

"I know." She sank into a chair and propped her head in her hands. "I picked out the brown for that pattern and this for this one…." She passed him a suit pattern that had a decided

74

Edwardian flair that even he recognized from an episode of *Downton Abbey*. Aggie and Vannie had rhapsodized over it long enough that he felt certain he'd *never* forget it again.

"But since they didn't have enough of this fabric, I decided to swap them out. No wonder I had so much brown left. I wasn't thinking." Vannie bent over and pulled the black and green striped fabric from the floor and dumped it on the table. "It was going to be hard to get darts right with stripes anyway." She punctuated her attempt at consolation with a sniffle.

"Well, you could use it to make something else. Perhaps as a skirt like your first couple? It's not what you planned, but it would still be pretty. Maybe wear it with that black sweater?" Luke prayed he hadn't missed some deeper issue with the clothing—prayed that it wasn't *really* about the vandalism. Again.

"True. I could cut on the bias. I'd still have quite a bit left, and I don't have anything for this pattern, but..." Her eyes widened. "Oh, but these stripes are the same size as the ones that Elspeth liked in that steampunk costume. I could tone it down and make her a church outfit. We've got all that black velveteen Aunt Libby found in her totes, remember?"

Though he nodded, a vague recollection of a pile of black fabric riding shotgun on the way home from his mother's one day hovering at the back of his mind, Luke felt like a liar. *Barely, Vannie. Barely.*

"I need her! And she rode to the library!" As happened at least once or twice a week, Vannie shot a mock glare at him. "Why did you have to buy a truck with a manual transmission? You *need* to teach me how to drive that thing!"

It took a moment to process the need for his truck, but understanding dawned after a few seconds of extreme darkness. "Vannie, just take the old blanket out from behind my seat and cover the backseat of the car. Put the bike in. Bring her home. Or better yet, call her and tell her you need her."

"She won't come unless I go get her, but I can call. If I tell her I'm coming, maybe she'll hurry up." Vannie hugged him and dashed for her purse. "I can't take the phone. She's got it."

Luke moved out and waited beside the door. As Vannie rushed toward him, he passed her his phone. "Just in case. Call Aggie's if you need us."

"But I think she's asleep."

"I'll go upstairs and snag it." He waited until she had her coat on before he added, "I'm proud of you, Vannie—making something for her instead. It has to be disappointing."

True to his word, Luke went in search of Aggie's phone. He found Aggie on their bed, a blanket covering her, Ronnie, and a restless Ian. He grabbed the phone and beckoned Ian to follow him. Once on the second floor, he offered play suggestions. "Want me to grab a tote of Legos or…?"

"Can I play outside? With the dogs? They missed us. Aunt Tina isn't as fun as we are."

You have a point there, son. Luke led him downstairs, handed him a jacket and pointed at his thicker boots. "Make sure you put socks on first." The disappointed look in Ian's eyes told Luke he'd predicted well. "Do it for Aunt Aggie. She doesn't need the stress."

"But socks annoy my toes!"

"Or, you can sit on the couch and watch the wallpaper fade…."

As usual, Luke's threat worked like a charm. The boy dashed for the laundry room and returned with a red sock that clearly belonged to one of the younger girls and a black one that looked more like Ronnie's. Against his better judgment, he kept his mouth shut.

The back door hadn't shut before a moan sent him dashing up the stairs to reassure his wife that she hadn't misplaced her phone—again. Instead, he found her leaning with her head pressed against the wall. "Mibs?"

"I hate stupid contractions. Why can't it just wait for labor?"

He rubbed her back, her shoulders, her back again. "I thought Hannah's explanation made sense—like workouts preparing for a marathon—get that uterus in shape before the big day."

"Yeah, well that's easy for you to say. You're not the one getting woken up by the stupid things." After another moan, she dashed for the bathroom. "And it's murder on the bladder," she groused. Seconds later, she groaned. "Two things. One, can you get me fresh underwear? Two, can you go start a load of 'em? I'm running out. I need to mark that down to ask her about on

Monday."

"Still have a weak bladder?" A pair of underwear flew out of the bathroom and landed at his feet. "I'll take that as a 'Yes, and will you add these to the washer, too?'"

Aggie's silence—eloquent in its simplicity.

Two flights of stairs—stairs that her midwife had credited for a first labor lasting less than eight hours. Stairs that Aggie believed would be the utter destruction of her bladder. She barely made it to the first floor before dashing into the bathroom.

As she entered, the sound of Vannie's indignant tone warned her of impending drama. *Can we go just one afternoon without it, Lord? Please? Begging over here.*

Confident in the Lord's agreement with her need for less stress and drama, Aggie stepped from the bathroom to see the girl shove the family cellphone in Luke's dismayed face. "Look at that! It's all along that side. The paint is totally ruined! And what's more, I don't think it's Drew this time. I heard Mr. Vaughn tell Mr. Markenson that he saw Drew get picked up this morning. It's his dad's weekend."

"Well, the tire we can fix, of course, but that paint job...." Luke hugged Vannie and apologized. "I just don't see how we can afford to fix that right now."

"I should *have* to live with it, anyway."

Aggie stepped back into the bathroom and gripped her stomach as a contraction ripped through her. It took every bit of self-restraint not to gasp as another one followed only a minute or two later. The baby shifted. Her bladder failed her. Again.

Lord....

Another contraction—this one a bit less intense—sent her shuffling down the hall and into the mudroom. The washing machine chugged away, but the red shirt that swished in the window hinted that whites had already made it into the dryer. Aggie opened the door and felt around inside. Nylon—the ones she hated the most—felt the least damp. With them wadded in her hand, Aggie waited until voices moved into the kitchen and made tracks for the stairs.

Her great plan to hide yet another bladder leak might have worked had the cooled off unders not proved damper than she'd first surmised. Aggie grabbed her hair dryer and blasted the things until she managed to fully dry them, but by the time she donned them and hurried out again, Ronnie had disappeared, and she heard the distinct sound of Luke's heavy shoes on the stairs leading to their room.

Lord, I really don't want him suggesting a bladder infection to Hannah.

Of course, her uterus decided to protest just as Luke arrived at the bathroom door. Aggie gripped the counter and gasped, despite her best efforts to keep her discomfort to herself. A low moan escaped as the baby shifted uncomfortably in its constricting and confining space.

"Mibs?"

Oh, how she despised the way that one pet name could weaken her resolve almost every time. "I think I'm dehydrated. Didn't Hannah say that could cause Braxton-Hicks to start up?"

It took no time for Luke to settle her in bed — on her left side, as her pregnancy notebook instructed — and retrieve a sports bottle of water. Her indefatigable optimism believed that would be the end of Luke's "mothering." Aggie couldn't have been more wrong.

He seated himself beside her on the bed, stroked her hair, nearly putting her to sleep, and fiddled with his phone. Only when he spoke did she realize what he'd done. "Lu —"

"Hey, Hannah. Sorry to bother you on the weekend, but I'm a bit concerned about Aggie."

When she realized she'd never get him off the phone without receiving an answer, Aggie made motions for him to put the midwife on speaker. He hesitated, but Aggie glared. "Putting you on speaker. Apparently Aggie wants to make sure I don't lie to her about what you say."

"I was just telling Luke that you shouldn't hesitate to call any time. Now what has him concerned?"

"I...."

"If you don't tell her, I will," Luke warned.

Only the fact that Luke rarely insisted on his way about anything kept her from snatching the phone from him and chucking it out a window. The irrationality of that temptation did hint that perhaps she might not be doing as well as she thought. "It's just a few Braxton-Hicks."

"And…." Luke and the midwife spoke in unison.

"Well, my bladder is a bit weak. I'm back to going to the bathroom every other minute—just like in the first trimester."

"And…." this time Luke spoke alone.

Aggie glared.

"Aggie, if you don't tell me what is going on, how am I supposed to reassure Luke that he's just being an overprotective papa-slash-hubby?"

The woman made a good point. "Well, like I said, the bladder is a bit weak. I've had to change my underwear a few times. I'm sure once the baby moves off it, and maybe I drink some more…."

A cough from Luke could have meant anything from a tickle in his throat to his opinion of her opinion. But when he began laughing, Aggie mentally reviewed her statement and sighed. "I *meant* that I think the baby is *standing* or sitting or something on one part of my bladder right now. If he shifts, maybe." Laughter filled her room until Aggie gave up and took another swig of water. "Meanwhile, I'm chugging water and lying on my left side thanks to Luke."

"Good man you have there." After a couple of questions, the midwife asked, "Do you have a fever?"

Luke bolted to the bathroom and returned with the children's thermometer. He gave her a grin when it beeped and shook his head. "Nope, Hannah, it's a perfect 98.6."

"Well, as long as it doesn't elevate before Monday, then I think you'll be fine until I see you then. Try to drink more and rest a bit. If I know you, you're trying to do everything at once. Slow down and enjoy the pregnancy. It's nearly over."

Not until Luke hung up, replaced the thermometer, and came to sit beside her did Aggie speak again. "I might forgive you."

"If…."

"You take the kids for a drive. My whole body just relaxed. I'm suddenly really sleepy." He opened his mouth to speak, but Aggie shook her head. "Do. Not. Say. It. I conceded defeat. That's enough, don't you think?"

Luke's kiss assured her she'd be alone and asleep inside ten minutes. "I'll let Vannie stay to work on her church outfit. I think she's trying to finish before tomorrow. That way if you need anything…."

"Do you need to do something about the car?"

He shook his head. "She had it towed to the gas station. Lem's gonna take the tire over to Brunswick and get it patched or replaced—whichever they say."

Aggie pulled him closer, gave him a kiss he wouldn't soon forget, and gently shoved him away again. "Then get out of here, mister."

"Love you." Luke waited for her reassurance that she loved him, too, and slipped from the room. "See you after a while. We'll figure out dinner. You sleep."

Aggie hardly heard him.

Sunday, November 30th

Vannie had just opened her Bible study notebook when Myra Vaughn leaned over her shoulder and whispered, "Can you help out with the four-year-olds this morning? Mrs. Flint stayed home with a cold, and I can't find Aggie anywhere."

"She's home—resting. It's been a stressful few weeks. Uncle Luke thinks it's irritating the baby—either that or a bladder infection." As she spoke, Vannie grabbed her notebook, Bible, and purse and slid out of the pew. "On my way. Know what they're supposed to be learning today?"

"I think Ellen was going to do something with the feasts, but you could just read a psalm or proverb or something and then do Bible quizzes. Marcus sent Josiah Ware to the market for snacks, so you should be good there. Keep him in the room if the kids are extra hyper. I'm sure he'd be willing to help."

Mrs. Vaughn's words looped through Vannie's mind on auto-repeat. *"Keep him in the room. Keep him in the room. Keep him in the room."*

"Right. So he can think I'm so pathetic I can't corral half a dozen four-year-olds."

Tavish stepped out of the restroom just as she passed. "What?"

Vannie blinked and kept going. "Just thinking out loud. Better get into class before Uncle Luke catches you loitering by the bathrooms."

The look of utter confusion as Tavish scuttled away made her rethink her warning. *Yeah. Like Uncle Luke would care.*

She hadn't been in the class for half a minute before two kids burst in with parents on their heels. "Mrs.….. Vannie?"

"Not a missus yet, but yep. You get me today."

Before anyone could reply, another child dashed inside. "I know my ver—huh?"

"Okay, parents!" Vannie winked at the little guy staring up at her in utter confusion. "If anyone doubted, Mrs. Flint is most beloved." She grabbed her Bible and began flipping through it, looking for the simplest Psalm she could find. Psalm 136 filled the bill quickly and easily.

Just as the final two children burst through the doors, both eager to inform Mrs. Flint that they'd learned their Bible verses, Josiah Ware arrived with a canvas tote bag bulging with what she suspected would be graham crackers, juice, and cups. *Please have gotten something other than purple grape juice or cranberry. A nice white grape… apple….* A little girl in a cream lace dress sidled up to her and smiled. *Please!*

"I'm sorry I'm late. Who knew little stores are that busy on Sunday mornings?" He pulled white grape juice boxes and gummy fruits from the bag. No cups needed. "I was going to get graham crackers, and then I thought maybe gluten-free kids couldn't have them." He glanced at a mother watching with evident curiosity. "Is there gluten in graham flour?"

"I'm pretty sure there's wheat flour in the crackers. Good call." Mrs. Kapinski gave Josiah a warm smile as she hugged her little munchkin. "Good call, Josiah. You're a treasure."

In no time, the room emptied of all adults and Vannie stood before the room feeling much too far out of her depth. *What was Mrs. Vaughn thinking? I can't do this!*

Josiah bustled the children into their chairs and offered to pray. Vannie sagged in prayerful relief as his words filled the room. Simple, direct, easy to understand—not preachy. She couldn't have been more impressed. Then her turn came.

"Okay, who knows their Bible verse?"

Hands raised — all but one. That little guy folded his arms in defiance. "I'm not thankful, so I won't say it."

"Well, we'll have to pray about that." The words sounded inane, even to her ears. "Well, who can tell me the reference? Is it John? Proverbs? Is it Genesis?" *Is it something that I can find quickly? Please?*

All five children cried out in unison. "Psalms!"

"Excellent. Which one?" She sat in the chair at the head of the semicircle of chairs and gave Josiah an encouraging smile. "If you want to go, I can probably —"

Laird burst into the room. "Can I help? Please? Tell me I can help." He rushed over to snag a couple of chairs for Josiah and himself. "Are we going to sing? What'll we sing?"

"Um, I was in the middle of Bible work."

"Great! What's the verse?"

Little miss lace dress piped up, "Psalm 136:1."

Laird took one look at the little girl — a carbon copy of her older sister — and turned green. "Hi."

How can I have chosen the right scripture for the week? Her eyes drifted toward the ceiling, even as she wondered why people did that. *What, like You're cottage cheese spread across a ceiling? Really? Anyway, um… thanks.*

"My sister likes you. *She* thinks you're *cute.*"

Vannie took one look at Laird and decided to divert. "Well, that's nice. We should all like nice people. Meanwhile, who wants to recite their verse first?"

Little hands did half-jazz hands as they vied for first position. Vannie chose "little sis" in hopes it would divert her attention from her sister's futile attempts at a love life. "Why don't you go first?"

"'Give thanks to the Lord, for He is good. For his lovingness is everlasting.'"

With an encouraging nod, Vannie praised the girl. "It was almost perfect. It's loving*kind*ness. Very good! Anyone —"

"Are you Lizzie's boyfriend?" The girl's eyes bored into Laird.

He flushed. "I don't have a girlfriend." Laird's eyes roamed the room. "Who wants to go next?" Josiah inched his way to the door, but Laird stopped him. "Let's see if Josiah knows it!"

That's all it took. The older boy seated himself and leaned forward. "When I was eight, my mom had me memorize the whole chapter, but the first verse is the easiest."

Laird clapped with excessive enthusiasm. "That's great. Let's see how many verses he can still remember, but first, who wants to go next?" His eyes slid sideways. "If that's okay, Vannie?"

The growing frustration fizzled at his question. *I'll give you a break since you're still freaked out over Lizzy and Kendra, but man. Really?* Aloud, she simply nodded and said, "Great idea." Vannie smiled at Josiah. "Do you mind?"

She'd had her fair share of guys interested in her, but something in the way Josiah Ware watched her felt... different. His eyes lingered for just a moment before he nodded. "That would be great. Maybe they can help me with the second part of every verse."

That's what I was going to have them do. Cool. She didn't say it, however. Instead she led the others in their recitations, made a note of the three word-perfect and the slightly off one from Lizzy's sister, and turned it over to Josiah.

They made it through the class period without *too* much floundering. The children were eager to sing, eager to tell about their Thanksgiving celebrations, and add what they were thankful for—even if every single one of them did name "Christmas is coming" as their number one reason for gratitude.

Laird planned to stay in the room—to continue hiding—but when Lizzie's sister dashed out calling for her, he decided he had a sudden need for the restroom. "Might be a while...." He whistled with an exaggerated innocent expression settling on his features. "Tell Uncle Luke not to worry."

The other children raced out to play before Vannie could stop them. "Oh, boy. I'm in trouble now. I think the parents are supposed to come get them." As she talked, she cleaned up the juice boxes, tossed them and the gummy wrappers, and tied the trashcan liner into a knot at the top. She rearranged the chairs—always just one step ahead of Josiah.

"I could help, if you'd let me."

"Well, you didn't get roped into this class. I did." The lack of appreciation for his help stung as she heard her words spoken. "But I didn't thank you. You were great. The kids were impressed with your memory work."

Josiah stood, hands in his pockets, and watched as she gathered her things. "It's an easy one to do. It looks impressive, but really, it's twenty six verses of two lines each. And one of those lines is always the same. That makes it just twenty-seven lines. Word wise, it's not much more than the Beatitudes."

A mother came to pick up her son just as Vannie started for the door. "Sorry. They all raced out. I didn't think—"

"No worries. I know where to find him. He's half in love with Lydia Rice. So cute."

For the first time, Vannie understood why her aunt and uncle found Kenzie's little crush on Rory MacKenzie a little unnerving. She turned to Josiah and shrugged as the woman disappeared into the hall. "Okay…."

"Why do parents encourage that?"

She stopped mid-stride and stared at him. "I was just wondering that myself." At the foyer, she grabbed her coat and slid her Bible and purse onto the shelf above the coat rack. "I'm going outside for a few minutes." She shook the trash bag in her hand. "Gotta take this to the dumpster. Thanks again for your help—especially for the snacks. The juice boxes were genius!"

Josiah took the bag from her. "I'll do it."

Her attempt to reach for it found it snatched from her reach. "I can—"

"Walk me out, then. But I'm doing it." Josiah pulled on his coat with one arm and transferred the bag to the other as he stuck his other arm in the sleeve. "That sounded rude. I just wanted to help."

How to answer? Vannie had no clue. Instead she crossed the foyer to open the door for him and found his hand already pushing the bar open. "Okay, now this is just embarrassing."

"My mother would kill me if I didn't show basic courtesies." As they stepped outside, Josiah added, "Even if I didn't want to do it anyway."

"Well, thanks."

Wind whipped at her skirt, making her wish once more that she'd found good wool for a coat. Josiah tossed the bag into the dumpster as they neared and turned to walk back. "By the way, nice outfit. You have such a classic style."

Oh, how she wanted to accept the compliment as it was given, but it felt dishonest, somehow. "Thanks, but it's a new style for me. I spent a couple of weeks in Fairbury — got to talk to Alexa Hartfield a few times. She encouraged me to wear what I liked. Then when all my clothes were ruined, I decided to do it." Again, her skirt whipped around her, this time flying up much higher than decency allowed. "Of course," she muttered as she jerked it into place, "it would look better if I actually had a dress coat, still. This thing doesn't do anything for keeping my clothes covered."

A strange rapping, tapping sounded nearby. She started to make a joke about Poe when Laird's face showed in the men's bathroom window. He plastered his cheek against it, palms on the pane, and slid down out of sight. "Oh, brother."

Josiah laughed with her all the way back to the church steps. "I know how he feels, though. Sometimes...."

Shocker. You're cuter than any teen pop star and not full of yourself. Of course, girls are going to like you. Aloud she just said, "I've usually avoided that problem, thankfully."

Just as the door closed behind them, Vannie could have sworn he said under his breath, "Can't imagine how."

Place to Place

Chapter Six

Monday, December 1st

With mud-caked paws, the dogs streaked through the house, leaving their mark on every floor, every rug, every bit of furniture they passed. Aggie stared at the melee, disbelief transforming into fury with each black mark on her once-clean floors. "I just *mopped* in here!"

Ronnie raced past, slid on a paw print, and landed on his backside. Ian, unable to stop, tumbled over him and landed at Aggie's feet. "Sorry, Aunt Aggie. They got out, and someone didn't shut the back door."

"That explains why I was cold all of a sudden, but it doesn't explain why you were getting in the dog pen without permission."

"They had it, Aggie." Luke's voice startled her as he stepped into the room. "I forgot how wound up the dogs've been lately, or I'd never have done it."

Rude? It was. Aggie knew it. But she just turned and strode—as much as a pregnant woman who waddles more and more every day can stride—to the mudroom and retrieved the floor vacuum and the steam mop. Luke offered to help—to do it for her—but Aggie shook her head and plugged in the vacuum.

Blissful noise filled the room.

I never imagined I'd prefer loud noise to the sound of my chil — The dogs raced past again. "Get. Those. Dogs. Out. Of. Here. I know the number to the pound, and I am not afraid to use it."

Four horrified eyes stared back at her as Ronnie and Ian stopped in their tracks. Ronnie opened his mouth to speak, but Luke ordered them to corral the dogs outside. He tried to pry the handle from her hands, but Aggie glared at him. With a shrug that could have meant almost anything, Luke followed the boys. A moment later, she heard him over the mini-cyclone in her hands. "They're out, Mibs!"

If you think calling me Mibs is going to fix anything, you're nuts. I have a midwife arriving in less than ten minutes and a house full of mud. Instinct kicked in with the motor, and she sang as she maneuvered the machine to the nearest mess. *"...wash me and I...."*

She'd barely made the first pass over the drying chunks when Cari came in from the library, wailing. "I don't know this word!"

Three... two... one.... Aggie took a deep breath and counted down once more. *Five... four... three... two... one....*

With the book thrust in her hands, Aggie stared at the words. "Which one?"

Cari stared over the top of the book, frowned, and snatched it back. Her lips moved as she reread every word until she got to the offender. "That one."

"'Ted jumped into the *sleigh*.' E-i-g-h says 'aye'. Like the long A sound." Aggie flipped a few pages back and nodded to herself. "Do you remember reading this?" She pointed to the reading lesson explanation of e-i-g-h and showed it to Cari.

"Yeah." Cari sniffled a bit. "I forgot."

Something in the girl's expression suggested another reason for the sudden tears. "I think you decided it was easier to cry about it and have me tell you the word than to go back and reread the lesson."

Genuine tears flowed. "I'm sorry."

"I think you're sorrier that I caught you than you are that you did it, but...." Aggie hugged the girl and pointed to the library. "Miss Hannah is here, so you're getting off easy this time.

Next time, you'll have to write the rule five times. Trust me; it's faster to look it up than do that."

Cari made it halfway to the library before rushing back to hug her. "I really am sorry. I can mop for you."

If she hadn't known how much Cari despised using the steam mop, Aggie might have assumed it to be a ploy to get out of more school work. Instead, she kissed Cari's head and sent her back again. "I appreciate it, but you need to finish your independent reading."

The doorbell rang before Aggie could even put away the vacuum. *Well, it's not like she doesn't know what life is really like here.* "Come in!"

Hannah popped her head inside the door. "Did you call me in?"

"Yep. Sorry. Stupid dogs got in the house and decided to 'stencil' my floor with prints. It's not the look I was going for. Too 'last year' or something like that."

"Could be worse. My sister's dog decorated her entryway with a different kind of package. I stepped right in it yesterday after church."

"Ugh!" Aggie propped the handle up into place and moved the machine out of the walkway. "Upstairs or in the guest room? Take your pick."

Hannah gave her an odd look. "If you'd rather not take the stairs right now —"

"Oh, no! But Luke suggested you might not like having to make the climb every other week."

The woman hoisted her medical backpack over one shoulder and pointed. "Lead on!" Halfway up the first flight, she asked, "Any more contractions?"

"Some. But it was better after a nap. I stayed home from church yesterday, too. Haven't had any today, though. I think I just needed some rest and hydration."

"Well, we'll see what's going on." Hannah's forehead furrowed as Aggie paused at the base of the second staircase. "Are you winded?"

As much as she hated to admit it, Aggie shook her head and muttered, "Stupid contraction. If I don't get up there soon, I'm going to end up with more bladder issues."

By the time she made it to her bathroom and out again, the contractions had grown worse—still irregular, but definitely worse. Hannah felt her belly with the practiced hands of a woman familiar with how a pregnant body works. She listened to the heart rate, took Aggie's temperature, and even tested the fluid that kept dampening Aggie's underwear, but everything looked good—good and normal.

"Well, the head is finally down. I suspect it's displacing your bladder a bit. If he shifts some or the head descends more, you'll probably get relief there. I don't like that your contractions seem to be activity and stress related."

A protest welled up in her, but Luke standing in the doorway changed her words. "Well, we don't *know* that. Luke just assumes...."

"You give every indication, anyway." He moved to her side and took her hand in his. "Okay, what should we look for—I mean, if something were to go wrong?"

Hannah gave Aggie's foot a reassuring squeeze before she answered him. "I'd say if normal activity increases it much more, or if they get even a little regular. And if the bladder leakage doesn't stop, we might want to have the hospital do a quick ultrasound—just to be safe."

"You did the litmus paper. It was fine!" Aggie glared at Luke. "I do *not* want another hospital experience. I want this baby right here in my room. Research—" She choked back her objections and opted for prayer. "Fine. If they get worse or regular, we'll go in. If I leak too much, we'll go in. But I'm having this baby right here."

Luke would have objected. Aggie saw it in his eyes and felt it in the way he moved closer as if to soften his words, but Hannah spoke first. "I don't see any reason you won't. Being cautious won't hurt anything. Having contractions won't either. It's common to have more with later babies. It's your body's way of gearing up for labor—conditioning for—"

"The real thing." Aggie and Luke grinned at each other as they spoke in unison.

"I've said that before, I suppose."

Aggie winked at Luke before she met Hannah's gaze. "A time or twenty."

They stood at the farthest corner of the property and spoke in hushed whispers. Laird argued, adamant that the vandals couldn't have been led by Drew, because he hadn't been around to do the car destruction. "It's just not possible."

"But he bragged about it. Maybe he got someone to do it for him—to throw us off his scent." Vannie wrinkled her nose. "I sound like a cheesy mystery sleuth. Ugh."

Laird stared out across the fields that flanked each side of the highway. "They had to have come through here. I wonder if there's anything—"

"I know. I thought that, too. But it'd be gone by now, for sure. We've had rain, and all the animals...." Utter frustration boiled over until Vannie threw back her head and gave a guttural yell. "That felt surprisingly good."

"Glad to hear it. Because now Aunt Aggie is going to come out here, contract some more, and Uncle Luke will make sure we suffer for it." Laird's head shot up and his eyes met hers just as he finished speaking. "Wait a minute. Wait. We're acting like it *has* to be Drew, or it *has* to be Troy, or someone like that. But what if it's not? What if someone did the first stuff and then someone else got the idea from town gossip?!"

"Or even *just* the car keying-tire puncturing thing. That could have been Troy piggy-backing off the others." Vannie frowned. "Except that the first stuff was just stupid kid stuff that got out of hand because they didn't close the doors. The second one, with the stuff directed at me—that's gotta be Drew. They didn't ruin anyone else's clothes—just mine. And after I told them off for making fun of them."

Laird gave her arm an awkward pat. "They deserved it, okay? Sure, you probably shouldn't have egged them on, but they asked for it."

"I'm the one who's supposed to be almost an adult! Two years, Laird. Two. And I let a stupid eleven-year-old bait me."

"I heard Uncle Luke talking to Mr. Markenson...." Laird hesitated as if uncertain.

"Yeah?" When he didn't finish his recounting of the conversation, Vannie pretended to throttle him. "Spill it, bro!"

The toe of his shoe kicked a rock free while Laird hesitated. "Okay, well, Mr. Markenson thought maybe Drew had a crush on you. Then you blasted him and it hurt his feelings." He stepped aside with exaggerated speed and movements, as if trying to avoid her wrath. "You have to admit. It makes sense."

Dread filled her. "Yeah. It kind of does. And then I went off on him again." Vannie folded her arms over her chest and shivered against a blast of wind that proved her aunt had been right. She did need something heavier than a cardigan with snow on the way. "I'm going to go find Drew. It's almost time for school to be out. I'm going to apologize. Maybe at least it'll stop future stuff. That's the most important thing right now."

"I'll go wi—never mind. I think I'll stay here. Take Ellie. Maybe he'll transfer his affections to her. She's too nice to hurt anyone's feelings, but she won't get all silly either."

As much as she wanted to do it, Vannie couldn't. "That's just mean. I almost thought about asking Aunt Aggie to say directly that I can't date so I could apologize to Troy, too. He'd ask again. I could say I'm not allowed. He'd think that's why... and if he was the one to do the keying or whatever, we'd be done with it."

"It's a good idea...." Laird sighed. "Yeah. You're right. I couldn't do it either. Self-respect—gone."

She left him there, still staring out over the landscape as if it held all the answers to life's questions. Each step through half-frozen mud led her nearer to the house but no closer to a plan to convince her aunt that she *needed* to apologize. *If I just tell her that I'm trying to get them to stop, she'll say no. I know it.*

Dogs yapped at her as she passed their pens. "I'll take you for a walk later, guys. I need to do something first."

Ronnie shot out the door and whizzed past her just as she reached the steps. "Mommy says I play with dogs!"

"Well don't let them out this time!"

"I won't!" A second later his voice carried back to her again. "But 'cause *Mommy* said so."

You're awfully articulate when you're being defiant. Has your mommy ever noticed that?

Kenzie and Ellie stood at the island rolling cake and cream cheese frosting into balls. *I swear she lets them do that to keep them out of trouble* and *because it means that cake lasts longer. Less junk food, even if we eat them more often.*

"Where's Aunt Aggie?"

"Laundry." Ellie leaned forward and whispered. "She keeps holding her stomach and going to the bathroom all the time. She's not going to have the baby *early,* is she?"

Vannie shrugged and inched her way toward the mudroom. "I remember Mommy doing that a lot with Ian. Like the whole time."

"Whew! I was afraid the baby would come early and end up in the hospital like that one we were praying for last month." Ellie rolled another ball and added, "She couldn't have the baby at home if it was early, could she?"

Another shrug, another step toward the doorway, Vannie tried not to seem *too* eager to get away. "I could ask...." Ellie turned to grab another baking sheet—a perfect getaway moment. Vannie snagged it.

Aggie stood at the dryer, door open and clothes spilling into a basket, but gripping the sides as if ready to shake out the contents. Just as Vannie started to ask if she was okay, Aggie sucked in a great gulp of air and exhaled loudly enough for them to hear it in the kitchen.

Great. Another one. Mommy did that. Not for the first time, Vannie chastised herself for still using the "baby" moniker for her mother, and once more, she ignored it. *I was still little. It's who she is to me.*

Though she turned to go, Aggie must have seen the movement, because without turning her head, she ground out, "Need something?"

"Just...." The temptation to add, "checking on you" made answering truthfully more difficult than she could have expected. "—wanted to go to town for a bit. Can I?"

"Wha—" Another contraction gripped Aggie. "Go. Ahead."

"Are you okay?"

"Fine." Aggie gasped out the words between gulps of air. "Stairs. Too much. Today."

All the way to get her coat, to find the keys and retrieve the phone from its charger—all the way out to the car, Vannie fought within herself. The engine hinted at not wanting to turn over. Ice at the end of the drive just as she pulled onto the street sent the back tires sliding for a moment. Fear coursed through her veins as she released her foot from the gas and tried to guide the car straight. Heart pounding, eyes wide with fright and a determination to keep the car from tackling Mrs. Dyke's mailbox, Vannie managed to regain control as she rolled past the neighbor's house and toward the stop sign.

It took three passes through town to find Drew and his little band of bullies. Vannie pulled her car into the space closest to them and stepped out. Drew laughed. "I heard about that. Doesn't look so great now."

It took more self-control to ignore the jab than Vannie had expected. The boy's expression showed mockery and disdain—nothing of the purported crush Laird had mentioned. Her foot slipped on ice near the gutter. She dove for the hood of her car and managed *not* to do a face-plant on the sidewalk. Drew and crew howled.

"Drew, can I talk to you?"

"Don't know. You can't walk yet. Have you learned to talk?"

Every step closer required her to order herself not to react. Two other boys flanked him, but the others scattered. "Very funny."

"She said it. Not me." Drew glanced around him and scowled to see his other buddies gone. A foul word spewed from his lips. She ordered herself not to react. Too late—Vannie winced. Drew howled. "The widdow giwl hewrd a bad wewd."

As she drew nearer, Drew swallowed hard. Then she saw it—some flicker of hurt in his eyes. *It's true. Great. I have to be careful.* Vannie stuffed her hands in her pockets and tried to look relaxed. "I owe you an apology." It went against every one of Aggie's rules for apologies, but Vannie tried something anyway. "You hurt my feelings when you made fun of my clothes, and I was mean and snotty about it. I'm sorry."

The boys on either side of Drew snickered, but Vannie ignored them. She kept her eyes trained on Drew's. He didn't waver. Second after second passed until he shrugged. "Okay."

That's it? I tell you that you hurt my feelings, and you can't even— Vannie cut off her own internal diatribe. "Anyway, that's why I came to town. I just wanted to say I was sorry." A new thought hit her. "Got any idea where Troy is? I was rude to him, too."

It worked. Drew's forehead furrowed, his eyebrows drew together until it became as close to a unibrow as a pubescent kid can get, and by the way his shoulders squared and his jacket moved, it looked like he balled his hands up in his jacket pockets. "What'd you say to *him?*"

"I told him I wouldn't go out with him." Answering truthfully—a calculated risk.

Drew grinned. "That's why he said he messed up your car and—" A kick from one of the others shut him up.

"Well, I doubt he did." The lie flowed from her lips with such ease that it almost frightened her. "He's probably just mad and talking big—blowing off steam. You know, like you saying you got even with us for me being a jerk." She turned to go. "Anyway, thanks for accepting my apology."

The thriving metropolis of Brant's Corners—all half-dozen mom and pop store's worth—showed no sign of Troy, but as she swung past the park, she saw him with a group of dubious characters. No, they weren't sketchy enough to make anyone in Rockland bat an eye, but their clothes, the way they sat on the outdated equipment—everything screamed, "I'm a force to be reckoned with."

Nerves rattled her as she parked the car and climbed from it. Her eyes scoured the ground, looking for any patches of ice. The last thing she needed to do was give them further reason for mockery.

A girl saw her first and elbowed Troy. From farther than she would have imagined possible, their eyes met. Troy pushed himself away from the merry-go-round and shoved his hands in his pockets as he wandered in her direction. The girl started to follow, but he ordered her back. Vannie watched with surprise and dismay as the girl slunk back and plopped down on the still rotating equipment.

From ten feet away, he called out, "What're you doing here?"

Vannie took another couple of steps before she answered. "Came to see you."

"Yeah?" He stood closer to her than Vannie felt comfortable with, but she refused to back away.

94

"I came to apologize."

"For getting me in trouble with the cops for something I didn't even do? Yeah. Too late."

Confusion flooded her. "What?" Vannie shoved her hands in her pockets and tried not to shiver. *Can't let him think it's because I'm afraid of him. That'd be a nightmare.*

"That cop—from your church. He came to my house and asked what I knew about the stuff going on at your house—all the break-ins while you were gone."

"Oh." She couldn't imagine why. "I just don't know why he'd ask *you.*"

At first, Vannie was certain he didn't believe her. A scowl darkened his face as he stared her down, but when she didn't flinch, he relaxed a little. "Huh. Then why apologize?"

Her throat went dry and she choked. It took a couple of swallows to moisten her larynx enough to talk again. "I just thought I was rude to you when you asked me out. You acted like I was, anyway. And I didn't apologize. That was wrong."

"Wait." Troy scowled at her once more. "You think I was mad that you wouldn't go out with me?" He turned to go. "Talk about full of yourself."

But Vannie reached out and grabbed his sleeve. From the corner of her eye, she saw the girl leap forward. "No, I said that I thought I was rude in how I said I couldn't go. I thought you got mad at me for being rude. So I wanted to apologize." She swallowed her pride and a lump the size of his fist and added, "And I'm sorry if I'm why Mr. Markenson came to see you. I don't see how, but Laird did accidentally tell Aunt Aggie about you asking me out, so maybe…."

Even as she spoke, something niggled at her, but Vannie's mind refused to cooperate. The girl appeared, but Troy ordered her back again. "If I want you, I'll call you." An expletive punctuated the command, and to Vannie's surprise, the girl slunk back to where she'd come from. Troy grinned. "You don't like that, do you?"

"Frankly, no. If I'd known that about you, I probably would have been even ruder." She sighed. Her mission had failed. "Anyway. I really am sorry. I want to say I didn't mean to be rude, but I can't even know that. And sorry for getting you in

95

trouble."

"You didn't. They don't have anything on me. Can't believe they haven't nailed Drew, though. That kid gave me details of what he did to your stuff. You totally—" Troy's next words gave a perfectly crass description of how she'd angered Drew.

The first snowflake fell just as three things exploded in her mind. She remembered William saying he'd speak to Troy, she remembered Drew saying Troy had admitted defacing her car, and she realized Troy had just provided detailed proof of Drew's guilt. "Anyway. I better get home. I don't know how to drive in snow yet."

"I could take you."

"Your girlfriend wouldn't like that, but thanks." The minute she heard her own words, Vannie cringed. *You sound jealous. That's just great. He's going to think you like him.* Before he could respond, she turned and bolted. At the parking lot, she almost slipped—again—and Troy stood there laughing at her, but at least he didn't look mad anymore. *Great. He's going to think that's "cute" or something. Oh, brother.*

A quiet house, something Aggie had begun to believe didn't exist, greeted her as Aggie descended the last steps and stood at the base of the stairs. Bathroom or couch? The question shouldn't have been necessary. She ached to sit and rest, but the past week had taught her that without bathroom first, she'd be struggling to extricate herself from the cushions.

No sooner had she finally seated herself, than headlights swept across the living room. "Aaah… Lu—" A midnight blue Corvette slid past the window. "Nope. William. Great."

As if to share her agreement, the baby kicked, and Aggie's uterus contracted. "Don't even start little lady or young man— whatever you are. Just don't even. I made it up and down those stairs half a dozen times in the past half hour without a twinge. Now just leave me alone."

A knock echoed through the room. Forehead furrowed, Aggie's eyes swept the area and realized the area rug in the entryway had not yet been replaced. *I can't afford any more mental notes. I need a notebook. I need something, or I won't get anything done.*

The knock echoed again. Aggie made a split-decision *not* to try to get up. "Come in!"

William peered around the door. "Did you say come in?"

"Yep. I'm not getting up until my bladder threatens to ruin the couch."

"Lovely mental picture, Aggie." William dropped into the chair opposite her and closed his eyes.

In an attempt to avoid whatever had brought him out after nine o'clock on a week night, Aggie opted for what she considered a safe topic. "Busy night? Drunk driver, or did the GIL escape from jail?"

"Spent all afternoon and evening talking to six different families. I *finally* got confessions for all three incidents."

Instead of the wash of relief she expected to feel, Aggie's throat went dry and a strong case of the shivers took over. She struggled to sit upright and inched her way out of the couch. "I'm cold. Want anything while I'm up?"

William said nothing. He just watched as she loaded the fireplace with newspaper, kindling, and a log she knew better than to lift. Sure enough, a contraction ripped through her. Then he spoke. "Um, Aggie?"

"Yeah."

"What do you think you're doing?"

A gasp escaped before she could stop it. "Building a fire."

"That log's too big for you to be lifting, isn't it?"

"I did it, didn't I?" Aggie didn't sound nearly as convincing as she tried to — and she knew it.

William stood and inched her away from the fireplace. "I'll get this."

He says after I've already done the hard part. What is it with men? They really do want to be chivalrous, but they're clueless half the time.

"Want some water?" What else could she do but ask? "Coffee? Cocoa? Might have a Coke or something in there."

"I'll get it. Just sit down. Luke's going to come home and blast me for you being over there in pain from waiting on me."

As much as she wanted to argue, Aggie shuffle-waddled back to the couch and eased herself back into the perfect cushions. *I don't think I thanked You for sparing this couch. So here it is, belated but genuine. Thanks.*

William's words hit her just as she heard him grumble at the sight of their door-less cabinets. "Um, William?"

"Yeah?"

"How'd you know Luke isn't home?"

"I wouldn't be much of a cop if I didn't have basic observational skills. No truck and an Aggie home means Luke is gone. Vannie can't drive the truck." William brought her a glass of water. "Drink. Vannie mentioned you needing more liquids."

Does everyone know what I do and do not need? Despite her irritation, Aggie accepted the glass, thanked him, and chugged about half of it before remembering how close she was to going to bed. "Thanks a lot. Now I'll be up every hour going to the bathroom!"

He appeared with a couple of cake pops and a glass of water. "I'm stealing one for me and one for Tina. I'll eat hers since she's not back from Yorktown yet. Wouldn't want it to go to waste or anything."

"You do that. Kenzie will be thrilled to know you appreciate her handiwork." The way William's face softened to hear Kenzie's name warmed her heart. "That little girl sure does love you."

"It's mutual." William glanced at his phone, up at the wall clock, and let his eyes rest on Aggie. "Know when Luke'll be home?"

Great. It's bad news. Another contraction squeezed her bladder until Aggie had to make a penguin-dash for the bathroom.

"Do *not* go into labor, Mrs. Sullivan!"

"Then do *not* freak me out with questions like that!" The bathroom door slammed shut behind her, but Aggie had already lost the battle with her bladder. Half a minute later, she staggered down the short hall to the mudroom and snapped on the light. A mouse scurried across the floor—across her *toes,* which *had* been firmly planted on said floor.

Her cry of fury must have sounded like a panicked, fearful scream, because William rushed into the room, hand on his hip, ready to do battle with whatever nefarious criminal he faced. "What?"

"I think your gun is overkill for a mouse—barely. Stupid

thing. Get me the broom, will you?"

"You're going to kill it with a broom?" His tone wavered between disbelief and amusement.

Aggie reached around him and snatched the broom from its hook. "They must do it in cartoons for a reason, right? It's like a golf club for dummies. Anyone can hit it with something this wide...." To prove her point, she poked the handle between the freezer and the wall.

Nothing.

"Why don't you leave it for Luke? Got any traps? I can set traps for you, if you like."

William tried to lead her out of the room, but Aggie just shoved the broom into his hands and went digging through the dryer for the underwear she'd almost forgotten. Success went to her head. Aggie caught herself half a second before she would have swung them in a triumphant arc overhead on her way out of the room. *Lord, I have officially lost it. Did You see that? Thanks for stopping me, but um... yeah.*

The ruddy tinge to William's right ear and neck hinted he might have guessed her near gaffe, but when she stepped around the couch minutes later, he sat with the phone to his ear and embarrassment etched in his face. "Tell Tina I said hi. She hasn't texted me all day. I think I miss the old messenger days."

"Did you hear that?" He hesitated and nodded. "She says the texts work both ways and that you need to hold out for labor until she arrives."

"I'm not in labor! Sheesh! This is just my body —" Aggie cut herself off and sat down before her bladder protested again. "Tell her she doesn't have to worry about me giving birth on the way to the hospital this time. That's the beauty of a home birth. No worrying about silly stuff like that. Besides, it only happens in movies."

Red shifted to green as her words sank in. William shook his head, disconnected his call, and leaned forward. "Okay, I wanted to wait for Luke, but I need to get going. We figured out the vandals. Vannie was right. There were three separate sets. The first set tried to impress Drew after she told all of them off. Then Drew used their mess to go in and get specific about Vannie's stuff."

"Wow. Really?"

"Like most bullies, he is too much of a coward to do anything on his own. He likes intimidation, but…."

"And the car?" Aggie closed her eyes and steeled herself against assurances that he didn't know.

"Troy Dulles. He didn't appreciate her lack of appreciation for *him*. So, he decided to use Drew's boasting as a cover for his payback."

She dug the heel of her hand into the side of her belly and rearranged the baby's foot into a more comfortable spot. "So what happens now? Do we press charges or what?"

"We'll let you know. These kids are all looking at some serious probation at the least." William stood and insisted she remain seated. "You might want to hint to Vannie that telling off people who annoy her isn't illegal, but it isn't always smart, either. This isn't her fault, but it might have been avoided if she hadn't antagonized them, too." He frowned. "Then again, I've said it several times lately. She probably got that memo."

Long after William left, his words tumbled over in her heart. *It sounds too much like, "It's your fault your husband hit you. If you hadn't egged him on…."* Her devil's advocate side argued against her compassionate one. *But by the same token, if you* sin *in your deliberate antagonizing, then you're still responsible for your sin, just as the jerk is responsible for his. Right?*

The questions worried in her mind until she fell into a fitful sleep. At some time in the wee hours of the morning, Luke came home from the house in New Cheltenham and urged her upstairs and into bed. She never did remember that.

Doctor the Nurses Are Paging

Chapter Seven

Wednesday, December 3rd

"...day coming... a great day coming...." Aggie's voice boomed through the downstairs as she wandered from room to room, supervising the children's work in between preventative maintenance with the little boys.

Vannie's eyes met Laird's as they passed in the kitchen and snickers followed. "Some things just scream, 'All is well,' don't they?"

He chugged a glass of orange juice before answering. "It's like the 'all clear' to decide something is good or bad. Just listen for Aunt Aggie's songs and you can tell."

Aggie waddle-dashed through the kitchen, dumping a pile of towels and dishcloths on the island as she passed. "Would one of you put those away? We are so behind on laundry!"

"I'll do a couple of loads after I'm done listening to my science," Vannie offered.

"That'd be great. Do the denim stuff, would you?" Aggie stopped mid-waddle and turned. "Why does denim remind me of something?"

An attack of nerves almost killed Vannie's answer. She knew exactly what it was and flip-flopped between wanting an answer and knowing that sometimes waiting meant a change in favor. Eagerness won out over patience. "Was it about my riding skirt?"

"Yes!" Aggie shook her head. "If I ever have another baby, I'm going to volunteer for a study on just how many brain cells pregnancy kills. I'm convinced I've lost half of mine—at least."

Vannie waited. Aggie stared. Laird, well, Laird chuckled. "I think Vannie's waiting for the verdict, and you're waiting for her to react."

Eyes rolled—something Aggie rarely indulged in—and impatience filled her voice. "Sorry." She snapped her fingers over her head. "Gone. It's like someone didn't pay the electrical bill for my synapses or something. Luke said to pray about it and be sure of what your parents would have allowed. If Allie would have said yes, then go for it. We'll trust you to be honest with yourself and us."

And with that, Aggie dashed through to the living room where two little boys had erupted in an argument over who owned a single Lego piece. *Five… four… three….*

Vannie didn't make it to two before Aggie called out, "Can you take that piece away from them, Vannie?" The bathroom door slammed shut as if punctuating her request.

She glanced over her shoulder as she bolted to stop Lego-ma-geddon. "Every time I think I can read what she'll do next, she ends up in the bathroom. Why don't I ever guess that one right?"

"Murphy's Law."

That's like the law of our house. *"If it can go wrong at Aggie's, it will." The guy just forgot that little prepositional phrase.*

In the library, Vannie popped in her earbuds, tucked her iPod into her skirt pocket, and listened to her science book on audio as she sliced through fabric with the confidence of someone with much experience and even more eagerness. *I just have to decide. Twill for the skirt or denim. Man, denim would be nice, but twill is more authentic. I wonder what Alexa Hartfield does. Does she sacrifice authenticity for practicality? Does it matter* what *she does? Isn't the point of this to let the clothes serve me, rather than the other way around?*

That thought stopped her in her tracks. *Weird way of putting it. So weird.*

As she learned about covalent bonds and molecules, Vannie

sat at the sewing machine and sewed the final ruffles onto Ellie's new Sunday outfit. Once those ruffles were complete, it would only be a matter of a facing and a single buttonhole. She became engrossed in the various button options until half of what her book said about bonds and molecules never registered.

Ellie passed the library, saw her stitching down the rows of ruffles, and squealed. Vannie jerked out one of her earbuds and beckoned. "Come look at this idea I just got!"

It took a couple of minutes to finish her ruffles, but she laid out the jacket and showed Ellie her plan. "What if we buy one of those ten dollar pocket watches from Walmart or something. We can take the glass cover off, paint the background something metallic, glue a few gears around it, and then put the glass back on. Then you can hook it to a button like a fob! It would be so cool!"

"That's awesome! Can we go later? Like when the kids are down for naps or something?" Ellie leaned closer. "Aunt Aggie started to make lunch, grabbed her belly, and went to rest on the couch."

Vannie's forehead furrowed. "I thought after the vandal kids were caught, she'd be fine again. I mean, that's what seemed to start everything—the stress and all."

"I know, but—" Sounds of boys bickering and Aggie snapping at them sent Ellie scurrying for the door. "I'm going to take them out to play with the dogs. Maybe…."

Vannie's eyes slid to the jacket—*so close to being done.* But conscience won out over desire. "I'll do it. You've been taking them out a lot lately."

"Just because you're working on that for me. I'll get Ta—Laird to help." A cloud darkened Ellie's face.

"Tavish still isn't himself, is he?"

Ellie shook her head and bolted from the room. Vannie heard her call for Ian and Ronnie. She hesitated once more, uncertain of the right course of action, but the idea of Ellie being disappointed at not being able to wear the outfit on Sunday decided for her. *And I have to make something more practical. Making dress clothes first might be more fun, but it's not exactly smart.*

At last, with earbuds firmly planted in place once more, Vannie pressed the seam, steamed it well, and pressed it again.

Her pin cushion grew empty as she pinned the large facing around the entire jacket and sat down to sew again. *It'll be done by lunchtime. Yes!*

A bundle of blue on the front porch unnerved Luke as he climbed from the truck. *Lord, that boy probably shouldn't be out here still.*

But despite his prayer, Luke grinned as he climbed the steps and dropped into a chair beside the bundled boy. "Sleeping bag — smart." When Tavish didn't answer, Luke tried again. "Need some peace and quiet?"

Tavish shook his head. "I was waiting for you. Vannie wanted to do it, but she's more help in there than I am."

A shiver rippled through him. "What's up?"

"It's Aunt Aggie. Vannie's worried. The only thing that kept her from calling you home was the idea of what Aunt Aggie would do if she found out."

Every part of him ached to bolt for the door, but Luke forced himself to remain calm — to listen. When Tavish didn't continue, he tried again. "Something particular concerning her?"

"She says Aunt Aggie is changing her underwear too often." His ears flamed red, but Tavish continued. "She says Mommy only had to do that a couple of times her whole pregnancy. But she thought it was just because different people are different...."

"Well...." Luke swallowed a lump that welled in his throat. "I'd say that's true. So what changed her mind?"

"She's contracting all the time. She gets up to do stuff and moans. She goes to the bathroom, changes her underwear — actually, she gets new ones before she even goes in now — and then she has to sit down again." Tavish gazed up at him, a hint of a quiver on the boy's lip. "She also told Vannie to go buy more when the kids go to bed."

A slow smile spread across Luke's lips in spite of himself. *It's strange how the kids talk about the younger children as if they're adults now.*

"You think it's okay?"

"I don't know." Though true, Luke could see that his words

hadn't been helpful. "But I'll find out. I promise."

Tavish nodded and stared out over the snow-covered yard. "The baby will be okay, won't it? It doesn't get hurt by all that squeezing?"

"As far as I know, no." He offered a hand up. "C'mon. Why don't you go read for a bit? I've got this." He dropped an arm around the boy's shoulders and squeezed. "Thanks, son."

Inside, he heard Aggie long before he saw her. "... *leaning... leaning... sss... and secure from... alarms....*" The gasps—loud enough that he heard them at the front door—and words reached him from the mudroom.

Lord....

The answer to his unspoken request came before he could formulate his thoughts. Aggie waddled toward him, a flash of white in one hand and a look of determination on her face. She gave him a wan smile and slipped into the bathroom before he could say hello.

As if confirmation, Aggie staggered out of the bathroom a minute later, holding her belly and puffing air out like a steam engine. Luke stepped forward to offer his arm, but he didn't need to. She grabbed him, hung on for dear life, and moaned. "Stupid. Contractions."

He pulled her close, cradling her head against his chest, and murmured a prayer for eased contractions. As an afterthought— and more than a bit of a warning—he added a request for wisdom. The hiss of sucked in air just as he murmured an "Amen" decided for him.

"Vannie?"

The girl appeared as if teleported from wherever she'd been. "Yeah?"

"Lunch and afternoon naps et cetera is on you. We're going in to get her checked."

Aggie's protest—right on schedule. Her adamant refusal to go—predictable. Luke's refusal to back down, however, stunned her into compliance. He led her down the steps, into the truck, and dashed back into the house for her purse. Vannie stood there with it and her coat.

"It's kind of cold."

"Good thinking. Thanks, Vannie."

"I'm just glad you're going in. I'm scared." Another lip trembling in the space of mere minutes. Luke's heart constricted as he hugged her and told her to pray. "It's probably nothing. Some women have more contractions with subsequent babies. Hannah said so."

"But she has no bladder control."

Luke nodded and gave her one last smile before he dashed out the door. *Assuming it is the bladder.*

The moment he opened his door, Aggie started in on him. If he'd thought compliance meant acquiescence, he could forget it. "—do not need to spend hours sitting in a stupid ER for them to tell me to buy Depends if I don't like all the leakage."

"You don't, perhaps. But I need you to do it. The *kids* need you to do it."

Her protest died mid-spew. "The—what?"

"I had Tavish on the porch, wrapped in a sleeping bag and waiting for me. The kid was trying not to cry, Mibs. Vannie is in there going out of her mind with worry because Allie didn't do this. They need to hear from the *doctor* that it's all normal and good. Allie didn't have midwives coming to the house. You didn't last time. This is new and scary for them."

She just stared at him. Blinked. Mouth gaped. Luke started the truck and was halfway to the highway before she spoke. "Really?" He didn't get a chance to answer. "Of course, really. Since when do you have that much to say in one sitting without even having to think about it?"

Again, she yielded, but again, Luke knew she didn't agree. He struggled to find words of encouragement but she spoke first. "You know this kills the whole point of a midwife, right? I was supposed to get to *avoid* hospitals and internal checks, and all that jazz. Now I'll be in there with monitors and ultrasounds and fingers digging around to find out what's going on." His heart constricted at the emotion that thickened her voice. "I hate it."

"I know, Mibs. I know."

For exactly fifteen seconds, he considered going to the Brant's Corners clinic. It whizzed past just moments later. He reached the highway and glanced at her. *She needs some semblance of control.* "Fairbury or Brunswick?"

He saw it—desire warring with practicality—and knew the

answer. "I'd rather go to Fairbury, but if something was actually wrong, we'd just have to transport. I say let's get it over with. We are behind on everything. Christmas, birthdays—we have Tavish and Ellie next week! I don't have time for this."

"And Christmas trees on the tenth." The minute the words left his mouth, Luke winced. *And why add that?*

As if proof of his stupidity, Aggie groaned and clutched her belly. "How could I forget? The kids keep marking off X's on the calendar. Some days have two or three." She stared at him. "Why is that again?"

"I just assumed that more than one kid wanted the privilege…."

"That'll work." She exhaled with much more force than should have been necessary. "I just hope we'll get everything done. I didn't get all our Christmas shopping done before Thanksgiving again. *Someday* that's going to happen."

Luke pulled into the hospital parking lot and hesitated. "Which would you prefer—shorter walking distance or me with you the whole time?"

He heard it. She started to say, "Stay with me," but another contraction hit and hit hard. "Better let me out. And I think I should have brought a pair of underwear. I doubt I'll make it in there for six hours before your *child* punches my bladder again."

Dinnertime came and went, but still Aggie lay on the uncomfortable bed in the ER with only a thin curtain doing its level best to block out the sounds of children screaming, grown men moaning as if giving birth, and machine alarms going off at intervals too regular to be true emergencies—or so she hoped. At her insistence, Luke had gone to take home pizza for the kids and ensure that Ronnie was behaving.

Of course, ten minutes after he left, she wanted nothing more than for him to be back again. A nurse appeared. "Time to take that temperature again." Seconds later, she backed out, but Aggie shouted for her. Red, frowzy hair—not even a pair of eyes appeared from behind the curtain. "Yeah?"

107

"What *was* the temperature, please?"

"Ninety-eight point six. On the nose." And with that, she was gone.

Well, at least there's no infection yet. Still can't believe I'm leaking amniotic fluid. She glared at her belly as the baby rolled about, likely trying to get comfortable. *Good luck, little one. Right now, though, I'll admit it. I'm mad at you. You are* not *allowed to come early. Got that?*

The baby responded with a well-timed jab at her ribs. "I would kick you back if it wouldn't hurt me more than you."

"That's what my parents used to say when I was about to get a spanking. I never believed it."

Aggie flushed at the appearance of the ER doctor. "Hi...."

The man laughed. "You aren't the first to say it and won't be the last *I* hear threaten it." He took her wrist and went through all her vitals again as if a nurse hadn't just been there—been there and forgotten to do more than take her temperature. "Did I see Amy come out of here a minute ago?"

"Yep. Took my temperature."

His hands slid over her softened belly. He nodded with some satisfaction. "The medication seems to be working already. Good." His pen clicked as he added something to a clipboard. "Stupid computers are down. And people wonder why I like things the old way." His pen light shone in each eye before he asked, "Did she tell you what it was?"

"What what was?"

"Your temperature." Even as he asked, he pulled out a thermometer.

"Perfect 98.6." At the smile he gave her, Aggie sagged in relief. "It's what I think, right? No infection yet?"

But the man didn't answer. Instead, he checked her ankles, listened to the baby's heart rate, and made copious notes on the clipboard. "As far as we can tell," he said at last. "No infection as yet. I think you have a small leak that needs a few days' rest to reseal."

Her eyes widened and relief washed over her. "They can reseal?"

"Common enough. I can't guarantee it, of course, but—"

"But it *could* happen?" Aggie shifted to sit up, but the doctor added gentle pressure to her shoulder. "Just stay down. You need all the rest you can to give that little one—you did say you didn't want to know, right?"

Aggie started to correct him—to tell him they just hadn't been able to see at her twenty-week ultrasound—but something stopped her. "I don't think I do. Did you see?"

"It's pretty clear."

Indecision wracked her. She clung to the idea of being "surprised" with an unexpected tenacity, but practicality niggled at her. *It would be so much easier....*

The curtain rattled and Aggie found herself alone. Forehead furrowed, she grumbled her complaints to the Lord. *And this is exactly why I wanted a home birth. No self-important doctors too rushed to let a woman take a moment to make a decision.*

But the man arrived moments later, shoving a piece of paper into an envelope as he did. He licked it, sealed it, and passed it to her. "Do you want this here, or should I put it in your bag of personal things?"

"What is it?"

A smile gave the funny-looking man a hint of charm. "The verdict. You can choose to open it or not—whenever you like. If you don't want the temptation, give it to someone else or throw it away."

Aggie accepted it and held it close. "Thank you. Thanks and sorry."

"Sorry?"

"I was thinking some pretty nasty things about you while you went to do me a favor." Her face flamed as she confessed. "Shows that what I tell my kids is true. It never pays to assume the worst."

As he listened, the man checked the levels, took her vitals once more—why, she couldn't imagine—and stared down at her. "Well, no harm done. I'd say a semi-laboring woman has the right to a bit of angst."

She felt it coming and winced.

"Contraction?"

"No, but I know what's next."

The man gave a shrug and smiled once more. "I can do it, or I can call in Amy if you'd prefer."

"How about we assume I'm permanently stuck at almost two centimeters?" Aggie gave him a pleading look. "Surely it can't be good to keep irritating the cervix like that, right? And some women stay semi-dilated for much of their pregnancies, don't they?"

"Have you been until now?"

Oh, how she didn't want to answer the question. The temptation to lie—never had it been so strong. Aggie shrugged and answered before she succumbed. "I don't know. Hannah hasn't been checking me."

"Hannah?" He flipped through his clipboard, and Aggie let him. It would be a half a dozen seconds of peace before he protested. "Oh, Hannah Olbrook. Your midwife. Has she been called?"

Aggie's throat went dry. "Um...."

Without hesitation, the doctor backed out of the cubicle, promising to return in a while. "We'll get her in here. She should know what's going on."

And you just won the "Least Obnoxious Doctor of the Year" award.

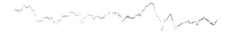

Just on the other side of the curtain, Hannah and the ER doctor spoke in low tones—much too low for them to overhear. At Aggie's glare, Luke inched his way to the end of the bed in hopes of catching a word or two, but he could only guess.

"What?" Aggie's whisper sounded like a shout to his ears.

Luke moved closer and bent low. "Can't tell, but Hannah either wants something he objects to or vice versa—or maybe both?" With his lips close to her ear, Luke kissed her cheek. "It'll be okay. They both think everything will sort itself out with rest."

"That's right."

Hannah's voice startled both of them, and immediately he saw Aggie wince. *Lord, please let it be a kick instead of a contraction or more fluid.*

"Fluid, contraction, or kick?" Hannah glared at Aggie with mock anger.

"Kick. It hit my bladder, but no fluid—yet."

In seconds, Luke had been relegated to the other side of the bed while Hannah helped roll Aggie onto her back and pulled on gloves. "Gotta check. We want that sack to seal. If it doesn't, you're looking at weeks in the hospital with nothing to do but annoy the nurses and worry about those kids." She winked at Luke. "It's my job to ensure you don't get that pleasure."

The doctor's hands slid over her midsection as Hannah swiped a piece of litmus paper and examined it. She held it out to the doctor who nodded and scribbled something on the clipboard. Aggie glared at him—a silent demand for answers.

"So…."

"Negative. This time." Hannah glanced at the doctor, waited for his nod, and continued. "But you *have* to rest until we see no sign of more fluid. Now, I think you would be more comfortable, and therefore rest better, at home."

Aggie nearly bolted up at those words. "Definitely."

With almost prescient clarity, Luke urged her to lie back down. "Listen to the whole thing, Mibs."

The doctor smiled. "Great nickname, by the way."

He gazed down at his wife and saw her relax a little. "I thought so."

"Anyway…." Hannah snapped off the gloves and tossed them as she spoke. "As I said, I think you'd be more comfortable at home. Dr. Pahl, on the other hand, thinks it would be best to keep you where we can monitor your progress—for about twenty-four to thirty-six hours?"

The doctor nodded. "Just as a precaution. I don't see how you can possibly rest in a houseful of children."

Luke winced at the doctor's words. Of all the things he could have said, *that* was the worst. "I think," he interjected before Aggie could speak. "I really think she'd worry enough to cause more stress-contractions." Another thought hit him. Luke steeled himself against the irritation he knew would follow and asked a question. "However, our room is two flights up—"

"Absolutely not." The doctor glared at Hannah. "You didn't tell me—"

"Because I assumed she'd go to the guest room downstairs!" Hannah sent Luke a warning look. "She can't possibly climb those stairs without reopening that tear."

Oh, how he wanted to promise that he'd keep her comfortably ensconced in the guest room, but experience taught him that he'd never be able to control her with promises made *for* her. *It's not like I want to control her just to be an overbearing jerk, Lord. But at times like this....*

"I'll stay downstairs for thirty-six hours, but then I'll *have* to go upstairs. That bed is not comfortable enough for much longer than that. My mom *loves* it, but it's too firm for me."

The doctor piped up. "Here, we don't even have to worry about her getting up to go to the bathroom. We can use a catheter—"

"No!" Aggie and Hannah grinned as they shouted in unison. Hannah continued, "The last thing she needs is another chance for infection. Getting up to go to the bathroom shouldn't be too much trouble—if she avoids stairs and lies right back down. It'll also help prevent blood clots."

Luke watched the exchange, trying to predict what the outcome would be, but a glance at Aggie told him he'd better step in. "I think we'll go home. Surely, you can send us something to stop contractions if they start. We'll get her home, up the stairs, and *then* start counting the hours—forty-eight of them, maybe— until she can try walking around. At the first sign of leakage or contractions of any kind, we'll call Hannah."

As he spoke, Aggie nodded. "Absolutely. Best idea of all. I can go up the stairs backwards on my bum—less stress on the baby that way?"

"I don't know about that," Hannah muttered. She turned to the doctor. "If I know Aggie like I think I do, this is the best way to get her down and keep her down until we have a good idea if that sack is going to reseal. Here, she'll be fretting, and that means contracting. Downstairs, she'll hear something the kids are doing and go out 'just this once'." Her laughter filled the cubicle as Aggie flushed and ducked her head. "At least upstairs it's quieter. She might hear less."

Dr. Pahl's eyes darted from Aggie to Hannah, over to Luke, and back to Hannah again. "I don't know...."

Aggie shifted. Luke could hear what was coming before she even opened her mouth. In a desperate move to preempt her, Luke asked the question he'd planned to avoid. "Okay, what would it take for you to be comfortable with this arrangement? I don't want our plan to be more important than the safety of the baby—which, I assume is why you are hesitant? Aggie herself isn't in any danger?"

"None that has presented itself, no." The doctor eyed Aggie and something in her face must have decided for him. "Okay, I don't like it. But I'll sign off if she'll agree to follow up with Hannah's backup physician on Monday."

"And just why do we care if he signs off on this?" Aggie gave the man an apologetic look. "No offense, but I can't figure out why we aren't just deciding what is best for me and doing it."

"If he doesn't sign off on it, then we have to leave against medical advice, Aggie." Hannah shook her head. "I can't do that. If you go against medical advice, my insurance will not allow me to retain you as a patient."

Before Luke could urge her, Aggie shifted, rolled over, and stared at the doctor. "I'll do it. I'll go home—even sleep in that stupid guest room if I have to—and I'll go see the doctor on Monday. But I don't have to *want* to." A wince, a grimace, a giggle. She turned to Luke. "Is it me, or did that sound like a perfect imitation of Cari?"

"With a dash of Ronnie, yeah." He grinned. "Let's get you home, Mibs."

Dr. Pahl shook his head. "It's really a great nickname."

Aggie's sigh almost tore at Luke's heart before he heard her say, "I guess this is one of those clay times. The Lord is molding me again. And once more, I feel like I'm losing my marbles."

THEY EYED WITH GLEE

Chapter Eight

Thursday, December 4th

The car hadn't even come to a full stop when Laird bolted from it and up the steps to the door. A scream and a wail erupted as the front door collided with a child's head—likely Ronnie's from the indignant protest. Even Cari hadn't been able to achieve decibels as piercing as that kid's.

"Ronnie?"

"You hit me! I tell—"

Luke stepped out of the kitchen and called to his son. "Ronnie. Come here. Now."

The boy, tears still falling and sobs growing louder, sent Laird a nasty look and fled to his father's side. His attempted ploy for sympathy fizzled at Luke's order to hush. "You're not injured."

"He hit me!"

Luke stared down the boy. "You were playing exactly where you were told *not* to play and for that reason. That door hardly touched you."

"But—"

Luke turned the boy to the corner and told him not to emerge without permission. "I'll deal with you in a minute."

Vannie burst through the door, arms full of bags. "Thanks a lot, Laird. You're *so* helpful."

114

Though he opened his mouth to apologize, Laird heard himself fling some angry retort—what he couldn't remember—at her and stomped upstairs. Halfway up, he remembered Aggie's bed rest orders and moved more quietly. Still, once he'd dropped to his bed, Laird found himself wishing he'd gone out back instead.

Several minutes later, soft thuds on the stairs told him Luke had followed. Guilt plagued him for a moment, but he hardened his heart and grabbed the nearest book. His Bible. *Great. I'm going to look guilty or like I'm trying to be innocent — further guilt.*

Luke's voice from the door drove those thoughts out of his mind. "Everything okay, Laird?"

"Yeah."

Silence. He waited for Luke to object, but instead, he heard only silence. After several long seconds, Luke cleared his throat. "Well, if you need me, I'll be downstairs."

That's all it took. Laird sat up and called after him. "Uncle Luke?"

"Yeah?"

The moment Luke stepped back in the room, the words spilled out in a rush. "What do you do when girls won't leave you alone?"

Luke grabbed the chair from beside the door and turned it around. How many times had he seen Luke, Chad, Uncle Zeke — any of the Sullivan-Tesdall men—do that when getting ready to listen? *Will I do that someday?*

"Most boys your age would consider girls hanging around to be a good thing...." Luke's arms rested on the back of the chair. "What do you mean, 'won't leave you alone'?"

He rolled over and sat with his legs dangling over the edge of his bunk. "At first it was just saying hi and giggling." Laird felt his face go red. "Annoying, but nothing too bad. But now...." He should have known better than to expect his uncle to fill in the words for him. "It's... *awkward.*"

"So who—"

His head dropped to his hands as he began reciting the names he could think of. "Kendra Vassili, Lizzie Leyton, Angie, Ashley—"

Luke's laughter cut him off. "Ahhh, our Laird is going to be a lady killer." He nodded at Laird's groan. "And it's not just giggling and saying hi anymore? What's happening now?"

"They ask me out now. I mean, c'mon! I'm *fifteen* – almost – *ish.*"

Usually, his uncle's tendency to take time before answering didn't bother Laird. That day, he wanted to shake words out of the man – words that would show him what to do and how to put a stop to something that both intrigued and almost terrified him. *C'mon. Just tell me how to make them go away.* A moment later, he amended that thought. *At least until I'm ready to deal with them.*

"Son, I don't know. I didn't have a lot of girls after me at your age. Then again, I wasn't half as good looking as you are, and I *was* a lot more socially awkward. You're a nice guy, handsome, kind to your siblings. A girl's going to notice that."

Not what I want to hear….

"But…."

Laird sat up and leaned forward with eager interest. "Yeah?"

"I'll see what I can figure out." Luke's eyes softened and a smile formed. "I suppose you had another encounter in town? Is that why you snapped at Vannie like that?"

A vague recollection of saying something rude prodded his conscience, but Laird just nodded. "Yeah. I guess. I'll apologize."

"So what happened?"

"Kendra's pushing for us to go on that Soul-Slopes trip. Vannie already said we weren't going, but she cornered me in the market and actually hung onto my arm. She kept insisting that if I just asked you guys myself, you might let us go." Laird's voice scaled up and cracked as he did. "'We could go to the banquet together….' Then –" As much as he wanted to continue, he couldn't. "I just want to be able to talk to people without it being all about if they're a guy or a girl."

"What else happened, Laird?" Luke stood and put the chair back in place before moving to his side. "The panic I hear in your voice is excessive for a girl trying to be your dinner partner on a ski trip."

Face flaming and vocal cords strangling, Laird shook his head. "I don't want Vannie to know. You know how she gets."

"Who said anything about announcing this at the dinner table? You asked for my help, and I can't if I don't know what the real problem is."

As Laird struggled to answer, he felt Luke's arm around his shoulder and heard the gentle whispers of his uncle's prayers. *Daddy would have done that, too. He would have prayed for me.*

How long they sat there, Luke praying and Laird struggling to speak words that both embarrassed and terrified him, he never did learn. Twice, Luke sent a child away from the door, and eventually he stood and shut it. Still, Laird couldn't find the words.

"What if I ask questions?" At his nod, Luke lobbed one after another at him with the gentle toss of an underhand ball to a little kid just learning to bat. "Did she try to kiss you?"

"Would have if I'd let her get close enough. I could tell." How he admitted it, Laird didn't know.

"Did she ask you out?"

He shook his head.

"Tell you she likes you?"

Again, Laird's head shook as he tried to imagine his uncle ever guessing the right thing. "No." Honesty forced him to add, "But she's told me that before."

A few seconds passed as Luke considered his next question. Laird almost told him it was useless, but Luke beat him to it. "Do you think I *can* guess it?"

"Probably not." His eyes slid sideways. "Unless you had your own cellphone when you were a kid."

"Nope. But you don't, either." Luke's eyes narrowed. "But she doesn't know that. She sees you with the family cell and assumes...."

The story spilled from him before he could reconsider. "She wanted my number. I told her I didn't have my own phone and that we're not allowed to give out the family cell number. I even used the thing with Ellie as an excuse—just like Aunt Aggie said. It didn't work. She didn't believe me."

"That doesn't surprise me. Most kids do have their own these days." Luke laughed. "Can you imagine our charging station with a phone for each of you guys? Our *bill*?"

The moment Laird relaxed, he realized the joke had been deliberate for that purpose. And it worked. "Well, when I insisted I couldn't, she tried to get closer again. I swear, if anyone else heard her, I'll beg to go to military school."

"It can't be *that* bad…."

That's what you think. Laird gathered his courage and looked his uncle in the eye. "She promised to send me a bra picture if I'd give her the number." He swallowed hard and forced himself to add the rest. "And when I didn't do it right away, she even said she'd get Lizzy and Angie to do it. She said no way would Ashley ever do that."

"Ashley's sounding better every second." What Luke *didn't* say drowned out the five half-choked words. Laird dreaded the next question. "So what did you do?"

"I bolted. Just left everything on a shelf and left. She actually chased after me. She was laughing." He dropped his head into his hands. "Uncle Luke, the car was locked. There she was coming right up to me, and I couldn't go anywhere she couldn't go, too."

Luke's laughter surprised him—surprised and stung. "Hint, Laird. Girls hate men's bathrooms. Library, gas station—even Cole Thanes would let you use his."

"Can't imagine why they'd hate ours. They practically live in theirs."

Again, Luke's laughter filled the room, but this time Laird joined him. "I think it's the urinal."

"Glad to know it. Works at church, but I thought that was because someone would say something if they were seen going in there."

If he'd expected to escape the rest of the story, Laird would have been sorely disappointed. But Luke's question came much swifter than he expected. "What did she say at the car?"

Seriously? I tell you some girl is trying to give me a picture of her in her bra *and you're just asking what else?* He cleared his throat. "Aren't you at all freaked out that a girl—"

"Don't like it at all. I'm just trying to get the facts straight."

It took him longer to tell than he wanted, but eventually Laird spilled the whole story. "She told me how 'cute' it was that I was embarrassed and promised that she wouldn't do it for anyone else—just me. She even hinted that she'd make out with me if I went."

"I take it you're asking permission to go, then."

Laird choked. "Wha—" His eyes closed as he felt rather than

118

saw Luke's smile. "So not funny, Uncle Luke."

"Sorry. Just trying to lighten the moment for you." Luke's arm tightened around him. "Look, I can't imagine what would make a girl make such an offer. I don't know if this is normal—not *right*, but normal—behavior these days or what. But I'm glad you told me."

"I'm just glad I didn't have a phone of my own," Laird whispered.

A thickness to Luke's voice hinted at the stifling of tears. "I am, too. It wasn't why we did it, but I can see that the Lord may have protected you with it."

"What do I *do*?" Laird winced at the whine in his tone. "Mr. Vaughn said we should treat the girls like sisters." He gazed over at Luke. "She'd take it as flirting. I know it."

"Good point. I hadn't considered that. It was what I was just about to suggest." Luke dropped his arm and fiddled with his ring. "You know, I am clueless about this stuff, but I will figure it out. We'll work on it together." He stood. "Meanwhile, you keep talking, okay?"

"Talking? About what? To who?"

"About all this stuff—to me." Luke gazed down at him for the better part of a minute before adding, "The minute you hide stuff like this, it holds you prisoner. The guilt makes *doing* something wrong a relief sometimes—at least then the guilt has a purpose. It's wrong and stupid, but it's how our brains work sometimes. Just talk to me. I'd rather know you were tempted to accept a picture like that—or might have been if it had been possible," he added with an understanding smile. "—than for you to hold it in until you just give in because you've given up."

They stayed like that for several minutes. Laird seated and staring at his hands, Luke standing and watching him. A cry downstairs sent Luke to the door, but Laird stopped him. "Uncle Luke?"

"Yeah?"

His eyes rose and met Luke's. "Don't tell Aunt Aggie—not now. She'll worry."

Several seconds passed as Luke considered the request. "I won't hide it from her if she asks about anything, but I'll wait to share until things are back to normal, okay?"

119

Laird flopped back on his bed as the door shut behind Luke and closed his eyes. *I think getting older stinks. All the stuff about it that was supposed to be cool is way too complicated.*

Despite the fascinating synopsis given in the homeschool newsletter, the book disappointed, page after page. Tavish stared at the large "9" on the page and debated whether continuing would be a lesson in fortitude or futility. *It's a complete waste of time. I know who's supposed to be the real bad guy, what we're supposed to think about the so-called good guy, and I disagree with both. Aunt Aggie would call it moralistic nonsense.*

That thought settled it. He flipped through the pages and stared at the beautiful cover. "Sure is pretty, though."

Excitement slowly filled him until he couldn't stand it. Tavish scrambled from the bed in his cubbie hole and stared at the book still lying on the rumpled blanket. A moment later, he slid it into an empty space on his shelf and hurried to the library.

The laptop stood open on one end of the table, and Vannie sat sewing at the other, earbuds in her ears. He waved. She stopped. "Huh?"

"Need this right now, or can I open a new tab?"

"Go for it. I'm not using it anymore." Vannie cocked her head and held one earbud ready to put it back in her ear. "What'cha doing?"

"I saw something on Pinterest the other day — when Aunt Aggie was looking for craft ideas for the little kids. I thought I'd see how hard one of the things was." Just as she started to wiggle the bud into her ear, he waved. "Do we have any old, ugly books no one would want?"

"There's that box in the attic. Aunt Aggie said we could use them for target practice if we wanted, remember?" At his nod, Vannie went back to sewing, and Tavish began searching Pinterest. It took exactly thirty seconds for the tutorial he wanted to appear. Unfortunately, it linked to YouTube.

For the first time, Tavish almost ignored the family Internet rules and just watched it anyway. He stared at the picture, trying to guess the steps and failed. Miserably. Several options lay open to him. He could ask Vannie to look for him. *She* was allowed to preview videos for the younger children, but then he wouldn't be able to surprise her with one. *And Aunt Aggie is out. Nothing that could stress her. That x-acto knife…. Yeah. And Uncle Luke would love one. I can't show him….*

A dozen people flitted through his mind. "Aunt" Tina, Mrs. Dyke, "Grandma" Sullivan—but when he thought of William, Tavish knew he'd found the perfect person. *I bet the only book he reads is the Bible, and I wouldn't do that to one.*

He bolted for the family cell phone and painstakingly typed out a text message—including the YouTube URL. WILL YOU PLEASE PREVIEW THIS FOR ME WHEN YOU GET A CHANCE? I DON'T WANT TO ASK ANYONE HERE OR IT WILL RUIN THE SURPRISE. IF YOU CAN'T, WHO SHOULD I ASK?

After triple-checking the URL to be certain he hadn't transposed any characters or forgotten to capitalize something, Tavish hit send. Then another dilemma presented itself. To delete or not to delete the message. *What's the point of sending it to Mr. Markenson if I am just going to leave it out there for anyone to see?*

With a quick punch of the delete button, Tavish erased any record of his text. A wail from the mudroom warned that Luke would be downstairs in a moment. Tavish closed out his Pinterest tab and left it at that. It was one thing to delete a text that they could request from William—another to dig into the history to hide his browsing. *I wonder if they know I can do that.*

Ronnie's cries grew louder just as Luke reached the bottom of the stairs. Tavish stepped out of the library and tried to intercept him. "Uncle Luke?"

"Be there in a minute. Have a son to silence before he drives his mother to early labor."

"But—"

"In a *minute*, Tavish." Luke made it three more steps before he turned around and backtracked. "I had no right to snap at you."

Embarrassment flooded Tavish as he apologized for pressing. "I'll go get a snack for them. Probably a low blood sugar thing or something."

"You think that. It's good for my parenting ego."

A glance through the fridge and the cupboards showed little in the way of snack foods. Apples were good, but the little guys needed more protein and the string-cheese was gone. No celery for peanut butter dipping.... Tavish stared at the apples and snatched two small ones from the bin. "Apples and peanut butter—probably amazing, and we've never even tried it."

The cores stared back at him as he placed wedges on paper towels and slid a ramekin of peanut butter between the two plates. *I bet they fight over that stupid thing. What happened around here? We didn't get away with stuff like that.*

Not for the first time, Tavish debated his aunt and uncle's wisdom in adding to their "collection" of children. *Even Ian is becoming obnoxious.* Fairness prompted him to concede that Ian hadn't been a problem until the past year. *Just as Ronnie got difficult. They feed off each other.*

Loud wails from the mudroom preceded Ian's appearance by mere seconds. Tavish pointed to the snack. "Hungry?"

"Apples and peanut butter?" The boy climbed up on the stool and picked up a wedge with some trepidation. "Really?"

Sounding more confident than he felt, Tavish shrugged. "Or eat them plain. You won't know if you like it until you try it, but c'mon. It's *peanut butter.* The only thing it'd be gross on is like spaghetti or something."

By the third wedge, Tavish concluded his experiment had been a success. But before he could reach for an apple for himself, the cores beckoned again. He pulled a paring knife from the magnet beside the stove and began digging at one. It split in half. Undaunted, he tried again.

"What're you doing?"

Without looking up from his impromptu project, Tavish began with the usual caveat. "Well, remember, I'm allowed to use knives. Anyway, I'm trying to see if you can carve an apple core— you know, like you carve wood—whittle." A face—rough and quite angry looking—slowly emerged from the core. Still, if you squinted just right and stuck your tongue out at the perfect angle, you could tell it was supposed to be a person. "Interesting."

"Certainly is." Luke's voice startled him enough to send the knife flying in one direction and the core directly into Ian's face.

"Aaak!"

Luke retrieved the knife, rinsed it, and popped it in the sink, apologizing all the while. "Didn't mean to startle you. I thought you heard us come in." He turned to a sniffling Ronnie and told the boy to climb up and eat his snack. "No more fussing."

That's all it took. Ronnie, while not exactly singing for joy, dropped the sour face and dug into the peanut butter and apples with relish. Tavish waited for the first skirmish, but it never came. Ian dipped just as Ronnie tried and their wedges crossed like swords. The boys gave each other challenging looks and began a duel of apples.

Luke sighed and folded his arms over his chest as he watched. Tavish watched. "Um, Uncle Luke?"

"Oh, that's right. You had a question." Luke nodded for him to continue.

"Well, I actually had a confession, and now I have a question, too." When Luke didn't respond, he just continued before he lost his nerve. "I went on Pinterest a bit ago — to look up something for a surprise. I deleted the tab so no one would see what it was."

Concern etched itself into Luke's forehead and the crinkles around his eyes. His jaw went a bit rigid. "You're supposed to leave tabs open, Tavish. That's the rule."

"I know, and you could find it easily enough if you wanted to. But I sent the link I saw to Mr. Markenson. You can ask him if it's okay. I just didn't want to ruin the surprise. Oh, and I deleted my text to Mr. Markenson. But he has it if you need to see it."

By now, both of the younger boys had abandoned the barstools to parry around the kitchen. Luke watched them for a minute before turning back to Tavish. "I think I understand what you did and why, but next time ask first. It's one thing to give misleading answers about gifts for a surprise. It's another to break family rules."

Luke's words struck home in Tavish's heart. He had justified his actions with that very comparison, but of course, he'd been wrong. "You're right. I'm sorry. I should have asked first."

"Tavish get swats?" Ronnie stood stock still in the kitchen and watched them.

Luke crossed the room and hunkered down on his heels. "No, no he's not. Can you guess why?"

123

"Because he's big boy? He almost big as you."

"Nope. Because he told me what he did. He didn't try to get away with doing something wrong. He just didn't handle it right. Now he knows, and I bet next time, he'll come to us first." Luke stood again, but something brought him back to his son's eye level. "And, he didn't try to hide it from everyone. He took it to an *adult.*"

Ronnie looked ready to protest, but instead, he stuck his bruised and browning apple wedge in his mouth and took a bite. "Okay."

Ian dipped his final wedge into the peanut butter and came up with a giant dollop. "Can we eat them outside?"

"Get your jackets on first." Luke offered the remaining peanut butter to Ronnie before bundling them up in their jackets and sending them out to play. "Stay in sight of the windows. I'll be watching."

Never had Tavish seen Luke look so weary. He plopped down on the stool and sagged. "Long day and it's not even dinnertime yet."

"Maybe you should go take a nap with Aunt Aggie. She's probably lonely up there anyway."

There it was—that special look Luke reserved for moments when he was particularly proud of one of them. "You're such an observant and thoughtful young man, Tavish. I'm proud of you." Before Tavish could object, Luke continued. "Unfortunately, I need to keep an eye on Ronnie—shouldn't have let him go out, actually. He needs a bit of tethering."

Tethering. How many kids would even know what that means? It's true, though. The little guys always behave better when they're not allowed to go off by themselves all the time.

"—said you had a question now?"

Jerked from his thoughts, Tavish stared at his uncle for a moment before nodding. "I think I just answered it myself, though. It's been a weird few weeks."

Luke went to peer out the window before he responded. "I'm sorry. Too tired to try to figure out what you mean."

Once begun, Tavish found himself asking a question he thought he knew the answer to. "I just wondered why the little guys get away with stuff we never would have—even Cari would

124

have expected to get in serious trouble for stuff that Ian and Ronnie get away with." His face flushed. "She'd have done it anyway—figured it was worth getting in trouble for—but she would have known it meant trouble."

Discomfort rose several notches for every second that Luke considered his words. Tavish felt ready to drown in a sealed room at any moment before Luke finally responded. "Thank you, Tavish. I needed to hear that my own concerns aren't me overreacting."

Another glance out the window sent Luke into the back yard. Tavish stood there, jaw agape. *Wow. I....* He blinked. *It's not even Aunt Willow and... wow!*

I'LL CRY TODAY

Chapter Nine

Sunday, December 7th

The closing hymn—one he'd heard Aggie sing a dozen times a week in the years he'd known her—rang hollow without her voice beside him. When his voice failed him, he prayed for wisdom—for strength. *I know You can change everything in an instant, but I'm not expecting it. I don't know why. But whatever the reason, I ask for the faith to trust. To hold fast to Your will, not my "way."*

A murmur behind him—one of the older women—of, "Oh, isn't that sweet," sent his eyes down the row. There at the end, Rory MacKenzie stood holding the hymnal for Kenzie. Twice the boy stole a glance at her. Twice he couldn't hide a grin. *Great. First Laird, now Rory. Lord, I can't deal with this right now. I still haven't figured out what to do about Laird.*

It wasn't a fair assessment. The little boy's crush had been immediate and long-lasting, never wavering. But Luke still struggled against the idea that his nine-year-old niece had a "boyfriend."

The minister called them to prayer, and just as Luke bowed his head, he saw Rory slide the hymnal into the rack and take hold of Kenzie's hand. A protest welled up with a ferocity that physically shook him. He inched his way around Cari and Lorna,

126

ready to separate Kenzie from the would-be masher and put an end to the foolishness. But just as he began to slide behind Kenzie, he saw Rory's other hand wrapped around Vannie's. *Lord, I've got to get a grip. He's just a kid. It's innocent. He won't be asking for bra pictures of my Kenzie. Sheesh, she doesn't even wear a bra... does she?*

Kenzie's voice jerked him from his moment of panic disguised as prayer. "What's wrong, Uncle Luke?"

"Nothing...." His eyes dropped to where Kenzie held her Bible—with *both* hands. "I did wonder if Rory wanted to come home with us after church."

The moment the words left his lips, Luke had to physically restrain himself from groaning. Rory's eyes lit up and clouded almost just as quickly. "I can't. We're going to take Aunt Clara Christmas shopping." His eyes slid toward Kenzie for a fraction of a second before he continued. "She's going to help me pick out stuff I want to get."

Before Luke could respond—or even sag in utter relief—Kenzie grabbed Rory's hand. "Then let's go play before you have to go!"

He stood there, staring at the empty space that had held two children much too young for the boy-girl silliness that threatened to destroy his peace. Vannie's voice cut through his thoughts. "Are you okay?"

"I think so."

"Well, I'm going to go make sure Ronnie isn't getting chased by Lyddie Palmer—again. Seriously. Three. The kid is *three!*"

This time, Luke did groan. He half stared at his empty arms, wondering when he'd set the boy down, and gathered the rest of their stuff from the pew. People stopped him, asked how his latest house was coming, if Aggie was feeling well, and two people asked for home repair help. Desperate to get away, Luke typed quick notes to himself to call later, and promised to do it by Tuesday. "I should make sure the children are behaving."

"Your kids are the best behaved I've ever seen," one older woman insisted. "Such joys."

As much as Luke needed to hear the encouragement, he offered a rushed "thanks" and bolted from the building, arms full of coats, Bibles, and the purse Kenzie had abandoned to play with Rory. He piled it all in the van—all but Ronnie's coat—and took off in search of his son. He found the boy ready to shove little Lyddie Palmer into a snowdrift. "Stop."

Much to his relief—and chagrin, at the idea that he had any doubt—it worked. Ronnie turned to him and screamed, "She kissded me!"

From behind, two ladies tittered and cooed, "How cute!"

How revolting is more like it. Determined not to get into a discussion on the appropriateness of childhood "romance" and the encouragement of such silliness, Luke shook the jacket. "It's too cold to be out here without a coat. Now let's go find Ian."

Lyddie's face screwed up in protest as she stepped forward with a demanding, "I want to play wif him!"

"I'm sorry, Lyddie, but Ronnie is coming with me. You'll have to play with someone else."

And at that, the child threw back her head and howled. Luke walked away, Ronnie in tow. The wails stopped. Seconds later, Lyddie raced ahead of them, stopped just feet in front of them, and repeated the protest. Luke saw her mother watching and smiled as he moved around her and kept going. Again, the cries stopped. Again the child moved forward and wailed as if tortured.

All the way across the parking lot to the church steps, the scene replayed itself. It would have been comical had it not been so telling. Sydney Palmer moved their way and tried to console the girl. "Sweetie, don't cry. I'm sure Ronnie wants to play too, but they have to go home now."

Luke just stared at her, stunned. Ronnie tugged his hand. "Can I swing?"

"We need to find Ian."

Sydney Palmer gave him a sympathetic smile. "I think Ian is on the swings."

A cheer from Ronnie preempted Luke's response. "We go!"

Hands stuffed in his coat pockets, Luke followed Ronnie to the swings. Lyddie rushed ahead, determined to stay with them. A glance back at her mother showed the woman smiling at the scene. *You just taught your daughter that throwing fits will get her what she wants. How will you like that when she's fifteen and angry that she can't have an outfit that is indecent or a brand new car for her not-so-sweet sixteen?*

Shame filled him and reddened his ears and neck as Luke heard the arrogance in his thoughts. *Lord, I'm doing it again. Help!*

Lyddie shoved Ronnie from the last swing just as he grabbed the chain. "You can sit with me, Ronnie."

The boy stood there, indecision sending conflicting expressions over his features. Luke debated between allowing him to try to make the right choice and guiding him into it. But before he could decide, Ian jumped off the swing he'd been using and landed in the snow at Luke's feet. "Swinging is super fun in the snow!"

Ronnie reached for the empty chains, but Lyddie snagged them and held them away from him. "You have to play wif me!"

The boy's eyes sought his, confusion filling them. Self-control almost gone. Luke considered the situation and decided to stand his ground. "Which swing do you want, Lyddie?"

"Bof!"

"Well, you can't have both. You need to share. So do you want the middle swing or the one on the end?"

The girl threw back her head and howled once more. Luke glanced over his shoulder and sagged in relief at the sight of Sydney Palmer striding their way. The moment she reached the child's side, Luke asked again. "Which swing would you like?"

"I want bof!"

"Oh, honey. You can't swing on both at once. Why don't you let Ronnie swing on one? You said you wanted to play with him, and Luke is staying longer just so you can do that."

Shock, dismay, frustration—they filled him one after the other. He almost dragged Ronnie home, but seeing the disappointment on his son's face proved too much for him. "Actually, I never said we were going home. I—"

"Now let's not confuse her, Luke. I *said* that you were being *nice*...." A meaningful glare told him exactly what she expected.

Lie to your child. Great.

Smugness filled the child's face. She passed the chain to Ronnie and kicked her feet. "Push me!"

He might have capitulated. For just a moment, Luke decided it wasn't worth the strained relationships at church. But Ronnie watched him, waiting for the decision, and Luke knew he couldn't do it. "C'mon, son. I think Mrs. Palmer is right. We should be going, now."

Ignoring the revived protests of Lyddie, Luke led Ronnie to the van. Halfway there, he knelt down and faced his son. "We'll go to the park and swing."

"Really?" Ronnie flung his arms around Luke's neck and held on as Luke lifted him and carried him to the van. "Why don't you go give the horn a couple of loud honks? We'll see who wants to go with us and who wants to walk down in a few minutes."

His children bolted for the van at the sound of the third honk. Luke shook his head, telling Ronnie to stop, and waited as the others arrived. "We're going to the park for a bit. Cari, Ian, and Lorna have to come with me. The rest of you can stay and walk down in twenty minutes or so." Kenzie started backing away again. He hated to do it, but Luke had to add a caveat. "Kenzie, you need to come with me if no one else stays."

Vannie piped up almost immediately. "I'll stay. Laird should go, though. Megan Ormond was talking in the bathroom about how she's going to get him to ask her out."

Laird turned green and hopped into the front seat. "I'm going."

Before Luke could open the side door for the others, Rory raced to his side. "My mom and dad have to do something in the classroom, so we're staying longer after all. Can Kenzie stay until we go? Mom says we can drop her off at home."

Oh, how he ached to say no. But the hopeful look in Kenzie's eyes, the respect in Rory's tone, the... *innocence* in his eagerness. Luke couldn't do it. "Go ahead. We'll be at the park for a bit if they want to swing by there first."

And the moment they turned, Rory tagged Kenzie. "You're it!"

Vannie backed away. "I'll stay anyway. Just in case they go before I walk down to the park. It'll save them a drive out of the way or get me a ride — one or the other."

With that, she turned to leave. Luke climbed into the front seat and stared at the steering wheel. A moment later, he turned to Laird and murmured, "Just how did Aggie do this before we got married again?"

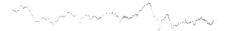

The article had burned in her thoughts for a week. So, as Ellie divested herself of the steampunk outfit that had inspired several compliments that morning, she made her decision. She'd try it.

Lunch dragged. Cleanup — it dragged even more. But eventually the family scattered across the house. Temperatures dropped as another snowstorm inched its way across the landscape and straight toward them. *It's now or never.*

With a roll of aluminum foil, a plastic bottle, and Drano from the chemical cupboard in the basement, she scurried out into the yard, as far from the house as she could get. Rolling an aluminum foil ball with gloves on wasn't as easy as she'd expected, but she managed to cram two of them into the bottle. A glance at the article made her roll up another one before she began struggling with the Drano lid.

"Why. Do. They. Make. These. So. Hard. To. Geeeet...." She growled. "Off?!"

"So that kids like you won't do something stupid like mix it with aluminum?"

She whirled and stared at Laird. "How —"

"It's not like everyone in the house couldn't see you if they were looking. What do you think you're doing?"

"An experiment. Did you know a girl in Florida got kicked out of school for making one?"

Laird stared at her for a moment. "Did you know that you could get *arrested* for making one? It's *illegal*, Ellie!" He frowned. "Well, it is in some states. I read the article you had up on the laptop."

Her face fell. "Nooooo. I have to come up with an experiment, do it, and report on it. This at least sounded interesting. The article said that the reason some don't blow up right away is because there's wax on the aluminum foil. I thought there would be enough time to pour it in and back away."

"And if it doesn't blow up? Are you just going to let it sit there until one of the little guys — ?"

"No!" Ellie stared at the bottle, disappointment filling her. "I

131

thought if it didn't blow up like the ones in Michigan, I'd just throw rocks at it until it did."

She saw it before he could cover it—admiration. "Well, at least you've thought it out."

"If I do it while the little kids are asleep, no one would know until it was over...."

"Is this my perfect little sister? The one who always does everything right—especially when she most wants to do something wrong?"

Ellie stared at the bottle. "I forgot the funnel." She screwed the cap on the bottle and gathered her things. "Great. Now what'll I do?"

Without a word, Laird took off toward the house. She stared at his retreating back and then down at her "supplies." It would only take a minute to pour some of the Drano in and screw on the cap. And once she did, no one would go near it until it exploded. Indecision wracked her as she stood there. Indecision and a little rebellion.

Noise at the back of the house turned her attention there. Luke bolted across the yard as fast as he could. "Don't—"

"I'm not!"

He reached her side and grabbed the Drano from her. "What do you think you're doing? Do you want to lose fingers? An eye? Really, Ellie?"

A protest welled up in her, but Luke tossed aside the Drano and pulled her into a hug fierce enough to hurt. "Don't scare me like that."

"I didn't—" she tried to explain, but until he released her and she could catch her breath, the words refused to leave her throat. "I didn't think it was a big deal. I thought the girl got in trouble because she didn't do it in class. The comments were all about people saying the school overreacted and...."

He stared at her, confusion and disbelief in his face. Ellie swallowed back tears of frustration and shame that she'd disappointed him and still hadn't managed to get her experiment done. But then he pulled out his phone and walked away without another word to her. Laird inched his way back and murmured, "What's going on?"

"I don't know. He came running out, grabbed the can of

Drano, and then hugged me like I'd half-killed myself."

"Well, you could have...."

"Thanks for tattling on me." She knew she sounded like a toddler, but at that moment, Ellie didn't care.

With hands shoved in his coat pockets, Laird turned to go. A few steps away, he called back, "I went to get his help. I thought if he did it, you wouldn't have to give up the experiment. I'll butt out next time."

"Laird?" When he didn't turn around, Ellie hurried to catch up with him. "I'm sorry. I shouldn't have blamed you. Even if you did tell, it's a safety thing. It's the rules."

Luke met them halfway across the yard. "Where are you guys going?"

"Inside?" Ellie held up the supplies. "I'll go put it away."

But Luke took them from her. "Go get kitchen gloves — rubber gloves. Oh, and take this with you." He handed her the bottle. "Put just a little bit of water in there."

Wide-eyed, Ellie stood there, staring at him. "Wha—"

"William says I can do it if I'm willing to risk my fingers. It's my private property."

They raced to the house, grabbed the kitchen gloves and poured a half an inch of water into the bottle. Tavish heard what they were doing and grabbed his coat as he followed them outside. Luke had them stand back — so far back that Tavish scrambled up to the treehouse and back down with his binoculars. "Here. Try these. It'll help you see better."

With yellow gloved hands, Luke shook some of the Drano into the bottle, capped it, shook it, and took off. Seconds ticked past as white smoke swirled in the bottle. The plastic stretched until Ellie thought for sure it would explode. It didn't. Well over thirty seconds passed until she'd just about given up.

"Maybe it's a dud?" Ellie stepped forward, but Luke jerked her back again.

"And this is why these things are so dangerous. I deliberately didn't put much Drano in. It'll work. Just give it a bit of time."

Another quarter minute passed — a quarter minute in which Ellie decided the experiment had failed. *He's wrong. It's* —

Pop! Though the plastic exploded with impressive force, the sound didn't do much more than pop and crackle. Ellie stared at Luke, confused. "Is that it?"

"Come over on this side so the wind doesn't carry those fumes to your lungs." Luke smiled down at her—not as far down as it once had been, she noticed. "A bit disappointing?"

"It *looked* cool, but...." Ellie shrugged and turned to Laird and Tavish. "Didn't it seem awfully quiet for something called a 'bomb'?"

"Maybe it's the snow?" Tavish inched his way closer from the upwind side. "Everything sounds quieter in snow."

Luke asked for a plastic bag from the kitchen before turning to Ellie. "Did you get enough for your science report?"

"Yeah...." The realization of what he'd done for her sent Ellie to his side. With arms wrapped around him, she murmured, "Thanks, Uncle Luke."

Minutes later, plastic bag full of Drano-coated pieces of plastic and aluminum in one hand and rubber gloves and leftover Drano in the other, Luke led her back to the house and offered a suggestion. "A good chemistry experiment has a positive outcome—either you learn something that will help you with your next experiment, or you get something tasty to eat."

"Eat? An experiment?"

He tossed the bag in the trash can and carried the gloves inside. In the mudroom, he rinsed them in the laundry sink and clipped them to the rack that hung over it to dry. "Yep. After all, cooking involves chemistry—especially baking. Mixing things like baking soda and cream of tartar—that makes a baking powder. You could compare using actual baking powder and substitutions and see if it makes a difference in the final product."

"Well...." She stared out the window where the boys still examined the snow where the "bomb" had gone off. "It sure would be tastier than Drano." And with that, she grabbed the can from the counter, carried it back downstairs to the chemical cupboard, and locked it up once more.

Stir-crazy. Her foray into a "life of leisure" had already

proven too much for her mental health. She ached to stand longer than the ten foot trips from bed to bathroom every hour on the hour. Each time she walked back to the bed, the temptation to take the long way around and swing past the window for a peek into the back yard grew stronger.

Libby's number one parenting advice—did it apply to pregnancy, too? She could hear the woman's gentle voice, see her soft, tender expression. *"Enjoy each day, Aggie. Don't feel guilty about not enjoying every second of every day, but find something in each day to enjoy. You'll never regret it."*

Now darkness made that less appealing, at least. "Sixteen more hours. That's all it'll be. They won't find liquid. I haven't had to change my underwear at all during the day, and it's good. It's really good." Her eyes opened and she stared at the ceiling. "Thanks, Lord."

The silence of the room—that had to be the worst. Music, for reasons she couldn't explain, seemed to intensify it. Instead, she grabbed her phone and slid her finger over the contacts. Libby… Tina… Savvy from church…. The sight of her mother's picture made her mind up for her. With a tap to the call button and another to speaker phone, she laid back and closed her eyes. "Hey, Mom! How's it going?"

"What's wrong?"

Aggie, had her eyes been open, would have closed them in utter frustration. "How do you *do* that? I try to sound as upbeat and normal as I can, and you *always* know."

"If I tell you, you'll stop giving it away. Nothing doing, Aggie. Now what's wrong?"

"Well, I don't think anything is anymore, but we had an exciting week—so to speak." Aggie hesitated before plunging into her story of endless laundry, a trip to the ER, and enforced semi-bed rest. "I get to take super short walks, though. That breaks up the monotony."

"How short is short?"

Once more, Aggie shook her head in disbelief. "Sometimes, you're scary. Ten or so feet—the space between my bed and the toilet. The doctor hinted that bed pans would be preferable, but I pretended not to get it. Tomorrow we go see Hannah's backup, Dr. Malara and get signed off."

"Dr. Malaria? Really?"

"Mah-*lar*-ah. No eee." Aggie snickered. "But I did the same thing when I heard Hannah say it."

From there, Aggie did a run-down on everything she knew about the kids—from Vannie's new wardrobe and apologizing to the kids who had vandalized the house, to Ellie's recent foray into chemistry. "I wonder what she would have done if she'd blown off fingers. I can imagine her painting with the paintbrush in her teeth or something. She's just that kind of girl. But man, Mom. Really? Of all my kids, *her?*"

"It sounds like Kenzie has a nice friend, though. She wrote to me about Rory. She said he's nice and doesn't let the other boys pick on her."

"He *is* nice. He has a serious crush on her, but at least it's just little kid stuff—like since she's his best friend, *and* a girl, she's extra special or something. It's not this mock adult stuff I see some of the kids doing."

Martha's sigh stretched across the miles and squeezed Aggie's heart as she said, "You know, Allie honestly believed she could keep that kind of nonsense completely away from the kids until they were in their mid to late teens. I never could make her understand that kids had been 'crushing' for millennia."

"I think Luke agrees with Allie. He came home from church just furious with one of the mothers—well, that's probably a bit strong. He wasn't very happy, though." Aggie rolled over, adjusted her belly until it felt more comfortable, and sighed. "Now, what's up in Yorktown? Are the deer out yet? Are you coming down for Tavish and Ellie's birthday?"

"Your father helped the neighborhood get the deer up by the first." Martha snickered. "And I've been treated to his blue-noses jokes ever since. You'd think he'd remember that he's *told me that a few dozen times already.*"

The familiar offers a particular kind of solace you can't find anywhere else, and that evening, Aggie found it in the backhanded scolding of the woman she called mother. "Sounds good to hear you say that."

"I was going to call you tonight."

Something in her mother's tone sent Aggie scrambling to sit up. "Oh?"

"That surgery? The one we've talked about?"

Aggie held her breath until she realized she hadn't answered. "Yeah...."

"I'm going to do it. They've scheduled me for the seventeenth. They think I'll be home for Christmas if I do it by then."

Her squeal brought the pounding of footsteps in waves. Luke burst through the door first, followed by Ian, Ellie, Vannie, and the rest of the children in one homogeneous clump. Luke found his voice first. "What?"

"Mom's having surgery — *the* surgery!"

Chaos erupted. Half the children cheered — the other half, not so much. Tears flowed — happy and sad. Questions bombarded her until Aggie felt battered beyond recognition. With a promise to call back after her appointment the next day, Aggie disconnected the call and tried to restore order from the confines of her bed. Tried... and failed.

SPEND THE NIGHT

Chapter Ten

Monday, December 8th

Nerves zinged, heart rates—both hers *and* the baby's—raced, and the dull ache in her back worked its way around to the front and down her legs as she lay on the paper-covered table and waited for the verdict. Just outside the half-open door, Hannah and Dr. Malara "spoke" in hushed whispers, while Luke sat beside her, squeezing her hand and trying to offer encouraging smiles. Her snark meter had broken, and sarcasm kicked into overdrive. *They look more like winces masquerading as grimaces.*

She struggled to sit up and swung her legs over the side of the table, but the draft from the blue paper half-gown sent shivers through her. "There has *got* to be a better way to do this. There just *has* to."

"Want your coat?" Even as he spoke, Luke jumped up to retrieve it, but Aggie shook her head. A new thought sent her arm waving and her finger waggling. "But grab my dress, will you?"

He wanted to protest. Every muscle in his face announced it, but Luke grabbed the coral knit skater dress and passed it to her. Aggie flung it over her shoulders and knotted the arms like a sweater. "That'll work."

Luke's hand slipped behind her ear and cradled her head.

The kiss—it could have lasted days, for all she knew. When his lips finally released hers, he brushed them once more across her cheek as he murmured, "And that's just one of the myriad of reasons I love you." He winked and sank back into his seat. "And I'll have you know I am using myriad in its proper sense—no 'hyperbolic nonsense.'"

A throat cleared. Aggie glanced up to see Hannah and Dr. Malara standing just inside the door, arms folded over their chests. Hannah eyed her with a look Aggie knew too well. She elbowed Dr. Malara and quipped, "You do know that that kind of behavior is what got you into this mess."

"And the problem is?"

Aggie snapped her head back and glared at him. "Really, Luke?"

"Are you complaining?"

Heat flooded her from her toes to her fingertips. A glance at the mirror over the sink added further mortification as she shook her head. "Not exactly...." A second glance showed her face flaming even brighter. She turned to Hannah. "Well, what's the verdict? Something is off or you'd have told me all is good. What's wrong? The baby looked healthy to me, and I haven't had to put in an Amazon order for a case of Depends...."

Hannah came and perched on the end of the table with her. "Well, there is great news. There's no sign of further leakage. I think your sack has definitely resealed itself—either that, or baby is pinching it shut. Whichever works for me for now. The good news—we don't need to hospitalize you or anything."

Bully for me. Aggie waited, and when Hannah didn't continue, her heart constricted. "But...."

"But you've dilated another centimeter. While normally that wouldn't be a big deal, that much that *fast* seven weeks out...."

"Six and a half."

Hannah glanced over at Dr. Malara. "Do you see what I have to deal with? You can *tell* she has a tribe of would-be lawyers at home."

"Can't wait to meet them."

Dr. Malara's words sent a shiver over her. *If that means what I think it means....* Aggie tried to ask, but the words refused to come. Luke, not blessed with the ability to read woman-ese, swung his

139

eyes from woman to woman until he couldn't take it anymore. "So, what exactly does this mean?"

"It means I'm not getting my home birth."

Luke reached for her hand, but his eyes caught and held Hannah's. "And why is that?"

"She's at high risk for early labor. I can't imagine her making it full term. If we can get her to thirty-six weeks...."

As she listened, Aggie pulled out her phone and began a new note to herself. "Okay, what do I have to do to avoid an early birth? And if I make it to say... thirty-seven weeks, then can I stay home? You said before...."

The two women exchanged glances before Hannah turned back and shrugged. "We'd have to reevaluate then. As of today, I am officially *not* your midwife. I don't have hospital privileges."

Tears spilled onto Aggie's cheeks before she knew they'd even formed. "I was supposed to have a home birth — not have to leave the house! This isn't how this is supposed to happen! Ronnie was a textbook pregnancy and birth!"

"And this little one is just a bit of a drama king/queen." Dr. Malara hesitated before adding, "You did prefer not to know, correct?"

"I suppose...." Aggie heard herself say the words, but they didn't register until she'd redressed and managed to make it outside to the car. In fact, nothing else that was said truly entered her consciousness. Instead, a numbness crept over her mind, her body, her heart. She rode through the streets of Brunswick with the radio filling the empty spaces around her. Luke held her hand, stroked the back of it, squeezed now and then.

Just as she opened her mouth to ask where he was taking her, the radio announcer's voice filled the car. "And in history, on this day in 1941, the United States of America declared war on Japan after the bombing of Pearl Harbor the previous morning."

"Figures."

Luke squeezed her hand again. "What does?"

"My body — or maybe it's this baby — declares war on me on the... seventy-somethingth anniversary of the US declaring war on Japan."

Seconds passed as she tried to take in the area. In the periphery of her mind, she heard Luke humming "Sound the

140

Battle Cry" just as she asked, "Where are you going?"

"I thought we were going to shop for Ellie and Tavish."

She stared at him—glared. "I thought I had to practically live in bed for the next six and a half—or at least four and a half—weeks."

"Well, you can't move around like usual, but surely you can ride around in one of those motor scooters—assuming PartyZone has one."

"I'm not squeezing into the front of a shopping cart. Just sayin'."

"I'll remember that. Be right back. I'm gonna go see if I can snag one of those scooters."

He was gone before she could warn him that his chances of success were slim to none. "We should go to Walmart. They've got 'em. Even if they have nothing but Disney princesses and superheroes for party supplies...."

Her voice echoed in the car, and that echo penetrated her heart with such loneliness. *It's like an omen or a prophesy or something. Merry Christmas, Aggie. Hope you like your four weeks in bed. Best gift you're going to get this year.*

A moment later a small smile formed and tried to tug at her lips. She slid her arms around her belly and cradled it there. *But next year... that gift is going to be more than worth the disappointment of this year.*

The sight of Luke sauntering back looking defeated proved her right—one of the rare times she didn't *want* to be correct. *Lord, just let him agree to take me home. I just want to go home. Stupid, I know. I'm stuck there indefinitely, but still....*

With Aggie propped up on the couch, taking most of the space, the Stuart children and Ronnie piled around the room wherever they could find a seat. Nervous glances, fidgety fingers, a quiver of Lorna's lip, concern-clouding Vannie's eyes. Laird slipped around behind the couch and knelt there. His arm slid over the back and squeezed Aggie's hand, as if seeking comfort before the boom of bad news fell on him.

Luke perched himself on the arm of the couch, his own arm

around her shoulders and allowed himself a moment to thank the Lord for children who cared deeply for one another and their often bumbling guardians. "As you know, we just got back from seeing the doctor." He felt rather than heard Aggie's repressed sob. With a gentle squeeze, meant to remind her not to unnerve the children any more than they would be already, he continued, fumbling for words as he tried to explain the situation.

"—just doesn't want to stay put, but it's much too early for Hermie to be born, so they want Aunt Aggie-slash-Mommy to keep resting as much as possible."

"But the baby is all right?" Vannie leaned forward. "I mean—" She shrugged. "I don't know what I mean. Hermie's okay?"

Luke gave her the most reassuring smile he could manufacture and nodded. "As far as they can see, the baby is well, but Aunt Aggie is just too eager to get to see herm."

"Aunt *Aggie* is perfectly content to let Hermie stay right where herm is. Her *body*, however, keeps trying to serve eviction papers."

Tavish on up snickered, but the younger children just stared at Aggie's belly in fascinated horror. Cari found her voice first. "Is the baby coming now?"

All order dissolved with those words. Lorna squealed. Ronnie tackled Aggie's belly, and from the sucked in air, precipitated yet another contraction. Cari rushed to get Aggie something—what, no one knew—and Kenzie burst into tears.

"No, not yet," Luke hastened to add. "They just want to keep her resting so the baby *doesn't* try to come too early." His eyes swept the room. "That's why we have to keep *calm*." He allowed himself to pause on Kenzie until she gathered herself together. "Because we don't want her to have to go to the hospital and stay for a long time."

Ronnie's eyes widened. "Spend the *night?*"

"That's right. She would have to spend the night—a lot of nights. So we want to keep—"

Explanation proved futile. Once more, Ronnie tackled her belly and insisted she stay home. If the pain that flooded her eyes and features meant anything, another contraction hit, and hard. Aggie took one look at Luke, shrugged, and wrestled herself out of the couch. "Sorry, I've got to get up there before I lose it."

Ellie and Tavish held a half-silent confab in one corner of the room, Vannie peppered Luke with questions, and Laird stood behind the couch watching the retreating form of his aunt with raw fear in his eyes. Never had Luke felt more alone than standing in his living room with the cacophony of his children crowding around him pleading for answers and feeling like something more than his wife's presence was missing.

"Hey, guys. Gimme a minute, okay? I want to make sure Aggie makes it upstairs all right, and I'll be right back down." Without waiting for an answer, or even to see if his son had listened, he bolted up the stairs—all five of them—until he caught up with her.

The slowness, the tension in her shoulders and the hiss of sucked in air hinted that the contractions had returned. "Are you sure you don't want me to go buy a new mattress for the guest room? You'd be nearer everyone…."

"And I'd get up. You know I would." A hint of a moan preceded her next words. "If. I. can't. hear. it, then. I. can't. be. tempted."

Never before had he wished he was larger, stronger. *If I could just carry her up there, Lord.*

"I swear. I wish you were Fezzik right now."

"Fe… the giant in *The Princess Bride?*"

A giggle melted a bit of the strain from his heart. "Yep. You could call me 'lady' and carry me up the stairs."

"And here I was just wishing I were bigger and stronger."

She didn't respond until she hit the landing. Then Aggie turned and slipped her arms around his neck. "There's just one flaw with this plan."

"And that is…."

With a kiss and a turn toward the stairs again, Aggie trudged onward. "Then you wouldn't be you, and I couldn't reach your lips without a step-ladder. Can you imagine how inconvenient it would be to wander around with one strapped to my back in case I had the chance to do a little canoodlin' when the kids weren't looking?"

That's my Mibs.

She gripped the newel at the top of the stairs and held on

tight. "Why did I think a house with *three* floors was such a good idea? Note, Mr. Sullivan:"

"Taking it now." Luke whipped out his phone and pretended to be ready to type.

"Our next house, should we ever be stupid enough to try to move all these people into some other place, will be a four-thousand square foot *ranch* home. One. Big. Box. Even if it means we have to have two side by side and connect them with an enormous living room in the middle somewhere. It could be a U-shape. An H... even a sort of 'A'. But a *ranch*, nonetheless."

"Got it. Ranch for Aggie when the kids are grown—or at least half of 'em are."

Once in their room, Luke pulled out her favorite pajamas and tossed them on the bed. "Might as well be comfortable."

Aggie stared at them for a moment before gazing up at him. "I want something."

"What's that?"

"A dress like this...." She tugged the coral dress over her head. "But sleeveless—like a jumper." Aggie rolled her eyes, sighed, and shrugged. "Whatever. I never thought I'd say *that*. But I do. Gray, black, brown—even white. I don't care. Just something neutral. I'll wear t-shirts and leggings in bed. Then if I have to get up, I'll throw that stupid jumper over them and voila. Instant modesty without the hassle of a skirt twisting around me in bed."

"We'll get you two or three."

Her fingers slid along the fabric of her favorite maternity dress. "In fact...." Decision flooded Aggie's features. "Take that down with you and see if Vannie can create one out of this. Just lob off those sleeves somehow. Maybe serge around the armholes and stitch 'em down or something."

"Will do." Luke helped pull her pajama top over her head and cradled her face when it popped through the neck hole. "I love you. It's going to be okay."

Aggie's eyes met his and held fast. "Is it? Really? Because it doesn't *feel* like it's going to be okay. Everything I dreamed for this baby is slipping away, one at a time. And it's taking all our celebrations with it. Ellie and Tavish have *nothing* for a party tomorrow. Nothing. And how am I supposed to make sure you don't buy a Charlie Brown Christmas tree on Wednesday? And what about Christmas, anyway? How—?"

It wasn't something he allowed himself to do often, but Luke kissed her mid-rant. She melted into his arms and all seemed well—right up to the moment the first hot tears splashed on his cheeks. "Oh, Mibs…." The words murmured on her lips only brought more tears.

Aggie buried her head in his chest and gripped his shirt as she struggled against her own emotions. Nothing he thought of to say would help, and Luke knew it. A quick prayer brought one thought. "I'll get Vannie and Laird to figure out the party. Once they have an idea, I'll send them up here to get your two cents. And we'll figure out something with the tree. Surely Vannie…."

She'd relaxed as he first began speaking, but the moment he mentioned the tree, Aggie stiffened. With a gentle shove, she stepped away and climbed into bed. Luke watched as she pulled the covers up over her shoulder, grabbed his pillow, and tucked it under her belly. Sobs—quiet but visible—wracked her body, and still Luke stood there, torn.

"Just go, Luke." A crack in her voice tore at his heart. "You can't fix everything."

They wandered up and down the aisles at PartyZone to no avail. Pirates—too kiddie or too sexualized. Detectives—not Ellie's thing. If they'd been a few years younger or older, cowboys would have worked. But turning twelve just screamed, "Make me special."

"How does she do it?"

Laird's voice ripped through Vannie's internal debate over the wisdom of going international. "How does she do what?"

"Come up with stuff like she does. She doesn't do 'Puppies' or 'Ponies.' But that's all they *have* here. Whole shelves of decorations devoted to soccer or…." Laird's voice choked and he turned around. Vannie glanced where he'd been headed and almost screamed in frustration.

"Seriously? What is that? A vampire prostitute?"

Laird took off down the aisle toward the door. "I don't

know, but I'm leaving. Let me know what you decide."

Vannie bolted after him and managed to beat him to the door. "Nope. We're going together. I don't want to know what else there is. That stupid nurse's outfit was almost as bad."

Once again, the Stuart-Sullivanmobile sat in the parking lot of PartyZone while those inside tried to find a way to create the best birthday experience possible — in less than twenty-four hours. "I get what you mean," Vannie muttered. "She forgets half the time — right up to the last minute. Then she pulls off this amazing retro fifties sock hop or an archaeological dig."

A snicker — a chuckle. Laird glanced at her. "The first ones weren't, though. Remember? Supermarket cake and an over-sized teddy bear? Who was that? Kenzie?"

"You got a camp-out on the front lawn, though."

"And Aunt Aggie got a sprained ankle and a bawling out from Mr. Markenson."

Something in his words seemed off. "Was that when she sprained it again? I thought that was the pillow fight."

"It was." Laird stared at her. "That wasn't the pillow fight night?"

"Don't think so. But, yeah. You're right. There were a few doozies." She sighed. "What do they *like?* She always does what we're interested in. Like the archaeological thing when we were studying Egypt and you were into all things khaki."

Laird leaned back the seat and propped his hands behind his head. "I still can't believe she *buried* my presents and made me dig them up. I was afraid I'd break something. I'm so glad she started that study for summer break. I wouldn't have liked it otherwise."

An idea had begun forming, and as she listened, Vannie pulled out her phone. Aggie answered almost on the first ring. "Did you figure it out?"

She punched speaker phone and assured Aggie they were trying. "How do you do it? You don't plan stuff until the week of — sometimes the *day* before! Like this time. You plan everything else way out."

"Because you guys change what you like almost daily. If I planned a sci-fi party today for next month, you'd all be sick to death of sci-fi by then and want something medieval."

Bet that's why you always wait to shop for Christmas until

146

December, too.

" — are you thinking about?"

Vannie snapped out of her thoughts and returned to the conversation. "Well, it *won't* be the prostitute vampire thing or the —"

"Um… Vannie?"

She swallowed hard and tossed Laird an apologetic glance before answering. "Yeah?"

"Are you sure you didn't end up in some costume area? Since when do party things have stuff like that? We need paper plates and tablecloths — a centerpiece. If they were littler, a piñata."

Laird piped up before Vannie could assure her that those things *were* with the groupings. "We should get one anyway — keep the little kids happy and out of the way of the gifts."

"Good idea." The sound of shuffling sent Vannie's heart racing, but it stopped too soon for Aggie to have gone anywhere. "Ugh. I'm going to get bed sores or something. My hips are killing me already! It's only been a few hours!"

"And several days from last week," Laird interjected.

Before she could consider the wisdom of it, Vannie punched him. "Shh…."

"No, he's right, Vannie. That does make me feel better. Okay, so what is Ellie into right now. Tavish is easy. We can throw books into anything and he'll love it. We just need to know what *kind* of book —"

"I've got it!" Vannie turned the ignition and put the car in gear. "Giving the phone to Laird. We're going to Walmart and maybe the craft store. It's so easy, I feel stupid."

Laird glared at her as she backed out of the parking space, somehow managed not to sideswipe a car that pulled in before she'd pulled forward, and shot down the row to the exit. "Feel like letting us in on this?"

"Steampunk! We can just decorate with some gears and some Victorian accents. Throw some books on the table as platter stands, and maybe make a hat piñata — like a top hat. We can totally do this!"

She heard the relief in Aggie's tone long before the words flowed through the airwaves. "That's perfect. But do a top hat all

147

decorated with a Brownie camera on it or something. Make a zeppelin for the piñata. It's easier *and* authentic."

Just as Laird started to say goodbye, Vannie shouted, "But what about the cake?!" The answer came to her before Aggie could answer. "Never mind. I got it."

Laird waited until she pulled into the Walmart parking lot before he asked about the cake. "I'm waiting…."

"The hat!" She grinned at him. "Took you long enough to ask! I'll stack a cake to make a top hat, use Rice Krispy treats for the brim, and cover it with that marshmallow fondant stuff that Aunt Libby makes. It'll be perfect! Centerpiece *and* the cake."

But as they climbed from the car, she could have sworn Laird muttered, "*Someone's* been watching too much Food Channel on the Internet."

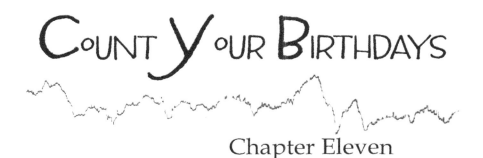

COUNT YOUR BIRTHDAYS

Chapter Eleven

Tuesday, December 9th

The rattletrap truck announced its arrival long before it pulled into the drive. Laird scribbled the last words of his essay comparing and contrasting American political parties and flipped the notebook shut. *Maybe he'll take me somewhere with him — anywhere but where we have to listen to Vannie snapping at everyone in sight.*

As Laird reached the first floor, he overheard Luke talking to Uncle Zeke in the library. " —never had to deal with girls like this. I just thought maybe you'd know how to help him. I just failed."

"We'll take a drive. Fellow over on the other side of Brunswick died, and I'm buyin' his milch cow."

"Thanks." Luke's voice dropped to where Laird almost couldn't hear. "Uncle Zeke, the girl offered him a picture of her in her bra."

Zeke's voice grew closer. "Just be glad he told you. That's the biggest thing. If you keep that communication flowing, he'll trust you with stuff like that." Silence hovered for a moment. "Tell me you didn't overreact."

"I don't think so. Not even when he admitted he was glad he doesn't have his own phone. I wanted to shake that girl for doing that to him."

As they neared, Laird decided he'd better get in there before they found him listening. *I'd also better confess when we get in the truck, or I'll mess up and give it away.*

"Uncle — hi!"

Zeke hugged him before Laird could speak his unrehearsed — and therefore, jumbled — greeting. "Good to see you, son. Want to help me get a cow? I could use a younger set of muscles for this one."

"Sure!" Laird dropped his voice. "Anything to get away from a stressed out Vannie."

"Laird...." Despite his reproving tone, Luke's mouth twitched. A second later, Vannie's screech reached the library.

"Get out of here! You're ruining everything!"

Luke took off for the kitchen. "Thanks, Uncle Zeke!"

The older man gave Laird a curious look and beckoned him to follow. "We've got a drive. Why don't you tell me about these girls Luke mentioned?"

Finding a way to explain it — harder than he'd expected. But Laird, after a bumbling start, spilled it all. "We saw Lizzy in Walmart yesterday." He couldn't bring himself to glance in Zeke's direction. "She's such a nice girl when she's not around Kendra."

"I wonder if this Kendra's parents would like to know the kinds of things their daughter is doing."

"I doubt it." Though muttered, Laird's words echoed in the truck. At Zeke's questioning glance, he tried to explain. "When she got caught making out with some guy at camp, the counselors called the parents to pick them up. It's the rules. They sign a paper saying they will and everything. Kendra's parents threatened to sue the counselor for 'defamation of character' or something like that."

The truck shuddered as Zeke pulled out onto the highway and shifted into a higher gear. "Well, son, I do see what you mean. They don't sound like the kind of folks to help their daughter through something like this. It's sad. A girl like that is searching for her worth in things that won't satisfy."

His internal self screamed for him not to ask, but Laird couldn't miss the opportunity. "Then why is everything about sex? They even show women practically making out with hamburgers to get you to buy one."

"That's true. That's definitely true." Zeke shifted again and glanced Laird's way. "But if it satisfied—that image of a woman with more showing than she should and 'making out' with the burger, as you say...." Zeke shifted down again as he slowed behind a car braking to turn. "There wouldn't be broken women all over this country—women hurting because they thought all they had to do was be like the girl on the shiny red car licking the dripping barbecue sauce from the burger and a good man would come running."

As much as Laird wanted to believe he understood what Zeke meant, he suspected there were more layers to the words than he knew how to peel. "I think I would have given Kendra my phone number—if I had one. I don't even know if it would have been for the picture." He swallowed hard. "But I would have opened it if she sent it."

"Most men would, Laird. It ain't right, and it hurts to think about it, but it's true."

"Would you?" The moment the words left his lips, Laird choked on his own saliva. "I'm sorry—"

Zeke interrupted him. "It's okay, son. It's a valid question. I'll be brutally honest. Today, I wouldn't. I wouldn't even be tempted." He winked at Laird and waggled an eyebrow. "Sixty years of marriage to a good woman helps with that kind of thing." A sigh escaped. "But what helps more is keeping your eyes and heart fixed on Jesus. It's easier to give into those temptations when you keep Jesus in your hip pocket like a handkerchief—just use Him to wipe up your messes."

He heard it—a long, silent, but demanding "but." When it didn't come, Laird tried leading for him. "But?"

"But I might have as a boy. I wanted to do right back then, but I hadn't learned that bit about not keeping Jesus tucked away until I needed Him. I sure might have." Zeke slowed and pulled onto a dirt drive. "Now, you said you would have given the girl your number, but not necessarily for the picture. Why, then?"

Disgust filled him at how weak he sounded, but Laird managed to answer truthfully. "To get her off my back." He gripped the door arm rest and said, "You know, I don't even think she really likes me. I think she just likes the *idea* of being my first girlfriend or something."

151

A sound—one Laird couldn't have described if he'd tried—of utter disgust filled the cab of the truck. Zeke pounded the steering wheel as if to punctuate it. "I remember when boys and men talked like that—conquests, they called 'em. Some guys talked about having 'notches' on their bedposts, like old gunslingers used to on their guns or gun belts. No girl I ever knew would've done it, though. They waited for a fella they liked and then sometimes they went after 'im. I seen that more than my fair share. But not just to be the first or something."

As a battered old farmhouse loomed before them, Laird grew desperate. "Okay, what do I do? I feel like I can't go anywhere anymore. Can you imagine what it'll be like this summer? It was hard enough to remember to avoid anywhere they'd be when they *weren't* trying to be in my face all the time."

"Not sure I follow."

"They don't wear much, Uncle Zeke. I could avoid them last summer, because they didn't care if I did. I'd see them coming and just go into the store or crossed the street or whatever. Laird glanced at Zeke again. "You know, like Uncle Luke said—avert the eyes. But this year, they'll be right there with their short shorts and their tank tops that...." He swallowed at the memory. "I really don't need to see."

Zeke backed the trailer up to barn doors and put the truck in gear. He turned to Laird, and the man's gaze seemed to pierce into Laird's heart. "As to what you do, you keep your eyes on *Jesus*." Laird's frustration must have shown, because the man shook his head. "No, I'm not saying that like it's easy and solves everything. It ain't the religious platitude that you think it is. But c'mon, lad. Think about it. Some girl sidles up to you and offers you one of those pictures."

"Okay...."

"What're you going to do?"

"Say, 'no thanks'?" He tried to get into the spirit of the conversation, but it had exploded exponentially from awkward to downright miserable. "I mean, because Jesus is right there, waiting for a peek?" Laird winced. "That came out wrong."

Zeke's laughter filled the truck and his hand pounded the steering wheel. "Oh, if you could've seen your face when you realized what you said!" After a few wheezed coughs, Zeke tried again. "Because Jesus is right there to *help* you resist. He's not there to shame you into doing what's right. He's there to *support* you in honoring Him with your actions."

Yeah, sounds good, but it won't work. I'll freeze or get an eyeful of something, and.... A sigh escaped.

"Laird?"

He swallowed a lump that welled up in his throat and tried to shrug off the defeat that tried to consume him. "Yeah?"

"You can do it. It doesn't feel like it, but you can."

"Not so sure about that. I think it's worse than when you were my age."

Zeke's chuckles rippled over him and soothed where they should have stung. "Son, I was tempted. Every man is. Women, too. Don't let anyone tell you otherwise. I didn't have girls wanting me just to say they got me. They didn't offer me pictures undressed. But there were always girls I knew would go one better, if you know what I mean. I could have."

"How'd you manage to hold out?"

"You assume I did."

That shocked Laird into meeting his uncle's gaze. "Wha —"

"I did — by the skin of my teeth and your Aunt Martha's good character, but I did. But, son, you shouldn't assume that because I'm telling *you* to, that I did. I'm just as human as the next man. I'm saying it because *Jesus* says you can. His Word says what?"

Pages of letters arranged into nonsensical words that wouldn't answer the question for him. "Don't know. " He ducked his head. "Sorry."

"Philippians —"

"Four-thirteen. 'I can do all things through Him who strengthens me.'" Again, he sighed. "Paul makes it sound easy, but it's not."

Zeke opened the door and hopped down. As he turned to shut it, his eyes caught and held Laird's. "Paul never even hinted at easy. He spoke a truth that we need to remember. That's it. The sky is blue, water is wet, Jesus is Lord, and we 'can do all things through Him who strengthens' us. That's it. It's just a reminder."

As Laird followed Zeke into the barn, the words reverberated in his mind. *Maybe I can do this. I get why Uncle Luke*

and Aunt Aggie don't want us doing the silly kid dating stuff, but sometimes it seems like it would be easier. We wouldn't be targets that way.

Despite Luke's evident disapproval, Aggie slid her bum down one stair at a time until she reached the living room. What should have taken twenty seconds took the better part of five minutes, but missing the party.... *I just can't. Those kids are missing out on too much, thanks to this mess.*

"Want a piece of cake, Aunt Aggie?"

"Did you get pictures? I want to show Grandma." As she spoke, Aggie peered over the top of the couch. "That seriously is an amazing cake!"

Beside her, sitting on the coffee table as if it were a bench, Luke assured her that he'd taken several. "Already zipped 'em to your phone, but I expect that's upstairs."

"Where I should be?"

He didn't answer. Her mind whispered that they both knew he hadn't even thought it, but her heart, deceived by hope deferred, insisted it was him punishing her for being foolish. The warring in her spirit produced the contractions her jaunt down the stairs hadn't even hinted of.

Eager to change the subject, Aggie pointed to the brim. "How'd you do that? Is that fondant?"

Vannie shook her head. "I tried. I really did. I ruined a ton of fondant. And I probably yelled at everyone in this family but you—"

"Some birthday gift," Laird muttered.

"Well, if you hadn't left me to do everything by myself—"

Luke's quiet voice interrupted the budding argument before it could become a full-fledged verbal battle. "Martha, Martha...."

That's all it took. Vannie's face crumbled into a picture of abject misery. "I know. I know. And I was glad he left when he did. What's wrong with me?!"

"The desire to make everything 'perfect' usually creates unrealistic expectations." Aggie gave the girl a weak smile. "Not that I'd know anything about that. I'm miss, 'who cares' and 'go with the flow', don't you know."

Even Cari and Lorna laughed at that one. *It feels so good to be down here like this Maybe I should have gone with the guest room.* She stared at the cake once more, trying and failing to figure out how she'd managed such a smooth surface. "What'd you do to it, then?"

"Chocolate. I melted a ton of it and just poured it over the whole thing and cut the excess away. Did you know if you heat a butter knife over the stove, it slices through hard chocolate like butter?"

The oven timer beeped, sending Vannie and Luke scrambling. At that moment, she realized that she had no idea *what* the menu would be. *I don't even know what they'll eat tomorrow for lunch or dinner.* One glance at the empty doorway to the kitchen sent Aggie flopping back against the couch. *I can't turn around like that all the time. It hurts too much.*

She got up to sit in the chairs opposite her and a contraction began in her lower back. *Noooo....*

Ellie brought her a glass of "steaming" punch. "They got dry ice to make it smoke. That's just so cool!"

Since when do you use the word "cool"? What, you turn twelve and suddenly have to sound like a teenager? I'm not ready for this!!!

"What's for dinner?"

A snicker preceded the girl's answer. "Ham-bur-*gears*. Laird cut cheese sections out to make it look like gears, but we think they're going to melt into a mess."

"Probably. But it's cute." Aggie caught the girl's hand. "Was it a good birthday?" Just as she asked, Aggie noticed that Ellie's characteristic braids were gone. Instead, curls and waves hung about the girl's shoulders. *Oh, man, you are growing up on me.*

"It is now that you're downstairs. It felt weird all day not having you ask how old I am now... if I feel older... do I have any clue how old I am *not*... all those questions you always ask."

If we did cellphones for the kids, I could have sent texts all day. At least it would have been sort of normal.

Aggie made a mental note to ask Luke if they should reconsider the idea of no cellphones for the kids until they graduate. "Can you ask Luke to leave the cheese off mine? I forgot. The last one I ate gave me heartburn. I think it was the cheese. I haven't been wanting much lately."

As much as she expected it—*waited* for it—the little ones didn't come to her side with stories of their day. Ronnie sat at the table, a fork in one hand, a spoon in the other. Ian sang a strange version of "Count Your Blessings" but substituted "birthdays" for blessings. Kenzie and Laird joked about who would eat the most hamburgers. Tavish, though. Every time she looked his way, he watched her with concern etched in lines his face didn't even have.

Her smile did little to reassure him. Aggie crooked her finger and beckoned him closer. He jumped up and almost vaulted the couch in his eagerness to get to her side. "Need something?"

"Just a hug from my favorite, newest male almost-teenager."

A strange look formed on Tavish's face. "Shouldn't I be too old to like to hear that? Feels like I should."

Her arms stole around his waist as he perched himself on the arm of the chair and she squeezed. "I hope you'll never be too old for you to be my favorite Tavish ever."

At Vannie's cry for help, Laird bolted from the table. *That's my Laird. You might not be as...* intense *about things, but you sure are consistent in your willingness to help.*

"Aunt Aggie?"

"Hmmm?" After a few seconds of silence, she gazed up at him. "Everything okay?"

"Yeah...." His eyes slid toward the kitchen, over to the table, and back to her. He leaned forward and murmured a question. "So, I was wondering." She watched his Adam's apple bob and still didn't know how to encourage him to open up. But he spoke again, his words tumbling out in a half-jumbled rush. "Is it against the *rules* to have a girlfriend—or boyfriend—like before you graduate. Or is it just you don't think it's smart? I was just curious."

Oh, no, no, no.... Don't go there. That's crazy foolish at your age. I can't stand it. But despite his evident desire to drop the subject, Tavish's eyes pleaded for an answer. "Well, I can't say it's against the *rules*, but I couldn't promise we'd allow it, either. Who's the girl?" She sank back and watched him. *There. That was reasonably calm and relaxed, wasn't it?*

"I—" His face reddened. "Me? No one." A crash from the

kitchen startled both of them, and Tavish bolted from the room.

Tears welled up in her eyes, but Aggie blinked them back again. The tune to "Tell It to Jesus" played in her heart, but before the first words could pass her lips, Aggie scooted out of the chair and tried *not* to waddle as she bolted for the bathroom. *At least the contractions are at bay for the moment.*

By the time she returned, Libby's voice reached her from the kitchen. *And, that's exactly what I needed today.* Aggie hurried into the kitchen and grinned. "Hey!"

Libby swung around holding a platter of foil-wrapped baked potatoes with—could they be *carrot* propellers poking out of the ends. Aggie giggled. "Zeppelins?"

"You're supposed to be resting, young lady!"

And that's the new theme song of my life. Sit down. Bake the baby. No, "Happy to see you. Can I get you a chair?" Nope. It's just, "Sit down and behave yourself."

"I just wanted to say hi." Without another word, Aggie turned and stro-ddled back to her chair. For just one moment, the temptation to scoot her bum back up the stairs and into bed sounded good—a relief, even—but the idea of missing the kids' party just to prove a point.... *Grow up, Aggie. She loves you. Stop making everything a personal affront.*

Arms slid around her waist from behind and a kiss seemed to plant itself on her cheek. Libby's voice, soft and ever-soothing, flowed through her ears and into her heart. "I'm so happy to see you. Sorry for scolding."

"I'm being ridiculously sensitive today. I don't know what my problem is." She turned and clung to Libby for a moment. "Is it utterly immature to want my mommy?"

"Of course, not!" Libby leaned back and smiled into Aggie's eyes. "Any chance of her being well enough for a visit?"

Aggie's heart constricted and she squeezed Libby again. "No, but I didn't mean that mom, anyway. This time, I just wanted you. And here you are!" A scent from the kitchen stopped Aggie mid laugh. "Wait. Is that... *fried okra?*"

"Yep! Vannie thought they looked a little like gears all sliced up, so she went with it for the veggie." Libby squeezed her once more and whispered, "I'm sorry I didn't come yesterday. I was working on the kids' gifts and convinced myself that if you didn't call, it meant everything was okay. Until I got Luke's call late last night, I just didn't know."

And this is why the world can eat its heart out. I've got the best mother-in-law on the planet. Maybe of all time, but I can't make a claim like that…. I suppose.

Long after the children were in bed and the party mess stripped from the house, long after Ellie had dismantled every single item in the monster chemistry kit they'd overnighted thanks to the wonder of Amazon shopping, and long after Tavish dismantled a piece of chipboard into semi-recognizable cutouts of gears with his new knife set, Luke and Aggie lay curled in bed, talking. Well, Luke, for once, did most of the talking. Aggie just listened and wrestled with whether she should bring up Tavish's girlfriend problem.

"You okay, Mibs? Was it too much for you?"

"No contractions, if that's what you mean."

With the perfect pressure, from months and months of practice during her pregnancy with Ronnie, Luke worked the knots out of her shoulders and lower back. "So… something was too much, but not being downstairs."

Irritation welled up, but Aggie tried to stuff it back down. Tried, and failed. "If you want me to admit I shouldn't have gone downstairs, fine. I shouldn't have done it."

"Mibs…."

"What do you want from me, Luke? I tell you the truth, and—"

Shock flooded her, cutting off her words as Luke rolled away from her. But a moment later, when the light came on, she relaxed again. *You're doing it again. Stop being over-sensitive.*

His finger traced the outline of her cheek and brushed back wisps of hair as his eyes searched her face. "What's really bothering you? Not what irritated you about the party or the way someone said something. What is hurting your heart?"

A flood of thoughts and emotions pressed against the dam of her heart, but Aggie snagged an idea that floated past and held onto it. "Tavish asked me a question tonight. Before that, I was

158

ready to ask you if you thought maybe we should revisit the idea of not allowing them to have cellphones until graduation. I mean, if Ellie had one, I would have gotten her take of the day all day long. Tavish would have asked a million questions. Vannie would have included me in the party planning. But then...."

"I should have told them to use the family cell like that. I'll let them know first thing." He watched her for another pregnant moment before asking, "Then, what changed your mind? Tavish's question?"

Aggie rolled over, nestled herself perfectly against Luke, and pulled his arm around her, holding his hand as she told the story. "A *girlfriend,* Luke. At twelve! I mean," she hastened to add, "I know kids do that at six now. They actually take six-year-olds out on 'dates.' But *our* kids, Luke. I never thought...."

"I don't think Tavish has a girlfriend in mind."

"Then why would he ask?" She glanced over her shoulder and tried to catch his eye, but couldn't do it. "It doesn't make sense."

Only the crackle of the fire Luke had made for her in the fireplace broke the silence as she waited for him to formulate his explanation. *I never imagined that I'd be married to a man who has to think about every. single. word. he speaks.*

"I think it's about Laird."

"Why?" This time she shifted in order to see his eyes. "What's going on?"

Dismay flooded her as she listened to Luke's story. Girls chasing her boy. Her boy tempted by those girls to look at things they'd worked so hard to avoid with their Internet rules. *What was the point of no Facebook if they're just going to walk up and offer? I mean, she could just snap that picture and shove it in his face next time she sees him.* Her stomach churned like it hadn't since the first weeks of pregnancy. *I wonder if monasteries accept non-catholics.*

And at that moment, something clicked that hadn't at first. "Wait, he told you about this, *when?*"

"Um? Thursday? Friday?" Her silence produced a sigh in Luke. "I knew you'd take it hard, but we didn't know what we were dealing with. I told him I wouldn't tell you unless it came up. He was worried about you."

Self-control flew up the chimney and into the night wind.

Aggie rolled back over and glared at Luke. "Don't leave me out of parenting issues again. I can't *do* this bed rest thing if I am wondering, every other minute, just what people are hiding from me."

She watched a million emotions flicker across his face — some twice — and then relaxed as he nodded. "You're right. I'm sorry. It seemed the right thing to do, but I wouldn't have been any happier than you are."

Their eyes met and held. Time passed on wings that fluttered in her heart and stomach. "I love you, Luke." She swallowed down a lump in her throat and sighed. "Tell me I can do this. Right now…."

"I'll tell you what Uncle Zeke said he told Laird today." But the kiss he began threw all thoughts of wise words from their beloved uncle out after her self-control. When he finally did speak, when he finally said, "'I can do all things through Him who strengthens me,'" Aggie's mind couldn't process what he meant.

She yawned and snuggled closer. "Huh?"

"Shhh…. Sleep. It'll make sense in the morning."

Or, at least, that's what Aggie thought he said. Slumber consumed her as the words filled her mind and dreams.

TREES, PERFECT TREES

Chapter Twelve

Wednesday, December 10th

Aggie shivered in the van, her coat buttoned all the way up, a blanket over her legs, and her cellphone in her gloved hands. Though the keys dangled in the ignition, she refused to turn on the vehicle—refused to give Luke the satisfaction of being right. Again. A giggle escaped—between chattering teeth.

"I wonder if he'll even notice. He's so obsessed with—" Her phone buzzed again, and a fresh round of giggles erupted as the latest in a long line of absolutely pathetic trees flashed on her screen. "—finding *just the right* tree."

Another buzz, another picture. This one of all the kids making goofy faces at the camera. Her heart squeezed. *This is more like it.*

A text arrived. SEEMS A SNOWBALL FIGHT IS INEVITABLE. YOU OK?

As much as she dreamed of telling him to hurry up and get a stupid tree, Aggie couldn't do it. GET A FEW GOOD SHOTS IN FOR ME.

It worked. The phone remained silent for several minutes. Aggie shivered once more and capitulated. The stretch it took to reach the ignition felt like it ripped a ligament from her side and strangled her with it. But, in less than a minute, hot air blasted through the vents and warmed her.

The book she brought—it didn't interest her. The music on her phone left her hollow and empty. Even the Christmas carols that usually accompanied their forays into tree finding goodness just filled the van. They didn't fill her heart.

But the next text that arrived did. A sign—one she'd seen a dozen times already—held by Ronnie in front of the biggest, most perfect Christmas tree she'd ever seen—flashed on her screen. The sign read, "This one?"

With a squeal and a wriggle that did a number on her bladder, Aggie zipped back a text message. YES!!!!!!

And the wait began. Would half the kids return to the van? Would they all crowd around the cocoa counter and guzzle hot chocolate and munch on Christmas cookies? With each ticking second, her guesses as to who might return first shifted from one to the next. Then she saw the first: Laird and Tavish carrying the front of the tree. As they turned around a slight curve in the path, Aggie pulled out her phone and tried to snap a picture of it. All nine children clung to the tree as if it would crash to the earth without their sole support.

"And you are probably just making it harder on Luke and the boys, aren't you?"

Kenzie saw her and waved—waved and tripped over her own feet, face-planting in the snow. Vannie tripped over her, and with a split-domino effect, all but Luke lay sprawled in the snow as the tree rolled a few feet away and stopped. Aggie knew what would happen before the first kid moved.

Laird nudged Tavish, who kicked Vannie's foot. With a scramble that would have impressed the world's best snow-wrestling coach, if such a person or sport existed, the three oldest kids tackled Luke. From the odd jig Luke did as he struggled to get away, someone had also managed to shove a bit of snow down his shirt.

"Man, I wish that could have been me. I'd give anything to fight him in the snow right now. Nothing warms you like snow kisses after a 'fight.'"

Of course, *getting* the tree to the van was the easy part. While the little ones piled in and helped each other buckle up, Laird, Luke, and Vannie wrestled the tree onto the top of the van and began the tedious task of tying it down. *Five... four... three....*

The annual argument on just *how* to best place and affix the tree to the van began before she could hit one. Kenzie giggled first. Cari and Lorna followed. In the rear view mirror, Aggie watched as Ian and Ronnie exchanged confused glances. Tavish offered to get out and help, but Ellie told him to hush. "It gets worse every year. Everyone thinks they're so smart, but all they do is make a mess of things."

"I just don't get why we don't bring the truck. We get the tree, we throw it in the back, we drive home. Win-win-win all around."

"Shhh!" Ellie's glare, had it not been so out of character, would have quelled a lesser twin. "Aunt Aggie can't *drive* right now," the girl hissed. "Don't remind her of it. I'd go nuts if I was stuck in bed all day for weeks, and weeks, and weeks...."

Not helping, kiddo. Not helping at all.

Luke pulled open the door and gave her a sheepish glance. "Loop around the trunk, bring through the little windows, and then crisscross across the top and loop again?"

"Yep."

"Relieved that you came. Vannie was certain we tie the ropes to the top first, then loop. But isn't that how it slipped off a couple of years ago?"

Despite her best intentions, a grin spread across her face. "Yep."

"And that was *my* genius idea, wasn't it?"

The entire van erupted in snickers. Aggie shrugged. "As I recall...."

"I'll get you for that."

"What?" Despite her protest, Aggie grinned.

"Mocking me. I can hear it in your eyes."

Aggie blinked, shook her head, and shrugged—all at the same time. "That doesn't even make sense."

"Well, we *were* talking about you...."

Oh, what she wouldn't have given for a handful of snow right about then.

Aggie stared at the bowl of taco soup and willed herself not to take offense at the pile of cheese and sour cream on top. *It's just how you like it. Luke has enough on his plate without having to remember that your body has betrayed you in the food area, too.*

Still, no matter how irrational it seemed, Aggie couldn't shake the niggling whispers that insisted if he *truly* cared, he wouldn't forget. Tortilla chips filled the plate around her bowl, but if she didn't dump the cheese somewhere, she'd be up all night. *It might serve him right.*

Shock, dismay, remorse — they filled her the moment the thought fully registered. Determined not to allow herself any further nasty thoughts, Aggie dumped the chips onto her napkin and scooped the cheese from the bowl and plopped it on the plate. Half the sour cream disappeared with it, but Aggie chose to consider it insurance against that causing heartburn, too.

"I will *not* become a… a… *preg*-zilla. Ugh."

A giggle preceded a knock. "Hey, Ags?"

"Tina!" The bowl of soupy goodness nearly spilled all over her duvet cover as she reached up for a hug. "Wow! When did you get in?"

"Just now." Tina helped settle Aggie's dinner around her and stood back. "Loving the life of leisure yet?"

"Not hardly."

A smirk — the one Aggie loved more than almost any expression of anyone she knew — formed as Tina shook her head. "I heard something about a '*preg*-zilla.' What's with that?"

Shame, followed by a healthy dose of justification, filled her as she pointed at the plate of cheese. "He *knows* it gives me heartburn, but he loaded it up anyway. I got all bent out of shape—" Aggie closed her eyes and shook her head. "I don't know what's gotten into me."

"Need me to go get him? Apologize? Make out—er, up?"

"He doesn't even know it, but thanks." Aggie ached to ask her to sit and tell about her trip home and everything coming up, but courtesy demanded she at least *offer* food, even if she couldn't provide it herself. "Did you eat yet?"

"Nope. Vannie said she'd bring me some as soon as she finished. I think Luke was going to, but with two bowls on the floor…."

Again, Aggie closed her eyes and asked the obvious question. "On the floor?"

"Apparently your youngest boys watched Laird and Vannie play table football with a packet of hot chocolate mix. They tried it with chili—"

"Taco soup." Aggie blushed. "Sorry. Habit. Bad, mother habit."

Tina eyed her with a curious expression and then shrugged. "Anyway. I think he was relieved not to make that trek up and down the stairs again."

I hadn't thought of that. How many times a day does he come to check on me? He replenishes my water, sits in there while I shower… "just in case"… the works. And I'm throwing a mini tantrum over a handful of cheese. It's like spilled milk all over again, but this time it's curdled. Her eyes narrowed. "Hey… does cheese curdle at any point?"

"No clue. I bet Willow knows, but…." Tina shrugged. "Probably?" As she spoke, Tina dug into her purse. "I brought these back for the kids for their birthday. Thought I'd get the okay from you before I gave them something you didn't think was wise."

The words stung. Tina's tone didn't even hold a trace of frustration or accusation—nothing to indicate any hint of expected disapproval. Nonetheless, Aggie bristled. "Are we that tyrannical?"

Shock, hurt, confusion—they flooded Tina's face. She kicked off her shoes, slid onto the bed, and folded her arms over her chest. "Okay, spill it."

"Spill what?"

"Since when do you take offense at a basic parenting courtesy? I'm pretty sure you've *thanked* me for getting prior approval before. Remember when I didn't know any better and bought those vampire books for Vannie for her birthday? I mean, they were in the stupid 'Inspirational' section!"

Irrational and unwelcome tears flowed at Tina's question. Whether or not she'd intended it to be, the words served as a well-timed and much-needed rebuke. Aggie sat with her bowl in her lap, staring into it as tears splashed off her cheeks and onto her lap. Two managed to make the bowl itself.

"Aggie...."

"I don't know what's wrong with me. It's like...." She dragged her eyes to meet Tina's. "It's like my brain—heart, really—is *convinced* the world is conspiring against me."

Tina fumbled for her phone. Once she found what she wanted, she slid it across the bed and nudged Aggie's leg with it. "There. Read that one."

The moment the reference caught her eye, Aggie knew what Tina had pulled up. "Taking every thought captive." She tapped the screen, pulled up the whole chapter of II Corinthians 10. "Maybe you should read it in context. We totally misuse this Scripture to say, 'Don't let your thoughts run away with you,' but that's not what it's talking about. This is spiritual warfare, Tina."

"And you think that lies—you know those things that Satan is the father of? You think even lies only to yourself aren't weapons in spiritual warfare?"

How could she argue with that? As much as she wanted to point out that it was a bit of a reach, Aggie just shrugged. "It's easy to say, "Snag that thought and lock it away in a dungeon, but it's not so easy to catch them." She tried to lighten the moment with a nudge and a joke. "Besides, they run fast, and I'm not allowed out of bed."

"Liar. You were downstairs yesterday, and you'll be downstairs tonight."

"Aha!" Aggie finally dug a chip in her bowl of taco soup and bit into the savory goodness. "Man, I love this stuff. Anyway, where was I?"

Tina shrugged. "Sorry. All I got was, 'aha!' like that means anything."

"Oh, right. Um... *aha!* But you see, I am not going down tonight. That's just my point."

"Why not? Luke said you got down and up without any 'contracting funny business' last night."

Just how long have you been here? Even as the question presented itself, Aggie knew the answer. *He sent a text last night— probably a reply to hers asking about the party. It's what we do. Why does everything have to be an affront today? It's ridiculous. Lord....*

But despite her natural instinct to turn to prayer, the words wouldn't come. Aggie just ignored it and answered the question.

"They watch me, Tina. I can't blame them. I mean, we told them that the baby is trying to come too early, and that's why I have to be in bed so much. And when I'm down there, everyone's nervous. I need to stay up here and let them have their fun." When Tina gave her a disgusted look, Aggie shook her head with excessive vehemence. "No, really. I'm not doing a pity party thing here, Tina. I do need to make sure their Christmas traditions aren't all ruined by worry. If I'm up here, they'll forget about me long enough to have fun—most of the time, anyway." Her forehead furrowed. "Can you watch out for Tavish for me, though? He seemed worried last night—more than the others."

Tina's hesitation spoke louder than her words could have. She hadn't planned to stay. "I was going to go to William's…." A glance at Aggie's belly seemed to change her mind. "I could get him to come here, though. Maybe we'd make it through an evening without fighting if he did." She winked at Aggie. "After Kenzie sweetens him up, everything works out great."

"I hate to think of you guys fighting."

"It's all we seem to do anymore." When Aggie didn't ask, Tina sighed and let her head flop back against the headboard. A soft *crack* followed, but she didn't seem to notice. "It's just the same old thing, Aggie. I'm not going to wait around forever while he decides if he wants to commit to something other than being my boyfriend. I love him, but I'm not going to have a fifty year first date anniversary instead of a ten or twenty year wedding anniversary. I'm just not doing it."

As much as she hated the idea of them breaking up, Aggie knew she'd feel the same way. "Do you have an idea of when you'll just say, 'forget it' and move on?"

"The first time I can bring myself to say it and know I'll stick to it, I'm doing it." Tina's voice quavered. "He's never going to do it, Aggie. I think he *wants* to, but some wounds never heal. I think he has a few of those."

Kenzie's head poked out as she peered around the doorjamb. "Uncle Luke says we're going to start on the tree as soon as dinner is done. Her eyes sought Tina's. "You should eat soon."

Tina sat up and slid off the bed. "I'll be back up in a minute. We can at least eat together."

"And pray together. Let's pray about this—either that you'll have the strength to do what you think you should, or he'll have the strength to trust the Lord for this."

Just as Tina reached the door, Aggie added, "Oh, and will you see if Ellie has done any experiments yet? The dread is killing me."

"Experiments?" Tina nodded at the bag she'd pulled from her purse. "There's no way you can object to those if you got the kid a chemistry set."

Left alone, Aggie opened the bag and pulled out a set of alcohol ink pens and a small book on coloring with them. Another bag held a book on aluminum can inventions—everything from a robot to intricate windmills. "You did good, Tina. You always do." The memory of those vampire books came flooding back. "Okay, *almost* always. No one's perfect."

"O Holy Night," sung by Perry Como, of course, filled the living room as Vannie ascended the stairs with the sole box of ornaments that survived the vandalism-induced flood. *A stupid box of frosted "glass" ones that no one likes anyway.*

Luke met her at the top, pain in his eyes. "I forgot—"

"I know. I found these." She swallowed a lump that threatened to take up permanent residence in her throat. "What're we going to do? The kids expect to decorate the tree!"

Her heart constricted as his eyes slid upward, as if he could somehow read Aggie's thoughts through the ceiling. "Maybe...." He shrugged. "I don't know. I just didn't remember. It's going to hurt her to figure this out." When his voice cracked, Vannie barely kept her emotions in check. "I think it's probably a good thing she didn't feel up to coming down."

Just hearing him flounder—the man who kept everyone on an even keel with his quiet, steady wisdom—was all it took for Vannie to kick into gear. *C'mon. Think. What would Aunt Aggie do?* The answer came all at once. She beckoned to Tina and pulled Luke a little further away from the others. "Can you go to the market and get cranberries? I think we have popcorn, don't we?"

"Not sure. I can get it. What else?"

"Um...." Vannie dashed for the library. "Tell Aunt Tina."

It took less than a minute to flip open the laptop, sign on, and open a page of easy ornament ideas on Pinterest. Luke and Tina stood behind her and pointed at their favorites. "Okay, we need applesauce, too. And candy canes. They look festive, right?"

"Not sure the market'll have any, but if they do, I'll get them. Anything else?" Even as he spoke, Luke's hand fiddled in his pocket for his keys.

"I don't think so. We need you to come back fast. These kids are going to flip when they find out the ornaments Mommy bought them are all gone." She stared at him. "How did they mildew so fast?"

But Luke shook his head. "I'll explain later. It wasn't that. And there are a few in a different box, but they need cleaning. Most, though...."

At that moment just *some* of the wonderful collection of ornaments felt almost worse than none. What if someone had nothing salvaged and someone else had several? *How horrible!*

Tina's voice broke through her reverie. "Now, what do you need from me?"

"Oh. Sorry. Um, these look easy enough. I bet Cari and Lorna could make a few. Think Aunt Aggie would mind if we used up one of the old hymnals? I could buy a newer one on eBay if she wanted me to."

"Just do it. Okay, I need ribbon and little bits of fake evergreen? What about those little pine cones?"

But Vannie shook her head. "I doubt you'll find them there. You can look, but.... Just find something. Oh!!! Mason jar lid ornaments looked simple enough. "What if we asked Ellie to draw quick sketches of everyone? She could use those cool pens you gave her for her birthday — you know, to color them."

"I think her water pen and watercolor pencils might look better, but that's a great idea."

Vannie stared at the black and white sketches and tried to imagine them in vivid color. "Maybe.... What else?"

Tina scrolled through her phone while Vannie skipped idea after idea as too time-consuming. "Okay, see this? Couldn't Ian and Ronnie use those stupid frosted balls and cover them?"

"If any survived the process, sure."

"Well, they aren't glass. They're just frosted acrylic that

169

looks like glass."

Tina shoved her phone in her pocket and bolted for the door. "Then get them on it. That stuff will take forever to dry. Do you have Elmer's glue?"

"Tons! Aunt Aggie—"

"—buys out Walmart during the back-to-school sales." Tina laughed as she wriggled into her coat. "Be right back."

William's voice called out from beneath the tree. "Where're you going?"

"Vannie put me to work. We're going to have a bunch more fun than we ever imagined!"

"Why does that scare me?"

As she scanned the instructions once more, Vannie muttered to herself, "Because it should." Louder, she called for Ellie. "Can you come in here?"

It took half an hour to get everyone working on *something*. Just as Luke burst through the door with bags on his arms, Vannie started up the stairs to ask Aggie if any gifts had been wrapped. "I'll be right back down."

Luke rushed to the bottom of the steps. "I think I should—"

"Just asking about gifts."

"Gotcha. I'll go pop the corn."

She found Aggie perched on one side, reading a book—one she thought she remembered from summertime. "Hey, Aunt Aggie?"

"Vannie! How's it going?"

"Great. Everyone is busy down there. I just wondered if you had any gifts wrapped." Her conscience niggled for a moment, but Vannie pushed it aside. "You know how the tree always looks better with a few gifts under it, but I knew you probably hadn't had time to do much wrapping after we got back, and then...."

Aggie's eyes clouded. "I don't even know what I have in there." She threw the covers off the bed and shuffled across the floor. "You should stand back a bit—just in case."

"Are you supposed—?"

"If I can get up and go to the bathroom, I can open a closet door in my bedroom." Aggie tossed a smile over her shoulder and winked. "And I'll take any excuse to get out of that bed. Besides...." Aggie smirked. "We can call it clot prevention. I'm

170

supposed to keep the blood moving while not moving much myself. Yeah. Right."

A moment later, Aggie flung the doors all the way open. On the shelf, a single box sat—brown and plain. Nothing to hint at what it could be. Aggie pointed. "One gift. One. Yours."

The pain in Aggie's eyes pierced Vannie's heart. "Well, like you said. You can't shop early. We're always changing our minds on things."

"And now I can't go anywhere or do anything." Aggie closed the doors with excessive caution and shuffled back to the bed. "Can you just go, Vannie? I can't deal with this right now. I'm sorry."

At the door, Vannie hesitated, but Aggie snapped off the light, rolled over, and pulled the covers up over her head. Heartsore, Vannie slipped downstairs and into the kitchen where Luke stood with a plastic trash bag under the popcorn popper and the little boys slathered frosted balls with glue and water and pasted torn bits of hymnal paper over it all.

"That's looking good!" She sounded overly enthusiastic, even to her own ears, but Vannie ignored the odd look Luke gave her and pointed to an empty spot on Ronnie's. "Why don't you put one there?"

A bowl of cranberries on the island reminded her that they'd need needles and thread. She dashed for the thread container and fumbled through it. Red... white... green.... Vannie snatched up a spool of green and dug through the tools box for a packet of needles. With thread, needles, and a pair of thread snips in hand, she hurried back to the kitchen to thread needles in anticipation of a stringing party.

"Did you get the applesauce? Should I mix—?"

Luke slid a bowl under the air popper and turned it back to the counter. A moment later, he wrapped his arms around her and held her for a moment. "Vannie? It'll be fine. Everything'll be just fine. We can make ornaments tomorrow and all week. Let's just get a few things on the tree, okay?"

"Vannie!"

"Cari calls." Vannie kissed Luke's cheek and whispered, "Thanks. I needed that reminder. Can't fix everything all at once, right?"

171

Just as she stepped out of the kitchen, William called, too. "Tina wants to know if she should get some lights."

Vannie blinked—twice. And blinked again. "I totally spaced it. Yeah...." Her eyes swept the colors she had. "How about white? Let's go with white."

A cry of protest came from the dining table where Cari, Kenzie, and Lorna worked on folding third-sheets from hymnals into fans and origami stars. Cari pointed to something that looked like a giraffe with wings. "Wha—"

"She decided to make a dove." Kenzie rolled her eyes. "Of course, she doesn't know *how*...."

Cari stared at it. "I just thought it would work. We did those other birds...."

Vannie tried a dozen ways to shorten the neck, but she couldn't do it in any way that looked remotely like a dove. "I like the idea. I think if we just tuck this back on itself, it looks like a normal bird. I like it." She fingered one of the stars. "I can't believe you remembered how to do this. I love them."

And that reminded her that they likely had no tree topper anymore. *It was wired. That's probably not even safe. And it was ugly when it was off.*

A quick sweep of the room showed Tavish missing. *This is not the time to be hiding out, Tavish! We need you.*

Determined to get him out and stringing popcorn, at the very least, Vannie strode across the room and jerked open the door to his under-the-stairs hideaway. "Wha—"

With tears streaming down his face, Tavish sat on the mattress holding a nutcracker doll that had once been beautiful. Now the hair was half gone, the gold ribbon accents hung limp. It looked like something a dog had drug home from the gutter. "Mommy gave me this after we went that last year—remember? It was Ellie and my first time. She got Clara." His voice choked. "Clara's not in here."

It's ruined. Now I know what Uncle Luke meant. Vannie knelt beside him and began putting the ornaments—most looking quite bedraggled—back in the box. "We'll fix these soon. Right now, I need you."

Red-rimmed eyes met hers. "What for?"

She used hugging him as an excuse not to answer

172

immediately. But the idea came just as she stood again. "We don't have anything for the top of the tree. Make a star, an angel — whatever you want. But can you make *something?*" When he didn't respond, she tried a joke. "Well, not *quite.* No 'weeping angels' but otherwise...."

It worked. Tavish grinned. "Tempting, but I've always wanted either a fierce warrior-looking angel or maybe a star that has a solid cross element to the middle of it. I'll see what I can come up with."

"Remember that army guy you got a few years ago? The one who looks like he's ready to take out anyone who looks at him wrong?"

Tavish nodded.

"Maybe he'd be a good angel? Get some white fabric and see what you can do with it for a robe?"

Ellie appeared before Tavish could respond. "I got one done."

As happy as she was to hear it, Vannie had to stifle a groan. *This'll take forever.* The little sketched portrait brought a smile to her lips. "I'm glad you did Aunt Aggie first. She'll be here that way."

"That's what I thought. Now what do I do with it?"

She never did get the chance to answer. Ronnie's wail in the kitchen sent her racing through the house. There he stood, beside the cranberry bowl with a needle sticking through a cranberry and into his finger. "Oh, bother. Ronnie, there's no thread on tha —" At that moment, she saw them. Half a dozen cranberries on the floor and red juice staining his fingers. "Where did you think the cranberries were going?"

But the boy only wailed.

Duh! Get the needle out of his finger! She jerked the needle and freed the boy from impalement by sewing apparatus. "Okay, why don't we put *thread* on this and use the popcorn, too."

White lights glowed between the branches of the tree, giving it an almost ethereal look in the darkened living room. Popcorn-cranberry strands looped and crisscrossed the tree from top to bottom, and a dozen hymnal plastered balls hung scattered over it. *Using the hair dryer to dry them – that was genius, Vannie.*

Luke stood to examine some of the ornaments closer—little fans with ribbons and holly at the base. The origami stars touched his heart. *They remembered how.*

Tavish's kindling star with the solid cross in the center and wrapped in white lights sat at the top—a reminder of the beacon that led the magi to Jesus in Bethlehem. Luke dragged a stool in from the kitchen and adjusted it to stand just a little straighter. *That boy is a genius with his hands, Lord. I'm grateful for him. He has the inspiration and ability to see what might look good. I've never had that.*

But the mason jar lid with the sketch of Aggie in it that dangled from the front center branch remained his favorite. He'd loved it from the moment Ellie brought it to him to hang on the tree. Instead, he'd taken it straight up to show Aggie. Now a sketch of him hung beside it. *Mom'll want a picture of that. She loves Ellie's art.*

Once more, he stood back and admired the result. Never had they had a tree so *bare*, but Luke loved it just as it was. *Maybe Vannie will stop with the cinnamon ornaments. That would be nice.*

He took half a dozen more photos with his phone and decided he had enough. With the stool still standing to one side of the tree, Luke turned off the lights and climbed the stairs to their room. *It's time to tell her, Lord. Please hold her a bit closer right now. It seems like one blow after another. I don't know how much more she can take without growing bitter.*

174

I Made My Gifts for Thee

Chapter Thirteen

Thursday, December 11ᵗʰ

Ornament construction—the art *du jour,* as Tina had insisted on calling it—consumed the household. The scent of apples and cinnamon filled every corner of the house. In the closet beneath the stairs, Tavish worked on his first gift—a piece for Kenzie.

The work—tedious. One at a time, Tavish folded each page one-third of the way in to the center and glued it down. Halfway through the book, he realized he should have glued each one together at the same time. "Has to be faster that way."

His back ached, his fingers grew raw from wiping them clean of glue so he didn't ruin the pages, and his eyes began to cross at the odd word combinations that formed as a result of the folding. Still, he continued to fold, glue, and glue again. With each section, he watched the progression with a curious and keen eye. Would it work? He could only hope.

Kenzie's voice neared—closer, and closer. Frustrated, he tucked the pictures he'd printed from screen shots behind the mattress, and kept folding. *If she sees it, she won't know what it is.*

A knock preceded the opening of his door by half a second. "Hey!"

"Sorry." Her wide eyes showed instant fascination. "I

knocked!"

"Couldn't wait for me to answer?"

Kenzie's forehead furrowed. "What's with you?" She pointed. "What're you doing?"

"Making a Christmas present. I saw these book art things on Pinterest."

"Book art?"

Tavish nodded, his mind racing to find truthful things to say without giving it away. *Yeah, lies might be allowed for Christmas and birthday surprises, but I can't keep up with them. Needs to be true.*

"I don't know what that is."

"Well, they take books and fold and cut them into cool art things. I saw one that had an artist's palette, brushes, and an Eiffel Tower in the background. I thought I'd do it for Ellie."

The skeptical expression Kenzie wore would have been discouraging if it weren't so comical. "That's an awfully fat Eiffel Tower. Doesn't it get skinny at the top?"

Without a word, Tavish pulled his new carving set from the shelf and passed it to her. From the light in her eyes, it seemed as if she'd inferred exactly what he'd hoped she would. With a swipe of glue and another seam creased, Tavish continued his process and waited for more questions. With Kenzie, there'd definitely be more.

"We're making ornaments."

"Well, I'm making gifts. You'll put stuff *on* the tree, and I'll put stuff *under* it."

That's all it took. Kenzie's questions fired at him faster than he could dodge them. "Now, are you making something for everyone? We're not drawing names this year? I was hoping Vannie would get me so she'd make me a cool dress like Ellie's. Will we all have to make our presents this year? Aunt Aggie can't take us shopping, can she?"

Tavish swirled his finger in the bowl of cloudy water and wiped it on the kitchen towel he'd confiscated. He watched her until she stopped. "I don't know."

"Huh?" Her forehead furrowed as she tried to connect his answer to the right question. Eventually, she gave up. "I don't get it. Which one?"

"All of them. I don't know if I'm going to make one for

everyone. I don't know how long this'll take." His heart thrilled, just a little, at the excited look in her eyes as he added, "But I'm going to try. Even if I have to scale it back for some. It'll be fun." His mind whirled as he tried to remember another question. "I think we probably *should* make presents this year. I mean, Uncle Luke has enough to do, and Aunt Tina is leaving for that wedding in Costa Rica in what, a week?"

The girl's face fell. "I forgot. She won't be here for Christmas." He waited for it and wasn't disappointed. "That means Mr. Markenson probably won't be, either." Her finger traced the folded edges for a moment before she sat back on her haunches and watched. "If we have to make presents, and the little guys can't, then we probably won't draw names, will we?"

That question—that one was a good one. "Not sure, but you're right. Maybe we should get everyone together and talk about it. If we can decide not to do that this year, Uncle Luke won't have that to do. It might be smart."

"Want me to go tell Vannie and Laird? Ellie?" In the way of little girls the world over, she sniffed and tossed a braid over one shoulder. "I won't tell Cari and Lorna or the little guys. They'll just blab it to Uncle Luke and he'll try to make it happen."

Tavish managed to stifle the smirk that threatened to insult his little sister and nodded. "Probably smart." However, he couldn't resist a gentle jab. "But, you aren't that much older than Cari and Lorna."

The front door shut and they heard Tina and William's voices in the entryway—voices that sounded snippy. Again. *I wish I understood what happened. The longer they're together, the more miserable they seem. I'd break up with her if I was that unhappy.*

"I'm going to go say hi." Kenzie inched back out of the cubbie and whispered, "Mr. Markenson is always nicer to her when I'm there."

Interesting observation, Kenz. I wonder why that is.

"Oh, and I'll tell Vannie. We can meet in the library while the little kids are napping. It'll be perfect."

Even as the door shut behind her, Tavish realized he'd have to come up with *something* the younger twins could make for everyone or things would get ugly. Even Lorna was likely to revolt over being left out of everything. *At least that's one Pinterest idea I won't have to hide from anyone.*

A wall of journals and notebooks danced before his overwhelmed eyes, each insisting that it offered the best hope for Aggie's mental sanity and emotional happiness. He, on the other hand, felt his mind and emotions swirling into despair of ever finding just the right one. Leather bound with straps, spiral bound with hard and soft covers. Little paperback notebooks that looked more like catalogs than anything, and all in a dozen sizes.

A perky girl who looked a day over twelve, but no more, stepped up and offered her assistance. "Is it a Christmas — I mean, *holiday* – gift?"

"It's not for Christmas, no." Luke smiled. "Even if I didn't celebrate, I wouldn't be offended at the word. Take a deep breath." And with an ease and willingness that would have surprised everyone in his family, Luke spilled the whole thing. Bed rest, no preparation for the baby or Christmas, Aggie's loss of control — the works. "I just thought maybe if she could write out her feelings or start making lists or *something*...."

"Oh!" The girl reached for one notebook and stopped. She slid sideways a couple of feet and touched another journal — one Luke had been tempted by himself.

Of course, I was tempted by pansies. Maybe she –

"You know...." The girl turned to face him. "I'm a name person. I can't *do* this without a name. I'm Fee — short for Fiona, of course — and you?"

For something so formal, their handshake in the middle of an over-sized bookstore felt more relaxed and casual than most introductions. "I'm Luke. And if my wife Aggie were here, she'd hug you."

"Well, you hug her for me. I can't imagine being stuck in bed around Christmas — " Her eyes darted around her to make certain she hadn't been overheard. "Okay, what I was going to say...."

Amazed, and a little unnerved, Luke listened to her swing from introductions to sales mode in the space of a breath. "You have different needs. If she's going to be making lists, she might like this." Fee passed him a packet of three notebooks bound

178

together by a slim band. "But if she is recording thoughts and...." The wince before she continued would have been comical had it not been indicative of an ever-shifting society. "—prayers?"

"Definitely."

"Then...." Once more, Fee reached for the pansy journal. "I can see this being more like it. The pages have inspirational—mostly Bible—quotes and lovely illustrations." She paused at one. "See? And since pansies are the flower for 'thoughts'...." She smiled over at him. "Did you know that? Flowers used to mean something."

"I gave Aggie pansies with a poem about them before we were married."

Fee thrust the book into his hand. "You *have* to get this one. She can write her lists in a cheap note—"

"No." Luke swallowed hard and shook his head. "Aggie needs something that inspires her to use it right now. How many times have I heard her say, 'If you love what you *need* to use, then you'll *want* to use it. And if you *want* to use it, you will.'" He shrugged. "It's what I call having the 'right tool for the job.'"

It took another twenty minutes to sort out what he thought she might want, but he left with four distinct options and more confidence that she'd love them than he had going *into* the store. At home, he pulled the gift bag and packaging suitcase from atop the library bookshelf, snagged a generic gift bag and some tissue paper, and rummaged through the silk pocket in the lid for a card. Assembling the gift—two minutes, tops. Writing a card to express how much he loved her and wanted to encourage her—next to impossible.

All around him, his family worked to create a festive mood, while Luke worked to arrange words that he'd never be able to speak into legible and comprehensible sentences. Laughter jarred him from the one coherent thought he'd managed—*William. Must be his day off.* Tina's laughter followed and Luke relaxed. *That's good news to tell her. Maybe I should just write a quick note.* Then it hit him.

He pulled out the journal, stared at the flower-embossed cover, and began drawing. Though not perfect, inside a minute, he had a decent copy of the pansies placed in the center of the card. He hesitated, nodded, and signed it. *All my love, Luke.*

Just as he reached for the envelope, Luke saw the lack of salutation and once more, hesitated. He loved the simplicity of a page with only the flowers and his signature, but he picked up the pen again and after a moment's consideration, wrote, *Aggie*. On the envelope, he switched it to "Mibs."

Bag in hand, he climbed the stairs and peered around the doorjamb. The bed was empty. A flushing toilet sent him bolting for the bed. He dropped the bag next to her pillow and dashed for the doorway again. He barely made it.

Aggie stepped out of the restroom and her squeal hinted that he'd made the right decision. *Should have been obvious. Even I'd probably need some kind of pick-me-up after a week or two of this. Ugh.*

"I know you're over there, Luke. Come sit with me while I open this."

Suspicious tears hinted that he'd made her happier than he'd imagined. Luke kicked off his shoes and propped himself up against the headboard. Aggie hefted the bag with one finger. "Books. Smart idea." As encouraging as she tried to sound, he heard the disappointment in her tone and wondered at it.

"Here." In a desperate move to delay the inevitable, he pulled the card from the top of the bag. "Start with this."

Oh, the agonizing slowness of a woman who is determined to savor every second of a moment. She traced her nickname on the front, unfolded the flap with such care that he wished he had licked it shut, and slowly slid the card from it. "Hey, I recognize this one. I was going to give it to you."

"Forgot a card at the store, so I raided the suitcase."

"I really liked it." She kissed him before opening it. "You have good—" A soft gasp stifled Aggie's next words. Arms around him, tears on his neck, murmurs of love and appreciation.

"Guess I didn't blow it with that, huh?"

Aggie leaned back against the headboard and stared at him. "You doubted?"

"A little… it's not very eloquent."

Once more, her finger traced the words, the shapes. "A thousand words…."

Bag abandoned, she set the card up on her nightstand and fiddled with the arrangement until it pleased her. Then, with the bag balanced precariously on her ever growing belly, Aggie began flinging tissue paper from it with utter abandon. "Such a waste of money, trees, energy—and I *love* it. If we ever try to 'go green', I'm not giving up wrapping paper or tissue paper." Her eyes twinkled as they caught his. "Thought you oughtta know."

The packets of to-do list notebooks changed her entire expression. Aggie stared at them, slid the band off, flipped through, and glanced up at him before staring again. "Wow! This is so... so...."

"Sorry. I—"

"*Neat!* I can't believe you did this. It's perfect!"

After the third kiss in just a few minutes, Luke made a mental note to consider more spontaneous gifts when things grew a little commonplace between them. "Well, the girl there, Fee, she said I should hug you...."

But the cuddling he'd expected never materialized. Aggie gave him a brief hug and dug into the bag. This time, she pulled out the largish hardcover journal-slash-notebook that Fee had insisted on. "Fee also said to look these up on YouTube. She says there are all kinds of neat videos on how people use them. I believe her words were, 'You can binge-watch planning videos for days without knowing you did it.'"

She slit the plastic covering, flipped through the pages, and stared at him. "It has an index. Is it for creative writing? A non-fiction book on how to have ten kids in four years?"

"I think she said a lot of people use it for a planner." Luke pulled the wrapper paper from it and tucked it inside the front cover for her. "She said to look up the name."

Aggie didn't seem to *want* to set it down, so she propped it up against her chest and reached for the next. Luke preempted her question. "She says you can buy leather or fabric notebooks that these fit in. They're just dot grid journals for whatever you want."

"They're pretty. I like that sunflower." Aggie started to set it aside, but she paused. "How—oh, I'll look it up. There's something else left. I felt it."

When Aggie pulled out the pansy journal, the bag toppled to the floor. Her thumbs caressed the embossed flowers for half a minute or more while she fought to gain control over her emotions. "Luke?"

181

"There are Scriptures and quotes on the pages." He pulled her close and held her. "I just thought it might help to write out what's going on in your head. Maybe if you find it hard to pray, you could just write your prayers, or you could write notes to the family for them to read... something."

"I'll have to think about it, but yeah. That's a good idea."

How long they sat like that, he didn't know. But it must have been well through lunch, because Ronnie appeared at the door with a petulant look in his eye and disgusted tone as he announced he'd been sent up to bed. "Can I sleep wif you?"

"With." Aggie's correction came so automatically that Luke almost laughed.

Some things never change.

"*With* you?"

He kissed her, ignoring the giggles of his son, and climbed from the bed. "You get up there and sleep, son." With a hug and a kiss for Ronnie, too, Luke inched his way from the room. "Need anything?"

She pointed at the plates on a chest of drawers by the door. "Just those taken down." Before he could question her, she added, "I dropped them off there when I got up to go to the bathroom. It's all good." She frowned. "Or is that *well?* I can't even remember!"

An emptiness filled him as he left the room. Luke pondered it as he stopped by Ian's bed and suggested the boy rest. He pondered it as he asked Cari and Lorna what books they planned to read during their quiet time. And he pondered it as he entered the kitchen to find William and Tina cleaning up the ornament mess... together.

I suppose it's a good thing when a man doesn't feel quite complete when his wife isn't by his side.

They sat around the library table — Vannie at the head, Laird at the foot, Kenzie and Ellie on one side, Tavish on the other. Vannie stared at her blank computer screen and shrugged. "Okay, we're taking on the gifts, right? Do we just throw out ideas for everyone? I can shop."

Kenzie spoke up before Vannie could look up from the screen. "I think we should make some."

At those words, both Laird and Tavish slumped in their chairs. *Then the guys are out. Shopping it is.* But Kenzie's confused expression stopped Vannie before she could voice her opinion. A glance at Tavish showed him almost glaring. "Well, we don't have to decide that right away, but we should figure out what we're going to do. I mean, Aunt Aggie could shop online, but does she *want* to? I don't know. If we presented a—"

Tavish sat up at those words. "I don't think we should be trying to take over their Christmas. If we want to do more than just the gift exchange this year, fine. But I'd be pretty tick— *annoyed*," he corrected at Vannie's glare. "—if my kids just bumped me out of Christmas decisions altogether."

"Yeah. He has a point. I mean, I think we should do *something*," Laird added at what felt like a kick from Kenzie. "I just think it should be us playing 'Santa' because we want to. Not because we are trying to make up for something."

This time, Ellie vocalized a protest. "We're not bringing Santa into this. No. Way."

"I didn't mean it like that. It was just a figure of speech. I know he's not 'invited' to our celebration, and I'm good with that. But, c'mon." Tavish's eyes swept the table before landing on Ellie again. "You all knew what I meant, right?"

In less than five seconds Ellie would apologize, Tavish would too, and things could continue. Vannie counted. Ellie hopped up and bolted from the room. Shocked stares followed until Tavish shoved his chair away from the table and shuffled out himself. She heard the cubbie door open and close again.

"Then there were three." Laird shook his head. "Look, I don't *mind* making gifts if that's what you want to do, but I'm not exactly good at stuff like that."

"Uncle Luke would help…." He blinked at her. She sighed. "I guess that *does* kind of defeat the point of doing gifts ourselves."

Before Laird or Kenzie could offer another idea, Tina and William strolled in, hand-in-hand. *At least they're not arguing right now. That's improvement.*

"What's going on? Ellie bolted out the back door and

wouldn't talk to me when I asked her what's up. William says Tavish is under the stairs again."

An expression—one she'd seen many times and still didn't quite understand—flickered across William's face and filled his eyes with pain. "I could go get him."

"He's fine, William. Not everyone—"

"Okay." William pulled up a chair next to Kenzie and dropped an arm around her shoulder. "All right, what're you plotting? I see it in those gorgeous eyes…."

As Kenzie flushed and ducked her head, trying to explain their mission, Tina slid in beside Laird. "Christmas gifts. I forgot all about those. I guess I could shop—"

"We were trying to do something just from us," Vannie interjected. "I don't think Aunt Aggie would like not getting a choice in what she did. Grandmother…."

William cleared his throat, but Tina ignored him. "Good point. Too much is still, well, too much. Now, what do you need from us?" She glared at William. "Don't even try to get out of it. This is what friends do."

"Did I—"

"Whatever." Tina turned back to Vannie and pulled the laptop closer. "Oh. There's nothing on here."

That's kind of the point. We need ideas, not your approval of them. As she heard the snarky tone in her mind, Vannie tried to tone it down. *Well, to start with, anyway. We should probably get* someone's *okay.*

William pulled out his phone and stared at the screen before tapping something. A few seconds later, he began swiping his fingers all over the place. "Now, how many gifts are you trying for?"

"Just one each, don't you think?" Vannie's eyes swung from Tina to William. "I mean, we usually do the gift swap anyway. So we can come up with one without messing things up too much."

"But!" Kenzie's protest fizzled the moment she began. William murmured something, and she shook her head. But in all of it, Vannie saw something that unnerved her.

That girl has something up her sleeve. Great. I do not *need this right now.*

Laird's voice broke through her thoughts. "—is going to do

184

what for whom. Who. Whatever."

"Well, I could do clothes for the girls, I guess. Or maybe for the little girls I could do doll dresses." Vannie looked at Kenzie for confirmation. "Do you think they'd like that?"

"Yeah…." She rocked back in the chair for a moment before adding, "Or you could do cool outfits for them like you did for Ellie. Or maybe make Ellie another one."

In other words, you want something different. I can do that, little sister. I can totally do that. But Vannie played along and just nodded. "I'll think about that. I could make a few pieces that would mix and match with Ellie's so she could turn it into several outfits."

"Well, Ian and Ronnie aren't going to want trench coats, bow ties, and fezzes, so we need to come up with something non-clothing for them."

This time, William interjected a thought. "Except that they might like dress up clothes. Robin Hood, or army guys, or even a…. I don't know." He winked at Kenzie. "Sheriff or policeman or something."

Tina shook her head. "No, no, no. Vannie won't have time to *breathe* if she has to spend the next two weeks sewing something for everyone in the house."

Those words prompted Laird to drop his head on the table and pound it a couple of times. "What about Aunt Aggie and Uncle Luke? What can we do for them? And what about the baby? What if it comes early?"

"I don't think it will, Laird. Not now." Tina reached across the table and ruffled hair that had needed a cut for a couple of weeks already. "But you're right. They'd like the baby to be remembered. I wonder if Ellie could manage a patchwork baby blanket or something. We've probably got enough scraps from your clothes over the years to make something semi-meaningful."

This time, William didn't try to suppress a snicker. "*We*?"

"Fine. You. Whatever." Tina rolled her eyes and threw up her hands. "If it were me, I'd go to the mall, buy for everyone, and be done inside two hours, okay? It's how I roll. But Aggie…." Her eyes met Vannie's and held. "This would mean so much more to Aggie than my way of doing things."

Before Vannie could respond, Ellie crept back in the room,

185

Tavish on her heels. "I'm sorry."

"It's all good." Vannie glared at Laird's fake cough. "Let's just figure out what to do for the little guys and um...." She turned to Tina for help. "What do we do about each other?"

"Let me handle that." Tina jumped up and beckoned for Laird to follow. "Let's go figure her out. Everyone else, figure out Laird while we're gone. We can repeat with Tavish and voila. All done."

Long after William and Tina had left, long after the others had disappeared to places unknown in and around the house, Vannie sat with her list of gift ideas and tried to calm herself down. *It's too much. I know it is, and I can't help it. I want to do it anyway. I sure hope Laird can figure out how to do the marshmallow shooters, or we're doomed.*

With that cheerful thought filling her mind and heart, Vannie climbed the stairs in search of her old doll. Only when she reached above the door to the shelf that now stood empty, did she remember the sliced open vinyl and butchered hair. *Great. I can't even use her for a model. I have to sew after the little guys are in bed.*

All Things Dark and Awful

Chapter Fourteen

Sunday, December 14ᵗʰ

Potluck Sunday — the Stuart-Sullivan highlight of the month. Luke had hinted he didn't want to stay, but the collective display of dismay had prompted a quick change of mind and a scramble for something to bring. Even still, with all that, he'd had to make a complete circle to return for the quick pot of taco soup they'd thrown together that morning.

So, while the rest of the church fellowshipped and prepared the meal, Vannie took off for the market. She'd made it to the corner and crossed the street, when she realized that she heard more than just her footsteps crunching in the snow. A glance over her shoulder showed Josiah Ware gaining on her.

"Something wrong?" Vannie backed toward him, ready to return to the church if Luke had decided he needed her.

"No, I came to ask you that question." Josiah reached her side and smiled. "I saw you take off and got concerned."

It wasn't the first time a guy had showed interest in her, but it *was* the first time it had been focused on *her* welfare. And it felt nice — really nice. "Just going to the market. We didn't have any chips for the taco soup we brought." Vannie took a step toward town. "I need to hurry."

"Do you think your uncle would mind if I came with you?"

There it was again—that *something* that she couldn't quite place. Whatever it was, Vannie liked it. "I don't think so, but I could ask." She pulled out the family cellphone and wiggled it. "For once, we didn't forget the extra phone."

Josiah nodded. "Well, then call. I'll at least walk until he says no."

But Luke gave approval almost before she finished asking and added milk to the order. "If you've got someone to help, I don't feel guilty about asking. Marcus brought ghost peppers. He's going to add some to his soup—and if I know him, mine."

"Got it. Anything else?"

Luke's silence suggested a probable answer in the affirmative, but experience had taught her not to press. It only made him take longer. "Well, if it doesn't get to be too much, stuff for salad with dinner would be great. We have tomatoes, but the rest of the lettuce is soup, and I think the boys ate the last cucumber for a pre-breakfast snack."

"Got it. I'll put Josiah to work—milk and salad stuff. Be back in ten." As soon as she disconnected, Vannie shook her head. "You'll think twice before trying to be nice next time, huh?"

The way Josiah chose his words carefully reminded her a little of Luke. While swifter, the boy's reply was too perfect not to have been well-considered. "I think having a next time would be worth a whole lot more than the effort to carry a couple of grocery bags."

He talks like someone from a book sometimes. I noticed that before.

Awkwardness filled the air between them until Vannie pounced on the first thing that she could think of to kill the miserable silence. "Someone said you guys live in Brunswick. What brought you to The Church?"

"My parents were looking for a smaller church. The Assembly is solid enough, but they're so big. We like a closer-knit community."

Vannie hurried across the street before replying. "Well, we're close. We have to be—tiny compared even to First Church in Fairbury. I think Aunt Aggie almost went to Brunswick at first, but we love Mr. Vaughn's humility and commitment to *just* the Word. He's great about saying, 'I used to think this means this, but then I found this, and in context, if you take them both,' and *bam!* We're all sitting there going, 'Which is it.' And that's when the best part comes."

"He did that the week before you guys got back. He just looked at us and said, 'Look, I was either right before, I'm right now, or I'll find out someday that I never did figure it out.'"

As they reached the market, Josiah pulled open the door for her. "Thanks. Yeah, I asked Uncle Luke about that once. I mean, you'd think it wouldn't be so confusing. Wouldn't you imagine God would make things understandable for us? But Uncle Luke said that we read things through misguided filters, based on prejudices and experiences, and it makes us miss the simple truth of Scripture."

"Makes sense to me."

"Then he complicated it and totally confused me." Vannie grabbed a basket and carried it down the chip aisle. "He said, 'And then there's that whole mystery thing, the glass darkly thing, and the thing about us being sinners, so it may just be impossible to get it right. Maybe God did it to keep us digging in the Word. Who knows?'"

Josiah reached for the basket as she popped a couple of bags of tortilla chips in it. "I've got this. And I think your uncle has a point there. Wonder what my dad would say about that." He frowned at the basket. "Did you say milk and salad stuff?"

"Yeah." Vannie led him to the small produce department and piled a bunch of spinach, a couple bunches of romaine, and two cucumbers in the basket. She eyed him. "You are totally going to regret taking that when I put a couple of gallons of milk in there."

He reached for a couple of anemic looking tomatoes. "Need these?"

"Uncle Luke says we have plenty of them for now." Her eyes caught sight of a bag of oranges—on sale, no less. "He didn't ask for them, but I think I'll get oranges, too. We have no fruit in the house." Vannie fumbled for the phone, reconsidered, and shoved it back in her pocket. "If he doesn't want them, I'll pay for them. He's probably busy with the boys. Or Cari. She's been a bit *too* angelic lately. It's about time for her to insult someone, or bop one of the older kids for being mean to someone, or something equally

189

mortifying."

As soon as the words left her lips, Vannie flushed deep red and hurried toward the checkout counter, her apologies trailing behind her. "That sounds awful. I'm sorry. You wouldn't get the joke. It probably sounds so mean."

"Sounds like an inside joke." Josiah nudged her toward the dairy case. "Didn't you say milk?"

"Oh, right. Thanks." All hope of carrying on a reasonably intelligent conversation evaporated with the deep chuckle and smile he gave her. Flustered, she almost grabbed 2% instead of whole—something that would have ensured more teasing than she thought she could endure. That's when it hit her. *I'm at the store with a* guy. *And he's being really nice.*

Without a clue as to how she did it, Vannie managed to unload the purchases onto the counter, find Luke's debit card, and swipe the thing without making a fool of herself. The screen flashed an error. She frowned, swiped again, and punched in the number. Again, it insisted she'd done something wrong. "I don't get it. It's always worked before."

"The machine's been flaky all morning," the checker offered with too much cheerfulness to be helpful.

Vannie blinked and pulled out her phone. "Let me make sure he didn't change the PIN numb—"

But Josiah whipped out his wallet and passed thirty dollars to the checker. "I've got it. No need to bother him. She could be mid-bop right about now."

It took Vannie until their purchases had been bagged and they'd made it out of the store to get what he meant. "I'm sorry about that. I didn't bring my purse. But I've got enough cash in it when we get to the church. Sorry."

"I think you said that already" Josiah looked ready to give her a friendly nudge, but it never came. Instead, he assured her he wasn't concerned about repayment. "I'm just glad I went with you, now. Going back would be a pain." He paused mid-stride and waited for her to look back at him. "Then again, I could have gotten to walk with you again."

Those words sent her heart doing somersaults. *I think that was his idea of flirting. Wow.* Vannie tried to find something both encouraging and somewhat neutral to reply with, but his smile wiped out any hope of coherent thought. "That's nice...."

She did manage to stifle a groan. *Nice? You sound like an old lady who isn't impressed that someone got to go to a mud fight yesterday but is trying to be polite.*

The screeches of playing children greeted them even before they rounded the corner. Vannie led Josiah to the van and left all but one gallon of milk and the chips in the back before carrying the rest inside. Still mortified, she said almost nothing all the way inside and even less as they stopped in the foyer to leave their coats on the rack. But there, Josiah finally spoke. "That's another great dress. I like your style. It's such a nice combination of modest without being dowdy."

A snicker escaped before she could help it. "Dowdy? I didn't know anyone else my age *knew* that word anymore." Something niggled at the back of her mind, and at his question about her inspiration for it, she realized what it was. "Oh, and thanks. Sorry. You just threw me with 'dowdy.' I can't wait to tell Aunt Aggie. She's going to like you."

It seemed that once she'd found her voice, it refused to stop. She snatched up the milk and the bag holding the chips, and started to rush off to the fellowship hall, but Josiah stepped in front of her and took the milk. He didn't move. He didn't speak. He just stared at her with an expression she couldn't quite read. Curiosity? Nervousness? What was it?

"I was wondering...."

Oh, great. He's going to ask me out, I'm going to have to say no, and then there goes any hope of a friendship.

"How would you feel about me talking to your aunt and uncle—getting permission to get to know you better?"

Well, that's different. He's not asking me out, per se. They might go for that. But exactly what he *was* asking, she didn't quite know. "Not to be rude, but isn't that what we're doing? I didn't know you, you talked to me, and now I know you a bit better?"

He cleared his throat, and now that undefinable expression from moments earlier became clear. *He's nervous! Whoa....*

"Well, I was hoping that we could get to know each other better—me visiting your family, you visiting mine—with an eye to a future courtship if we find we have enough mutual interests and convictions."

191

The words all sounded innocent enough. Get to know each other. Visit families. Mutual interests. Convictions. She didn't hear anything that sounded like a date in there anywhere, but Vannie decided to be certain of it. "Well, if that's your way of talking about a date, the answer will be no. Not until I graduate, anyway. But…."

"We don't date in our family." Josiah glanced around him and stepped just a bit closer. In an irrational moment of inconsequential thought, Vannie wondered if his arm wasn't growing tired holding that gallon of milk. "My parents have encouraged my brothers and me to be very purposeful in getting to know someone, without getting emotionally invested. It sounded easy enough, but I'm starting to wonder."

Vannie's throat went dry. *Okay, if that's not saying, "I like you" in whatever language he's speaking, I don't know what is.*

" — if you'd rather I not ask, I'll understand. Maybe in a few months…."

She snapped out of her thoughts and shook her head. "I don't mind." Again she shook her head. "I mean, I think I'd like that. Sorry. You um…." Vannie blinked. "Well, you surprised me is all."

Josiah pumped his arm up and down and gestured for her to go ahead of him. "Then let's get this down there before someone needs it. I'll talk to Mr. Sullivan."

Though Vannie heard every word, little of it registered. She led the way downstairs, overly conscious of every move she made and hating herself for it. *This is so cool. Not dating, but getting to know a guy — for later. And no pressure of having a boyfriend to break up with, because we're not even "courting." Just getting to know each other. Doesn't that mean he'd ask if we could "court"? I wonder what that even means. I should ask Aunt Aggie.* That thought solidified it all. *I'll do that.*

They made it to the tables with the food before she remembered that he'd paid for it all. "Oh! I need to go get my purse! I need to pay you back."

"Let's eat first, okay? Can I sit with you guys?"

And right about there, Vannie melted into a puddle of useless thought. "Um… yeah. Thanks."

When twelve-thirty came and a dead silent house mocked her every whisper, Aggie flopped over onto Luke's pillow and groaned. "I forgot the fellowship meal. Ugh. They'll be there for hours!"

A glance at the remaining half dozen chips in the bowl Ellie had brought her hinted that she might just starve before they got home. "I could go down... slowly. It would be *some* exercise. That has to be good for me. I'm going to have a terrible labor."

It took half an hour to get downstairs, and the sight of her house almost sent her right back up. Though he managed to keep their room quite tidy and appealing, the rest of the house looked as if toddlers had been allowed free-rein. That thought set her teeth on edge. "And that's because they *have*. They *have* had free-rein. Or should I say r-e-i-g-n, reign?"

But finding something she could eat *and* carry upstairs proved more difficult than she thought. Finding leftovers— impossible. Finding anything remotely tempting... nope. Nothing.

She debated fixing something and instead, grabbed what was left of a bag of Doritos and shuffled back to the stairs. But the third time the bag bounced against the step, Aggie stood and climbed the stairs. "I'm not. Going to. Scoot." A contraction began in her back. "Up. These. Stairs. Again."

Of course, by the time she arrived in her room, the contraction grew to uncomfortable proportions. She eased herself into bed, pulled covers over her legs, and relaxed against the headboard. It made no difference. The next one came even stronger, and on its heels, fear rippled through her.

"I have *got* to get this under control before they get home." Left side, laptop open, long sip of water, head resting on pillow. Set and ready to go, she searched for downloaded sermons, chose the next one in the "Fruits of the Spirit" series, and punched the play button.

Eyes closed, she listened as the teacher began from the beginning of the passage. "'...the fruits of the Spirit are love, joy, peace, patience, kindness, goodness, faithfulness, gentleness, self-control.' Today we'll be looking at self-control."

Aggie snagged a chip from the bag and chomped on it as the words of the teacher filled the little space around her, working their way through the strain and stress of the contraction and, mercifully, relaxing the muscles. *There's nothing like the Word to soothe mind, body, and soul.*

No sooner had she achieved ultimate "soothedness" than the teacher's words plucked a sour note in her heart. " — tend to think of self-control in terms of what we avoid. If we are self-controlled, we don't lash out at others, we don't drink or eat to excess, we don't squander our money. But there is much more to self-control than a list of check boxes to tick off at the end of a difficult day. Self-control is all about what we *do* do. It's about choosing to redirect our hearts into correct thoughts when they try to go into wayward directions. People often call this 'taking our thoughts captive,' but I submit to you that it is self-control, self-*regulation*. It is the choice to do what is *right* rather than the absence of choosing what is wrong."

Her throat constricted at the expectation of what would come next. Aggie could almost predict it word-for-word. Her lips pursed, her eyes squeezed shut even harder, and she waited.

"Brothers and sisters, I am telling you, self-control is about accepting the Lord's will for your life with a yielded heart to that will. It is about handing over our dreams and embracing *His* for us."

She snapped the laptop shut with such force that it should have damaged some vital component. "You're reading into Scripture there, buddy."

But despite her complaints, the words wouldn't leave her mind. She rolled over, grateful that at least the contractions had stopped. *Yeah, they stopped while you were sticking to the Word...Now that you're getting all loosey goosey with some wild interpretation....*

The laptop mocked her. She stared at it with contempt before rolling out of bed. "Shower. That's what I need."

Hot water filled the bathroom with steam and pounded the aching muscles in her back. Her ire slowly melted into a relaxed puddle of goo that swirled and disappeared down the drain. Inhale... exhale... each breath a calculated decision to calm her.

"Be still my soul; the Lord is on – " She choked over the next few words but tried again. *" – patiently the cross of grief or pai – "* This time, Aggie snapped her mouth shut. She shook with repressed emotions until nothing sounded better than being cocooned in her blankets. But the moment she stepped from the shower, she stepped back in again.

"Rinse hair, *then* get out. And it's time to figure out how to plan for this baby… and Christmas. Must do something about Christmas."

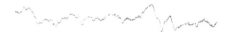

With laptop in hand, Ellie picked her way through the mess that liberally coated the living room floor and went in search of the ingredients on the screen. Laird passed through the kitchen as she set the laptop on the counter. "What'cha doing?"

"I'm going to see if we have the stuff to make rolls."

"Like… *dinner* rolls?"

She nodded. This says it takes three hours. That would get them out of the oven at about six."

"If everything went right. You know how that baking stuff is. Nothing follows the plan."

Irritation welled up in her, but after the sermon on being "peaceable," she managed to stamp it down again. "Well, so we have them late—with honey… for dessert."

"Good idea." He stared at the screen. "I think we've got it all. Might check the yeast, though. That's the only thing."

But, with the methodical care of a scientist, she lined up each ingredient on the counter, in projected order of use, and double-checked amounts. Satisfied that she could do it, Ellie left everything there and went in search of Luke. Cari and Lorna sat playing Connect-Four on the dining table. *How did I not see them there before?* She brushed aside the question and asked if they'd seen Luke.

"He went outside, I think." Lorna eyed her with frank curiosity. "What are you doing?"

"Just an experiment—if Uncle Luke says it's okay."

Ellie didn't give them a chance to ask if they could help. She dashed out the back door in search of Luke. She found him out by the dog's pen, checking the heating system. "Uncle Luke?"

"Ellie, the answer is no. I cannot have the dogs in the house. This helps keep the chill off, and they have those lovely fur—"

"But I wasn't asking about the dogs."

Luke stood and shoved his hands in his pockets to warm them. "I'm sorry, Ellie. That wasn't fair of me."

"It's okay." Hope welled up in her. *He'll let me now. He always does.* She jerked her head toward the kitchen. "I wanted to make rolls for dinner. I checked. We have everything. Is it okay?"

For just a moment, Ellie thought she'd been mistaken. He looked ready to say no, but then a slow nod began. "I suppose.... Well, no. Don't, Ellie. I want to say yes, but we already have such a mess, and I think—" His words cut off with uncharacteristic brusqueness.

"I'll clean up the mess—and the living room, too. That way you don't have to make the kids do it."

He almost said no again. Ellie saw it in the set of his jaw, the way he swallowed first. But a slow nod began. "Sure. You have fun. If you need help, gimme a holler. I've made lots of bread with my mom."

She squealed and hugged him before dashing off. But her excitement fizzled as she stepped into the kitchen and found Cari and Lorna standing in front of the now dark laptop, guessing what she might make. "Can we help?"

How do you guys always speak in unison like that? It's scary. Tavish and I don't do that! But instead of asking, Ellie just shook her head. "No, I have to clean up the mess by myself, and you guys can't *breathe* near flour without coating everything in sight. Just go play—make a nice big mess in the living room. I have to clean it anyway. You might as well get—"

Luke stepped into the room mid-sentence—something he *never* did. "—llie, when you took chips up to Aggie, did you just take the bag, too?"

"Just the bowl, why? Want me to take the bag up, too?" She moved to get it, but Luke stopped her. "No. They're not there. Thanks." And with that, he disappeared out the door.

A glance at the counter explained everything. *Either someone ate them when we got home—not likely if he's asking—or she came downstairs. Great. Thanks a lot, Aunt Aggie. He's going to be grumpy all evening.*

Lorna and Cari whispered together in the corner before inching toward the back door. Absentmindedly, Ellie reminded them to put on their jackets. But then it clicked. "And don't bother Uncle Luke. You're *not* helping me." Drooping lips prompted her to add, "But if it works, we can see if we can make more tomorrow."

Both girls still looked unconvinced, so Ellie fell back on the one thing that usually worked like a dream. "Do you want to know what I used to like to do when I was your age?"

The girls' heads shook until their braids flopped against their cheeks. Ellie led them into the dining room and pulled out one chair. She crawled under and beckoned the girls to follow. "I used to take my dollhouse people and make apartments under the table. Mommy played sometimes, too. Sometimes, it was a mansion instead of an apartment, and each chair was a room." The memory washed over her and choked her. "She even let me put the hand towels on the seats so each room could have 'carpeting.'" She pointed toward the mudroom. "I think Uncle Luke did towels last night. I bet there are towels in there."

Cari scrambled out and dashed for the laundry room, but Lorna hesitated. "But if they're clean...."

"Just don't let them be on the floor, and put them back before dinner. They won't be dirty then."

To her relief, it worked. Ellie crawled out and made it to the kitchen before the squabbling over colors began. But she ignored them and began the process of measuring. *One-fourth cup of water... pinch of sugar... two and one-fourth teaspoon of yeast....* "Wonder what would happen if I doubled that. Maybe it would rise faster?"

Laird's voice behind her made her jump. "Won't work. Remember? Vannie tried that a couple of years ago. Made a mess and it tasted nasty."

Oh, go away. But despite feeling snappish, Ellie thanked him and kept working. *Half a stick of butter... melted. Three-fourths cup of milk... heated.* While those heated, she beat sugar and egg together and stirred in the salt. *The Bible says 'a little leaven leavens the whole lump'... so why so little salt?*

197

A scorched scent sent her flying for the stove. She stared at the pan and frowned. "Oh, well. Maybe it'll give it more flavor." Without reading the next line of the instructions, Ellie dumped the boiling milk over the egg and sugar mixture. Instant scrambled eggs floated to the top and her heart sank. "Now what do I do?"

It took much work with a whisk to beat the egg pieces small enough to hope that they'd do their job in the mixture. Just in time, she touched the butter-milk-egg mixture and put down the frothing cup of yeast. A glance at the flour tempted her, and temptation won out. She stirred the first two cups of flour into the bowl and touched it. Another cup. That seemed to cool things enough to dump the yeast in as well.

All seemed to go well, but the more flour she added, the more impossible it became to stir it in. "It… says… that… it's supposed… to stop. being. so. Sticky!"

She stared at the pile of goo masquerading as dough and stalked through the house. "Vannie! Laird! Tavish?"

Vannie appeared from the library with a mouthful of pins and a bunch of fabric in her hands. Her eyes demanded, "What?"

Before Ellie could answer, footfalls pounded down the stairs. From the sheer loudness of them, Ellie assumed it to be Laird. That left Tavish under the stairs. She scurried around the stairs and kicked his door. "Tavish! Help!" She then turned to Vannie, shook her head, and pointed to the library. "Go ahead. I just need help stirring. I can't stir the flour in. I'm not strong enough."

It took all three of them to work enough flour in the dough to turn out onto the counter. Right about then is when Ellie remembered flour for the counter. "Oops."

"Aunt Aggie forgets sometimes, too." Tavish elbowed Laird. "Like when we're snitching pieces of dough."

"Well, I don't have that excuse."

Laird stopped at that. His hands still buried in dough, he turned to her and laughed. Ellie sniffed and offered her best, "We are not amused" expression, but Laird only laughed. "Not that you take yourself too seriously, or anything."

"I—"

"C'mon, Ellie. Your turn. Just knead that stuff in there. It still needs more flour."

"How do you know?" She stared at the lump with suspicion. "It says it takes about four cups of flour! I've used at least six!"

Once more, Laird's laughter filled the room. He waggled the measuring cup and eyed her. "Is this the 'cup' you're talking about?"

Ellie snatched it from him and stared at the handle. "Three-fourths. It was just the biggest one. I didn't know they had a three-fourths."

"This new set does. That's why Aunt Aggie bought it." Laird scooped another "cup" into the flour and sprinkled it over the dough. "It has to take more. It's still all wet and sticky in places."

But with the dough on the counter, Ellie found it easier to mix and knead. The boys eventually disappeared as Ellie worked every bit of flour into the dough, kneaded it, rolled it in a ball, and plopped it back in the bowl. She set the timer for an hour, set it on the stove with a towel over top, and began scrubbing down the mess she'd made.

Why is it so much more fun to make a mess than clean it? You'd think making something look pretty again would be fun, *too.*

Two hours later, Ellie pulled golden-topped and semi-charred bottomed rolls from the oven and half-dropped them onto the stove top. "How can the tops be so *perfect* and the bottoms be so gross?"

Before she could think of what to do, the family crowded in to see the results. Even as she struggled against tears of frustration, everyone but Kenzie praised how great they smelled and looked. "They're charred!" But her protest fizzled in a wave of requests for one.

Only Kenzie seemed to understand. With the skill of Job's comforters, she patted Ellie's arm, picked up a roll, and reassured her that she could "Cut off the bottom." Just as her "comforting" seemed to reach its epoch Kenzie upped the ante with, "It's okay. I get it. I'd be embarrassed, too."

Can I just crawl in a hole now? I can't do experiments without getting the law called on me — so to speak — and I can't bake them without ruining them. My career as a scientist is over before it even began.

THE DARK CLOUDED DAY

Chapter Fifteen

Monday, December 15th

Time to take charge of this thing. No more letting bed rest control my life. I can take it back.

With the YouTube video playing, Aggie flipped through her notebook-slash-journal assortment and considered which one would be best. The hardbound book with the index seemed to make the most sense, but it was so sleek—so pretty. If she messed it up, Aggie knew she'd regret it. "No regrets!"

That left the packet of pretty dot grid notebooks or the to-do list ones. She set the to-do lists aside and pulled out the notebook with sunflowers on the cover. "Oh, I love sunflowers."

Ellie appeared just as she paused the video and picked up her phone to call and see what happened to the requested office supplies. "Sorry. Ian and Ronnie had been playing 'office.' I think that's boy for 'seeing how much of the office supply cabinet we can destroy.'" The girl winced. "But I have it all cleaned up now. I just did it while I was looking for everything on your list." She inched her way closer and stared at the notebooks. She pointed at the one in Aggie's hands. "Soooooo, what is that?"

"It's a notebook Luke got me. I'm going to turn it into a planner—like this video. Want to watch it with me?"

For a moment, it looked like Ellie would say yes, but her

shoulders drooped and she backed away. "I'm still not done with my math, and Uncle Luke isn't home for lunch to help yet. Oh...." She blinked. "But Vannie is watching the little guys. She's got it covered."

Ellie paused at the door, glanced back at Aggie as she pulled a ruler from the supplies box, and scurried from the room. With a sigh, Aggie punched play again and began struggling to measure off things. "I don't even know my kids anymore—and it's been a *week*." Her conscience reminded her of the days *before* enforced bed rest, but Aggie ignored it.

A couple of minutes later, Ellie appeared again. "I went and got Vannie's skinny little ruler—you know, the one she uses for sewing. I thought it would be easier."

"You're the sweetest Ellie ever." Aggie smiled. "And that's not just because I don't know any others. Note the 'ever.'"

"Maybe when I figure out this math, I can come watch you for a bit. If Vannie doesn't need me, that is."

She knew better, but Aggie heard herself offer to take the boys. "They can play with their trains over there—make tracks that last for miles, for all I care."

But Ellie wouldn't hear of it. "Uncle Luke would kill me. But I'll tell them to do it in the dining room. Like Cari and Lorna's dollhouse under the table. They wanted to play. Now they can." She hurried back to the door. "Better go tell them before the girls remember and get it first."

Why do I feel like that shouldn't be something that should concern her? Is it because she's too young to have so much responsibility or to have to think *that responsibly, or is it because it hints that my kids are too prone to squabbles?*

It might not have been the most mature thing she'd ever done, but Aggie lobbed that question in the "to consider later" pile and tossed a match after it. "Too much to wonder about," she muttered as she placed the little ruler where she needed it and grinned as it stayed exactly where she put it. "Genius, that Ellie. Total genius!"

Inside half an hour, Aggie had the next two months set up like the video stated—with lots of pages between the months just in case she needed them. *Love how these lists can go wherever— doesn't matter. You can find them because you have that cool index. No more guessing and hoping your pages don't get wasted.*

She wrote in every appointment—from the one the next day through to the second week in January. "The power of positive thinking—or something like that." Buoyed by that feeling of success, Aggie took one of the blank pages after the approximate right number of pages for January and titled it "D-Day!" With space above for a photo, and space below for a date, she added the necessary vitals.

Name:
Time:
Weight:
Length:
Daddy's first response:

The word, "name", bored into her mind and worked its way down to her heart. Aggie glanced at the drawer in her nightstand. *It's in there. Boy or girl. He said there was no doubt. If I knew which, I could get so much more done from here. And I'll be playing catch up for weeks afterward—won't have time to do things like I did with Ronnie.* She gazed at the drawer. *We know the boy's name. Douglas Allan. I could write it in if that paper says boy....*

That thought did it for her. She fumbled for the drawer, nearly knocking the laptop off onto the floor, and reached for the envelope. Once in hand, she hesitated again. *Should I wait for Luke?* That question fizzled. He wouldn't want to know. He liked that element of surprise, and so had she—with Ronnie. Everything had changed this time.

Probably means it's a girl. And then I'll have to come up with a name.

Before Aggie could talk herself out of it, she ripped open the envelope and stared at the single word on a sheet from a prescription pad. The doctor information had been torn from the top, but the bottom remained intact enough to show her what it was. The single word thrilled her, much to her surprise. "I didn't know how much I wanted a girl," she whispered. "A girl."

Immediately, the baby's name came to her. "Alanna Olivia—Lana. She can't be Lani or Allie. She just *can't*." The word on the page filled her with joy again. "A girl..."

Aggie started to wad up the paper, but couldn't bring herself to do it. She shoved everything off her lap, carried the envelope to the fireplace, and dropped it in the dying flames. Back in bed, she tucked the paper on that page and pulled out her phone. Without hesitation, she called Tina. "I need something."

"What's that?"

"Washi tape—it's like this cool tape—"

"That you can pick up and down. Paper tape. Pretty colors." At Aggie's cry of surprise, Tina snickered. "You think I don't pay attention to what is cool these days? Luke says he got you some stuff for planning, and I did research. Apparently, no one can hope to plan anything without a few hundred rolls of the stuff."

Aggie's growing blush faded at the joke of a few hundred rolls. "I was just thinking two or three—baby colors. Maybe a blue, a pink, and a yellow? Plaid or stripes or something?"

"Gotcha. I'll bring it later. What's it for?"

Without thinking of the ramifications of abject honesty, Aggie answered. "I wanted to tape the doctor's note on the baby's gender into this planner I'm setting up."

"I'll bring anything you want, under one condition."

"What's that?"

"You tell me what it is."

Should have seen that coming. This bed rest thing is eating my brain cells. Aggie considered for a moment and countered. "I guess that depends on your washi-buying skills, then. You get good stuff, and we'll talk."

With that, she said goodbye and rang off. A few squeals and shouts downstairs hinted that Luke might be home for lunch. "For the day is probably more like it." Aggie tucked the paper into the notebook and set it aside.

The "to-do" notebooks came next. She grabbed the address labels she'd requested, slapped one on the blue cover and one on the green. Before she realized what she'd done, Aggie wrote "General" on the blue one and "Baby" on the green. They looked so boring, so plain, so *clinical* compared to the videos she'd watched. Aggie picked up a pencil and tried half a dozen ways to embellish the label, but none looked as nice as what she'd seen. "Great. Now I have to learn to draw, too?"

"You could always ask Ellie. She's amazing, if you recall."

Aggie's head snapped up and she smiled at the picture of Luke standing there, leaning against the doorjamb, arms crossed over his chest. "There's my handsome man. Want to see what I did with your gift?"

"Sure. I also have a proposition for you." He sat on the edge of the bed and watched as she flipped through the pages she'd created. "That's impressive. Did you come up with that yourself?"

"No, but your friend, Fee, is right. There are a million videos out there. I think I'm going to love this. I could even adapt it for school planning. It's *that* cool." Aggie picked up the to-do lists again, setting the planner out of reach. "These are for just daily stuff that maybe I can't do, but there's too much for the planner. I'll just write stuff down the minute I think of them, and while I'm planning for me, I'll do something—maybe highlight—the ones the kids can handle or whatever. One for general stuff. One for baby."

Luke nodded and tapped the labels. "Thanks for clearing that up. I wasn't quite sure…."

"Oh, be quiet. Now, what was this about you propositioning me?"

"Definitely need to do that, too." Luke's kiss nearly drove all thought of anything else from her mind, but a moment later, he sighed. "You met the Wares, right?"

"Yeah? Please tell me they don't want to visit. I'm not up to the embarrassment of what Ellie just called, 'seeing how much of the office supply cabinet the boys can destroy.'"

Luke gave her an odd look—one she could only see in the laptop screen's reflection—before he explained. "Looks good down there now. The little guys have trains set up all under the dining table. We're eating lunch in the kitchen so they don't have to put them away." He pulled her close and held her. "No, the oldest boy—Josiah. He called and asked if he could come over and talk to both of us. I think he wants to ask Vannie out."

Her heart sank. "We said no dating until after high school."

"Does this mean we're not even willing to listen when a young man comes to *us* about this? He asked Vannie if he could. I thought that was kind of a nice compromise between bypassing the girl or the parents."

"And if this is what he wants?" Aggie turned and searched

his face. "Are you going to say 'Sure, you can take her out. Just have her home before midnight and still pure?' Really?"

"I was thinking more like, 'You're welcome to take her on group outings—get to know her better—but she has two years before she can officially date.'"

I hate it when he makes sense in just the areas I don't want him to.

"I thought I'd come up, get you, help you downstairs, and back up again. I just thought, after being cooped up here for the better part of a week and a half, you'd enjoy a change of scenery."

That bait—she snatched it and gobbled it down, bypassing the hook altogether. "Done. What day?"

"In about two hours?"

Aggie nodded. "I'll be ready. I can get down by myself, but I might need help going up." She winced. "How, I have no clue."

As he heard Aggie scooting down the stairs, Luke gazed out the window again, watching the clouds darkening and growing more ominous by the second. *She didn't confess about the chips, Lord. That's not like her—not like her at all.*

Shuffling on the floor told him she'd made it down. Luke turned and couldn't help but smile at the picture she made. One arm cradled her belly, the other checked her dress to be sure it hadn't bunched up as she descended the stairs. "Have I ever told you how beautiful you are?"

"A thousand times or two." She grinned at him. "And you finally got me used to it—liking it even. So you'd better never stop or I'll wonder."

He heard a car pull into the drive just as he got her settled into the couch. "Looks like Josiah is here."

Aggie's eyes darted around the room. "Why is it so quiet? There's no one in here!"

"Vannie took them downstairs to work on projects so we could talk uninterrupted—we hope," he tacked on without confidence. With a quick kiss and a moment of whispering to baby, Luke strolled to the door, ready to open it when the boy knocked.

Nothing came. Luke peered out the side windows and saw

Josiah sitting in his car, head on his steering wheel... was it, praying? *That's a good sign, isn't it, Lord? Surely? He'll understand our caution if he's seeking the Lord.*

The moment the boy opened his car door, Luke stepped out onto the porch and shivered at the arctic blast from the coming storm. "Cold one, today!"

Josiah nodded. "My dad said they're expecting six inches by nightfall. It better get going or that won't happen."

As the boy stepped onto the porch, Luke held out his hand. "Thanks for calling. I've got Aggie downstairs and ready. The change of scenery is probably good for her right now."

"And I almost didn't call until after the baby was born." Josiah shrugged. "But...."

"C'mon in and tell us what's on your mind." Luke led the boy inside and re-introduced him to Aggie. "You met Josiah, didn't you?"

No one could have accused Aggie's welcome of being excessively warm, but she did manage a hint of a smile. "Briefly."

Luke had already decided Josiah would ask to pray. He didn't. He also didn't make small talk, circumvent his purpose—nothing. He seated himself across from them and, with hands folded together in nearly a death grip, he began speaking.

"I wanted to ask permission to get to know Vannie better." He frowned. "I meant to ask. Is that her full name or...."

"It's Vanora—some obscure name of Scottish origin, as far as I know." Aggie leveled a no-nonsense look at him. "She's been 'Vannie' since birth. Only her grandmother—many bad memories there—calls her Vanora."

Josiah swallowed visibly. "I see. Well, *Vannie* seems like such a wonderful girl."

With each word Josiah spoke, Aggie grew more agitated. Luke finally took pity on both and laid out the decisions they'd made. "She is, or at least, we think so. You should know, we've told the kids that we likely won't approve dating before they've graduated. At Vannie's rate of work, it'll be at least a year—year and a half."

"Um, I'm not asking to *date* her!" Both Luke and Aggie relaxed a bit. "Our family doesn't *do* recreational dating."

Luke watched Aggie stiffen and her arm encircle her belly

again. *What? You didn't want her to date either! We'll tell him to keep it to group stuff like we planned, and everything will be great!*

"I just noticed Vannie at church. I won't pretend that I haven't noticed how pretty she is and everything, but what I find most attractive is just how mature and focused she is on the Lord and her family. My parents and I talked about it, and we all agree that she seems to be exactly the kind of girl I had hoped to meet." His face reddened a bit. "You know, she has such a good sense of humor. From what I can tell, she doesn't take herself too seriously."

Luke and Aggie exchanged amused glances. Aggie found her voice first. "I think you might need to spend more time with her. Like almost every girl her age, she often takes herself far too seriously."

Josiah just listened and finally nodded. "I can see that. Okay. Another thing I liked," he added after a moment, "is how she isn't always putting herself down or trying to attract attention." The boy strained at his swallow until Luke prepared to do the Heimlich on him. "I guess I'm just trying to say that I think she's an amazing girl."

Oh, yeah. You're crushing hard, so—um, boy. Luke frowned at the weirdness of starting to call a kid in his late teens, "son." *I'm not old enough to have a son your age!*

When Josiah didn't speak, Luke waited for Aggie to say something and then gave up and urged him to continue. "Well, we think she's a wonderful girl, but I'm not sure that helps you with your errand."

"Right. Sorry. I've never done this." Josiah stared at his hands clasped before him before raising his eyes. They swung back and forth between Aggie and Luke before he added, "I wanted to ask if we could spend some time together—purposeful time with our families—with the hope of beginning a courtship within a year or two?"

Luke's throat went dry. *Lord, help her control herself.*

A glance sideways showed Aggie's white face and lines around her eyes. He knew those lines all too well now—pain lines. She shoved herself from the back of the couch, scooted to the edge, and struggled out of the couch. "I think I should go lie down now." She gave Josiah the briefest smile. "I hope you understand. Thank — have a nice day."

Wide-eyed, Luke stood to follow. He gave Josiah an apologetic look and promised to be back in a couple of minutes. Josiah shook his head. "I can go...."

"No, really. We should talk. It's just these contractions, you know."

He followed Aggie to the guest room and shut the door behind them. "Wow. Not what I was expecting."

"Ya think?!" Aggie began pacing.

"Why don't we get you sitting, at the very least. Those contractions —"

"Should have thought about that before you brought *him* here!"

Never had Luke been grateful for these early contractions. But this time, it turned her shout into a hiss. She allowed him to set up the bed and get her into it. As he worked, he tried to calm her. It failed. "Mibs, what's wrong?"

She stared at him as if he'd grown horns or something. "You can ask — he's talking *courtship!*"

"Shhh! He'll hear you." He chose each word with great care. Too yielding and she wouldn't take him seriously. But if he showed much support for the idea, she'd put up walls to lock him out as well. Luke tried the humorous approach. "And yeah. So he used the dreaded "C" word. Not all are evil like you saw. Mel had a wonderful courtship — wouldn't have it any other way. It *can* be a beautiful thing."

Despite his best efforts, they failed. Aggie got comfortable, fluffed the pillow, and pulled the blanket over her. "*Our* Vannie is not doing this, Luke."

When nothing he could think of would reassure her, Luke tried logic. *At least it'll soothe my spirit.* "Aggie, we need to balance our feelings with wisdom." Her glare prompted a new idea. "I know it's not what we anticipated, so, instead of giving him a definitive answer — yes or no, I mean — why don't we just tell him we're going to pray about it, discuss it, and get back to him."

She closed her eyes in an evident attempt to control her temper. After a huffed exhale, Aggie sighed. "Fine. I don't care what you tell him as long as it's not *yes.*" She met his gaze, winced at the concern she *had* to see there, and shook her head. "Right now, I just need to be alone."

Luke bent, kissed her cheek, and crept from the room. He closed the door behind him and waited. Silence. Seconds passed — nothing. Concern drove him to open it again, positive she'd be doubled over in pain from a contraction. Her eyes flew open. "He already left?"

"Wha — no. Just — never mind." Again he shut the door. Again he waited. Again, not even the faintest trace of a hymn wafted through the door. His mind raced over past days — over the past two weeks. *She hasn't sung much at all. It could just be that she's up there and we're down here, but...* Luke shook his head. *No, Lord. No. I can always hear her anywhere in the house. The way she belts out those songs....*

In a bit of a daze, he returned to the living room and seated himself. "Sorry about that. I'm sure you can imagine that we were a bit taken off guard."

"I know. I didn't know how — I'm sorry."

But Luke shook his head. "No reason to be sorry. We're actually appreciative that you spoke directly to us and Vannie instead of leaving your parents to do everything. I know that wouldn't have set well with Aggie." He gave Josiah an apologetic smile. "She watched a very ugly formulaic approach to courtship once, and it does make her uncomfortable."

"Well, I can wait until things are less stressful for her, sir. There's no — "

Luke interrupted before Josiah could make it any more difficult for him. "There's no need. We're going to pray about this, discuss it, and get back to you. It might take a few weeks, and if the baby comes, that could delay us." His mind whirled with the injustice of stringing the boy along like that, but Luke couldn't see any other way. "We'll try, though — to get back to you in a week or two. Meanwhile, you're welcome to spend time with the family *as a friend.*"

Josiah's grin made Luke wonder if he may have been too encouraging. But, not knowing how to take his words back, he just pointed to the basement steps. "The kids are down there if you want to go hang out for a while. I have some school work to look over." Another thought hit him. "And probably a tub of ice cream to purchase. I think Aggie could use something sweet right now."

As Josiah disappeared around the corner, Luke sagged against the couch. *And I could use fifteen minutes in the car alone with You, Lord.*

THIS IS MY MESSED UP WORLD

Chapter Sixteen

Wednesday, December 17th

The third time Vannie found herself halfway up the stairs, she forced herself to make the rest of the "journey" to the top room. It had always been a favorite place—the creamy tan walls, the snowy curtains, the touches of green everywhere.... *I wonder if I should redo colors in my room since we have to replace everything.* Another thought formed a lump of discouragement in her throat. *I bet that's all I get for Christmas. New curtains, new bedspread, new area rug.* Before she could work herself up into despair, Vannie stuffed down her predicted disappointment and reminded herself that she'd created the problem.

Aggie looked up from the stack of endless lists—and a small mountain of the funky new decorative tape Tina had brought—and smiled. "Need something? How is everything down there—really?"

"I'm trying. But they make a mess before I'm done cleaning or getting them to clean up the last one. How do you *do* it?"

"I've got a bit more authority than you. That helps." She patted the bed beside her. "Come help me figure out Christmas for Ellie."

Oh, the struggle not to ignore Aggie's request and demand the information she most wanted. Instead, Vannie seated herself

211

cross-legged across from Aggie. "Okay, so what do you have?"

"I thought maybe some of this cool plastic paper and some ink refills for those markers that Tina got her. I saw this video...."

Vannie's patience wore thin as she watched several videos—in their entirety—and pronounced it "fun" looking. "It's kind of chemistry-ish, too. She's so into chemistry right now. And that's all about showing what water and inks do to each other."

"Chemistry?" Aggie nodded. "That's right—her birthday. We got that set." She frowned. "I could try to find more—like how to mix your own paints? Inks? That might be cool... making dyes from natural things? She would do that at Willow's...."

Each question agitated Vannie's already irritated nerves. A squeal downstairs made her jump up from the bed. "I better go see what's up."

"I suppose...." At the door, Aggie called out, "Did you come up for something specific?"

Just ask. Then you won't have to come back. Vannie winced at how selfish it sounded and swallowed hard. "I just wondered why no one said anything about Josiah's visit. He asked, came all the way out here, and then it was like he didn't even come. No one said anything."

The longer she spoke, the more frantic the words became. Aggie stared at her with evident dismay. "Well—"

"I just think that since this whole thing *was* about *me,* I might have the courtesy of being told what's happening with *my* life!"

Shock, hurt, anger—emotions flitted across Aggie's face and then settled in around her eyes and lips. Before she got scolded like a two-year-old for daring to voice a reasonable opinion, Vannie shook her head. "Whatever. Never mind." And ignoring Aggie's calls, she stormed downstairs.

She passed Ronnie and Ian fighting over the same train, grabbed her coat, and bolted outside. "I do not want to be in there when one of them whacks the other with it. Not. Happening. They aren't *my* kids. Why do I always have to be the third parent around here?"

At the end of the drive, she had choices—return, go left toward town, go right toward Tina's, go across the street to Mrs. Dyke's. Across—out of the question. *It's too close. I need to get a break. Town is just full of jerks who think they know everything. Back...*

not *happening right now.* That left Tina's house over on Cygnet.

She arrived long before Tina would. But a key hidden, used, and replaced gave her the solace she needed. Crisp, clean, contemporary—Tina's house was everything theirs wasn't. The only thing out of place was an open Bible on the couch with a note in the margin beside Ephesians 6:1. "'Children, obey your parents in the lord, for this is right. Honor your father and mother(which is the first commandment with a promise).'" The note read, *Even when it means a stupid wedding in Costa Rica while your friend needs you.*

"Lord, that's just not fair." Her heart insisted that Aggie technically wasn't *her* parent. "Yeah, but I bet it's the same thing. I'd never let *my* kid get away with those kind of messed up semantics."

Despite the resistance in her heart, Vannie hauled herself back up off the couch with such slowness her movements looked like a mockery of Aggie of late. Door locked, key replaced, Vannie took off for home again, rehearsing a speech that was both true and respectful.

Chaos greeted her the minute she stepped through the door. Ronnie ran from Ellie who seemed to be trying to convince them to pick up half their mess. Vannie stood in front of him and crossed her arms over her chest. "What are you doing?"

But instead of answering, the boy tried to wriggle past. Her arm shot out and caught him just under the neck. How many times had she seen Luke do that with Cari over the years? She pulled him close and murmured, "Would Mommy like how you're behaving?"

"Mommy not here!"

Vannie knelt before him and brushed tears of frustration from the boy's eyes. "But she is. She's upstairs trying to keep the baby safe. But she can hear you, you know. And it hurts her. And eventually she's going to get up and come down here to fix whatever is wrong. And you know what?"

The boy shook his head.

"It'll be our fault—" Vannie bit back her true thoughts and revised. "For making her feel bad." She pointed at the string of toys from the library to the dining room. "It'll take you one minute to pick those up. Just do it."

When Ronnie looked like he'd hesitate again, Vannie moved for the phone. "I guess I'll have to call your daddy."

"He upstairs, too." Ronnie didn't say it, but she heard it in his tone. *So there.*

"Good." Vannie smiled. "It won't take him as long to get here."

Ronnie's eyes widened and the boy dashed to pick up his toys before she could reach the phone. Considering that problem sorted, Vannie climbed back up the stairs. Just outside Aggie's doors, she heard her aunt weeping to Luke about her outburst.

"—don't know what brought it on. We were talking Christmas presents and then she just—" A low moan filled her ears, followed by Luke telling her to relax, to get on her side, to breathe.

"I'll talk to her."

"Don't, Luke. Her plate is so overloaded, trying to do my work, that she's overwhelmed. It's not like her."

His chuckle even soothed the rising panic in her own heart. "I meant that I'd explain what we decided about Josiah. I doubt we need to reprimand her for that. She'll be back apologizing before long."

Silence. Vannie struggled to hear a whisper—anything. When she didn't, she stepped around the corner and found them kissing. *You guys....*

"Um, sorry."

They didn't even stop—not for another few seconds. Luke turned, squeezed her shoulder as he passed, and murmured, "Come see me when you get time. We'll talk."

Oh, man. Why can't you guys just yell at us like normal parents. This is just the worst. Aggie beckoned her closer, but Vannie stood, half-frozen in place. "I came to apologize."

"I know you did."

She swallowed hard. "I don't know what got into me."

"You're forgiven. Will you forgive us for leaving you hanging?" Aggie wiped a few straggling tears from her eyes.

"Yeah...." *Don't do it. Don't try to one-up your sin. She'll kill you for it.* Vannie smiled. "I better get back down there. Ronnie...."

Aggie nodded. "I heard him a bit ago. I think he's going to

have to spend a lot of time in here."

Her emotions unshackled her feet, and Vannie flew across the floor to Aggie's side. "I won't do it again," she whispered as she hugged her aunt. "I love you."

"We love you, too. Now get down there. Luke's probably getting worried about you."

Vannie made it halfway down the second flight of stairs and paused, her ears straining. *Where's Aunt Aggie's hymn?*

Squabbling voices — *do we hear anything else these days?* — reached him from the mudroom. Luke strode down the hall, ready to let Cari have it — what for, he could only imagine. *Lorna will be pleading —*

But mid-thought, Luke heard it. Cari's plea! "—can't do it. It's wrong."

"No one will know! And I'm hungry. I didn't get seconds. *Again.*"

"Some kids don't get firsts!" Despite the protest, Cari's outburst sounded a little more like a question than an assertion.

Luke's heart constricted as his usually compliant niece-slash-daughter showed a nasty, rebellious side he'd never known she possessed. "Well, I'm having one. And you'd better not tell on me, Cari Stuart. I don't tell on you for all the stuff *you* do!"

In the silence that followed, Luke could almost hear Cari's dilemma. He decided to step in and put a stop to it before Lorna *did* blame Cari for her getting caught. "Just what are you having that Cari thinks you shouldn't?"

Contrition. He waited for it. Instead, Lorna whirled, stared at him for a moment, and jerked open the freezer. There, a box of ice cream sandwiches — a treat he'd brought home for after dinner — waited. Open. *Someone has already had one.* Double shock filled him as he watched the self-satisfaction wash over Lorna's features. *Oh, boy. That's it. I have to sell that house as is. We're losing money every day, and I need to be here.*

As Lorna reached for the box, Luke pulled her hand back and shut the freezer door. "Cari, will you leave us alone for a minute?"

215

To his astonishment, Cari's eyes welled with tears. "She's just missing Mommy—and Aunt Aggie. It's my fault. I'm a bad in... well I'm bad for her."

"I think the word you want is 'influence.' And you're just fine. Go up and see Aunt Aggie. She's lonely up there. We'll be up in a few minutes."

Left alone, Luke prayed for a moment, hoping the time would soften Lorna's hardened heart. A moment later, Cari burst back through the door. "Just put your pants on again, Lorna. We have to be good for Aunt Aggie and the baby." Then, as an absolute afterthought, she tossed out, "And Jesus. We have to be good for Jesus." Her features screwed up as if something in that statement didn't work well. "Because He made us good—with His blood. So if we're not good...." Her eyes sought Luke. "We're liars? Or He is?" Before Luke could hope to formulate an answer, she shrugged. "Doesn't matter. It's not good." And with that startling homily, Cari disappeared down the hall—this time, for good.

Lorna stared after her. "Put my pants on again? How? We're not allowed to wear them."

Luke's lip twitched and he managed to stifle a chuckle before he explained, "I think she means, re*pent*. Weren't you guys studying prefixes today? Be, de, and *re*. I think she remembered that and...." Lorna's eyes glazed over. "Anyway, I thinks she means repent."

"Well, I'm not going to." Lorna reached for the freezer door.

Luke stared her down. She tried again. "It won't work, Lorna. I can stand here all night if we need to, but you're not *stealing* anything from me."

"It's *our* food. It's not just *yours*."

He refused to argue. Instead, he waited, hoping the child's usually tractable spirit would yield. *What happened to our children? To us? Lord, I'm drowning here.*

"You used to be nice. Now you're just mean."

"Because I won't let you get away with doing wrong?" Luke shrugged. "I think I'm okay with that. But if you continue to defy me, we'll have to have a conversation with a 'teacher.'"

The girl's eyes widened, and Luke suspected she couldn't remember the last spanking she'd had. He sure couldn't. It looked, just for a moment, as if she'd yield. He hoped for it—prayed for it. But it returned—that look of utter defiance he usually saw in Cari's face. Had he not overheard them himself, he'd have sworn that Cari had somehow convinced her twin to stand in for her this once.

His heart wept as he administered a spanking he'd rather have foregone and led Lorna upstairs. "You need to spend the rest of the afternoon with Aunt Aggie. You will not leave her room, and you *will* obey her." At the top of the stairs, he knelt before her and held her gaze for a moment. "Do you understand?"

Lashes still wet from weeping, Lorna nodded. "I will. I'm sorry."

He held her, his own grief and confusion blending with hers. "I am, too. It's been a bit rough lately, hasn't it?"

"I miss Aunt Aggie. She always says nice things."

And we've gotten into the habit of only noticing what isn't *going well. No wonder she's not herself. Lorna thrives on affirmation, and you know it.*

"Well, maybe the rest of us haven't because there are so many nice things to say to you that we don't know where to start." Her eyes lit up and he winked. "You know, like how helpful you are when Tavish needs all the dishes from the table, or how your giggle makes me smile, or how smart you are to get your school work done before I get home so I can look at it in case you need help."

"Yeah...." She flung her arms around him once more. "I love you, Uncle Luke."

He stood in the doorway, watching as Aggie made room for the girls, one on each side of her, and began asking about their days. That simple act of mothering relaxed her. *You once found it draining. Now it's such a part of who you are. You need more time with the children—even up here. Even stuck in this room. Even if it's more work for the rest of us.*

Luke jogged back downstairs, but his heart turned heavenward. *Got it, Lord. Thanks.*

The house hummed with familiar sounds and scents—*tones.*

But amid the orchestration of it all, each note seemed just a tad off pitch—slightly sharp. Slightly flat—never right.

A hymn warbled from the library. "'...*all is calm....*'" It would have been perfect—should have been. Just *hearing* those beautiful lines as afternoon drifted into evening should have filled Luke's heart and warmed it. But Vannie sang, and as sweet, clear, and true as her voice was, it couldn't replace Aggie.

No one can.

A voice—extra quiet and without its usual confidence—tore Luke's thoughts from his wife. "—said I should come help with dinner now."

The memory of the earlier unpleasantness reminded Luke of what he needed to do. "Well, she knows that you'd my best helper. Let's go see what Ellie's cooking up for us."

Lorna's wide eyes met his and her hand froze on its way to catch his. "She isn't making peanut butter and jelly lasagna again is she?"

Laughter and nausea—an odd combination, but Luke felt them in tandem. "It was... different."

"Exgusting is more like it."

"Don't you mean *dis*gusting?"

Lorna clasped her hand in his and walked with him toward the kitchen. "Nope. It's in the past and hopefully it stays there, right? So it's *ex*gusting." Luke's mind whirled at her words, but Lorna continued, eagerness filling it. "But, if you did the 'c' sound instead of the 'g', there could be no *excuse* for something that dis*gusting*." She giggled. "That makes me feel smart."

"Well, you *are* smart. But yes, that was particularly clever."

As he stepped into the kitchen, Luke realized what other "sour note" had spoiled the family symphony. Fennel—about twice as much as would be necessary for any good spaghetti sauce or meatball—assaulted their senses as they entered the room. Ellie stood at the pot, tasting, nose wrinkling, and reached for yet another can of diced tomatoes. Half a dozen littered the counter.

"Everything okay in here?"

Ellie whirled, dropped the can of tomatoes on her toe, and burst into tears. Lorna sprang forward, ready to bandage—even "kiss it better" if Ellie wished—but Luke pulled her back. "I think the tears are more for frustration than pain, sweetheart. Why don't you get started on that table?"

Taking his cue from the afternoon's lessons, Luke wrapped his arms around Ellie, held her fast, and murmured, "Have I thanked you for all your help lately?"

"You shouldn't." Ellie pulled back and tossed a malevolent glare at the pot before reaching down to pick up the can of tomatoes. "I ruined the spaghetti sauce. It said a half a teaspoon of fennel. I mixed up the lines and put in a tablespoon. It's *overpowering!*"

"And your solution is to triple the recipe?"

She blinked. "I didn't — oh, that's — okay!"

The girl became a whirlwind. She pulled out two more cans of tomato sauce, reached for the jar of minced garlic, and ticked off double of each item as she dumped them in the pot. Once finished, she reread the recipe again and nodded. "Got it."

Luke just stood there, smiling, proud. Happy. "That's my girl."

"Can you do me a favor, though?"

"What's that?"

Though she turned back to the stove, one hand flapped at the island behind her. "Would you *please* clean up that fennel for me? I spilled that bottle, and now it's mocking me."

"Not to mention assaulting our nostrils — smells like a licorice factory in here."

Ellie's nose wrinkled. Luke couldn't see it, but he had no doubt. Ellie Stuart despised black licorice. "That's just cruel."

His mind whirled to think of a good retort, but Kenzie burst into the room. "Rory's here. Can they stay for dinner?" Her eyes took in the mountain of discarded cans. "We've *got* to have enough! Look at that!"

"They can stay if they want." At Ellie's yelp of dismay, he squeezed her shoulder and added, "I'll help — starting with the fennel eradication process." Luke turned to Kenzie and found the girl gone. "Well, okay then."

Scrubbing the counter did little to kill the overpowering fennel assault on his nostrils. Desperate, he pulled out a bottle of lemon juice and shook it all over the counter. It improved, but not enough.

Savannah MacKenzie stepped into the room and her eyes

bugged. "Whew! A bit of fennel overkill much?" Luke's pointed glance at Ellie sent her cheeks flaming. "Of course, it might go away if you didn't have that rag full of it just swirling around that counter...."

"Duh." Luke dashed for the laundry room, returned, poured lemon over his hands, and the kitchen already smelled a thousand times better. "Hmmm.... I wonder what lemon-fennel muffins would taste like."

"You make 'em, Uncle Luke. I've decided fennel is gross *and* grossly overrated."

Luke and Savannah snickered in unison. Not surprisingly, Savannah spoke first. "We brought gifts." Her eyes rolled. "Rory wanted to get something for Kenzie, and then he couldn't leave out the others, so...."

Just in time, Luke saw a stack of packages appear by the tree. "Anyway, he bought for everyone." His heart soared and flopped at the same time. "That was thoughtful of him."

"But not necessary. I know." She smiled. "But who wants to tell a kid he can't be generous to his crush's family."

It wasn't the time, and Luke knew it. But after debating for several long seconds, he stepped a little closer and murmured, "Are you guys okay with this crush business?"

Mac joined them before Savannah could find her voice. "Is everything okay?"

"Luke seems upset about Rory and Kenzie."

His protest sounded excessive—defensive—even to his own ears. "It's not that. I just see some of the silliness at church with the kids, and...."

Relief softened both their features. "Okay. *That* I get." Savannah rolled her eyes. "I've seen Lyddie Palmer chasing Ronnie, trying to *kiss* him. It's ridiculous. We told Rory he has to treat Kenzie like a favorite sister—special, but not like a grown up girlfriend. He was good with that. 'Kissing is gross.'"

And that's why you should talk to people. Luke just nodded and thanked them for understanding. "I know Kenzie has been hinting at gifts for Rory. Would that be okay?"

"It'd be fine, but we're heading to Ohio tonight." Savannah's eyes slid toward the kitchen stove. "Kenzie offered for us to stay, but we promised Rory Sonic on the way."

Mac's half-repressed chuckle earned him a dirty look from Savannah and a smile from Luke. "Hey, I'm calling it like it is. Rory isn't so smitten that he'd give up Sonic for Kenzie—yet."

"Hey, Dad? Can we take Kenzie to Sonic with us? Vannie said she'd come get her!" The cry started faint and grew louder with each pounding step and ended with nearly a shout in their ears. "Hmm… over shot that one."

"I don't even know what that means," Savannah groaned. "I don't know what to *do* with this kid."

But Luke saw Rory's eyes flip-flop back and forth between him and Mac. "Sorry, son. Can't do it. I need her help to eat up enough spaghetti sauce for an army." He leaned close. "And she can put away the spaghetti."

The boy's face brightened. "Something else we have in common! I *love* spaghetti. Yum!" Without even a blink, he turned to his parents and said, "Okay, then. I'm ready *and* star—very hungry."

"Good save, little man. Good save. Get in the car. We'll be there in a minute." Savannah waited until he was out of earshot before adding, "We'd bring her back if it would help."

Panic welled up in Luke. "Not really a good night, but thanks." He choked back a strangled apology and instead, forced a smile. "Lots going on."

The whole family—sans Aggie—stood out front and waved the MacKenzies down the driveway and away from the house. One by one, they went inside and returned to their previous projects. Vannie worked on something in the library—Tavish under the stairs. Laird helped Ian with a Lego project, and Luke managed to rescue it from Ronnie's impatient fingers. Cari and Lorna disappeared upstairs—likely to bother Aggie again—and Ellie stirred the sauce with a cautious eye.

"Uncle Luke?"

"Hmm?"

Her quiet voice, her drooping shoulders—everything hinted at what she'd say, but he winced anyway as the words found their way to his ears—almost inaudible in their quietness. "I miss Aunt Aggie."

He squeezed her shoulders, kissed her cheeks, and sighed. "Me too, lovely Elspeth. Me too."

Long after dinner. Long after the children went to bed and fell asleep. Long after Aggie took a shower and climbed back into bed, finally exhausted, Luke sat at the dining table, his phone waiting to hear word of Martha's surgery, his Bible open, his eyes unseeing. Prayers welled up in his heart and lodged there. He ached to unburden his heart to the Lord—pleaded for clarity to read and allow Scripture to soothe the wrinkles in his spirit. Nothing worked. Instead, one after another, tears splashed onto the table before him as he struggled to make sense of everything. As her friend, he missed Aggie's laughter, her jokes, her joy. As her brother in Christ, he missed the spiritual strength she drew from her hymn habit. But as her husband, as her husband he missed *being* a husband. He missed *her*. *If the doctor says we can't be together until after she heals from birth, then it's best, but it's tougher on both of us than I ever imagined it would be.*

The phone's ring tone sent him scrambling to stop it. "Hello? Dad?"

"Hey, son, you know, that never gets old."

And you say it every time we talk. But Luke stuck to his usual line as well. "For me as well. I miss hearing my father call me son. How's Momtha?"

"She's been out for a few hours now. They say it went well. Looks like she might be able to do things she hasn't in years. They want to start her on a treadmill by Saturday."

"Already?" Luke's heart constricted. "How will they know?"

But Ron insisted all would be well. "They've got monitors and everything. I just wish she'd have done this years ago. It was too experimental in her mind."

"But she's here, she's alive, and all is well. This is wonderful. I can't wait to tell Aggie."

Ron cleared his throat. "She's not awake?"

"Sorry, no. I can go see. Lying around in bed means that sometimes she wakes for a few hours, but...."

"We'll call tomorrow. Martha's worrying, so if she was awake, I thought...."

He knew better, but Luke bolted for the stairs. "Just let me check. She needs the connection. It's killing her that she can't come."

"Martha is taking great strength from Aggie's faith and trust in the Lord over this."

If only Aggie *were as faithful and trusting as her mother thinks she is.* Luke asked a few questions — generic things about when Martha would get out of bed, how long physical therapy would last, if she would be home for Christmas still.

Aggie woke at the sound of his voice in their room. "Hey, Dad? Aggie looks like she's awake after all. Hang on." He passed her the phone and whispered, "Sorry. It's Momtha."

She put the phone on speaker, but Luke didn't hear a word they said. Instead, he watched his wife, and at last, he prayed.

PLEASE, JUST BUY IT ALL

Chapter Seventeen

Thursday, December 18ᵗʰ

The familiar honk of the UPS truck sent Aggie to the window — heedless of the fact that Luke had determined he was needed at home so he could and likely *would* arrive in the doorway the very moment she stirred out of bed to do anything but take yet another fascinating trip to the bathroom. The brown-uniformed man dashed up the front steps four times. Two boxes were reasonably sized, one was large. The other, one could only identify it as enormous.

Footfalls on the stairs below her sent Aggie scrambling back to her bed and her Amazon lists. *It's the only way anything would get here in time anyway.*

"Aunt Aggie! Grandmother sent presents! How could she do that? She's in *jail,* isn't she?" Laird stared at her, eyes wide. "Do they let old people out for good behavior?" Relief washed over him the second the words left his lips. "Well, that's not likely to happen."

Ain't that the truth. Aggie didn't allow herself to say it, but she *ached* to. Instead, she pointed to the door. "Can you tell Luke to bring them up here? Who knows what she sent?"

As he disappeared through the door, she could have sworn he said, "It would save you the hassle of trying to shop from bed if they were okay."

Lord! Wha — Aggie forced herself to redirect her thoughts. *Fine. I am* not *allowing this to happen.* "Hassle of shopping for presents." *I shouldn't* feel *that way about* gifts. *That's just* wrong.

Luke appeared before a separate idea came through. "Laird told you?"

"Yeah."

He produced an envelope with half-torn pieces of tape protruding from it. "One box had this taped to the top."

As much as she hated it, her fingers trembled as she tore at the envelope. "She hasn't done this since *before* the thing with Ellie. Why *now?* Why *this* year?"

"Because she's had time to be alone? Because the woman is getting *old?*"

Aggie stared at him, jaw agape. "You feel *sorry* for her! The woman who *stole —* "

"Aggie, she's old, lost everything. Of course, I feel sorry for her. I think she's where she belongs, but that doesn't mean I have malice in my heart toward her."

"And I do, I suppose. Because I don't trust her? Because I think she's done nothing but antagonize my sister's family — and mine?"

He slid onto the bed beside her and pulled her close. "I'm not criticizing —"

"Well it *feels* like you are. Can't you just —" Aggie wriggled away and unfolded the letter — or note, rather. The few lines made it difficult to call it a *letter.*

Dear Agathena,

I have instructed my lawyer to arrange for the children's Christmas presents. He has consulted a personal shopper that took the children's ages and genders and tried to come up with gifts that would be appropriate. I rejected a few ideas as things I didn't think you would approve of. I hope the rest are acceptable. Please forgive the lack of wrappings. I thought you would prefer to examine the gifts before allowing the children to have them. I wish you all a Merry Christmas.

Sincerely,

Geraldine Stuart

As she passed him the letter, Aggie asked, "Did you open the boxes?"

"The boys are bringing them up for you to open — all but one of the smaller ones. I opened it and saw it was presents. Then I found this letter and sent Laird up."

Vannie arrived carrying the two smaller boxes. "Where do you want these?"

Luke pointed to the end of the bed. "Just set them there. Thanks. I'll probably get you to wrap them if everything is okay."

She nodded and smiled at Aggie. "Just think. There'll be something under the tree. And it won't be a big stress on you. It was nice of her to try — after... everything."

A lump welled up in her throat, but Aggie managed not to choke it out with words she knew she shouldn't say aloud. "We'll wrap together, okay?"

At the door, the girl hesitated. "Do you think they'll be okay? You know how she is."

As much as she didn't want to do it, Aggie waved the letter. "This is promising, anyway."

Laird burst through the door with the next largest box and set it at the end of the bed. "Tavish is waiting for help with the last one. It's not that heavy, but it is huge."

"Need help?"

"We've got it." He beamed. "I think it's cool. She didn't forget us. She can't hurt us anymore, but she didn't forget us."

The words pierced Aggie's heart. The moment Laird was out of sight, she turned to Luke. "Doesn't that sound like every abused woman you've ever seen in a movie. 'Now that he can't hurt me, I'm thrilled that he's trying to get back with me.'"

The "large box" turned out to be even more enormous than she imagined. Almost large enough for a washing machine, the thing barely fit through the door. "Oh, wha —"

"She didn't say how many gifts she bought each one. You know how excessive she always is." Luke smiled. "Some things don't change."

The moment the boys left the room, Luke closed the door and ripped into the box. Games, dolls, fine quality art supplies, two laptops, and four e-readers. Stuff spilled from each box,

226

complete with "suggested" recipients taped to each item. Aggie watched, waiting, almost *hoping* for inappropriate choices. None came.

It took prison to teach her some semblance of appropriateness. At what, eighty? What is wrong with this picture?

When yet another gift idea that she had on *her* lists appeared, Aggie lost her temper. "Um, how do we get *rid* of this stuff!"

"Didn't you want to give Laird—?"

"Yes! *I* wanted to do it. If we give them all this stuff from her, *we* won't have any gift ideas left. They'll have too much stuff. We can take it back and give the kids the cash from Grandmother—these. *We'll* give the gifts."

Luke didn't respond, and as a testament to her physical and mental condition, she missed the significance. As she fumbled through the box on the bed for some kind of receipt envelope, she almost didn't hear him when he finally spoke. "I can't do it, Mibs. I'm sorry, but it's a week until Christmas. I don't have the time and can't take it away from the kids to return all that and buy it again. Put our names on it and give the kids the cash from our account. I don't care. But I think they'll know who did what. It's not worth the bother."

The weariness in his tone, the haggard look about his mouth and his eyes—they pricked at her heart, but Aggie hardened it. "I'll take care of it. You just go do whatever you've been doing with them. You're certainly not helping *me* keep a relationship going with them." His protest died as he stared at her. She narrowed her eyes and turned away. "Just go, Luke."

And when he did, she wept.

Guilt filled her as Tina listened to Vannie's gift ideas. *You should be here, helping. You shouldn't be three thousand miles away sipping fruity drinks at a wedding reception that you don't even want to attend!*

"What do you think? I mean, if the girls were teenagers, it would be easier. I could do more complicated—cool clothes—or easy. Bath bombs or scented lotion or something. But even Elspeth is kind of young for that."

227

"She loved your steampunk outfit. Maybe a piece to coordinate with that?" She sounded like she was clutching at straws, and Tina knew it.

Vannie cocked her head and considered. "Well, I *had* thought of that. I was afraid it would seem like just doing it to be doing it instead of because it's what she truly wanted. Mommy hated token gifts, and I'm trying, but...."

"No gift, made with love, is ever 'token.' The fact that you chose to do something to make Christmas extra special is beautiful in itself."

As relieved as Vannie looked, something held the girl in the grip of uncertainty. A voice upstairs called for her—a panic-tinged tone, no less. Vannie backed out of the library with an apologetic grimace. "Something happened. Who knows what, but apparently I'm the only one who can fix anything anymore."

Though Tina tried to offer to go, Vannie was out the door and half up the stairs before she could make it out of her chair. The list of Christmas gift ideas wrung her heart. *Why isn't Libby helping with this? She's usually on top of this stuff.*

A voice beside her tugged Tina out of her thoughts. "Aunt Tina?"

Thanks to William, she too held a special place in her heart that only Kenzie could fill. "Hey, Kenz. What's wrong?"

"Nothing. I hope. I wondered if Uncle William could help me."

"Well, if he can't, maybe I can. What do you need?" Though she asked the question, the tablet in Kenzie's hand held her full attention. "Whatcha got?"

With a surreptitious glance around her to ensure no one could see—exaggerated and utterly adorable, of course—Kenzie passed the tablet to Tina. "I want to make these—for Christmas presents. I tried on one of my old shirts. I can do it. If I make one a day—well, I'd have to do two on a few days—I could have them done in time."

Sweatshirts appliqued with monograms stared back at her. Whatever had given Kenzie the idea to make gifts for her siblings, Tina couldn't imagine. If they *all* got the notion to solve Christmas all by themselves, the house would overflow with unneeded gifts. But just as she started to hint that maybe everyone didn't *need* another sweatshirt, and maybe Kenzie should make something smaller—perhaps for stockings—Kenzie's full request burst into her thoughts.

"Why do you need to talk to William about it?"

"I need someone to help me get the shirts, and you're leaving."

Way to make an "aunt" feel like a heel, kid. "What about Luke?"

"Uncle Luke's too busy. And besides, Uncle William likes me. He'll help. But I can't call without permission." She pointed at the screen. "And can you delete that? So no one can find it? I'm not allowed."

Do you even know how? A glance at Kenzie hinted that the girl just might indeed know how. *I'm not even going to ask. It may be irresponsible, but sometimes ignorance is bliss. I think I finally get the attitude that says grandkids are best because you spoil 'em rotten and send them home.*

Kenzie lowered her voice. "Will you—ask him? Please?"

She knew better—really. But Tina couldn't resist the mental image of William shopping through stores, trying to find the right sizes and colors. "Okay, make me a list of what color you want and for whom. I'll write down sizes when you're done. Do you have the fleece?"

"We've got lots of scraps. I looked." Kenzie ducked her head. "I took some out, too. I'll print out the letters and cut them out today. That'll make things go faster." With arms flung around her neck, a squeeze and a kiss, Kenzie disappeared through the door, and once more, the room lay silent.

"Oh, boy. Why do I feel like I just got taken for a ride?"

Aggie's Amazon lists lay spread out before him, but Luke couldn't bear to look at them. Instead, the laptop screen beckoned his eyes—taunting, teasing, tempting him to look at the rapidly dwindling balance of their checking account. The credit card was double its usual monthly total. "And it's only halfway through the month."

His eyes slid toward the lists—printouts of their shopping cart—the cart with a four figure total. "And she said she's not

229

done, Lord," he whispered. "How am I supposed to tell her we can't *do* this? I can't do it." The numbers burned into his eyes. "I can't *not* do it."

All it would take is a toggle—just a click of the trackpad. One bit of pressure with his thumb and seven figures would open up to him. Luke grabbed a pen and made a note. *Move the kids' funds into a different bank—one with a two or three delay transfer thing.*

Another account in the list held the month's Social Security deposits. His job—transfer it to the main account and record each child's deposit in his or her spreadsheet. But once again, temptation reared its glorious head. *It's not wrong. It's there for their maintenance. Would it be so bad, just one month… to use it for their Christmas?*

His less prideful-self insisted that the money was there to pay for their food, clothing, shelter, education, fun. That's why the checks came every month. But prideful Luke insisted on providing for his family without the aid of Social Security and the children's inheritance. *Christmas isn't a* need. *Why shouldn't their parents pay for the gifts they would have given if they'd lived?*

One by one, Luke entered the check amounts into the spreadsheet and closed out that window of the bank website. Instead, he stared at the remaining balance and shivered to see less than three months' income in there. *I have to sell that house.* Now. *We can't afford to be without the extra three or four thousand I should get out of it.*

His email chimed. When Luke saw the name, he steeled himself with a cover of prayer. *They're going to be late with the rent. It's Christmas. I shouldn't be surprised.* The date on the email prompted him to amend that thought. *Make that "even later."* One click confirmed his suspicions.

```
To: luke.sullivan@letterbox.com
From: dryan342@letterbox.com
Subject: Rent check

    Luke,
    Sorry, but I can't get you the rent check
until the first. With Christmas and my tire
blowing out, I just don't have it all. If you
want half, I'll drop it off, though. Sorry.
```

Merry Christmas,
Dale

He zipped an email back assuring Dale that full payment on the first would be fine and offering an extra week in January to catch up. *Sucker.* But despite his self-deprecation, Luke knew it would work. They'd be one week late in January instead of two, and he wouldn't end up losing two weeks on the back end of the lease.

"Did that once. Won't do it again."

Luke's voice echoed in the library. He glanced around and sighed. *We work through these things together.* Together. *Now I'm down here trying to hide the truth from her to keep her from feeling bad about it. How is this right? Lord, what do I do?*

With a great shove, he pushed himself away from the table and retrieved a Bible from the shelf. Fingers familiar with the Word flipped through the pages until Ephesians chapter five opened before him. Luke read the admonition for husbands to love their wives. His heart cried out to the Lord for direction in how best to love Aggie *and* their unborn child. Was this a time to carry a burden *for* her or would that cause her to lose respect for him?

His eyes skimmed the next verses — admonitions to children, to slaves, to masters. Verse ten struck him with the opening word, "Finally." *After all these things… after all these verses that tell us how to interact with each other, he ends with, "Finally" and tells us to fight against Satan. He tells us to pray for our brothers and sisters — for the saints.*

Before he could stop himself, Luke pulled out his phone and composed a text to Tina. EPHESIANS 6:18-20. I'M ASKING FOR IT. PLEASE PRAY FOR ALL OF US. I THINK WE NEED TO ACCEPT THAT THIS SITUATION IS CREATING SPIRITUAL WARFARE. DISCOURAGEMENT. LACK OF FAITH. WE NEED THE LORD. PLEASE PRAY.

Redundant? Yes. But Luke hit send before he could over-think his words. An answer came before he could turn back to the dilemma still before him.

YES. YOU ARE LOVED WITH AN EVERLASTING LOVE. JEREMIAH 31:3. I WAS JUST THINKING OF AGGIE WHEN I

READ THAT VERSE TONIGHT. SHARE IT WITH HER.

Another Scripture tugged at the fringes of his consciousness. Luke flipped to First Peter, skimmed the first chapter, skipped to the fourth, went back to the third and found the verse he sought. "'…live with your wives in an understanding way, as with someone weaker, since she is a woman; and show her honor as a fellow heir of the grace of life, so that your prayers will not be hindered.'" *I'd say this is a weaker time for her, yes. Usually, I'd say she's stronger than me, but that's not saying she is weaker. I'm just supposed to be understanding and compassionate — as I would to someone weaker. How did I never catch that before? And I need to do this so my prayers — those things I just said I needed for us — won't be hindered.*

Luke pulled out the sheets of gifts and scrolled through the shopping cart, moving one gift per child out of the cart and into the "saved for later" section. It still reached four very high figures. He moved another set of gifts back. This dropped it down to eight hundred and change. The bank screen had long timed out. He logged back in, reexamined the balance, compared it with their projected budget for January and February, and winced. *It's better, but….*

The memory of boxes of Christmas gifts that Aggie wanted to return and repurchase choked him. *We can't do that. I have to find a way to live with her "in an understanding way" and not neglect my duty to the entire family. We have to be able to eat, and I promised her we wouldn't rely on Doug and Allie's money to provide for these kids.*

Hands in his pockets, Luke wandered through the downstairs, down into the basement, out into the backyard, and up to the kids' rooms. He peered into closets, on shelves, in toy boxes. Back in the library, he opened the game cupboards and stared into their depths, pleading for the Lord to give him wisdom. And the answer came in a quiet nudge. Luke snatched up the laptop and the gift sheets and bolted upstairs. He found Aggie making another of her myriad of lists. This time — things to do with each child during the day.

"I need to keep connected. Maybe I'll do the Susannah Wesley thing. I'll snag half an hour or an hour a day with each kid. This'll be good. It makes me be still and know my children!"

But the verse says to "Know that I am God" not "know your kid inside out." Despite the thought, Luke nodded. "They'll love that. I know they miss you."

"You'd never know it from my end. They're never in here. It's like they're afraid early labor is contagious or something." Her voice dropped to a whisper. "I was sure Dr. Malara would say I could be on light duty around the house. She said until thirty-seven weeks, I'm stuck here."

I heard her. Trust me, I wanted the same. Luke gave Aggie a half-smile and settled in beside her. "Um, I've been going over the budget...." His throat constricted as he heard Aggie sniffle. "We can't buy everything on these lists without dipping into this month's Social Security. I was supposed to have had that house finished and sold by now."

"This is my fault. I—"

"That's ridiculous, and you know it." He pulled her close and held her, the laptop and papers abandoned. "Mibs, it's just a setback. We'll be fine. But I can't spend twenty-four hundred dollars on gifts when I have two tenants late for rent and a house that will be hard to sell unfinished."

"Maybe you shouldn't sell it. I mean, we don't have a construction loan. It's not like we're losing interest every day. Maybe you should just—"

But Luke couldn't do it. "You know as well as I do that we need not to have that hanging over us. The baby will come; I'll be home then, too. We just can't. The money we'll get out of it, even unfinished, will help."

Aggie sighed. Her body sagged against him, and a ragged quality entered her voice. "We have to keep the GIL's gifts, don't we?"

"If you want a big Christmas for the kids...."

Again, the sigh. Again, Luke's heart constricted. Aggie nodded and wiped away a few tears. "Silly—crying over her doing what Allie wanted all those years. I'm being ridiculous."

"I did have an idea, one you've talked about before...."

He played with her hands, amazed at how the slim fingers had swollen in recent weeks. But Aggie pulled them away and shifted to look at him. "Well, spill it. What idea have I had that you're trying to steal now?"

But Luke's eyes took in the changes in her features, the dark circles under her eyes, the roundness of her cheeks, the limpness of her hair. His thumb caressed her cheek, and his fingers traced the lines of her jaw, marveling—full of wonder. "Sometimes, I can't believe that you're really *my* wife. The Lord has been so good to me."

Every word softened the edge he'd felt in her, but that last sentence sent her bristling again. "Stop trying to change the subject. What idea?"

Lord... help! To reprove or not—was it the time? Scripture on being understanding trumped taking thoughts captive for a moment. Luke ignored her demands and kissed her, holding her lips captive as well as her thoughts for a minute or two. "Oh, Mibs...."

"I love you, too."

For the first time that night, Luke felt as if she meant what she said. His heart sagged in relief. "Okay, you know how you keep saying you want to do family gifts at Christmas and then personal gifts for birthdays?"

Aggie stiffened, but before he could try to explain, she relaxed again. "It would be a good year for that. Everything is different already, and they *do* have personal gifts—from the GIL. Then birthdays... it could be a good start for a new tradition."

Luke took that admonition regarding supplication to heart and pleaded with the Lord for her to make a decision that both soothed her heart *and* didn't strain the budget. Seconds, minutes—for a moment, he thought she'd fallen asleep—but once she thought through it, everything changed.

"Let's do it. What've we got in the cart?"

His throat stuck together. A cough, a strangled plea for water, and a second try left her eyes wide with panic. "It's nothing that bad. Sorry. I just moved out of the cart what we absolutely couldn't afford without dipping into the kids' money. Just don't panic. I saved them."

Hours later, lights still blazing in the room, Luke awoke and found Aggie curled against him, half-reclining and asleep. The laptop teetered precariously on his knee. One unfortunate shift and it would have crashed to the floor—another expense they couldn't afford. He closed it, slid it onto the night table, and

234

stacked all the papers he could reach on top of it.

It took longer than it should have, but he managed *not* to wake her as he shifted and squirmed his way into a prone position. Back and neck—they screamed and then sighed in relief. Aggie rolled onto her other side and Luke slipped an arm around her, cradling her ever-expanding belly. The baby kicked his hand. Love—overpowering and deeply intense—filled him as he massaged the area until the baby settled once more.

Thank you, Lord. Thank you for a wife with eight children already, willing to do this not once, but twice. After this one, I don't know if she'll be up to another, but I got to hold my Mibs while she slept — hold her and soothe our baby. I'm grateful.

FAITH IS A BOTHER

Chapter Eighteen

Friday, December 19th

The doorbell rang, but Tina ignored it. *If you know me, you'll come in. If you don't, I don't have time for you.*

The latch clicked and feet tapped along the hardwood in rhythmic staccato movements. "Tina? You're home?"

"Back here!" Tina grabbed a stack of shorts and t-shirts and began rolling them into pairs. The footsteps came closer. Her heart pounded as it always did. The sound stopped just at her door. She ordered herself *not* to speak first, but as usual, it happened. She looked up.

"Hi."

Oh, you know how to turn my heart into mush at the bottom of my stomach. Tina folded her arms over her chest and tried to meet his gaze. To her disgust, her eyes landed on and refused to leave his lips. "Hi."

"You mad at me?"

"Should I be?" The question flew from her lips with an edge to it she never intended. Before he could respond, before he could grow defensive, she gave him an exaggerated wink. "Been flirting with Kenzie again? I'm getting jealous about that girl."

Relief washed over her as the dark cloud that formed as she spoke blew away at the wink. "Well, she does think I'm perfect.

236

Some people have figured out the truth. Of course, waiting ten years to be a male cougar—what *do* they call guys who marry much younger women?" His forehead furrowed. "Can't think."

"Sugar daddies if they're rich. Otherwise, no clue. Jaguar?"

"Yeah, well…." His eyes drew her closer until he could reach out and grasp her hand. "I'm going to miss you."

She shouldn't have asked. Her heart demanded she keep her thoughts to herself. But despite it all, the words flowed from her lips and, if the pained look on his face meant anything, pierced his heart. "Will you? Why?"

"Tina…."

She turned away, her hands grabbing the next set of clothing and rolling with a practiced flick of the wrist. "You need to get some things for Kenzie. I left a list on the fridge."

Heart constricting, throat aching, Tina gripped the roll and tried not to cry at the sound of his shoes retreating. *We're never going to work. There's no hope for us. Why do I even try?* The answer came just as quickly. *Because you don't give up on people you love.*

Despite her best intentions, Tina knew the words meant little. *Because if you come home to the same old-same old, you're going to dump him, and you know it.*

Footsteps returned, and with them came the racing of her heart. *Why do I love someone who is incapable of a normal relationship? Why couldn't I have fallen for someone without baggage? Or, at the least, one who isn't commitment-phobic!*

"Sweatshirts in nearly every size and color on the planet? Why?"

Tina couldn't help the giggle that erupted. "She's making Christmas presents for everyone. I wanted to talk her out of it, but I couldn't bring myself to do it." Her eyes sought his once more. "These kids are not handling this as well as Aggie and Luke think. Vannie is stressed to the max trying to be a little mother, Laird has checked out in an attempt to seal off his heart, and Ellie is trying to keep up with Vannie as much as she can. The little guys are getting away with murder, and where is Libby? I swear that woman has a sixth sense for when people need her—even the tiniest bit. What gives?"

And, in a move that would keep her going, make her ache to come home again, William stepped forward, wrapped his arms around her, and just held her. He didn't speak, didn't move. He just waited for her.

"The old William would have tried to 'fix' this."

"The old William's approach wouldn't work here. I have no intention of being a cougar cub."

Tina's head jerked back as she stared up at him. "What?"

"Well, the last time I tried to fix Aggie's children problem, I tried to marry her. This time, I'd have to marry Libby, and ugh."

Laughter—it solved more of their arguments and strained feelings than anything else. Tina's giggle blended with his half-stifled chuckles in a way that always soothed her heart. "Okay! I'll admit it." Tina shoved him out the door. Standing in her hallway, Tina leaned in and kissed him. "I'm going to miss you, too."

"You're still hurt—angry."

"Yeah. But we'll work on that when I get back. Maybe after the first?"

His fingers brushed a wisp of hair off her forehead. "I love you. I know it's hard to believe it sometimes, but I love you. And I'm trying...." William pulled her close again—fierce. "I know, I know. I'm *very* trying."

Why she did it, Tina couldn't imagine—so out of character—but she asked before she could stop herself. "Come with me? I'll get you a ticket right now. *Please?*"

"How can I?" He waved the list of colors and sizes. "You put me on Kenzie duty."

A note of desperation entered her tone. Tina kissed him again—lingering long past the safety zone before she whispered, "I'll get Libby to do it."

"I couldn't get anyone to take my place, or I'd be tempted."

"Would you?" Again, she ached to kick herself. *Why do you do this? Why must everything be a challenge? You know he's thinking it!*

"Want me to try?" Even as he asked, William reached for his phone.

But Tina threw her arms around him and held him tight. "Of course, I want you to. But the fact that you didn't even hesitate to start means more than anything. I'll go find tickets. If you find someone, I'll hit the purchase button. You might get stuck in coach, though."

William's laughter sent cartwheels through her heart. "Most of society does, Tina. I'll be fine." He kissed her cheek as he turned away, his fingers already sliding over the surface of his phone. "Hey, Megan? Got a huge favor."

Wow, he's doing it. A tiny part of her ached to buy the tickets outright—a sign of her faith in the Lord's ability to grant this one desire of her heart. *It's not about him being there—not really. But he said he'd go. He's willing to* try. *That has to mean something. And if he can't does it mean I should stay? Show him he means more than a cousin who probably won't notice if I'm there or not? Aggie could use the help....*

A hint of William's progress drifted through the house and to her room. "... fine. I understand. I'll try Gabe."

Lord....

She pawed through her closet and pulled out a couple of her favorite sun dresses—and William's. A smile formed as she laid them out and considered the best shoe options. Another hint of William's progress reached her ears. Tina sighed. *Aaaannnd, he's on to Mike. Argh! C'mon, Lord! Please?!*

Toiletries, Kindle, DSLR. One after another, she packed things into her packing cubes and added said cubes to her suitcase. She'd half-freeze between the car and the entrance to the airport, but leaving her coat behind would be worth it. She rehung that. Instead, she pulled out her warmest sweater and a sleeveless, collared cotton shirt. *That'll work.*

Five minutes passed. Fifteen. When she could still hear his voice out there, talking—almost *pleading* with whoever his latest victim was, Tina forced herself to let him off the hook. She closed out of the airline app, shoved her phone in her pocket, and went to find William. He stood at the kitchen sink, gripping it, talking on speaker phone.

"—it's late and I volunteered, but something came up. If you can't do it, I understand, but—"

His voice cut off as she slipped her arms around his waist and laid her cheek against his back. "It's okay," she whispered. "Thanks for trying."

"I'll call you back, Kev."

"Sorry, man. Wish I could—" But William punched the phone off, turned, and buried his cheek in her hair.

"I'm trying...."

"I know. But you can't. I get that. I'm sorry for putting pressure on you." Tina prayed the words would be true—sooner rather than later. "C'mon. Help me finish packing. You can still take me to the airport, right? Or should I call a car?"

William didn't answer. He didn't move. He didn't release her. They stood in each other's arms until time demanded she finish her job. "I have to go." She raised her eyes to his and said, "Unless I stayed."

"You know I want you to. The kids would love it. But your dad doesn't ask as much of you anymore. He asked for this. You should go."

Tina dropped her forehead to his chest. "He's going to spend the whole time harping on our relationship. He'll try to set me up with clients who just *happen* to be vacationing right where we're staying. Who knew?"

Several long seconds passed before William spoke. She noticed a shift in him even before he formed the first word. "If you decide that *we* aren't what you want, I'll understand. I'll hate it, but I'll understand. But don't let your dad confuse you. Please." A chill rippled through her as he added, "I hope I'll see you when you get back."

Kenzie met him at the door with a smile and the cutest wrinkle of her nose as the cold air bit it. "We're going to get more snow! I can feel it in my nose!"

"Mrs. Dyke says that, but she says she can feel it in the knee she twisted a few years back." He hefted the bags of sweatshirts like a Santa's sack and grinned. "Where do I put these?"

She beckoned him to follow. "I'm going to hide them under my bed. No one will look there—not while Aunt Aggie is in bed. Uncle Luke hasn't had us change our sheets since we got home from Aunt Willow's!" Kenzie giggled and led him into the house and up the stairs. "Shh... don't tell."

An eerie quiet hovered over the house. "Where is everyone?"

"Vannie and Ellie took the little kids out to try to find birds.

They're calling it school. A 'winter nature walk.' I was supposed to go, but they forgot me when I went to the bathroom. Then when I went to go out, I saw your text on the phone." She giggled. "I just stayed. Vannie will yell, but it's worth it."

Once in her room, Kenzie peered into the bag. "It's going to be so cool!" She pulled out a mini safe and twisted the dial. Three times. Nothing. Tried again. Nothing. In a fit of frustration, she thrust it at him. "Laird always has to do it. 17-3-32."

"Which way first? Left or right?" As he spoke, William realized that she had no idea what he was talking about. "I'll try both." Right failed. He spun the dials again and tried left. It opened without a hitch. "Okay. Next time, go left—like opposite a clock. Then right. Then left. If you try to go right first, it won't work."

Eyes wide with hero worship, Kenzie nodded. "Okay. Thanks. How much do I owe you?" She reached into the little safe and pulled out a fistful of bills. "I have a hundred and eight dollars. Is that enough?"

As much as he hated to do it, William pulled out the receipts and passed them to her. "Just round them. I think one was for forty-two something and the other was thirty-seven. That's seventy-nine, but you can take care of it whenever, Kenzie. I know you're good for it." He smiled down at the girl as she counted out two twenties and a stack of fives and tens. *And maybe you'll forget about it.*

"Okay. I don't have enough ones, but you spent gas." Kenzie passed him the bills. "Here's eighty." The pride in her voice and shining in her eyes stopped William's protest before it crossed his lips.

"I'm proud of you." He tweaked the girl's braid and grinned. "They're going to love whatever you do with them."

"Want to see?" Kenzie didn't wait for an answer. She dug into the bottom drawer of her dresser. Piles of summer shirts appeared on the floor and a mess of fabric scraps filled the rest of the drawer. But from under the scraps, at the back, Kenzie retrieved a few folded pieces of paper. "See! Everyone will get a sweatshirt—just for them. I got Doctor Who blue for Laird. I'm going to use that font for his. It'll be so cool. And I'm going to make some gears to put behind Ellie's, because she's all into steampunk now." One by one, she shifted paper after paper to show her plans for the sweatshirts.

"That looks complicated, but I bet you'll do *great*. Don't be afraid to ask for help if you need it. Luke or his mom—"

"I want it to be a surprise." The interjection would have been rude if she hadn't been distraught at the idea.

William ignored it, something that Tina would have blasted him for, and helped her replace the shirts into her drawer. "I'll help. I don't know what I'm doing, but if you need it, I'll help."

Laird's voice filled the downstairs, calling for her. William nudged Kenzie toward the door. "Go. I'll put this stuff away."

Her smile brightened her semi-panicked face. "I love you! Thanks!"

It took less time for him to finish than it did for her to dash downstairs and out the back door. He made it to the stairs before that mudroom door slammed shut. But a crash above him, followed by a cry that sounded like pain, sent him up instead of down and out the door. "Aggie?"

"William?"

He burst through her bedroom door and stared at her as she scowled at the floor. "Wha—"

"I dropped my planners."

He folded his arms over his chest. "You screamed like you'd gone into labor because a book or...." William scanned the area. "—five fell to the floor?"

"When you're not supposed to get up except to relieve yourself, *yeah*. It's frustrating." She eyed him. "What're you do—"

Aggie snatched up her phone and held up a finger. "It's Mom. Hang on."

You must *be desperate for adult conversation. Or maybe* any *conversation.* But William relaxed against the doorjamb, hands in his pockets, and watched as Aggie spoke with her mother.

"—feeling today?"

Oh, right. The surgery. All attempts to block out the conversation vanished. William listened as she asked questions about incisions, about physical therapy, and about when they could see her.

"Are you still going home on Monday? That's good, right?" Aggie's grin lightened the tone in the room all by itself. "That's

242

great. And you're managing the pain? You can sleep and everything? You don't want—"

Stop mothering your mother. There's something incongruous about that.

The conversation switched from surgeries to Christmas, and William's heart squeezed at the pain in her tone. *You know, Tina was right. Where's Libby in all this? I think I'll have to ask.*

The conversation dragged until William begged the Lord to let him go. *I just need out of here. And maybe a trip over to see Libby Sullivan.* The minute the thought occurred to him, William winced. *Who am I? This isn't my business. Luke can hand—*

Aggie tossed the phone on the bed, beaming. "She's still recovering—going to be a long, long road—but my mom is going to be healthier now than she ever has before. Wow."

The pile of books on the floor beckoned him. William stacked them on the table and inched his way back to the door. "Glad to hear that. Do you need anything? I have the day off. Took Tina to the airport and did some shopping, but I can go get you something—cravings? Ice cream? Pizza? Pickles?"

"Before I talked to Mom, I think I would have begged for adult conversation." She grinned. "You could tell me about your latest hardened criminal—you know, like the kid who TP'd the school or something. But now…." Aggie slid down into the covers. "All I want is a nap. But come back." Desperation entered her tone. "Please. They're always so busy. I go crazy up here alone. I'm trying, but…."

It wasn't any of his business, and he knew it. But William couldn't stand it. He stepped closer once more and leaned his knee on the corner of her bed. "Aggie, you have an important job. I get that it's boring. I get that you want it over. But you *need* to do that job. Just rest and keep that baby safe. Nothing else matters. You don't want to regret not doing everything you could to give it the best start in life."

Defeat washed over her features. "I know. I do. But it's easier to say from where you *stand.* Me, I'm not even supposed to *sit* that much."

"I'll keep praying for you, and you keep singing. That always cheers you up."

"Yeah."

243

William jogged down the stairs and paused. Something seemed off. He almost returned to ask Aggie if she'd called, but when a repeat didn't come, he assumed it had been his imagination. However, once he reached the first floor, the problem struck him hard and fast. *She's not singing. She must have been* really *tired if she didn't sing.*

And his prayers winged heavenward.

As Luke stepped from his truck, an arm looped with several grocery bags, screams pierced the frosty afternoon air. Visions of severed limbs and shredded entrails filled his mind as he took the steps three — well, *all* — at a time. He flung open the door, dropped the groceries in the entry way, and bolted to the mudroom from whence the presumed carnage seemed to originate.

Ronnie stood in the middle of the room, arms wrapped around a single remaining ice cream sandwich. Melted vanilla ice cream drizzled out of one corner of the wrapping and onto his arm, his leg, the floor. The boy didn't care. Ellie ordered him to fork it over. He stomped on her toe.

This one act galvanized Luke into action. He sent Ellie from the room with a smile and a whisper of appreciation, before turning to his son. "Drop it. Now."

"It's *mine!* I *call* it!"

"You didn't ask." Luke held up one finger. "First swat. I said to drop it and you didn't obey. Shall we go for two?"

"But—"

"Two. Three?" His eyes bore into the boy's and tried to imagine what could have gotten into the child. *Since when is a stupid ice cream treat the catalyst for misbehavior in this house? I'm never buying them again if—*

Almost nauseating relief washed over him as Ronnie dropped the ice cream. The boy took one look at it on the floor and burst into tears. "Now it's icky!"

Luke gathered the boy in his arms and held fast. "Sorry to tell you, bud, but it was ruined long before you dropped it. That's what happens when you're selfish."

"But Ellie gots *two*. Lorna gots *two*." Ronnie held up one finger. "I only got *one*. See." He pointed to the single digit pointing upward. "I got one. I wanted...." His second finger struggled to rise without any others messing up his count. "Two, too!"

"Well, I think I can get you a tu-tu, but I don't give little boys things that they tried to steal."

Again, Ronnie protested. "It's *not* steals! It's in *my* house. That's not for steals!"

"I think the word you want is "stealing." Luke stroked his son's hair—the faintest niggle of a hint that the boy needed a haircut breaking through to his consciousness. "But you didn't pay for it. Without permission it isn't yours." When Ronnie's eyes glazed over, Luke tried again. "Did you use your money from your bank to buy it?"

Understanding dawned and sent a dark cloud over the boy's face. "No."

"Then you can't touch it without asking. Just like Ellie's coloring pencils, just like Tavish's Legos. Just like Mommy's markers and notebooks." Luke let those words sink in.

Ronnie's eyes slid past Luke's face as he spoke. Something in the boy's face hinted that he wasn't listening. Luke glanced over his shoulder, ready to tell whatever child stood there that he or she needed to give them privacy. Instead, Aggie stood there, tears streaming down her cheeks.

"Mibs? What are—?"

"My kids are falling apart! I heard him screaming for five minutes, and it sounded like he'd impaled himself or cut off a finger at the least." Her eyes darkened as a wave of pain ripped through her. He'd seen enough to know what it looked like, and this one was a doozy.

Ronnie's misbehavior forgotten, Luke jumped up and tried to urge her to the spare room, the couch—even back upstairs. "You look ready to drop. C'mon."

She shoved his hand away as Luke tried to lead her from the room. "Just. Don't. Touch. Me."

"Mibs—"

"I *have a name!*" Tears sprang to her eyes. "I'm sorry. I don't know what's wrong with me. I love your nickname for me. But so help me if you try to make me do one more thing, I'm going to get

245

ugly."

Going to? *You're already there, Aggie. But what do I do about that?* A dozen thoughts whizzed through his mind, slowed, and raced back. Luke's brain couldn't keep up. "Um...."

"I think I'll make me a sandwich—grilled cheese sounds good."

Jaw agape, Luke stared after her. He choked as her voice called back to him, "Don't forget. You owe him two swats. I heard."

By the dejected look on Ronnie's face, Luke suspected the boy had counted on him forgetting. Never had Luke wished more that he could just let it go. But he'd learned the hard way—hard on him *and* Ian—that inconsistency only made it harder on the kids. The temptation to rush—equally strong. *But he needs to see you taking this seriously.* A niggle in his heart suggested that perhaps not *too* seriously. *Okay... first offense in this area. No molehills here.*

Minutes later, through residual tears and occasional sniffles, Ronnie worked at cleaning up the liquid puddle of cookie and ice cream soup that half-remained in the confines of the wrapper. Fifty paper towels—or so it seemed—returned the floor to sparkling. *Now, if only the rest of the mudroom floor were as clean.*

As if he could read Luke's mind, Ronnie frowned. "The floor is dirty. *That—*" Ronnie pointed to the wide oblique in the middle of the floor. "Is clean. I make it clean."

"I'll get the rest later. You go apologize to Ellie. You deliberately tried to hurt her. Go tell her how sorry you are."

For a moment, Luke feared the boy would insist that he *wasn't* sorry. Everything, from his stance, the way he refused to meet Luke's eyes, and even the stubborn set of the little jaw, screamed, "I won't!" But in a flash, it all changed. Ronnie's lip trembled and wide eyes filled with unshed tears. "I don't want her step on my foots."

"Go on then." With a last hug, Luke sent Ronnie upstairs in search of Ellie while he went to work on Aggie's cooperation.

Aggie stood in front of the stove, one fist kneading her back, the other hand flipping a sandwich every three seconds. The temptation—nay, *desire*—to take over nearly overrode Luke's common sense. He stood at the island, and his heart pleaded with her to rest. "Feeling better today?"

Wrong question. Aggie shoved the pan off the fire and stormed from the room as effectively as anyone can with contractions sending shock waves of pain down her legs. *That's what she said, right? That the contractions start in back and work down the front of her thighs? Sounds horrible.*

Time was against him. He needed to get her calm and resting again, but nothing irritates a pregnant woman more than someone *trying* to calm her when her hormones have determined agitation to be the rule of the day. To finish the sandwich or follow his wife? The question produced more confusion than answers. A dash around the house found Vannie wrapping gifts in the basement.

"Hey, they look great. Aggie is going to be relieved to know there are gifts there." He spun one at the end of the table and sighed. "Of course, *yours* won't look this good. I'll do my best, but...."

"That's okay." Vannie held up a computerized robot for Laird to assemble. "She did find neat stuff this year. It fits us better than usual."

And why does that both impress and terrify me? Luke ignored the question and confessed his reason for coming. "I wondered if you could do me a quick favor."

"What's that?"

"Aggie came downstairs—"

Scissors clattered to the table as Vannie's head snapped up. "What? She can't *do* that, can she?"

"Well, she did. Ronnie was screaming—"

"Yeah. I heard him, but by the time I got done wrapping the one I was on, it stopped." Vannie eyed him with wary curiosity. "Tell me he didn't chop off an appendage."

You can be frightfully like me sometimes—out of the blue and never when I'd expect. Luke's thoughts nearly made him forget to reply. "No, just an argument over a liquefied ice cream sandwich." *Get back on track!* So, before she could respond again, Luke added, "But anyway, Aggie tried to make a sandwich. Can you go finish grilling it for me? I need to make sure she made it upstairs all right."

Vannie didn't hesitate. She abandoned the half-wrapped

247

package and skittered past him. "Got it."

Though he didn't think he could spare the time, Luke stood at the top of the stairs and prayed for wisdom, patience, understanding, and, if necessary, the exact amount of firmness she needed from him. *I'd want her to make me do what was necessary for my health, even if I didn't like it at the time. Matthew 7:12 here....*

The sounds of heavy breathing, moaning, gasping reached him as Luke started up the stairs. He found her clinging to the newel, her face contorted in pain. "Aw, Mibs."

"I—don't—think...." She couldn't finish speaking, but he heard her loud and clear.

"I've got you. Hold onto me."

How he lifted her and carried her up the stairs, Luke would never know. His muscles strained, and even he could feel the veins bulging in his neck as he staggered up one step after another. Once in their room, Aggie lunged for the bathroom. *Lord, please. Not again. It's too soon.*

But a minute later, she stumbled from the bathroom and crawled into bed, spent. "It's just sick that I'm so out of shape already that I can't make it up and down the stairs without nearly passing out from exhaustion."

As much as he wanted to react, Luke forced himself to reconsider every word until he found the least offensive ones he could. "I think it's more the fact that your body keeps trying to make you stay in labor for the next five weeks."

"Well, I'm sick of it. And where are the gifts we bought? No UPS man... *again!*"

"I got the shipping notice today. They'll be here Monday — all but two. Those'll be here Tuesday or Wednesday — I think."

She jerked the covers over her shoulder and turned her back to him. "If you'd have ordered what I wanted when I gave you the lists, this wouldn't be an issue. Now we'll have nothing." And, as if it made perfect sense, she added, "And are you ever going to send up Tavish? We were supposed to meet an hour ago."

"He's finishing up something. He sent up Kenzie. Didn't she ask—?"

"Oh, great. Now I'm worthless *and* forgetful." His heart ripped open as she whispered, "And utterly forgettable, it seems."

Luke tried to sit beside her — soothe her. His heart prepared words of encouragement, but when she growled and snapped for him to leave her alone, Luke changed the direction of his thoughts—his prayers. "Mibs, when is the last time you read your Bible? Prayed? Spoke to us in 'psalms and hymns and spiritual songs?' When did you last make 'music in your heart to the Lord'?"

"Go preach to someone else. Until you've been trapped all alone in a room with a body that has betrayed you, I don't want to hear your sermons."

A shuffle behind him hinted that Vannie might have made it upstairs. As much as he wanted to ignore her words—to brush them off as the pain talking—he couldn't. Vannie needed to hear him speak the truth in love, and even if they pricked a little. "Aggie, you know that is wrong thinking. Truth doesn't change based on experience."

"Yeah, well experience can sure put it into context. It's taught me that all the lofty ideas in the world mean nothing when life vomits all over them."

He'd decided against it, unwilling to cause her more pain, but the bitterness in her tone illuminated what she'd actually said. Luke stood close, gazed down at her, and tried to speak truth to her heart. "When we swallow the lie that says only those who have lived through our exact difficulties can share the Word of God with us, we're saying that *God's Word* is insufficient. You know better, Mibs."

"Luke, I don't want to say what I'm about to, so just go away. *Please.*"

He found Vannie standing outside the door, the sandwich growing cold, and a look of utter shock and horror on her face. With patience and tenderness he didn't know he possessed at that moment, Luke led her downstairs, into the kitchen, and only then did he speak. "She's not herself. She'll come around. Just pray, Vannie."

L○VE W as M ine but N○w Is Rebelling

Chapter Nineteen

Saturday, December 20th

A blank journal page lay open before her, but Aggie's pen lay capped and untouched. Pride warred against raw honesty for preeminence. *Write what I'll wish I'd been thinking or be "real"? Those are the options. Why isn't there a middle ground?*

Aggie blinked. The page beckoned her. The pen demanded she give her thoughts a chance to make a concrete impact in her life before she stuffed them down again. For the first time in over a week, Aggie sent a heartfelt prayer heavenward. *Help me be real – authentic.* The journal with its lovely pansies and iridescent butterfly beckoned. *Even if only for myself.*

It's almost Christmas – my favorite time of year. All our traditions and celebrations are either non-existent or happening without me. I can't decide which is worse.

When you have nothing else to do but navel gaze – and when your navel is as flat as a pancake thanks to a stretched out belly – you discover things about life and yourself that you didn't know or even want to know. How can I feel like the Lord gave me a bait and switch with my life when I know I wouldn't change any of it?

I was going to be a teacher. I wasn't <u>against</u> marriage and family. If it happened, I would have been good with it. But really, Lord? Eight

250

children at once. Why did You think I could do this? Really? <u>EIGHT?</u> And two more? What were You thinking? I'm supposed to be making lesson plans for high schoolers — trying to revive a passion for the past to help ensure a brighter future. Instead, I'm lying around in bed trying to keep from having a baby living in NICU for the next month. This wasn't in the plan.

I can't sing. I can't pray. I can't read the Word. And I can't even write about what I can't do. I'm staring at this page and I don't know how to explain my heart.

I miss my kids. I miss my husband. My mother is recuperating from what might be a life-changing surgery, and I'm sitting here staring at four walls that I'm learning to hate.

I want

With evident hesitation, Luke stepped into the room and gave her a weak smile. "How do you feel about going 'on a date'?"

Excitement welled up in her. "Going for a drive? Yes!" His face fell and with it, her heart plummeted to her stomach.

"The kids thought we needed a date. They're making dinner, want to decorate the room for us — everything. Vannie says you have to take a shower and let her do your hair and…." Luke gave every appearance at choking down twice what he could reasonably manage. "Your makeup."

"Really? Makeup? Since when — ?" She closed her eyes. "Fine. I'll take a shower. She better be glad that I've had an agitation-free afternoon."

Luke hadn't looked so miserable since he'd paced the floors in prayer for Ellie a few years back. "I know, but I didn't have the heart to remind her."

"You don't have to act like it's torture." The words flew from her mouth before Aggie even realized she'd thought it. Her mouth opened again to apologize, but the words never came.

He stood there, arms folded over his chest, leaning against the dresser, unspeaking. His eyes held hers, pain filling them until she thought they'd overflow in tears, daggers — *something*. But still he didn't speak. She tried to think of something to say — something that didn't include an apology she didn't feel. When he did speak, it choked her.

"Mibs, it is torture. It's torture every time I step into this room and feel like an instant adversary." Luke's eyes focused on some indiscernible thing on the floor. "It's torture to feel like my wife sees me as the enemy." His heart wrenched to see her shocked, grieved gaze. In a ragged whisper, he added, "It's torture to feel like my wife has lost her first love."

A white-hot fury filled her. "And who would that be? You? The Lord?"

Luke turned away. "I guess you just answered your own question. Obviously both."

Great sobs welled up in her chest. The pain — excruciating. Never had she imagined such a staggering ache. Her heart pleaded with the Lord to release — to cry. But the tears never came. Aggie watched him disappear — listened as his feet thudded down the stairs with such a melancholy ring to each step.

What have I done?

The downstairs rippled with repressed tension. Luke stood in the bathroom, combing his hair and pleading with the Lord for wisdom. *I've never not wanted to spend time with her. I feel like we're allowing this situation to drive a wedge between us. Is it the situation? Is Satan testing our faith and our commitment to one another? What's going on? What do I do?*

A tie hung loose around his neck. As much as he didn't want to tie it, he knew how much Aggie loved when he wore one to special occasions. Vannie had even picked it out for him. *"Wear this. It'll make her smile. She doesn't smile much anymore."*

The truth of her words squeezed his heart once more. Luke adjusted the tie, flipped it around twice, and pulled through the knot. Done. Simple. Easy. A small thing to do for the woman he claimed to love.

That thought beat into his mind and heart, and he rejected it. *I do love her. Always have. Lord, I feel like that day when I thought she was going to fire me. She wouldn't, would she? Not now. It's just the hormones, right? The cabin fever. She doesn't even have that. She has bed fever. How would I feel, trapped there all day every day and without any guarantee that it would work?* His words the previous day

252

haunted him — taunted him. *"When we swallow the lie that says only those who have lived through our exact difficulties can share the Word of God with us, we're saying that* God's Word *is insufficient."*

All set, Luke stepped from the bathroom, still mulling over his words. Had they been right? Of that, he had little doubt. Had he chosen the best time to speak them? *I just don't know.*

Ellie's voice reached him before he even stepped into the dining room. "Vannie, listen to this. Does the colon go before or after the but?"

"I can't imagine how it could come after a colon, but...."

Vannie's reply faded into oblivion as his mind tried to work out how a butt would ever come before a colon. *Enema, perhaps? What* is *she studying?*

Disaster — it defined the collective explosion of children, dishes, scraps, and spills that littered every surface of the room. Ellie stood next to Vannie, showing something in a notebook. As Luke neared, he saw what the girl meant. "You should know," he managed to gasp out after laughing hard enough to receive semi-horrified looks from the girls. "From the other room, it sounded like you were talking about anatomy, and I was *really* confused."

Blank expressions. Double blinks. Furrowed foreheads. It all culminated in a burst of laughter that drew other members of the family in almost a desperate attempt to be a part of semi-normalcy. Cries of, "What? Tell us!" reverberated through the kitchen and pierced his heart. *We need a break, Lord. I just don't know how to get it. I'm so lost.*

" — to go upstairs. Can Aunt Aggie eat at the table we made her, or should it be lunch in bed?" Vannie ladled her baked potato soup into a bowl and dumped a fistful of cheese onto it. "She can't eat the onions right now, right?"

"I think she's good with green onions." Luke scowled as he tried to remember. "Didn't she add them to her baked potato the other night? It's just brown onions, right?"

Ellie nodded and reached for the sour cream. "I'll just put some in a ramekin just in case she wants some. I think she said something about needing to avoid empty calories now that she's stuck in bed."

The words stung more than he thought they should, but Luke just nodded and managed to remember to praise her. "Is

Laird back with the flowers yet?"

Silence answered for him. *Do I go up without them, or do I just wait? It's hard to know what to do anymore.*

"Can I use your phone?"

Luke dropped his phone in Ellie's outstretched hand and watched, impressed, as the girl's index finger slid across the screen without hesitation. "I'll... just ask... if he's almost...here."

A minute later, the boy burst through the door. "Sorry I'm late! Was that you, Uncle Luke?" Footfalls thundered through the living room, across the dining room, and into the kitchen.

"Ellie with my phone, anyway." Luke grabbed the flowers, thanked Laird for risking frostbite — or at least icicles in his nose — and dragged his feet toward the stairs. *Since when am I not eager to spend time with my wife?*

The answer hit him just at the base of the second set of stairs. *Since I don't know her anymore.*

Foolish, ridiculous, pretentious, even — the words mocked him as he knocked on their bedroom door. *Why did I agree to this again?"*

"Door's open. You don't have to—" When Aggie saw him standing there, flowers in hand, her eyes rolled. "Oh, brother. They're playing this up all the way, aren't they?" Despite the sarcasm, Aggie's eyes softened at the sight of his hesitation. "Of course, I have no vase up here, but they're awfully pretty."

He stepped inside and zipped a text to Laird. VASE PLEASE. However, he just shrugged at Aggie's words and gave them a weak sniff. "I'd have brought pansies — somehow. Laird rode to the store for these."

"I'll have to thank *him* then."

Everything about her, posture, facial expressions, even her tone, said it was a joke. But something sounded off still. Luke fought a wince and offered them once more. "Not much scent, but the carnations have a bit."

Had he not just asked for a vase, Luke would have been certain the thundering up the stairs meant that someone had done something horrifying. Instead, he turned, hand outreached, waiting for the vase. Laird burst into the room with a sheepish grin. "Sorry. Should have sent one up with you." He waved at Aggie. "Lunch is almost done. Do you want to sit at the table or...?"

"Table. Definitely. It's not the bed!"

He helped her to her seat. Offered to get her a cardigan. One of Willow's candles waited to be lit, and Luke obliged. He brought the flowers over and tried to set them in the center, but it failed. "Can't see you with those in the way." A glance around the room didn't help, so he moved to grab his "night stand."

Aggie giggled as he tried to give it an artistic look beside their lovely laid table. "You're... something. Absolutely something else."

"Well, you should be able to see your flowers." A smile at her showed her looking better than she had in weeks, but as he began to compliment her, Luke choked back the words again. *Yeah... because saying she looks good only after she gets a face full of makeup isn't going to be insulting.* He tried a dozen different things in his mind, but they all sounded like a backhanded compliment at best.

"I look ridiculous, don't I?" Aggie dropped her eyes and stared at the table.

His heart wrung again. "You look beautiful." Luke waited for her expression of disbelief before giving her a weak smile. "I kept trying to figure out how to say it without making it sound like you look awful any other time."

Her arm cradled her belly as it did every time she felt the least bit vulnerable—often these days. That thought explained much and left even more to confusion. Luke struggled to find a way to reassure her, comfort her, encourage her. Words, as they often did, failed him.

"Would you *want* me to wear makeup more often? I mean, more than the occasional mascara?"

That is such an impossible question! How can I answer it? Nothing will come out right. When any hint of a reasonable reply eluded him, Luke shrugged. "Only if you want to. I love *you*—not just your face or your hair or your clothing style. I want *you* happy. That's when you're the most beautiful."

Her entire countenance shifted in half a second. Aggie made it half a dozen words into a semi-tirade on *him* trying to be remotely chipper in similar circumstances, when Vannie walked in with a tray of soup bowls and a panicked expression on her face. "Are you hungry?"

To Luke's relief, Aggie grinned. "Starved, and that looks *good.*"

"It was hard to guess what might be good, but I wanted to be sure I could *make* it, too." She set bowls in front of each of them and gave Aggie a smile. "We're making paninis. Do you want roast beef or turkey?"

Only Providence could have prevented Luke from answering for them both. He opened his mouth to say they'd both take roast beef—as they *always* did—and snapped it shut as Aggie said, "Oh, turkey sounds delicious!"

At Vannie's questioning glance, Luke managed to choke out, "Roast beef, please."

They ate soup in silence, and their sandwiches with little more conversation. Laird appeared with the basement TV and set it up on the makeshift dining table. It wobbled—twice. Luke tried to ignore the impending doom of the TV they'd *just* replaced, and helped Aggie back to bed—after two trips to the bathroom, no less. To his relief, Laird got the streaming stick loaded and managed to pull up the movie they'd chosen—*Anne of Green Gables.* Aggie's favorite.

With Luke leaning against the headboard, Aggie curled herself half around his chest and rested her head over his heart. It pounded with nervous anticipation—much like it had the first time he'd held her hand, touched her face, kissed her at their wedding. She didn't stiffen, didn't resist. It was the first time they'd had some semblance of normalcy in weeks.

The opening notes to the soundtrack filled their room, and Aggie sighed. "I love this movie."

"You just want to hear Gilbert say, 'Hello, Anne.' I think I should be jealous." He stroked her hair, twisting silken strands around his fingers and letting them spiral down into straight locks again.

"Maybe…." Aggie raised her eyes to meet his. "If I had a single-syllable name, you might be able to equal him. But Aggie…." She wrinkled her nose. "Not the same."

Rachel Lynde burst upon the screen with a keen eye and enough vim to her sweeping to ensure that the dust just settled right back into place again. Luke almost missed his cue, but the moment the nosy woman's husband mentioned the possibility of courting, Luke snapped back to the present.

"Um, perhaps then I should just say, 'Hello, Mibs'?"

A giggle escaped, despite Aggie's best attempts to appear unimpressed. "It could use some work, but…."

He dropped his voice a little deeper. "I'll remember that."

Aggie swooning—he'd never have imagined it, especially not when her emotions were so unpredictable, but swoon she did. A kiss followed—three. The movie played out before them, but neither took notice until Anne's impassioned cry of hatred jerked them apart. She winced. "I always hate that scene." Another wince. "And then I use hate to describe how I feel about a scene about hatred. Lovely, Aggie."

From that moment on, the movie worked its magic in both their hearts. Luke relaxed and reminded himself of just how much he loved her, just how hard being confined would be on any woman, and just how discouraged anyone would be at two or three *more* weeks of inactivity. *The pain from lying around all day— excruciating when sick, but at least it's only a day or two. Why didn't I think of that?*

Telling her—apologizing. Luke worked at finding just the right words to keep her from misunderstanding what he meant. He couldn't apologize for speaking truth, but he could apologize for not trying to make things easier on her.

Aggie's voice jerked him from his thoughts. "—totally get Anne. Do you see how she is always thinking, moving, going, doing? Even when she's just enjoying the beauty of something, there's *action* in her somehow. I feel like that's been stripped from me."

She is a doer—always working, always fixing, always moving, going, teaching, training, cleaning, improving. This kind of idleness—

"—idleness is killing me."

"I was just thinking that myself. You're never idle."

His heart raced at her unexpected kiss. Every one of the doctor's warnings pummeled his mind and helped him resist… *more.* Her whispered, "I didn't think you understood," tore at his heart.

"I understand, Mibs. I do. I just think that fighting it means you're making it twice as hard on yourself. And I hate seeing you worn down by it all." He pressed his cheek against her hair. "I want to fix it. I can't, and that hurts. I'm sorry for appearing unsympathetic. It wasn't intentional."

The faintest edge entered her tone as Aggie spoke. "You are a fixer — like most guys, I bet."

That sounds reasonably innocuous. Maybe I'm reading into things.

Matthew's death tore at his heart. Aggie sat, hot tears soaking his shirt, and tried to breathe through the pain of the scene playing out before them. Luke only hoped that was *all* the pain she endured. "Every time he says that — about only wanting her...."

"That's how I've always felt about you. Right from the start. Just like he said."

He'd either said something right again, or Aggie had decided to kill him by constriction. His chest ached from the force of her arms squeezing tighter and tighter. Her next words came out in a ragged whisper. "I don't know how I'll make it another week or two. I can't *do* this, Luke!"

Luke worked to put all the comfort, love, and encouragement he could into the only thing he believed would get her through the long days ahead. "Perhaps the Lord has given you a gift, Aggie. Perhaps now is the time to learn to 'be still.' To embrace that He is God and let Him comfort and hold you up in ways you wouldn't — "

He never got the chance to finish. Aggie rolled away from him, pulling the blankets over her shoulder, and wrapped herself around one of her pillows. He tried to pull her back again, comfort her. But she shoved him away and growled, "Just leave me alone. Go back downstairs or work on a house or ... whatever. Just leave. Me. Alone."

"Mibs — "

"Luke, I'm not asking." He waited for her to turn and look at him, but she didn't. It took several great gulps of air before she spoke again. "I'm telling you. Go away."

William bolted from his car and raced for the steps, but the sight of Kenzie standing there waiting for him halted him in his tracks. "Did you text me?"

"Yep! You got it!"

He choked. "Um... you typed 9-1-1. That usually means an emergency. You should know that."

"This is! I didn't *call* 9-1-1. I just sent a text so you'd know it was important." Kenzie hopped down the steps and dragged him inside. "I made Vannie stay out of the library until you got here."

Incapable of speech, William followed without a word as she led him through the house to the library. There, laid out on the table, were four sweatshirts. He grinned. "Wow! They look great, Kenzie! I'm proud of you." His eyes met the troubled, confused gaze of his favorite Stuart, and he choked. "What's wrong?"

"They look *awful!* My stitches are all crooked and the letters keep stretching out all weird. Look at that L! It's more like one of those funny Ls for British money."

As much as he didn't want to, he couldn't help but nod. "I can see that. But it's clearly an L and there aren't any of the little cross lines on it. Don't those things have—?"

"But it looks *awful!* Laird is going to hate it. And he won't wear it. And it's all my fault."

The words seemed a bit extreme for a slightly wonky L. He draped an arm around the girl's shoulder and hunkered down a bit. "I think you're being too hard on yourself. I bet he'll wear it because *you* made it." *Even if it means he wears it to bed or under a jacket or something.*

"I wanted them to be *perfect,* but instead, they're just awful. And this one...." She grabbed one of the little raspberry colored sweatshirts he'd gotten for the twins and pointed at the C. "It got all twisty, too. I couldn't make it stop. It's almost an O!" Her voice cracked as she continued. "I tried to take it off, and look."

Even William's throat constricted at the obvious hole in the sweatshirt. "Oh, we need to get a new one, don't we? I'll go as soon as I get off work, but Kenzie...." He stood and squeezed her shoulder once more. "Just next time, send a note with the 9-1-1. Say, something with it like, 'project' or whatever. That way I know you're not actually hurt. But I'll get another sweatshirt for Cari. It'll be okay." He pointed to Laird's sweatshirt. "And if my name started with an L... and I was as scrawny as Laird, I'd wear that with pride."

"But it's so crooked!"

"I think it looks more like it to you than it does to me. I didn't see what you were starting from. All *I* see is a great looking shirt." Something Mrs. Dyke once said flashed in his mind. "You know, when we look at what we've done, we usually only see the tiny details—the imperfections. But when others look at it, they usually see the overall effect. To them it looks great."

"You think so?"

"Mmmhmm." His eyes darted around. "Where's Luke?"

Kenzie's giggle—a bit strange seconds after a semi emotional meltdown just half a minute earlier. "They're having a date. Vannie and Ellie cooked and everything. Uncle Luke is wearing a tie. Vannie made Aunt Aggie wear makeup."

I didn't know she wore any. That's weird. Luke in a tie. William managed to stuff back a snicker. "Okay, I'll talk to him later."

"Talk to who—?"

Kenzie's scream pierced their ears. "Uncle *Luke!* You're supposed to be upstairs!" The girl dove for the table, shoving her projects off the other side and standing in front. "You're ruining the surprise!"

William jerked a thumb at the door. "I'll hide them. You go see if Aggie needs anythi—"

"No, don't. She needs rest right now. Why don't you go help Vannie and Ellie clean up the mess in the kitchen. Then we'll work on your division."

The moment she stepped out the door, Luke sagged against the jamb and rubbed his hand over his face. "If you tell me that Ian or Ronnie called for 9-1-1...."

"Nope."

Relief—he'd never seen such a perfect, physical manifestation of it. "That's the last thing we need right now."

"Um, but Kenzie did send me this text." William pulled out his phone and flipped through texts to hers. He passed it across to Luke and grinned.

The look on Luke's face—priceless enough to make a credit card commercial's heart go pitter patter. "Kenzie wants to walk on the beach with you at *sunset?* What?"

Heat flooded his face, burned his ears, choked him. "I think my finger slipped." Shouting a thousand silent insults at himself, he nodded. "Scroll down one."

Luke frowned. "What? Why—"

"Project malfunction." William chewed on a thought for a moment or two before adding, "She needs help with something. I just don't get why she came to me instead of you."

His suspicions proved correct. Luke winced at the words. It wasn't the first time Kenzie had turned to him for help or advice, and as much as he loved the little girl, it didn't seem right. The speech—rehearsed many times over the years. And it seemed that the perfect moment had come. "Look, I'm not a dad. Have *no clue* about parenting. But it seems like I 'rescued' Kenzie and the others from a mean grandmother right after I met them. I was nice to her. And she, in a vulnerable time just losing her own father and everything, transferred all her loyalty to me."

"Yeah. I've often thought the same thing. I'm just glad she has someone she trusts that *I* can trust with her."

"Well," only the memory of Tina's insistence that Luke needed to be Kenzie's "hero" kept him going. "I'm not complaining, okay?" His training kicked in. He squared his shoulders and delivered the rest of his speech with calm, impassioned directness. "I just agree with Tina that Kenzie needs someone she can rely on more than me. You're her father now. She needs that stability of knowing the primary man in her life lives under her roof."

The defeat that fogged Luke's eyes wrung William's heart more than he'd ever have imagined. But Luke's words—they jabbed him in the gut. "I can't make her prefer me, William. I can only love her and trust that the Lord knows what He's doing in my crazy, mixed-up family."

Maybe it's not the time. With Aggie.... But the text message nudged him to try again. "You can't, no. But you can...." He rounded the corner of the table and pulled out the ruined pink sweatshirt. "This is for Cari." He pulled out Laird's. "And this is Laird's. She hates them both." He stuck a finger through the hole on Cari's. "And she needs a new one. If you could help her figure out how not to stretch out her pieces, she'd consider you the greatest man alive." He shook his head. "I've heard of perfectionistic women, but Kenzie's utter disgust over her imperfect letter...."

"I've seen that with her schoolwork sometimes." Luke glanced over at an abandoned math book and frowned. "It might actually be the problem with her division. She's probably irked by remainders or something. Hadn't thought of that."

"Get the sweatshirt for her. Do it now. That way you can honestly say you could do it before I could." He pocketed his phone and shuffled back a step or two. "Let me know if I can do anything for you guys."

Once he'd climbed back into his cruiser, William pulled out his phone again and zipped a text message to Tina. FINALLY TALKED TO LUKE ABOUT KENZIE. ALSO ACCIDENTALLY SHOWED HIM YOUR TEXT. A BIT EMBARRASSING. STILL WISH I COULD WALK THAT BEACH WITH YOU.

Oʜ, Sʜᴀʙʙʏ Dᴀʏ

Chapter Twenty

Sunday, December 21ˢᵗ

"Oh, I thought we'd see her by now." Mrs. Ware's words held a hint of a rebuke—likely unintentional, but it rankled Vannie.

"I'm sure she'd like that, too." She offered the most genuine smile she could but a sigh escaped—one that didn't escape Mrs. Ware's notice. Vannie tried again. "It's hard with her upstairs and all alone. We're all trying to keep everything going, but between school for everyone, laundry for everyone, three meals and half the time four snacks a day, not to mention Christmas—"

Mrs. Ware's expression stopped Vannie mid-sentence. Her eyes bugged and her lips formed into a large O. "She's confined to her room?"

"Actually, her bed. I mean, she can take a quick shower when she needs it, and obviously she has to go to the bathroom, but...."

Panic filled Vannie as Mrs. Ware jumped into action. She pulled out a notebook—the very one she'd taken sermon notes in—and drew lines down the pages. Vannie tried to follow, but all it looked like she did was write her name, some word, and a phone number. Myra Vaughn passed, and Mrs. Ware stopped her. "I'm setting up meals for the Sullivan-Stuarts. Did you know Aggie is confined to bed—as in full bed rest?"

Mrs. Vaughn turned to Vannie eyes wide and looking nearly as shocked as Mrs. Ware had. "Is she, really? I thought she just had to take it easy for a couple of weeks—as a precaution."

What if I wasn't supposed to tell? I didn't know. I am totally dead. Vannie's throat stuck together as she tried to answer. "I think you should talk to Uncle Luke. He knows more than me. I just know we're going to be glad when we see her more than once or twice a day. We miss her."

The moment she finished speaking, Vannie regretted the words. *Too much... that was too much. When will I learn to keep my mouth shut?*

But before she could try to fix it, Mrs. Vaughn pointed down the pew closest to her. "Can you try to do a sweep of the pews? Make sure all the hymnals are in place and that the note paper isn't used up? We'll take care of this."

"Please talk to Uncle Luke. I didn't know that people didn't know," she murmured. "Maybe it was more private than I thought."

Nothing Mrs. Vaughn could have said would have comforted more than her assurance that if she wasn't supposed to say something, he would have told her. "He's probably just too busy to think, 'Oh, if I called the church, maybe they could handle a meal or twenty to save us some of the hassle.'"

Ears straining to hear anything she could, Vannie moved through the rows at the front of the building as quickly as possible, but as she reached the middle, she slowed. Josiah found her there, flipping through each individual piece of notepaper as a diversionary tactic. "Forget your notes?"

"Just making sure they're all unused. Mrs. Vaughn asked." She gave him a weak smile. "Are you going on the ski trip?"

"No, not really my thing." He stepped a little closer—not too close, but enough to hint at a desire for a bit of privacy. "Our family goes caroling with The Assembly every year. It's tonight at six-thirty. Maybe you and...." He hesitated before adding, "Laird would like to join us?"

Everything in her laughed at the idea that she could leave for an evening, but Vannie couldn't bring herself to say it. Instead, she shrugged, replaced the notepaper, and straightened a hymnal. "I'll ask Uncle Luke. It might make Aunt Aggie happy. She's feeling bad that we can't do all our usual stuff." As much as she didn't want to do it, Vannie added her own caveat. "But I think I'd need to bring Ellie and Tavish, too."

"Great! I'll be praying for that." He pointed to the other side. "I'll go get those. Then maybe we can go watch the kids play for a bit?"

His words couldn't be mistaken. *You want to talk to me with relative privacy. Wow. Well, Uncle Luke and Aunt Aggie didn't say anything about that!* She nodded. "Sure. Thanks. Mrs. Vau—"

Her eyes swung to where the woman spoke to Mrs. Dyke and Bertha Seaman. *I messed up! Now I don't know what they said. I blew it. Just—*

"Vannie?"

"Yeah?" She spoke, but her eyes didn't leave the other ladies.

"Mr. Sullivan isn't upset. He said he just didn't think about it, but meals would be helpful. He's not going to be angry."

Nervousness did triple back flips in her stomach. Try as she might, Vannie couldn't meet his gaze or even search out Luke. Instead, she bit her lip and stared out the window, unseeing. "It wasn't my place...."

A gentle tap on her shoulder made her turn. Josiah stood just inches from her. "You answered a simple question. I was right there. I heard you. You weren't...." He fumbled for the right word. "—indiscreet."

"Are you sure?" Vannie couldn't tear her eyes from his. "They don't talk about it much—just between them. And they're so—" Again, she snapped her mouth shut and shrugged. *If they wanted us to know what's going on, they'd tell us. I'm sick to death of worrying about her, but maybe that's why they do it. Trying to get us to lean on the Lord or something. Yeah. That's probably it.*

Luke called to her from across the room. "—need your input."

A glance at Josiah—she expected an "I told you so" expression, but instead he just nodded encouragement. "Don't forget to ask about caroling. It'll be fun. I'll go watch the kids. Come out if you can?"

With a smile and a wave—and a determination to get

approval for caroling—Vannie hurried to help Luke. "Sorry. What?"

He pointed to Mrs. Ware and Mrs. Seaman. "They're planning meals for us—"

"At least until the first of the year—probably through a week or two after the baby," Mrs. Seaman insisted.

Luke and Vannie exchanged unnerved expressions, and Vannie spoke before he had a chance. "That would be great except for Christmas Eve and Christmas. We have those all planned. The kids are excited." Though she spoke truth, Vannie definitely exaggerated a bit. Luke backed her up, looking more relieved than irritated.

Mrs. Ware just nodded and smiled her approval. She turned to Luke and sighed. "You are blessed to have such wonderful helpers. We wanted a large family, but the Lord chose three sons for us. We're grateful, but sometimes…."

He must have seen the wince she tried to hide, because Luke nodded. "Trust me, it works the other way, too. Right, Vannie? We're grateful for every single one, but sometimes…."

"It used to be, 'But sometimes Cari….'" She sighed. "Now it's more like, 'But sometimes Ronnie….'"

"Most of the time it's that now. That boy…." Luke rolled his eyes. "I was sure we'd have him settled before the baby came, but now I'm not certain."

Though she hesitated, Vannie could see it in the woman's eyes. She had something to say—some nugget of wisdom that would either bless them or irritate them to no end. She waited… impatient. Dreading.

"Someone once told me somthing—back when the boys were all little, rambunctious, and in constant need of training and redirection."

"I'd love to hear it." Luke waited, eyes trained on the woman. Vannie watched him.

"She said, 'You keep acting like you can impart some knowledge, training, or wisdom and boom. You'll be done.'" Mrs. Ware sighed. "She said, 'You actually seem to think that *they* will be 'done.' Well, let me tell you this. Children are people— humans. And all humans are growing and changing, and hopefully improving until the day we die. Even Paul said we

266

were being 'perfected until the day of Christ.' You'll never be 'done' with your children. They aren't a check box on your to-do list.'"

Well, duh! He knows that.

"—ank you. I needed to be reminded of that. It's one thing to know it in your head, but it's easy to get caught up in the idea that it's our job to 'finish' them. They might finish *me*."

She didn't want to hear any more, but nothing Vannie could think of didn't sound rude and demanding. She stood there waiting, watching, weary. And Luke, in his usual quiet, observant way, caught her discomfort. "Vannie, they were wondering what meals Aggie might like most. I think it should be something that isn't time consuming for others as well."

Her first thought spilled from her lips before Vannie could stop it. "We have enough spaghetti sauce to last us until we hate it." She winced. "Sorry."

"Honesty is important, Vannie." Mrs. Seaman squeezed her arm. "I'll put 'no spaghetti with marinara' on the list. That way, if someone wants to do chicken or something else with a white sauce, they won't think it's just the pasta."

Only you could use being helpful as a chance to correct people. Yeah. Spaghetti is the pasta, not the meal. Anyone who has ever been to Olive Garden knows that. But, come on! People call it that. Everyone knows what we're talking about. It's just —

"Vannie?"

She jerked her head to Luke. "Sorry, I missed that. What?"

"They wondered about chicken. I think roasting chickens would be a bit much. We'd need two, wouldn't we?"

At least. With Tavish and Laird.... Vannie scrambled to make an alternative suggestion. "I think it would be easier and less expensive just to put some leg quarters in a disposable pan, douse with barbecue sauce and bring them over to pop in our oven." Another idea hit her. "And soup is easy, cheap, and filling. We love soup."

"Isn't she a treasure?!" Mrs. Ware beamed at her. "I told my Josiah, 'That one has a good head on her shoulders.'"

Why do people say that. Do people have bad heads? Are they malfunctioning?

Once again, Luke's voice called her from her thoughts.

Vannie's face flamed as red as her hair. She knew it—even without a mirror. As she tried to meet his gaze, he grinned. "Go on, now. We've got this. Give a ten minute warning to anyone you see, okay?"

As she buttoned her coat, Vannie sighed. "So much for being a 'treasure'. Can't even stick with the conversation."

He found Kenzie under one of the counter desks in the basement, working half-curled in a ball. "Kenzie? Can you come out here?"

"Um, don't come any closer!"

Luke managed *not* to smile or in any other way show his amusement of her "secret club" attitude. Kenzie's braids bounced as she scrambled from the cubbie hole she'd created for herself. The blanket that covered half the opening slithered to the ground in a puddle of fuzzy fleece. "What?"

He handed her the sweatshirt. "Heard you needed this."

Kenzie's eyes widened. "Mr. Mark—"

"Told me you needed it fast. He knew I could go before him, so he told me what to get." Luke leaned back against a folding chair and smiled at her. "You could have told me you needed help, sweetheart. I—"

"But they are supposed to be a surprise!" Her lip quivered. "I didn't think he'd tell."

"He knew I would want to help. And I won't look at anything you don't want me to, but I've done a lot of crafty things over the years with Grandma Libby. If you need help, just tell me."

Her protests grew louder. "But you can't. You have too much on your platter—plate—platter?"

"Both, I imagine." Luke grinned at her. "Maybe I do. Someone probably thinks so. But you know what?"

"What?"

His grin grew. "You're more important than most of the things I have to do. But I can't help you if you don't ask."

Tears erupted—flooding her cheeks and creating a river

flowing from her nose. Luke winced and pulled her close, preparing himself to become a human handkerchief. "I just want it all to be nice. Aunt Aggie is all lonely up there. And—" She couldn't continue.

Lord, are we putting our burden on them? I didn't think... With a quick prayer for wisdom, he pressed his cheek against her hair and tried to explain. "Sweetheart, Aunt Aggie would be proud of you for trying to surprise everyone, but it would break her heart if she thought you felt a burden to do it. That's not a gift, Kenzie."

"But Ta—" Kenzie snapped her mouth shut and buried her face in his chest again. "But...." She choked back another sob. "I just want them perfect."

His mother would rip his lips off for it, but Luke found himself sharing a story he'd heard once. "Remember when we drove up north and saw the Amish farms?"

"Yeah, that was cool. The girls in their pretty dresses and white aprons."

"Well, when we were in that store where we bought that quilt for Grandma Libby, the woman showed me this triangle that was supposed to be blue in the pattern, but it was green. She said, 'The Amish believe that only the Lord is perfect, so they make sure there's an obvious mistake in all of their quilts.'"

Kenzie crawled away, and Luke's heart constricted. *Now what do I do?*

A moment later, she pulled out an olive green sweatshirt with a wonky A on it. "Mine isn't on purpose. Mine is just messed up!"

One look at the letter showed the problem. "Did you iron down the adhesive?"

"What 'hesive?"

His forehead furrowed. "Do you have directions?"

Again, the girl scrambled under the desk and back out with a sheaf of papers in her hand. "This. Mr. Markenson printed them for me. I tried to follow it...." Again, dejection entered Kenzie's tone. "I just can't make it work."

He glanced at the page and zeroed in on one line. "Did you iron down the stitch witchery really well? I think—"

"Uncle Luke! I didn't use any witchery! I know better. Mommy—"

269

But Luke shook his head and tried to stop her. "It's not like that. It's just a name for fabric glue that holds the pieces together until you can sew it down. I bet Vannie has some."

Kenzie, eyes wide and shock plastered on every centimeter of her face, shook her head. "I don't think so. Not Vannie."

"Want me to go see? I can show you how much easier it would be."

Oh, the uncertainty and *guilt* on the girl's face. She wanted it—badly. But the part of her that still considered anything even hinting of witchery as utterly unacceptable—it warred with her desire for perfection. "Well, if she has it, maybe you could pray over it?"

"It's not necessary, Kenzie, but I'll do it if it'll make you feel better. You get your stuff together and put it out there on the table. I'll get the iron and the stuff and be right back. We'll call it, 'stitch gluery', okay?"

"I like that better." Just as his foot landed on the lowest step, he felt Kenzie slam against his back. Her arms flew around his waist. "I love you, Uncle Luke. Thank you!"

It took time—time he felt as though he didn't have—but Luke turned, held her, promised her there was nothing he'd rather do than help her with her presents, and hurried upstairs.

An hour later, he counted out seconds for her while she ironed down her letters and he picked the stitches out of contorted ones. She picked up a navy shirt with a gold fleece "I" and held it up to show him. "Look how great it looks!"

"It's wonderful." He waited to catch her eye and smiled as she beamed at him. "I'm having fun, Kenzie. I needed this. Thank you for letting me help."

" —re I come!" Ian raced through the downstairs, into the library, under the table, and behind the chair. He scrambled into the living room, checked every nook and cranny, and back out again. Not under the dining table. Not under the kitchen table. Not in the pantry, the coat closet, or the mudroom. He shouted down into the basement for Luke. "Is Ronnie down there? Rules say he's not supposed —"

"He's not down here."

From his perch on the kitchen bar stool, Tavish listened, his mind whirling with possibilities. "Maybe you should try outside. Ronnie's not that good of a hider."

Ian appeared at his side. "The rules...."

"Well, he never follows the rules anyway. I'd try it." Tavish balled up his paper towel, aimed for the garbage can, and missed. *Of course.* Four tries—it took four. But the last one arced so perfectly, that it proved worth the wait. "Score!"

A primal yell preceded Ian's arrival. He glanced around and said, "Wait—where?"

Guilt pinged, but Tavish ignored it. "Sorry, no. Just made a perfect basket. Um, you really can't find him?"

"He's not *anywhere.* Where could he be?"

Tavish moved into action. "Okay, you go look outside— maybe try the tree house. You know how he loves that thing."

Again, Ian stated the obvious. "But we're not *supposed* to go up there without asking!"

"Sometimes Ronnie doesn't listen very well. Go look. I'll see if he went up to Aunt Aggie's room and work my way down." Ian made it to the door before Tavish called out, "If he's not out with the dogs or in the tree house, check with Mrs. Dyke and Ms. Murphy."

Ian's tone perked up as he dashed for his coat. "Okay!"

Bet you don't think to ask for a cookie for the brother who sent you when Mrs. Dyke offers you one. Hmph. It's Christmas cookie time, too.

Ronnie wasn't in Aggie's room, but she had a good suggestion. "Look and see if he crawled behind something and fell asleep. He always needs a nap after church. Luke probably forgot." Her eyes tried to hold his. "Is everything else okay, though? You look... upset."

"I might need help with a project, but I'd rather keep it a surprise if I can." Tavish paused at the door. "Can I get you anything? Are you hungry or snacky? Maybe a new book or movie?" His eyes moved to the stacks of school books lining one short wall. "Want to start on school planning? I could come up in a bit and show you where I am."

Her laughter—when was the last time he'd heard real

271

laughter from her? It filled the room and smoothed the rough patches on his heart. "You must be bored stiff or something, because you're not only offering to visit with me—voluntarily—you're offering to talk school."

"I didn't know we were allowed to come up and visit. I thought you had to rest—to take it easy. I keep trying to stay away except when you call for us when you feel up to it." Guilt weighed him down as he chewed his lip and watched emotions flickering across Aggie's face. "I'm sorry."

Her hands beckoned, arms outstretched, and she squeezed him tightly as he crawled up next to her. "I'm sorry, kiddo. You shouldn't have to feel like that. Maybe that's why I only see you guys when I call for you—if *everyone* is trying to keep from 'bothering' me, of course I'd be left alone."

Tavish wanted to stay—to listen to her fun ideas for after the baby was born, to hear her sing a line of a hymn right in the middle of a conversation as if it were the next logical statement, to have her push him to open up about what he was doing in his life. She always made him talk, and as much as he resisted, it always made him feel better. "As soon as we find, Ronnie, I'll come back. Maybe I'll bring my project."

"Please do. I love seeing the things you make. That clock you made this summer...." Her eyes slid to the mantel where the steampunk-styled birdhouse clock rested in a place of honor. "So cool."

"Thanks. I like it. I'm thinking it might be neat to do one in an old book—for Ellie. Make wires come out of the pages with paper gears or something."

He saw it in her eyes—reluctance. She didn't want to do it, but Aggie sent him on his way. "Let me know when you find him, will you? Now I'm getting worried. And don't forget the bathtubs. He does like to crawl in with his blankets and pillows. Odd duck that he is."

Laughter—who could help it? Tavish shook his head and inched away again. "Good one, Aunt Aggie."

Bathtubs—clear. Bedrooms, under beds, and all closets—also clear. Tavish looked everywhere, including the basement. Ian arrived with a half-eaten cookie in one hand and a zip lock bag full in the other. "Mrs. Dyke sent lots of cookies. Want one?"

"I'll wait until Uncle Luke says it's okay. He might want them for dessert or something." Tavish looked around him. "Where's Ronnie?"

"Oh! They didn't see him. I looked in the van and the truck, too. The car's gone."

"Vannie went to get stuff for hamburgers."

"Chips?" Ian nearly dropped the cookie in his eagerness for his favorite snack.

It took more effort than maybe it should have, but Tavish did manage not to roll his eyes. "Yeah. Whatever. Probably. Look, if we can't find Ronnie, I think we should tell Uncle Luke. And Aunt Aggie." He winced at hearing himself couple her to the end of his train of thought. "I'll tell Uncle Luke and grab something to take up to show Aunt Aggie."

Luke's feet thundered to the top of the stairs. From the pitter-patter Tavish heard seconds later, Kenzie was right behind him. "Okay, where have you looked again?"

"Um, everywhere? Ian went next door and across the street—checked the truck and van."

"Tree house?"

Tavish nodded. "Yep. And all the bathtubs, closets—"

Before he could go on to mention every piece of furniture the boy could hide behind, under, or in, Kenzie piped up. "I can't believe he's not in your cubbie. He loves—"

Tavish's eyes widened, and he dashed for the door to his under-the-stairs closet. "Noooo… he wouldn't!"

"You didn't check?" Luke sighed as he followed. "He'll be in there."

He was—sound asleep atop the covers Tavish had used to hide his latest creation—just in case someone opened the door while he ate his snack. "Noooooooo!"

"I think you're being a bit—" Luke didn't have a chance to finish.

"Is he on—"

Angry tears—tears that shamed and embarrassed him—sprang to his eyes, but Tavish blinked them back. "It's gotta be ruined. I don't know why I try to do anything with him around. He always finds a way to ruin everything. And of course, we're getting another great little demon-lition engineer. Aren't we

273

lucky?"

Before Luke could reprimand him—before Luke could *stop* him—Tavish rolled Ronnie off the crushed masterpiece. With the rumpled, wrinkled mess in his arms, he tore up the stairs to Aggie's room. He plopped it as close to her "lap" as possible, watched it slide off again, and flopped back on the bed, still fighting back repeated waves of unexpected emotion.

"What happened?"

"Your son ruined it. Went in my room and crawled all over the bed where I had it hidden. Fell asleep on it."

The words didn't sound serious enough—not at first. Tavish tried to reword them to show the gravity of the offense. "I spent hours on that. There's no way I'll finish another one in time. Or if I do, someone else won't get theirs. He never *listens!* Why can't he just do what he's told?!"

"Someone has been watching Narnia a bit often. That's not quite verbatim—"

Tavish jumped up and raged as he inched to the door. "I don't care! He ruined more than just all that work. This was my most intricate one yet, too! He ruined someone's Christmas gift, because I'll never get one done now. I was pushing it as it is. If we had schoolwork this week...."

Aggie beckoned him and waved someone at the door back. Tavish suspected it was Luke. *Great. Now I'll be in trouble with both of them. And I don't even care, I don't think. This is just not fair. And I don't care if life is fair or not. If we couldn't get away with that stuff, how come he gets to? It's like we're the unwanted step-children and he's the bratty favorite who can do no wrong.*

" —have to do something about Ronnie. Every time I think we've got him settled, he proves we don't."

Got that right.

"But, Tavish?"

Here it comes. The criticism sandwich. Admit you blew it, chew me out for being honest about him, and then admit you'll have to do better. Five... four.... Tavish realized he hadn't answered. "Yeah?"

"It doesn't matter how right you are, and you have every right to be upset, you can't just lash out like that at everyone."

"But he can lash out and kick Ellie because she wouldn't let him have his way. He can ignore rules and ruin things—"

"Stop!" Aggie waited for him to stop outwardly seething before she continued. "Again, I think everything you're saying is right, but you know what isn't right?"

He nodded and pushed off toward the door. "Yep. It's not right that the 'wards' have to suck it up and deal with the fact that the bio kids get everything their way and we're just *in the way*."

Aggie's voice followed him all the way to the first floor, but Tavish ignored her. He snatched up his jacket, ignored Luke as well, and bolted from the house. The worst part—with six inches of snow in the yard and more along the ditches, he couldn't walk fast and there wasn't anywhere but Mrs. Dyke's to go—not without getting cold.

"I wish Daddy was here—or I was there."

The living room pressed in around him. Instead of enjoying the magical glow of Christmas lights with the rest of the house blanketed in darkness, Luke felt each one as a pin prick. *I suppose it's a good think they aren't "twinkling," or I'd be poked repeatedly.*

While he sat and waited, the house and nearly everyone in it slumbered. Aggie had mocked him for his over-confidence. *Perhaps she was right, but….*

A creak—was it a stair? A floorboard? A piece of siding shifting in the fierce wind doing its best to break through the cozy walls of their house? *Strange… a house this size – cozy. Who would have thought?*

The faintest whisper of a voice reached him, but no one stood there. "Uncle Luke?"

Oh, thank you, Lord. I'd almost conceded to Aggie's superior intuition. "Come on in, Tavish."

Just a year or two prior, the boy would have raced across the room and flung himself into Luke's arms. This time, he shuffled in and curled up in the corner of the couch where Aggie usually preferred to sit. Luke's throat constricted at the realization of just how long it had been since they'd sat just like this—talking. A nightly ritual had become a semi-distant memory in such a short amount of time.

"I need to apologize."

He heard a "but" in Tavish's tone. Waiting didn't work. The boy sat there, not meeting his gaze, not saying another word. After a minute or so, Luke tried to draw him out. "Finding it hard?"

"To do it honestly? Yeah. I'm *not* sorry. I want to be, but I'm not."

Again, his heart squeezed. A single light flickered and faded on the tree. There was something semi-symbolic in that. Luke tried again. "I can work with that." As his heart prayed for wisdom, Luke tried to say the rehearsed words he hoped were right. "I hope you know that I'm not upset with you for how you feel."

The boy's head shot up. "You're not?"

Luke shook his head. "Not at all. But I bet if you think about it for a minute, you'll be able to tell me just what bothered me."

"I don't have to think. It's what bothers *me*."

Am I going too far if I say it? Lord, stop me if I shouldn't. "There was a lot of truth in what you said." Luke allowed those words to sink in for a moment before continuing. "Then again, there were a lot of false assumptions, too." He tapped Tavish's arm and gave the boy a weak smile. "No one ever thinks you are anything but our beloved family. Life without every single one of you— unbearable. Never think otherwise."

Tavish tried. Luke watched his head move as if to look up and then drop down. "Sometimes...." Despite every effort to explain, the boy shook his head and released the world's most dejected sigh.

"Can you do something for me?" Even as he asked, Luke begged the Lord for mercy. At Tavish's nod, he tried yet another experiment. "Do you remember when Aunt Aggie first moved into the house in Rockland?"

"Yeah...."

"Remember when Cari cut off her pony tails and when she and Lorna did the spit balls all over the ceiling?"

Tavish grinned. "Toilet paper bombs. They got them all wet and threw them up there—they stuck. It was so funny." He sighed. "Aunt Aggie was hurt then, too—the first time she sprained her ankle."

It seemed wrong—*unkind*—to bring up a person's past

mistakes as an object lesson for someone else. But what else *could* he do? Desperation drove into a potentially disastrous turn to the conversation. "Do you remember what Cari was like back then? Do you remember how Aggie despaired of ever getting her to stay out of trouble?"

"You're saying it's the same thing?"

"Well, I'm saying Ronnie's about that age, and we've had a bit of upheaval right in the middle of it—just like with Cari and Lorna." He swallowed hard. "I don't want to make excuses, Tavish. I also don't want to cast Cari's mistakes up to her. She's older, better behaved, and more self-controlled. But she was a toddler then—just entering the preschooler age."

Tavish slowly nodded as he listened. "I guess...."

"I'll be honest, Tavish. I was pretty cocky. I had a mom who helped Aggie get past the rough spots. I thought I knew everything I needed to do in order to avoid that kind of trouble, but we're not usually as diligent as we think, *and* we are raising children, not plugging formulas into a computer or robot. We let things go. We let other things be more important to us than our children."

Tavish frowned. "Like what? You're always doing stuff with us. I—"

"But we let those kinds of things come before Ronnie's training. Homeschooling, the houses, even this house. I could have gotten a bathroom repaired, fixed the furnace, and we'd have been fine here. Aggie didn't need me to be gone all day every day." A new thought—one that sickened him—drove out all others. "Tavish? Oh, man...."

"What?"

The words had almost spilled from his lips before he could stop them. But only after a moment's pause, he spoke anyway. "I think we—or *I*, anyway—have been counting on you kids to help notice and keep him in check. That was wrong of us."

"Well, we see stuff—"

Luke interrupted him. "No, Tavish. No. If you happen to, sure. But it's wrong of me to rely on that, and I have. Helping one another is one thing. Families do that." A deep sigh emptied his lungs. They ached. His heart ached.

Everything in the conversation shifted. Tavish stood to go.

"Thanks, Uncle Luke. I'm sorry that I was so rude—now I am, anyway. I'll apologize to Aunt Aggie tomorrow."

"You can if you want, but I can tell her, too."

He saw it—that strange expression Tavish always got whenever the children's father came up in a conversation. "Daddy wouldn't like it. He'd say, 'You blew it. Now apologize.' So I will." Halfway to the stairs, Tavish turned back. "Uncle Luke?"

"Hmmm?"

"I love you."

His eyes closed with the speed of a garage door opener. Luke exhaled almost as slowly. "Love you too, son."

"Know what else?"

Luke's throat constricted. "What's that?"

"I love that you call me son. It feels like I still have a real dad—not just an uncle that got stuck with me because he fell in love with my aunt."

"No one could ever feel stuck with you, Tavish." Throat aching with repressed emotion, Luke tried once more. "You made my dreams of being a dad come true overnight. Most guys don't get that."

A suspicious sniffle preceded Tavish's next words. "If Daddy had to die, I'm glad God gave us you for a second dad."

And how can anything be better than that?

OH, IT CAN'T BE

Chapter Twenty-One

Monday, December 22ⁿᵈ

As Luke dressed, he shared the previous evening's conversation. Aggie seethed in a stony silence that would have been dangerous had she not been shackled — or so it felt — to her bed. With each word her anger grew and her despair increased in exponential increments.

"—thought you were right. I mean, it was long after everyone was in bed, but he's always come before."

"He apologized?"

"Not at first. He was feeling like he *should*, but it wasn't genuine—"

That, she couldn't let him get away with, husband or not. "And you have the right to decide if his repentance is genuine? Really, Luke?"

"No...." He turned to her. "Are you feeling okay?"

"Stop blasting me with my supposed hormonal issues and answer my question, please." Aggie almost forgot to tack on that "please" and it rankled. *I can be civil, even if he's being overbearing. He drags me into the doctor's office against my will and thinks he can just run my life after it. Well, that's not exactly Biblical. I vowed to submit, not to allow myself to be coerced into submission.*

"Ooookay. Mibs, I don't see how this is a profitable

discussion. You're obviously—"

"Stop it! I'm serious, Luke. I just want a stupid answer!"

Shock, horror, pain—they rippled through his expression much like breaking news scrolling across a TV screen. Luke swallowed hard, stood with his eyes trained at the end of the bed, lost in thought—or prayer. Likely both.

And it'll take an hour for you to come to the point.

"Aggie, *Tavish* said he felt like he should apologize, but he didn't feel it. It wasn't *genuine*. That's all I meant."

Before Aggie could formulate a retort, Kenzie burst into the room. "Cari and Lorna decided to do the dishes for us—and squirted the wrong soap into the dishwasher. There are bubbles *everywhere!* What do we do? Vannie's trying to clean it up, but they just keep coming."

Luke bolted from the room. Aggie flopped back on the pillows, whacked her head on the headboard, and tried to fight back the tears that sprang to her eyes. Her phone buzzed with a picture of the Costa Rica shore and a selfie. A moment later, a Snapchat arrived. "Hey, girl. I was just thinking of something. You know how we're always talking about how you need a break—a vacation from all the work? Well, you *got one!* How cool is that? Now, I'd rather you be here with me on this gorgeous beach, but you know what? Find some cool ocean videos, play 'em on the laptop, and kick back. Get one of the kids to make you a fruity drink and have Luke massage your feet. It'll be like you're in the spa with me. Love you! Miss you. Gotta go. Love ya! Bye!"

"Good thing you aren't here. I swear, I'd throw a pillow at you."

Screeches and squeals from downstairs sent her scrambling for her ear buds. With her journal on her lap, Aggie reached for a pen as well. *Might as well write it out before I spit it out at the wrong time.*

What do I do now? I've got kids feeling like we're playing favorites, a house that is in chaos—dish soap in the dishwasher!!!! And of course, nothing is going right. I spent the past three or four years trying to create a routine that kept us afloat. I'm used to being focused—competent, even.

Look, I'm reasonably intelligent. But right now, I feel stupid and probably look even stupider. All the people who said, "Don't you think you have enough kids already?" Maybe they were right. Maybe having another baby was just too much. I mean, we made it through morning sickness — the worst time ever — without too much hassle. We made it through the second trimester with everything just perfect. I felt confident. Okay, I kind of felt like, "In your face!" about it. I'll admit it. I mean, our house didn't fall apart while I was puking. The kids kept up the schoolwork. And Ronnie wasn't making enemies of his cousins.

Then Luke drags me off to the doctor because he decides I'm in some kind of early labor, and now look. I'm stuck in bed. My house is a shambles, the kids are a mess, and our relationship is shot. I don't even want to pray anymore. What's the point? Yeah, I know. The baby will come, my hormones will make me all lovey dovey and voila. Instant love of the Lord again. But seriously? Shouldn't I be leaning on Him more than ever? Why does that sound like some kind of cruel joke?

The sudden urge to relieve herself of the half ounce of water she'd consumed in the twenty minutes since waking sent Aggie scrambling from the bed. Her journal lay open, pen marking the spot. Her heart suggested that she should close it — hide it. But Aggie refused. *I should be able to leave something personal out without everyone digging into it.*

Her conscience protested. *You told Luke he could read it whenever he wanted. He's going to come in....*

But Aggie resisted — rebelled, even — at that idea. *He should know better. Just because someone tries to be transparent doesn't give someone else the right to take advantage of that.*

The accusation — unjust, and she knew it. But Aggie shuffled into the bathroom, out, and right back in. Constipation — something the doctor hadn't warned her about. Despite a daily regimen of stool softeners, guzzling water despite the increased trips to the bathroom, and a half-eaten bag of prunes that now resided permanently on her bedside table, relief eluded her.

Washing her hands — the most mortifying part of every day. Aggie stared at her reflection, her limp, greasy hair hinting that she'd have to ignore Luke's concerns and take yet another quick shower. For the first time in days, her heart constricted at the idea of worrying him — again.

You're too hard on him. You're being awful — a spoiled, bratty child who doesn't get what she wants so she makes everyone around her miserable. Libby would spank you if she knew it. Iris.... That thought produced a lump in her throat that Aggie doubted she'd be able to swallow. *Repent! Must. Repent.*

Aggie jerked open the door, determined to make a new start with her family, saw Luke standing there reading the journal entry she'd just penned, and embarrassment flooded her. Her lips parted as she struggled to explain, but Luke turned and stared at her, pain filling his eyes. He closed the journal and stepped back. "I know you said I could read it. I don't think I will again." He gave her a weak attempt at a smile — one that didn't even turn up the corners of his mouth — and backed toward the door. "I'm praying for you. I love you. I'm sorry."

With those words, Luke bolted for the door.

Aggie gripped her stomach, squeezed her eyes shut, and gasped for air.

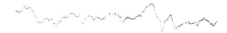

Breathing — impossible. Instead, Luke stumbled down the stairs with his chest squeezing the life out of him. Another week had arrived, and with it, a wife he didn't recognize any more. *It's like what Mrs. Vaughn said a few months ago about how she'd never take Marcus up on his request for her to nag him about things. "He'll want it — or thinks he will — until I actually do it. Then he'll get mad at me for doing exactly what he told me to do. I'm not doing it. If he wants a nagger, he can find an app for that."*

I knew better than to think she could handle me reading what should be private stuff. She's not Willow. I know that. I need to apologize — later.

Just as those thoughts broke through the barrier to his lungs and allowed him to inhale once more, he overheard Lorna crying in the library. A glance around the corner showed her head pressed to the table, her hands stretched out before her — utter dejection in every syllable she spoke. " — but nothing is the same now. Not since Aunt Aggie got stuck in bed all day."

"I know, but the baby will come soon. And then she'll be better. And now that we have people bringing us dinner and offering to help with laundry and stuff, maybe they can spend more time together."

"Why do *they* need to spend more time together? *I* need to spend more time with her." Lorna's voice now rang out clear, true. No longer muffled by the table.

Cari spoke over Vannie's nebulous words about how married people needed time to talk and just *be* together. Cari had no such discreet scruples. "Because all they do is fight now. Aunt Aggie needs a lot of hugs and a good dose of Jesus."

A snicker escaped before he could stop it. Vannie couldn't control a giggle either. "What?"

"That's what she told me when I got in trouble last time. She said, 'I think you need a great big hug and a good dose of Jesus.' And it worked! I think *she* needs one, too."

"Well, I don't know how to get her one. I doubt Uncle Luke does, either. I sure wish Grandma Libby wasn't so busy. She always makes Aunt Aggie see things." How something as simple as a workbook sliding across a table could be so recognizable, Luke didn't know. Vannie clicked a mechanical pencil and asked Lorna to write her spelling words three times each. "Don't forget to look at the words. Practicing the wrong way isn't going to help."

That's it. I've got to go talk to Uncle Zeke. If the kids.... His heart constricted. Luke stepped into the library and called Vannie out. It took every bit of self-control he possessed not to break down at the concern in her eyes. "Look, I've got to go do something. Can you hold down the fort? Aggie's... not herself today. I wouldn't leave if it wasn't im —"

"Go ahead. We're good. And Mrs. Dyke is right across the street if we need anything." Her quick hug hinted that she might know exactly what he needed.

You've become a young woman overnight. Luke couldn't help but take a moment and cup her cheek. "I'm so proud of you."

Luke grabbed his coat and jumped in his truck. The heater blasted cold air for the first two miles, but his half-frozen heart almost didn't notice. Fields whizzed past — farms. The highway to Brunswick. But at the road to Uncle Zeke's, Luke sat idling in the middle, avoiding the plowed drifts on either side. A moment later, he backed up the road, back onto the highway, and sped away from Brant's Corners and Brunswick. One farmhouse — two. Chad and Willow's place. The road to Fairbury. He rounded the curve that led to the highway and Lake Danube.

A memory emerged—slow, painful. As the truck whizzed past the rest stop and sped toward the Rockland Loop, Luke remembered the afternoon after his father had died and the dozen or two times he'd made that trek around the Loop before his gas tank insisted on a refill, and his wallet sent him back home again.

The day felt similar. Equally cold, equally bleak—both outside and inside his heart. Luke merged onto the Loop and allowed himself to increase his speed just enough to keep up with traffic. At the halfway mark, he saw the exit for Westbury. Auto-pilot kicked in and drove him off the Loop and onto the city streets. Through one division—to another. The neo-classical houses loomed before him, and nerves took over once more.

Do I even have the right to go to them without telling her? Asking *her?* Luke glanced around him, as if anyone could see or hear his thoughts, before continuing. *Fine. If Uncle Christopher is home, I'll go on in. If not, back to Uncle Zeke's. Or Mom, maybe—no. She's too close. She might just side with me out of maternal whateverness. Maybe.*

But Christopher Tesdall's new sedan sat parked in the drive, killing Luke's expected argument that he couldn't see through the garage door. *He's either just getting home or on his way out. Either way….*

But he couldn't escape the fact that if he did it—if he drove off again, he'd still have no help. *And Uncle Christopher has such a soft spot for Aggie.*

He backed up in front of the house and parked. Snapped off the ignition with such force it should have broken the key. Luke's hands gripped the steering wheel as he begged the Lord for wisdom, direction, and most of all, discretion. Then, before he could talk himself out of it, he bolted from the truck and scrambled up the half-shoveled walkway. *It's kind of slick. Needs some work. I'll do that before I go.*

Marianne opened the door; her head turned to answer something. "Just the mail—" At the sight of Luke she added, "—child of Libby's."

Luke stepped inside with a grin. "Different way of putting it."

But Marianne's eyebrows drew together and her forehead wrinkled. "That is probably the most painful grin I've ever seen.

What's up?" She led him to the kitchen, offering him half a dozen different food choices all along the way. "Oh, and there's some left over pot pie."

Saying "no thanks"—not an option. Instead, Luke latched onto the one that he hadn't had in a while. "Pot pie would be great. Thanks."

Christopher stood, abandoning a bowl of steaming chili, and pounded Luke's back in a big hug. "We don't get to see you often. How's Aggie and the kids?"

Those words destroyed any hope of him keeping his self-control intact. Tears flowed down his cheeks. He jerked out a chair, dropped into it, and covered his face with his hands in a weak, futile attempt to gather some self-control.

He couldn't say when Christopher first began praying aloud, but rather than calming his emotions and the fears he could no longer repress, the prayer only intensified them. Each word wrapped snake-like cords around his heart, every one squeezing tighter than the last, until Luke feared it would break. Arms wrapped around his shoulders. A cheek pressed against his hair— *Aunt Marianne. Everyone underestimates her.*

"Why don't you tell us about it?" she whispered. A kiss, another squeeze, and Marianne returned to fixing him a plate as if she'd never stopped.

As much as he ached to unload the burden that crushed his heart, Luke couldn't manage to speak. Christopher began a round of twenty-questions—all yes or no. "Is anyone hurt? The way he hastened to add, "I mean physically," told Luke that Marianne had growled at him.

He began to shake his head and stopped. With effort that felt superhuman to him, Luke shrugged and murmured, "Well, Aggie...."

"Libby said she's had to rest a bit this time—something about lots of Braxton-Hicks?" Marianne retrieved a plate of food from the microwave and set it before him. "Milk, water, or coffee—it's about all we have right now."

Luke started to say coffee, but the steaming plate of beef pot pie changed his mind. "Milk, please." He reached out and grabbed Marianne's hand. Though he couldn't meet her gaze, Luke stared at her hand, squeezed, and whispered, "Thank you."

Once more, he found himself engulfed in a hug. Eyes closed, Luke inhaled the fragrance of her clothes, the aroma of the meal, the hint of lemon from the kitchen cleaner she always used. The scents mingled together into something nearly tangible. It said "home" despite his home and his mother's home never having the same scents. *It's family — there's something undeniably familiar and warm about anything connected with a loving family.*

"Luke?"

When his eyes flew open, Luke blinked, confused. "Yeah?"

"You fell asleep, son."

Raw emotion balled in his throat until he couldn't swallow. *I get you, Tavish. Having someone care enough about you to love you like a son when your father isn't there anymore — more priceless than any Hallmark story.*

"Luke?"

"Sorry." He picked up a fork and stared at the glass of milk before him. *Where'd that come from?* Christopher's words came back to him. "Wait, what? I *fell asleep?*"

"Just sitting there. I only woke you when I thought you'd land face first in your plate like Ronnie did that time. Remember?"

Ronnie, Tavish, Aggie — why he'd come all flooded back at him. "Yes." One bite told him he'd slept longer than he thought. Marianne hopped up, grabbed the plate, and nuked it again.

"You're scaring me a little, Luke," she scolded as she passed it back. "What's wrong?"

Between bites, and vain attempts to choke back tears that only made things worse, Luke spilled the story. The further vandalism, Aggie's enforced bed rest, the children's neediness, and his inability to cope. "I'm doing my best. I am. But nothing seems to go right. Vannie's got a boy following her, and Laird has a dozen girls, it seems. He hides in the van after church, but only *after* trying to get me to let him stay home and...." Luke added air quotes, "take care of Aggie. Ronnie is so out of control that the other kids resent him. And who knew that ice cream sandwiches are like crack for little kids. Turns them into monsters — even *Lorna.*"

Christopher's and Marianne's chuckles filled the room. Christopher found his voice first. "Oh, I wish I'd recorded that.

You would love to hear it—in about three weeks."

As much as he craved the released tension that comes with a good laugh, all Luke could do was fight not to cry again. He wiped away tears with the back of his hand and dove into the pot pie. "Remind me. Right now…."

"It sounds a bit overwhelming, I know. But surely your mother can help with—"

"She has Christmas to deal with—all the grand kids, and you know how she is about gifts. Speaking of which, I can't work. That means there's no money coming in. Our accounts dwindle every day—twice as fast as I expect them to. I don't know how we're going to meet January bills without dipping into savings. And it's lower than usual now. I *need* to sell that house."

Marianne dropped into a chair and pulled it close. "Just *why* is everything so expensive right now? You've never been extravagant. Are the doctor's bills—?"

"No." Despite his rudeness, Luke interrupted with an explanation that would likely make things even more confusing. "We have good health insurance—thanks to the trust."

"But surely the Social Security and the annui—"

"Goes straight into their accounts, Aunt Mari. I'm not using it to support my family."

Christopher cleared his throat—a sound that usually meant one thing. Rebuke. "Son, that's pride talking. Those kids had wise parents who knew how to provide for them. They intended—"

"And it'll be there—for college or starting a business. Hey, at the rate it's growing, and with everything they left, they could each buy a house if aren't extravagant." At Marianne's next protest, Luke shook his head. "I have a family. I want to—*need* to, even—provide for them. The money is hard, but it's not the biggest problem. If we hadn't had all those repairs. Don't even *mention* the electric bill to Aggie. I don't know if she's thought of that. Who knows how long the doors and things were open before the power shut off after it all flooded."

Silence hung heavy over the table. Christopher broke it first. "What's wrong, Luke? Nothing you've said fits the… the…."

"The word you want is despair." Marianne's voice trembled just a little. "Is something wrong with the baby, Luke?"

He wanted to reassure them—insist that the baby was well,

but instead he shook his head.

Christopher's voice broke this time. "Aggie?"

Heedless of the basics of dining etiquette, Luke propped his elbows up on the table and hung his head in his hands. Marianne gasped. Christopher groaned. To no one's surprise, Marianne found her voice first. "Should you have left her? Why did you come here? What if she *needs* you? How serious is it? Are they considering a C-sect—?"

Luke's head snapped up. "What? Why would they do a C-section?"

"Well you said Aggie—"

The chair wobbled as he sagged against it once more. "It's her mental, emotional, and spiritual state. She's... she's not *Aggie*."

"Surely—" His agitation must have been visible, because Marianne stopped short. "Is it really that bad?"

If he answered, any hope of keeping Aggie's condition—or *conditions*, rather—would be gone. But he couldn't help her, despite every effort. *And what if I'm wrong. What if I'm the one who is out of sorts and seeing things all messed up? Then again, Uncle Christopher would tell me. He would.*

With his heart racing and his nerves pulled tauter with each word spoken, Luke described life in their home. "—and the kids miss it. They—"

Marianne's shock ripped through his explanation in one three-word question. "Aggie isn't singing?"

"No. And if I'm right, she isn't praying or reading her Bible, either. She's just *up there.*" Every bit of him resisted saying what he thought. Even his throat rebelled and choked as he added, "It feels like she's seething. It's like she considers this some kind of betrayal, and before I left—"

Again he hesitated, chewing his lip until he tasted blood. Admitting he'd read the journal would look bad on him. But maybe it should. *Maybe it doesn't matter what someone says. Maybe it's just another one of those, "Willow is different and no one else should try to emulate her" things.*

"We can't help if you won't talk, Luke." The absence of Christopher's "son" drove a knife into Luke's heart.

"Okay, we spent all that time at Willow's and Chad's place,

you know? Aggie loved Willow's journals and how Chad would read them to keep up with what was happening while he was away from home. He said it helped him see when she needed time alone or to know she was cherished. She said she loved knowing there was a record of their days and that she didn't feel guilty about not telling him about something. He could just read it."

"And Aggie wanted that?" Marianne winced. "Oh, Luke!"

"She's usually so self-aware. She knows what she likes and doesn't or if she doesn't know! So, when I gave her the journal, she said to feel free to read it anytime. And I did. And the words—" This time, all hope of hiding his tears failed. Luke broke down, weeping. His words—incoherent, and he knew it.

Marianne's arms engulfed him, and Christopher's hands gripped one of his and held it fast; he prayed. Marianne whispered words of love and comfort. Luke wept.

Despite the resistance that almost strangled his words, Luke found himself choking them out in choppy, semi-incoherent sentences. "—blames me. Don't understand. How did taking her in to see if everything was okay *cause* her early labor?"

"Oh, Luke, I don't think—"

He shook his head and jerked his hands away. Arms folded over his chest, he glared at the half-empty plate before him. "'*Then Luke drags me off to the doctor because he decides I'm in some kind of early labor, and now look. I'm stuck in bed.*'"

Luke blinked. "Didn't know I'd remember it that well, but I think that's verbatim."

"It's the hormones talking, Luke." Marianne pulled the chair closer, plopped down in it and rubbed his back as she spoke. "Pregnancy can create a sort of temporary insanity in some women. I wouldn't take it too much to heart. I'm sure once she's six or eight weeks postpartum, you'll see the wife you knew."

"I've been telling myself that. Or trying…." Luke gripped his hands before him in an effort to stop their shaking. "But I keep thinking of words being like seeds. In a sermon last week, Marcus kept saying that when we water the wrong seeds, we germinate wrong thoughts— ideas, even—and they grow in our hearts."

Christopher's nod showed he knew where Luke would take the conversation, but Marianne looked utterly confused. Luke directed his question to Christopher. "But how long can you water seeds of disbelief, despair, betrayal, faithlessness—how long can you do that and leave the ones that sprout the fruits of the Spirit dry…?" Luke swallowed a lump in his throat and finished in a ragged whisper. "Just how long can you do that before you kill the fruits you do want and grow the ones you don't?"

Half an hour passed—half an hour in which Aggie waited, almost praying for Luke to return. She picked up her phone half a dozen times to apologize. Each time, she set it back down, not sure she'd done anything wrong. *I was honest about my feelings. I didn't chew him out for reading it.* He *decided* —

A knock jerked her from her reverie. Kenzie stood just inside the door, a wad of fabric in her hands and a half-panicked look on her face. "Can you help me? I think I ruined it!"

Relief washed over her—*finally* someone *needed* her again. "Sure, honey. C'mere. What've you got?"

"Christmas present for Gramby Libby. See…."

The problem—glaringly obvious. The girl had tried to iron fleece to a white sweatshirt—probably using steam—and the fleece had bled. "I didn't even know fleece *could* bleed." She stared at the sweatshirt before picking at the letter. "I think I can get this off. Can I try?"

A couple of tears escaped the girl's overfull eyes, but Kenzie nodded. "If we *have* to…."

"We'll try to get it out, first. If not, I think you can make your letter thicker and it'll cover the pink."

It took a moment, but as Aggie ripped off the large red "L", Kenzie nodded. "Oh, I see what you mean. That'll work."

"Well, if it doesn't, we can put a big circle behind it or something. It'll be cute. I promise." She eyed the shirt. "Go down to the mudroom and grab that bleach pen. We'll try to wash it out." She winked at Kenzie. "Well, I'll get it on there, and *you* will wash it out or Uncle Luke will get grumpy at me."

"He just loves you."

The defensiveness in Kenzie's voice sent ripples of surprise through Aggie's heart. She nodded, murmuring something about knowing and understanding that, but the words tumbled about in her mind as she waited for Kenzie's return. *What's up with that?*

The experiment began the moment she squeezed the last of the bleach pen onto the last bit of pink. "Okay, let it sit for a minute and go throw this outside into the trashcan. I don't want the little guys deciding to try to play with it. When you get back, you can try to wash out the pink."

"Will it work?"

As much as Aggie wanted to reassure her, she'd had mixed results with those bleach pens, but no way would she let Kenzie work with a bottle. "One way or another, we'll make this shirt work. Or, if it doesn't, we'll ask Vannie to go get another one. It'll be okay."

"She can't. Uncle Luke is gone. No one else can drive in an emergency."

"Where's Luke? He didn't say he was going anywhere."

Only when Kenzie said, "Vannie thinks he needed some time alone with the Lord," did Aggie realize she'd spoken aloud.

"Oh, okay. Well, go toss that thing and we'll try this when you get back." Aggie waited until Kenzie made it out the door before she flopped back on the pillow, her arms cradling her now contracting belly, and struggled not to cry.

Each wave that came intensified, until she found it difficult to breathe. Panic threatened her, but Aggie stuffed it back down. *I've been through this before. I just know how to irritate that uterus. It's like it's connected to my emotions or something. So not fair.*

Kenzie waltzed into the room, ready to attack the shirt and stood stock still, staring. "Are you okay?"

"Fine. Just practicing for the real thing. Remember how I did that with Ronnie?"

The girl just blinked.

"Well, I did. Anyway, I want you to go in there and use the *cold* water to rinse out that bleach. Rub it together really well, and when you're done, use soap on your hands. I should have you get some gloves—"

"Wouldn't the water and bleach just soak through?"

Oh, brother. Never mind. Aggie grinned, hoping it looked like she laughed at herself instead of her niece, and nodded. "Probably. Go on ahead. Tell me how it works."

A scream a moment later told her how it *hadn't* worked. "Aunt Aggie! It's getting *bigger!*"

As Aggie crawled from the bed, she groaned. "So am I! Sheesh!"

But Kenzie hadn't exaggerated. You could see quite a discernible L where the red had once been—an L that feathered out onto the rest of the shirt. "I'm sorry, Kenzie I didn't think it would do that." She sighed. "We can do two things. Either we soak it in a bowl of water with bleach in it and wash it, or we do the circle we talked about. Which one do you want to do?"

Seconds passed—seconds that felt like quarter hours. Aggie gripped the counter and tried to ignore the pain radiating across her back and down her legs. *C'mon. Just choose. I* need *to get back in bed. Hate it when Luke is right when I want him to be wrong.*

"Which one would you do?"

Argh! But the blessing of the question hit her hard and fast—just like the contraction she couldn't hide this time. "Okay, I have to lie down first. But…." She managed to avoid a gasp—barely. "I would try the bleach in the bowl first. Because, if it doesn't work, *then* you can still do the circle. But the circle adds work." Each word sounded labored, even to Aggie's ears. She crawled in bed, took a huge sip from her glass of water, and sank down on her left side. "Go get Vannie. I'll tell her what to do."

Kenzie burst into tears. Another contraction ripped through her with a ferocity that she couldn't disguise. Pain overrode any hope she had of being patient and understanding. A primal yell she didn't know she possessed exploded from her. "What's your problem?!"

Shock, hurt, and worst of all, *fear*, filled Kenzie's face seconds before she bolted from the room, leaving the sweatshirt still dripping all over the bathroom floor. Aggie tried to call out for her again, but another contraction, less intense, but just as long as the others, began. She snatched up her phone and zipped a text to the family cellphone, praying Vannie was watching it. *I'll give it two minutes, and then I'm calling Luke.*

The thundering of feet on the stairs suggested Vannie *had* gotten it. "Hey, I just yelled at Kenzie." She couldn't continue.

This time, contractions couldn't be blamed. No, the hurt and angry expression in Vannie's eyes stopped her.

"I know. Laird's with her."

"I need to apologize, but can you help her with something, first? There's a shirt in the bathroom—probably still dripping all over the floor. Can you soak it in bleach for her? We need to try to get the dye out of it."

Vannie just stared—both at Aggie and then into the bathroom. If light bulbs actually did glow when understanding dawned, Vannie would have resembled a stadium at nightfall. Her face lit up as she bolted for the bathroom. "That's what she was talking about. I was lost. She's trying to keep this a secret from everyone—and succeeding in making sure we all know about it, of course—so when you said for me to help, she lost it. Then you yelled…."

Timing—it couldn't have been worse. A contraction began just as Aggie tried to acknowledge her wrong. "I *know!* I *said* that. Now will you *send her back in* so I can *apologize?*" Aggie took a long, slow breath, a swig of water, and another breath as she waited for the contraction to subside.

"Um, can I make a none-of-my-business observation?"

"Sure."

"Maybe it would mean more if you weren't still irritated when you apologized." And with that, Vannie disappeared.

The minutes slipped into the better part of an hour. Aggie, half asleep, didn't hear Tavish come in, but she did hear him whisper her name. "Aunt Aggie?"

The ligaments holding her baby in place screamed as she rolled over, but the contractions seemed to have abated. "Yeah?"

"I'm having trouble with something. Can I show you and get your help?"

Relief bubbled up inside her as she shifted into a semi-sitting position. "Of course. What's wrong?" Aggie stared at the large box in Tavish's hand, wondering what kind of crazy, likely robotic, concoction he'd produce. Instead, he pulled out a half-carved book. A top hat emerged from the page on one side, and on the other, a winged zeppelin slid around the page.

"I can't decide if this should be suspended from the book on a wire—you know, so it hovers over the top like it was really flying."

"Why wouldn't you do that?" Aggie picked it up and held it overhead. "Especially if you could make the little ribs on the wings to give it a bit of a 3-D effect. It would be cool!"

Tavish nodded as she spoke, but each nod added a degree of concern to his face. "I just wondered if it wouldn't mean that the book would be too fragile to survive. It's Ellie's Christmas present. I tried a few different ones for her, but then I found this book, and I had to try."

"And you're afraid that if you do it how you think you'll like it best, something will happen to destroy it?"

His face turned a mortifying puce as he tried to hide his embarrassment. "It's been known to happen around here."

"I'll buy a glass case for it—one of those things for footballs or whatever. We can keep it safe long enough for that to get here. Just give me measurements for it as soon as you can. I'll order it, and it'll be here in a couple of days. Gotta love that 2-day shipping."

It took longer than she would have expected for him to wedge the book into the box to his satisfaction, but once he did, he hugged her, asked if she needed anything, and rushed from the room—whether to get away from her before she bit *his* head off for some innocent remark or to work on the project, Aggie couldn't say. She could only hope for the latter.

Laird entered only a moment later. "Um, we have a mini problem down there—nothing too earth shattering, but...."

Her exasperation showed before she could hope to hide it. "What's the problem?"

"I can wait for Uncle Luke, but he looks beat." Laird inched toward the door. "I shouldn't have bother—"

"I shouldn't have made you feel like a bother." Aggie managed a smile she felt sure would look genuine and tried again. " Sorry. It's me, not you. Now, what's up?"

"Well, the tree got bumped—you missed the annual almost tree-tastrophe. Aren't you blessed?"

She grinned at the familiar joking. It *sounded* so normal. Something in her craved more. "What a *tree-mendous* joke."

"Ha!" Laird beamed. "Well, it jarred something in the stand, and now the tree is leaning *way* to the right. I swear I heard Ellie call it the 'leaning tower of Tree-za.'"

"This I've got to see." She inched her way to the edge of the bed, stood, and waited. Not a hint of a contraction emerged. Aggie grinned. "Yes! I've stopped irritating myself." She winked at him and shuffled toward the door. "See, it's not just you guys irritating me when you haven't done anything *to* irritate me. It's just my body's aching desire to be irritable. I swear, I don't recognize myself."

A glance over her shoulder showed a nightstand full of litter—a tissue or two, a few crumpled sticky notes, an empty bag of chips. She couldn't take it. "Can you dump that for me? And maybe fold back the blankets? I haven't changed the sheets in at least two weeks. That's just gross."

All the way down the hall, she found little things to correct. A crooked picture, a Lego that sent her dancing in pain and Laird panicking. "Are you okay? You should go back to bed. This isn't safe."

"Just promise me," she hissed between clenched teeth, "that you'll have them straighten out the Lego boxes later. I bet they're a mess."

Dust on the banister. Somehow she found it. A sock on a step. The first floor loomed with jackets strewn about the floor near the door. A trail of toys looped around the house without any evident connection from one to the next. Laird picked up each item as quickly as he could, but each successive toy increased her stress level until Aggie felt as if she'd pop.

She eased herself onto the couch, took a deep breath, and tried to turn straight in front of the tree. "Oh, I guess that wasn't necessary."

"What wasn't?" Laird, toys, shoes, and books spilling from his arms, paused beside her.

"Trying to face the tree. I can see it leaning without trying to be directly in front of it. Wow. How is it even upright?"

Laird dumped everything in a half-empty laundry basket on the dining table and came to shake the tree a bit. "It's surprisingly sturdy. I just think it looks like something out of Charlie Brown or Dr. Seuss."

"Aunt Aggie!" Vannie stepped into the room, hands on her hips and eyes flashing. "What are you doing down here? Are you trying to get me in trouble with Uncle Luke? Argh!"

Aggie and Laird exchanged amused glances. "The tree's crooked," he tried to explain. "I just wanted her opinion and she—"

"Had to come down herself." Vannie stepped closer and growled, "Couldn't you have just taken a picture with the tablet or something?"

"Didn't think about it?" Laird winced. "Sorry." Aggie listened as he pulled her aside. Ears straining, she barely heard him whisper, "She's freaking out about the house—much worse than usual."

"She's probably nesting up there with nothing to *do*. Now we'll spend the next week scrubbing the place from top to bottom to keep her from going nuts. Thanks a *lot* Laird. Christmas is in *three days!*"

Oh, how she ached to protest—insist it wasn't true. But even as she opened her mouth, her subconscious hinted that it wasn't such a bad idea. *You don't want to bring the baby home to a messy house. Maybe just a general pick up and rewash all the infant stuff. That shouldn't be too much.*

Just then, Aggie saw a streak of fingerprints across the wall. She swallowed hard. *And maybe scrub a couple of the worst walls. It can't hurt….*

"Um, I gotta get out of here."

"What?" Vannie stared at her. Laird's eyes widened.

"You don't mean—"

Aggie wrestled herself to the edge of the couch cushion and pushed upward. "I mean that if I stay down here one more minute, Vannie's predictions will come true." Her rear plopped back onto the couch before she could make it halfway up. "I'm seeing all kinds of stuff that. Is. Freaking. Me…."She hefted herself upward again. This time, she made it. "Out. Whew!" Aggie propped one hand on her back and slid the other over her belly. "Okay, time for me to—"

A contraction ripped the rest of her sentence from her mouth. A second later, it also ripped open the amniotic sac. Water poured down her legs and splattered at her feet. Aggie stared in shock. *Why is that puddle cloudy?*

Laird and Vannie stepped forward, their eyes trained on the

ever-growing puddle in fascinated horror. "Is that—?"

"Yep. Call Luke." When neither moved, Aggie clapped her hands together. "*Now!*"

Laird leapt for the land line. Vannie raced for the family cell—in the library. *She must have been keeping it close in case I needed her. Great.* A new thought hit her. "And someone has to call Dr. Malara."

Ellie wandered out from the basement with arms full of sketching supplies. "Why do you need to call your doctor? Do you have an appointment today?"

"I do now. Can you get me a towel and some clean, *dry,* clothes?"

Fifteen minutes—that's all it took for Aggie to go from calm and collected to near frantic. Contractions piled, one on top of the other, until she could barely walk to the door. "We've got to get everyone in the van. If Mrs. Dyke isn't home, you've got to take me. We can't wait."

"What about an ambulance?" Vannie's question came out in a half-panicked wail.

"Not happening. Talk about overkill. Just get me down those steps and in that van. We can do this. You'll just have to find Luuuu…." She exhaled with excess force. " —kkkeeehhh later."

Children screamed and ran out the door as Ellie ordered everyone into the van. With Vannie on one side and Laird on the other, she made it to the passenger seat, but hung over it, van heater blasting in her face. Aggie couldn't hope to get in. Another contraction held her captive, wringing every ounce of strength and endurance from her. She whimpered. "Call. Libby."

Don't know why I didn't think of it sooner!

Six and a half minutes—Aggie counted every, single one—is what it took for her to be able to half-climb, half-be-shoved into the seat. She reclined it as far as she could, propped her feet against the "dash" and exhaled long and slow. "Get me there. *Now.*"

"I can't *drive a woman in labor!*"

"Well, you don't have a *choice.* It's you or Laird. Pick one, but do it now." A glance in the rear view mirror showed Laird turning a particularly gruesome shade of green. "I take that back. *Drive,* Vannie!"

The van lurched forward before she could brace herself. Aggie could have sworn it shoved the baby down a couple of centimeters. "I thought being down like this meant you were pushing *uphill!*"

Laird found his voice. *"Don't push!* Whatever you do, Aunt Aggie. Do. Not. Push!"

A fit of giggles sent her next contraction into overdrive. She moaned—low, deep, guttural sounds—through the worst of it. "Vannie."

"Yeah?"

"Speed anywhere it's reasonably safe."

Deep emotion—*tears*—entered the girl's voice. "It's *never* safe to speed. *You* taught me that!"

"I mean if there's no other cars or children, just *do* it. Oh, and someone call William. Tell him to find us. *Now!*" The urge to scream nearly overpowered her.

"Aunt Aggie is mean when she's having a baby."

The words came from somewhere near the middle, but Aggie couldn't decide if it was one of the twins or Ian. "Sorry."

At the highway, Vannie floored it, and Aggie nearly slid off onto the floor. Her groan turned into a wail that then became another moan. Once more, she fought the urge to scream. "You. Must. Hurry."

A familiar—oh, how she wished it wasn't—burning began. Aggie's whimper became a full-fledged scream. "Noooooooooo!" A gasp. A scream. "No! Faster, Vannie!"

"Aren't you supposed to be breathing or something?"

That helpful tidbit came from Tavish. Aggie made a note to get him with an ice-cold squirt gun the first opportunity she had. "Do you think I'm holding my breeee*eeaath?!*"

Vannie snapped at him as she snapped on the turn signal. "Shut up, Tavish!"

The entire van erupted in an almost perfect, unified, "Don't say, 'shut up!'"

The turn-off to Brunswick loomed ahead. "Ooooh, I don't want the corner." The burning sensation intensified, and at that moment, Aggie realized she'd *changed* her underwear, not just removed it. "Heads up, eyes closed!"

Thank the Lord they listened without question this time. The semi-prayer of thanksgiving preceded her flinging the underwear over her shoulder and wriggling out of her coat.

"Aunt Aggie, what are you doing?"

"Trying to prepare to catch this thing!"

"Do. Not. Have. That. Baby." A whimper followed before Vannie added, "*Please!*"

Another giggle. Another gasp. A stronger burn. Aggie screamed when the next contraction ripped through her. "Can't. Stop. It!"

Deep breaths did little to stop the baby. And her body kicked in, despite every attempt to stop it. She bore down against her own will. With the involuntary push, that primal growl erupted and filled the close space of the van.

Cari and Lorna clung to each other. Ian screamed in abject terror. Ronnie sobbed. Laird covered his ears and prayed at the top of his voice. What the others did, Aggie couldn't tell. Another contraction ripped through her just as Vannie screeched into the Emergency Room drive and shot down the ramp to the ambulance bay. Aggie tried to tell her she wasn't allowed, but another yell—louder than the rest—filled her chest and exploded from her. And with it, the baby's head emerged.

"Help. Vannie. Catch." Again, she yelled. This time, Lorna and Cari joined the melee.

Vannie bolted from the van and scrambled toward the double doors. Laird screamed, "Noooo!" and bolted after her. Somewhere, in what felt like an out-of-body-experience, she heard him order Vannie back to help her. "I'll get help!"

Before Vannie could jerk open the door, Aggie felt the baby's shoulders and then that blissful relief when the baby's body slipped through. Her coat did little to provide the traction needed to keep the baby from slipping, but it did slow the child's descent to the floor. Cold air blasted her as Vannie jerked open the door.

Her eyes widened at the sight of the baby wriggling, half on the floor, half on the coat. Aggie screamed for Vannie to wrap the baby in the coat. "Hand her here!"

"How do you know it's a her?" A pause. A gasp. "It *is* a her!"

Two nurses—both men, of course—bolted from the building, Laird on their heels. The baby wailed. Aggie shivered. Vannie burst into tears as she handed the baby to Aggie. "I'm sorry. If I hadn't tried to go get help —"

"It's okay, really. It was smart." Aggie winced as another contraction attacked. "I didn't even think of it."

A gurney — where had it come from? — appeared. The men helped her to it, and as they half-lifted her, Aggie thanked the Lord for men. *Who knew I'd be grateful for that?*

A woman took the coat-wrapped baby from Vannie's arms. Aggie watched as she jerked her head toward the van. "You'll have to move that. Sorry."

From her spot on the gurney, the last thing Aggie saw was the van with her children backing out of the ambulance bay and disappearing from sight. She turned to the nurse holding her baby. "I'm early — too early. And I think my placenta just detached." She frowned. "Did you clamp the cord? Cut it?"

The woman nodded.

"When?"

"It's the first thing we did, hon."

With that, she collapsed in a fit of weeping. "I want Luke!"

LUCAS, THEY OUR CHILD HAVE TAKEN

Chapter Twenty-Two

Wrapping paper rolls lined the counter, and boxes with names written in Sharpie marker stood piled around the floor beside her. Libby Sullivan stood at the island with a box marked "Rodney" and eyeballed the paper selection. Cutesy animals and elegant foils—definitely out. That left plaid, stripes, and winter birches with cardinals in the branches. She rolled the cardinals aside and stared at the rest. Candy cane stripes rolled away, too. Wide green and red stripes, or Stewart plaid?

It took half a minute to decide on the plaid. "It will match the—"

Her phone sang out "What Child Is This?" mid-decision. With a sigh that immediately produced guilt, Libby set down her scissors, snatched up the phone and stared at the name without bothering to tap the screen. "Oh, Marianne, I can't take time for last minute shopping today. I'm sorry, but I *need* to get this done. I want to go see Luke and Aggie and the kids." The phone seemed to grow louder with every word. She capitulated. "Hello?"

The voice on the other end didn't sound quite like Marianne—hushed, gravely, it sounded as if she had a cold or a sore throat. "Why didn't you *tell* us Aggie and Luke needed help?!"

"Marianne?"

"Who else would call from my phone? Libby, your son!"

301

Cold pain gripped her heart. "What about Luke? What are you talking about?"

"Aggie's pregnancy? Why didn't you tell us they were struggling? We'd have come. Willo—"

Again, Libby repeated the question. "I don't know what you're talking about. What about the pregnancy? She's on limited duty—as a precaution. I've been over there a few times during the past couple of weeks, but she's usually been resting. Everyone—"

"No, Olivia! Aggie is on strict bed rest. She's struggling, too. If you could hear your son…."

Libby grabbed a chair and lowered herself into it. A calm, steadying breath, closed eyes, a cry for patience. She tried again. "Luke? Why are you over there?"

And the words spilled out. Libby sat transfixed by the story unfolding before her. Silent, remorse-filled tears slid down her cheeks as innocent phrases from the children filled her mind. *"Can't, because Aunt Aggie needs to rest." "Uncle Luke can help me — maybe. He has to make dinner first." " — play a game with us? Vannie is getting groceries, and Uncle Luke is trying to help Aunt Aggie."*

"They didn't say. I kept hearing that she needed to take it easier this time. No one said—" An enormous lump choked back her words. She strained to swallow it and finished. "No one said that there was any real risk. I've been so busy I didn't *look* at what was going on."

Dead air—it lasted for what seemed like an hour. Marianne's voice broke the silence with a ragged sigh. "I want to say I would have noticed, but I probably wouldn't have either. You know how Luke is. He can be very close with personal stuff. And he's so stubbornly determined to do this parenting thing on his own."

"Well, so were we!" Libby couldn't let that one go, but her conscience urged her to soften it. "I remember telling Mama, 'You had your turn. I want to do it myself.'" A chuckle escaped at the memory. "She said I sounded like I did when I was two!"

"No, no. I'm talking about stuff like the money. Did you know they're struggling financially with all this, but he *still* won't touch the insurance or benefit checks?"

Libby did know they wouldn't dip into what they considered to be the kids' money, but she hadn't realized things had gotten that lean. "I'll talk to him. Why did he go to your place? Why didn't he talk to me?" The words flew from her lips before Libby could consider the wisdom of them. She hastened to correct her gaffe. "Don't tell me if you shouldn't."

"I think I just heard him tell Christopher that he didn't want you to feel torn between them. Libby, they're having serious troubles in their relationship. Aggie is…."

"A pregnant woman. I'd say that whole living in an 'understanding way' and her being the 'weaker vessel' fits right about now. I thought better of Luke."

Marianne's gasp would have been funny, had Libby not been irritated with her son. "I think you've forgotten that there are two sides to every story. I love Aggie. I am not condemning her, but she has left Luke in what sounds like an impossible position." Marianne coughed to cover her last—much too loud—words. "But that's not why I called. I called to find out why we weren't included in helping them. Obviously, no one knew. They either tried to manage it on their own, or never got the chance to share—probably thought they did, if they meant to at all. Anyway, what are we going to do from *here*? Christmas dinner? Presents? How are they on those? I can go shopping today if you just tell me who needs what."

Libby jumped up and began gathering things—a few freezer bags of stew, rolls from the freezer, and the box of Christmas cookies she'd planned to drop off the next day. "I'm on my way over. I'll let you know what I can find out." With the car loaded, she backed out and drove off down the street.

Five minutes down the road, her phone rang just as she pulled up to a four-way stop. Against everything she had ever preached at her grandchildren and children about cellphones not being choke-chains, Libby sat at the intersection, one eye on the rear view mirror and the other on her hand as she fumbled through her purse for her phone. The name did it. She tapped the screen and put it on speaker. "Hey, Vannie, honey. I—"

"Gramby! Aunt Aggie had the baby—in the *van!* I was driving and couldn't help her and—"

"Whoa. Slow down. She *had the baby?* As in *delivered?!*"

"Yes! And we can't find Uncle Luke anywhere. They're in the room getting checked, but I'm not old enough to take the kids in, so we're stuck in the lobby until someone comes. *Why isn't*

Uncle Luke picking up his phone?!"

Deep breaths—one after another—Libby took them until she felt ready to deal with an understandably hysterical teenager. "Vannie?"

"Yeah?"

"Inhale." A second passed. Two. Libby rolled her eyes and infused every bit of patience she could into her words. "Now exhale."

A burst of air filled the phone. "Okay. You're right. I was freaking out. But the baby didn't make much noise. I—"

"It's here early, sweetheart. It is probably quieter than most newborns. So it thinks it's screaming its head off, and you're hearing it barely fussing. That's what I've seen before, anyway. Take heart. The Lord has that baby in His hands. Everything is going to be exactly as the Lord wants it to be."

Vannie's next words, preceded by a predictable sniffle, came in almost perfect unison with her thoughts. "That's what I'm afraid of. I want the Lord to want it how *I* want it to be. How do we make *that* happen?"

"By asking Him to make our desires *His* desires. That's the best way. Now, I think I know where Luke is. Let me call him and then I'll head right over—Brunswick Community?"

"Yeah. Gramby?"

Libby's heart constricted at the vulnerability dripping from Vannie's tone. "Yes?"

"Hurry? I'm scared."

For the next mile, Libby prayed over the phone, each word chosen to point the girl to Jesus and take her mind from the situation. "—and above all, we ask You to give us the faith we need to trust You when we don't understand."

"Thanks, Gram. You're the best. Should I call Grandma Millie?"

"I'll ask Luke when I talk to him and then get right back to you."

She heard it—the relief in Vannie's tone when the girl realized she didn't have to do it yet. "Thanks."

"Okay, going to pull over and call Luke now. You go keep those kids from getting you guys kicked out until I get there." Vannie's giggle gave Libby just the relief she needed. She'd almost disconnected when a thought hit her. "Wait! Vannie!"

"Yeah...?" The hesitant waver made Vannie sound a bit childlike.

"Is the baby a boy or a girl?"

"Oh! Sorry. It's a girl! They're playing 'guess the baby's name' right now. Ronnie insists it's Stevie. I've given up trying to point out that most Stevies are little boys—*very* little *boys*."

Olivia pulled into the Brant's Corners Post Office parking lot and swiped through her phone for Marianne's number when Luke's phone didn't pick up. "This is *not* the time to let your phone go dead, young man!"

"I'm not a young man, and my phone is just fine." Marianne didn't *sound* like she was joking, and her next line proved it. "If you're just going to beat that boy up further, you can go away. He's doing a fine—"

"The baby's here. I need to talk to him. *Now.*" As much as she dreamed of leaving the authoritative demand as it was, Libby couldn't help but tack on, "Please."

"Wait, *here?* As in—"

"Please let me talk to Luke before he hears it accidentally." The ugliness in her tone made her backpedal a bit. "Sorry, Mari, but I need him *now.*"

Slow, painstaking fractions of minutes passed as she waited to hear her son's voice—minute fragments that she used to rehearse a gentle way to share the news. But when his voice came on the line, heavy traces of emotion lingering in his words, her heart filled her throat. "Oh, Luke, why didn't you tell me?"

"Sorry, Mom. It wasn't intentional. You came, you saw—I was just on auto-pilot, I guess. Can we talk about this later? I—"

She had to interrupt him, but every maternal instinct revolted. Interrupting a sister? Not a problem. Interrupting the *child* she'd trained out of it—awkward at best. "Luke. Shhh.... You need to get in your truck and head to Brunswick. Aggie's at the hospital. She needs you."

"Wha—"

Libby heard it. Luke scrambling—probably trying to find jacket, keys, and hug his aunt and uncle. She heard mumbles that sounded like gratitude. Marianne's voice came through with unexpected clarity. "We're praying, Luke."

Not until she heard his truck door slam shut did he speak again. "Is the baby okay? Did they say? Who called? Why didn't they call—oh wait. I've got Aunt Marianne's phone. Why didn't you call mine?"

"Deep breath, son. Take Marianne her phone and charge yours on the way. Meanwhile, your child—tell me if you want to know what it is—is here."

"Of course, I d—no. Wait? The baby is *here?*"

A smile—she couldn't prevent it spreading across her lips and entering her tone. "It's here. That's all I know. Now, do you want to know if it's a boy or girl?"

The answer came immediately. "Don't tell me. Mibs will want to do that. But thanks for thinking of it."

She knew better—almost stopped herself, even—but Libby couldn't help but add, "Are you guys truly having the kinds of trouble Marianne thinks? She's truly concerned, Luke."

"It feels like it, Ma. I don't know her anymore. I keep thinking that it's just the bed rest, but I don't want to do that—assume. It seems like a great way to ignore a problem." His voice trembled, and only her sister's demand that he come in out of the cold hinted that it could be anything other than raw pain. "That's not true. I *want* to, but I know I shouldn't."

"Hang on, Luke. Hang on and trust the Lord. He'll carry you. Now give that phone back to Marianne and get out of there. You've got a long drive and a wife waiting for you."

"Yes, ma'am."

Nothing felt better at that moment than to hear a hint of confidence return to her son's voice. *Thank you, Lord. Now… what to do next?*

The great fans whooshed as Luke stepped up to the automatic doors. They slid open and seemed to suck him into the lobby rather than push him out. As if the Lord's gift to him, the first face he saw was his mother's. Libby sat in one of the chairs, Ronnie on one knee, Ian leaning against the other, and the twins on either side of her. *Why do we always think of Cari and Lorna as "the twins" when we have Tavish and Ellie?* He blinked. *And why do*

306

irrelevant and inconsequential thoughts always occur at the least opportune times?

Ellie saw him first and rushed to his side. "The baby—is it okay? No one will tell us anything."

"I don't know." His eyes met his mother's, but Luke saw no answer there. "I'll find out, though. Okay?"

As much as he ached to go to his wife, the kids clung to him—all but Tavish and Laird. The boys stood as close as they could and seemed to draw strength from his presence. Vannie, after just a moment of enforced "bravery," leaned against his back, arms around his waist, and sighed. "I'm so glad you're here."

"Let me go find out what I can. I'll come tell you before I go see Mibs, okay?"

Everyone but Ronnie peeled themselves from him and moved back to their "assigned seats." Libby stepped forward, cradled his face in her hands, and spoke reassuring wisdom into his heart. "The Lord loves you. I love you. These children love you." She waited until he met her gaze and added, "And Aggie loves you."

"I love you, too."

While Libby took charge of a very reluctant Ronnie, Luke gave the children one last reassuring smile and went to learn what he could. At the reception desk, they directed him to the OB wing, refusing to call for an update. He stood in the elevator, hands shaking until he shoved them in his pockets. *Lord, the baby. Please, not the baby. I don't think Mibs can take it right now. I just... Please....*

A nurse met him at the elevator doors. "Luke Sullivan? Aggie's husband?"

"Yeeesss...."

"Your mother called to say you were coming up. She's in room 304. Just arou—"

He stopped her. "Look, I want to see her, but the children are down in the lobby terrified. I think they saw the birth or—" He swallowed hard. "I just need to know how Aggie and the baby are and then go tell everyone before I go in. Once I get in there—"

"You're not going to want to leave. Of course. The baby is down there in the NICU. She's fine—doing well for a baby that aspirated meconium."

Luke nodded as the woman spoke—more for something to do than encouragement. "Meconium—that means distress before the water broke, doesn't it?"

"It can. But sometimes it just happens. We're keeping an eye on her, but she's doing well. Aggie is, too, but she's agitated. She wants *you*."

His heart pushed him toward the room, but Luke stepped back and punched the down button to the elevator. "I'll be right back. I just can't leave them wondering down there, and I promised I'd come back. I think we all assumed the worst, and they should be reassured in person. I'm not going to break my word now."

When the elevator didn't rise fast enough, he glanced around him for stairs. The nurse just pointed to a door at the far corner. "Over there."

"How—well, doesn't matter. Thanks!" With that, Luke bolted down the short hall and to the entrance to the stairwell. The exercise—refreshing. Having a purpose—even better.

The lobby had filled with teenagers holding balloons and waving pompoms. Luke wove around and through them to the corner where his family sat huddled together. He dropped to his knees before them and grinned. "They're both fine. Okay?" A collective sigh of relief greeted him before Luke could continue. "The baby is getting extra special attention because it came early and it swallowed stuff it shouldn't have. But the nurse said she's doing well. Aggie needs me, though. She's fine, too, but she's all alone up there and the baby isn't with her, and that always scares mommies. Anyway, I'm going up there to be with her, and I'm going to ask Gramby to take you back to the house. You can all visit after I've seen what's going on and I know Aggie is rested enough."

Libby stood and nudged him. "Get out of here. Your wife needs you. We're going home. If you want Vannie to bring you dinner, just call—with your *charged* phone?"

He patted his pocket. "The only advantage to a long car ride. Plenty of time to charge—charge and pray. Thanks, Ma."

When he left the lobby, Luke didn't know. Whether he rode the elevator or took the stairs? That he didn't know either. He made it to the floor, found the room number, and knocked on the door before he entered. "Mibs?"

"Luke! Where've—"

"Phone died. Sorry." Luke rounded the curtain and tried not to react to the pale, wan woman on the bed. "How're you doing? Sorry—"

But her arms reached for him, and he couldn't speak. Luke moved to her side and held her. To him, Aggie's voice sounded weak, weary, empty. "They say she's okay, but...."

"She?" Even as he asked, a vague memory of the nurse mentioning a "she" filled his mind.

"Oh!" Everything changed in that one moment. Aggie's eyes lit up, her smile became genuine, and her hand reached for his as naturally as if she hadn't stop making those gestures in recent weeks. "She's so little, Luke. And she fell to the floor, but I got to see her after they cleaned her up—wheeled me in for just a minute. You should go see her. She's beautiful."

Don't react. The order came from deep within him. *How did she fall to the floor?* Again, he ordered himself not to react and focused on the only thing he could think of. "We don't have a na—" Luke shook his head at the sheepish look on her face. "I think I was going to say that better than I realized. *We* don't have a name for a girl, but it looks like *you* do."

Just the faintest hint of pink tinged her cheeks. "I thought Alanna Olivia."

Luke kissed her forehead, closed his eyes, and sighed. "Little Lana. I like it."

"I like that you knew not to call her Allie or Lani."

He pressed his cheek against her head and murmured, "Too painful and too close to all the other 'eees' we have."

"Exactly." A tear slid down her cheek. Another followed, with that slow, steady drizzle of raindrops on windowpanes. "I've never been more scared. I think I probably scarred the children for life."

"Did you come in an ambulance or...?" He brushed the hair out of her face and reached for the cup of water by her side. "Here, you look a bit parched."

But she just stared at the cup, her eyes unseeing. Aggie blinked and whispered, "They didn't tell you?"

"Well, you said she hit the floor. Upstairs, or were you—?"

"The *van* floor, Luke. We were just pulling into the emergency ambulance spots and I couldn't stop pushing. I tried to catch her, but—"

Luke couldn't help it. His eyes slid to the door. "What did they say—?"

"Just that they're watching her. She's not struggling or anything. But they did give her oxygen. I saw that much. They hardly let me see her."

As much as he ached to go ask, Lana was in good hands. Aggie needed him more. But another look at her concerned face made the decision for him. "Do you want me to ask? Specifically about—"

"Would you? Oh, and if I can take a shower? I am *gross*. I *need* to get out of this bed! I feel like I've been trapped in a bed for *decades*."

"Just a few weeks." Luke kissed her forehead, lingered, and kissed it again. His eyes met hers, and pain ripped through his heart when she glanced away. "I'll be back in a few. I'll get you that shower, too. If I stand right there in case you get woozy? We could ask Hannah—"

"I didn't call her!" Aggie's eyes widened. "All I could think of was to get here when I saw that cloudy water." She winced. "It's probably my fault for—"

Luke kissed her head again, squeezed her hand, and left before she could begin another self-flagellation session.

Alone in her room, Aggie waited with agitated nervousness. Every beep, every page, every cry of laboring mothers intensified until she found herself with hands over her ears, fighting the urge to whimper. The curtain rattled—that ugly, pathetic excuse for an aqua and gray striped curtain. Aggie's eyes lit up and she sat up a little straighter.

"Well, let's check out that fundus, shall we?"

Why don't we stop talking to me like I'm going to be doing anything. Talking about yourself in the third person is condescending at best. Especially when you're about to inflict obscene pain on someone.

"You sure look... are you always this pale?"

She shrugged. *I don't know! Compared to you, yes. Not everyone gets to have rich, chocolaty skin.*

"Well, we'll see what the doctor says when he comes back for his rounds. He's a little put out at you, you know." At her questioning glance, the woman flashed a row of startling white teeth. "Because you preempted him—didn't let him do his job!"

Do you think you're funny? Because – Aggie bit back a scream as the woman kneaded her belly with force that suggested a history in bread making and managed to transform it into a guttural groan instead. *– when you're torturing a woman who just gave birth, jokes like that are just digs.*

"You probably don't think this is funny, do you? I getcha. I do. I've had five kids myself—all without drugs." She grinned again. "Bet you're annoyed about that, aren'tcha? I would be." On and on, the woman chattered as she kneaded Aggie's belly.

Aggie, on the other hand, winced with every push, every squeeze. "I'm making a horrible mess in the bed. I can feel it." Her voice sounded far away—outside herself.

"Wha—" The woman shifted the covers, and Aggie almost passed out at the crimson blob. "Okay, honey. I'm calling Dr. Malara back in. You might have retained a lobe or something. Just hang tight. Are you cold?"

She shook her head. "Tired, but not cold. I just want to hold the baby—try to feed her."

"That's good news right there. You probably just pooled the whole time, but to be safe, we're gonna get her to take a look, okay?"

Like I get a choice. This is why I wanted to be at home. Everyone doesn't freak out about every little thing. Hannah promised. I can't believe the Lord did this to me.

A gasp filled the room. The nurse turned and stared at her. "Something hurt?"

"Yeah. My heart—the figurative one."

With an understanding nod, the nurse helped her stand in order change out the soaked pads covering the bottom sheet. "Missing your baby is normal. They'll bring you to her—or her to you, if they can—as soon as possible."

"Ever feel like God has betrayed you?"

Nothing could have surprised her more than the woman

311

dropping clean sheets on the floor, wrapping arms around her, and holding tight. "Aw, honey. There ain't one of us who hasn't felt that way. Doesn't mean it's true, of course." She stepped back and grinned at Aggie again. "But look at you! You got me to say ain't again after years of workin' to get rid of it."

After another squeeze, she went back to work as if she hadn't just given an impromptu mini-counseling session. Aggie stared at the bed, wondering. *What would Luke say if he knew? Would he be disappointed in me? Probably. I should care more... shouldn't I? Well, I don't care that I don't care — I don't think.*

She shifted and a gush of blood ran down her leg. Another surrealistic wave washed over her. "I sure am bleeding more with this baby. Is that because she was so little or something?"

"You think you're bleeding more?" The nurse turned and stared at the floor. "Tell me about this birth while I get you changed into new briefs and a fresh pad — new gown, too."

"I want a shower—"

"Not happening without the doctor's okay. Sorry." The nurse — Maya according to the white board near the door — gave Aggie a pat on the back and began peeling clothes off her. "Don't have the authority."

"Is it too much blood?"

"Hard to say. It always looks like more than it is. I've been doing this for years and I *always* overestimate how much is there."

The answer — too evasive for Aggie's comfort, but by the time Maya got her back in bed and covered with a blanket, she almost didn't care about her coveted shower. Luke stepped into the room, saw the puddle of blood, and blanched. "Um...."

"We're looking into it." The nurse pulled out her phone, snapped a picture, and went to work cleaning up the floor. "We'll get this taken care of. I've got to go get someone with a mop. Be careful there until I get it all cleaned up, okay?" Maya stripped gloves from her hands — when had she put them on? — and hurried from the room.

Aggie closed her eyes and exhaled in one long, weary breath. "She's going to call Dr. Malara. She's trying to act all calm, but that freaked her out a bit. Especially after seeing my bed."

"Should I be worried?"

"Probably not. She has a point. I've been sitting in the exact

312

same position since I got here. The blood probably all pooled in one spot, but they can't just ignore it either, I suppose." Aggie sighed. "She's nicer than I thought, though. Even gave me a hug."

Luke settled himself beside her on the bed and slipped an arm around her shoulders. "I can do that, too...."

"You wouldn't if you heard what I told her."

Was it her imagination? Did he stiffen a little? Aggie couldn't be sure. But Luke's voice sounded just as calm and steady as it always did when he finally spoke. "What was that?"

Will telling him damage our marriage? I'm already so angry. If he lectures me.... That thought sealed it. "I don't want to hear it, Luke."

"Try me."

"I told her that I feel like God betrayed me."

He squeezed her closer. "What'd she say about that?"

"That everyone does at some point or another." Her voice dropped to a whisper—one she almost hoped he wouldn't hear. "Have you ever lost your faith?"

It didn't matter how feather soft his lips were or that he only brushed them against the top of her head, Aggie felt it—every time. "Not really, Mibs. I've had times where holding on was difficult, but I've never lost it—not yet."

What prompted her to speak the words she'd tried to hide for weeks, Aggie couldn't say. But she heard them slip through her lips and felt a certain bit of finality in speaking them. "Well, *I* have. I have absolutely lost my faith through this mess."

Aggie braced herself for his shock, his rebuke, his withdrawing from her. None of it came. Instead, she heard that same calm, steady voice rumbling near her ear. "I've got enough for both of us right now. It's going to be okay, Mibs. You're weary—weary 'in well doing'. But you haven't fainted—not yet. I'll trust the Lord for us right now. You just try to keep your heart open to Him."

"How?" The word exploded from her in a combination wail/accusation.

Never had she been more impatient with the slowness of his replies. Twice, she tried to face him, but weariness sent her sagging against him each time. Luke's arms just pulled her tighter against him. "Try to sing, Aggie. Remember what your Sunday

313

school teacher taught you. You memorized all those Psalms with the kids earlier this year. Just recite them. Consider it practice. Trust me."

What if I don't want to? What if I'm just done with it all? Oh, how she ached to ask—to hear him reassure her that the Lord knew—that He understood. She swallowed hard. *That He'll forgive me if I ever get to a place where that sounds good again.*

And in that moment, Aggie realized two things. She wasn't thinking clearly, and Luke hadn't told her what he found out from the nurses. *Oh, boy. Lord, I am* not *praying. But if You want to take my lack of prayer and turn it into one, I'm okay with that.*

"Luke?"

"Hmmm...?"

Aggie steeled herself against whatever he'd say and asked, "Why haven't you told me what the nurses said?"

Oh, how his characteristic quiet squeezed her heart until it ached. She longed to scream at him, pound his chest, berate him for being so infernally cautious in his speech. Instead, Aggie waited, doing everything she could to avoid an outburst.

His answer came as slow and comforting as she should have known it would be. "Because my wife needed to know she's loved—not just by me, but by the Lord. And...." Luke shifted so he could watch her expression—always did if possible. How had she not noticed that before? His eyes smiled at her as he spoke. "You want to know how our beautiful little Lania is?"

Aggie's eyes rolled before she could stop them. "I should have known you'd find a way to put an 'ee' in there. And, *yes!* I do want to know. The only thing keeping me from beating it out of you is the fact that I couldn't if I tried. I'm worn *out.* Her eyes drifted closed. "Can you pull that blanket up?"

"You're cold?" He tucked the blanket in around her and pulled her to his chest. His hands rubbed her arms as he described all that the nurses had said. "There are two nurses working with her and two other little ones. Those babies—Aggie, did you see them?"

"No, they only wheeled me in long enough to see that she was there and fine."

"Well, they're tiny." His voice cracked as he spoke. "The one—I don't think it's going to make it. It's too small—too many

314

problems. One of the nurses never left its side."

Her heart clenched as he spoke of monitors and wires. The mother—a young teenager—watched through a window but refused to come and stand by the incubator. "But Lania is doing well. They have her on a respirator just to help until her lungs clear. Her temperature is good, and according to her favorite nurse—"

Aggie snorted. "Favorite nurse?"

"No joke. She has a favorite. She actually fights the other one. Julie says she thinks that there's something about her that reminds Lania of you."

"You know everyone is going to call her Lania, right? There's no way we can avoid it."

He shrugged. "Probably. It's a pretty name, though. It fits her."

"Now, tell me more. She likes Julie, she has good temperature… fingers and toes? What was her Apgar score?"

"Sorry. Didn't ask. But they said as long as she doesn't have any episodes, they'll probably wean her off the respirator tomorrow and see how she does." He grinned. "Oh, and get this! She weighed *exactly* four pounds."

"That's half Ronnie's weight!" Aggie sighed and yawned. "I can't believe she's so tiny!"

"You know that photographer you wanted? I think you should call. The chances of getting that picture of a baby in my hands is never going to be better. She's going to snuggle perfectly in there."

Aggie's heart melted a little at the mental image of Luke's strong, calloused hands cradling the delicate body of their infant daughter. "Hmmm, will they let us?"

"Mibs… she's going to be tiny for weeks. But she's going to need clothes. You could fit two of her in what we have."

The mental image of her mother's excitement filled her with joy until she realized that her mother probably didn't *know*. "Um, Luke?"

"Hmm…?" His lips brushed her temple.

"Did anyone call Mom and Dad?"

His silence—absolutely unhelpful. For most people, it would imply that no one had. For Luke, it could mean anything. But the words eventually came. "I don't think so. I'll see if Mom did." Even as he spoke, Luke dug for his phone.

Aggie yawned and shifted. Another gush told her she either needed to stay put or something was wrong. "Can you tell the nurse I gushed again? I think they should check me." And with that, everything went black.

Gone The Love, I'm Now Confessing

Chapter Twenty-Three

Tuesday, December 23rd

Tina's call came just after the latest attack on Aggie's uterus. Luke, sleeping in the uncomfortable chair beside her, stirred before his head flopped back to one very awkward angle. Aggie tapped the screen and tried to keep her voice low. "Hey. Thanks for calling me back."

"I can't believe I missed the birth. This was supposed to be my acid test for motherhood."

"The nurses say she's the most stubborn thing they've ever seen. They're calling her 'fierce princess.'"

A few irritated, muttered words filled the phone as Tina ordered someone to leave her alone. *Your father introduced you to someone else. Great. This won't make things even worse with William.*

"Fierce princess...." Tina's response came through as if she hadn't been interrupted by what was likely a very attractive and wealthy man. "I like that. What'd you name her?" Before Aggie could speak, she laughed. "I can't believe I asked that. You named her Alanna, didn't you? Now is it Martha, Grace, or Olivia?"

"Since you're so good at guessing...."

Tina's response came without hesitation. "Grace. I don't see you doing 'aah, aah' together."

"Yeah, well, you're wrong. I should do Grace, but I can't. So,

I want Olivia. Because, as much as I love Mom and Aunt Martha, I do *not* love that name."

Everything shifted. "Okay, when I called last night, Luke said you were struggling. Something about losing too much blood?"

"They talked about an infusion, but since I'm otherwise healthy, and since they got the bleeding to stop, they're giving me until noon to get some level or another up. I was kind of out of it."

A nurse entered the room and gave her an apologetic smile. "Sorry, Tina. They're about to torture me, and I'm probably going to cry. Can you call Vannie? Oh, and as soon as Luke wakes up, I'll get him to send Lania's picture to you."

"Lania. I like it. Fierce Princess Lania. Hey, look." Everything went quiet for a moment. When Tina spoke again, it was in a hushed whisper. "I've got a new return flight—takes off right as the reception should be ending. I'm not telling Dad. I'll just get on the plane and text from Dulles."

As much as Aggie ached to tell Tina not to antagonize her father, she couldn't do it. "If I wasn't so selfish…."

"Well, you are. And I'm glad. Look, I'll be there as soon as I can. Send me texts, emails, whatever. Sometimes I miss those instant messenger days."

With that, Tina disconnected. A moment later, Aggie's phone buzzed. *POOFS*

We hung on longer than all of our other friends. Call me stupid and nostalgic, but I miss those hours on the messenger instead of the phone or texts. It blended the best of both worlds—needing to be on at the same time for a real conversation, but the privacy of typing thoughts we might not bring ourselves to say aloud. Now, the closest we get is a Facebook message now and then. Yeah—miss the old days—even with our goofy sign offs and dramatic reactions. Why do I feel old, thinking about it?

"Was that Tina?" His voice thick with insufficient sleep, Luke shifted and smiled at the sight of her. "You have more color."

"Good. I hear I looked ghastly." Aggie shifted in the bed and sighed. "Yeah. She's coming home early."

A slow smile cracked the deadpan expression on Luke's face. "William will be glad. He showed up while you were sleeping, and man...."

"Why aren't they engaged, at least?!" Aggie shifted again. "Seriously, I am *done* with beds. I need out of this thing!"

Once more, the nurse popped in. "Did I hear my name? No? Well, you're off the phone, so I'll make you a deal."

"That is?"

"If you don't gush this time, we'll walk down and see the princess."

As Aggie lay there, determined not to cry but with tears streaming down her face, she ordered her body to behave. So when she felt the same gush as before, her heart sank, and sobs accompanied the tears. "I don't get it! I feel better. No more dizziness, nothing!"

"You felt a gush, eh?" The woman shifted the covers and peered at the pads covering the bottom sheet. "I don't see anything on the pads...." She rolled Aggie to the side. "Yep, the only spots there are old." She helped Aggie stand and waited. "How do you feel? Woozy or...."

Even as Aggie shook her head, honesty demanded she be completely truthful. "Not woozy at all, but I do feel a bit unsteady."

"Well, that can be from weeks of bed rest followed by near hemorrhage. Why don't you go try to use the bathroom? Tell me how that pad looks, okay?"

"Can I take a shower? *Please!* I just want a shower. Luke can stand right there. He won't let me fall. I promise."

Without a word, the woman disappeared. Aggie turned to Luke and shrugged. "Does she have to get permission? I know Maya said that yesterday, but I know Dr. Malara said you could do it today if the bleeding was under control." stared at the white board. "I don't know her name."

"Nonni. And here are your towels." Nonni passed two to Aggie and one to Luke. Her eyes never left Luke as she spoke. "You get in there with her. You hold her up. If she falls, you'll regret it. That's all I'm sayin'."

Aggie gulped. "Is that necessary? I wanted to wash my hair."

"He can do it. You stand there and hold onto the handrail." As Aggie's protest began, Nonni shook her head. "Oh, no. It's him

319

or me. And I know I'd rather my husband joined me than some strange woman. Just sayin'."

Her eyes slid to Luke. "She wouldn't...."

"Do you want to take that chance?" He grinned. "I can't wait to embarrass Lania with *this* story someday."

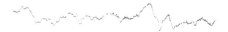

Ocean breezes teased her hair and sent wisps curling around her cheeks. *William wouldn't recognize me with curly hair.* Tina had never been much of a "selfie" taker, but Tina whipped out her phone, snapped a picture, and zipped it to William. SEE HOW LAZY I AM WHEN YOU AREN'T AROUND TO INSPIRE ME TO DO SOMETHING WITH MY HAIR?

The phone rang seconds later. Tina gazed at the picture of him—a rare one he'd allowed her to take—just because he loved her. *You do love me. I can't pretend you don't. But we're at four years and no commitment in sight.*

"Hey!" Her greeting sounded forced—even to her.

"You are beautiful just as you are. I wanted to tell you that." He cleared his throat. "Have you spoken to Aggie?"

Change the subject again. Just like you always do when you feel like you've offered me a morsel of hope. Tina closed her eyes, tilted the shade over her beach chair, and tried to stifle her sigh. "Just got off the phone with her. They're calling Alanna, 'Lania.' I kind of like it."

"She's such a tiny thing." Emotion choked him. "I didn't get to see Aggie. She was sleeping. But the nurse let me go in and see the baby. Uniforms have their advantages." William cleared his throat. "Her favorite nurse flirted with me."

"Oh?" The admission—weird. Tina waited with some trepidation for his next words. *Since when do you notice flirting, much less tell me about it?* Her heart hardened a bit. *If this is how you're going to break up with me, you will regret it, and I won't have to say or do a thing. Aggie'll handle that.*

"I told her about you—how much I miss you. How much I hope that when we have children, we won't have to do the NICU thing." William cleared his throat. "She looked so disappointed, Tina. Anyway, I told her if we *did* have to, I hoped there'd be a nurse like her in there."

Heart pounding, Tina wrestled a reason for his story from within and took a semi-wild guess. "She was even more disappointed, wasn't she?"

"How'd you know?"

It had been years, at least two, since she'd allowed herself to be vulnerable with him, but Tina could hear the effort he put into each word—words that tried to share his heart. "Because I would have been. Cute guy like you, *in uniform*, saying all the things that would make any woman's heart melt—to a *nurse*. Duh!"

"I meant it, Tina. Everything I told her. But...."

She'd worked and struggled to get him to open up—to face his fears. He'd always picked a fight and left. This time, she used distance and prayed it would make the difference they needed. "William, what are you afraid of?"

"It's never been about you—my commitment issues. You know that, right?"

She ached to say the words he wanted and probably *needed* her to say. But lies at this juncture of their relationship would serve only to drive in a deeper wedge. "No, William. I didn't. We talk about us; you run. What am I supposed to think?"

"You know my mom. You know the statistics."

The emotion in his voice. The dead silence for several seconds. The ragged breath. Tina's throat constricted. "William?"

"Yeah?"

"I'm coming home—early. I'll be there in forty-eight hours." She cleared her throat. "And then we're going to talk about the rest of the story—about how you protected your siblings. About how you aren't a statistic. You're a person with the Holy Spirit indwelling him."

Another ragged breath. "Yeah?"

"And then we're going to let ourselves dream about those kids you were talking about." Her heart demanded she stop there, but her mind told her now was the time. "I hate that I'm going to say this, but I've got to. I'll wait another year, William. One more. But if we aren't engaged by next Christmas, I'm going to take it as your way of saying I'm not the one for you."

William's protest came right on schedule, but Tina just repeated, "I love you," until only her voice remained. "See you

321

Christmas night—it'll be late. Bye." Her thumb tapped the disconnect button and her eyes closed. *Okay, Lord. I finally handed this over to You. Please don't break my heart.*

Lania's protest at the removal of the diaper she'd worked so hard to fill reached them just as Luke and Aggie stepped into the NICU. Luke steered Aggie toward the corner recliner and helped get her situated before turning to Julie. "Is she hungry? Aggie's concerned that it's been too long."

A glance back at his wife gave Luke the impetus he needed to continue. *She looks infinitely better.* With a reassuring smile, he turned back to Julie. "Even if Lania can't *eat*, surely the stimulation is good for later?"

"Yes. And we'll get her pumping, too. It'll help with production, and at least our princess will get the best milk for *her* when Mama isn't around. Dr. Hyashi pushes for that." Julie carried the baby to Aggie and helped hold her as Aggie positioned Lania for nursing. "Mama knows what she's doing. That's always a relief."

"Mama feels like an idiot. I'm convinced I'm going to break her. She's so tiny!"

Julie pointed at a pillow on a shelf. "Luke, can you bring that over here? She needs a bit of support."

How did I forget that? We carried her pillow all over the house last time. She had that special pillow, but she only wanted hers.

The picture of Aggie holding their daughter filled Luke's heart until he thought it would explode from happiness and gratitude. *They're both here—alive! And it looks like they're going to be just fine. Thank you, Lord. Just hold her up until she gets her eyes off the waves that threaten to overwhelm her and back on You.*

His phone buzzed. Luke pulled it out, took a picture of Aggie trying to nurse—trying without much success. Tiny rosebud lips refused—or perhaps, couldn't be expected—to open wide enough to do much good. Still, the picture of Aggie's hair spilling over her shoulder in a perfect modesty curtain for a photo—he couldn't resist. A glance at his recent calls showed half a dozen missed calls—both of their mothers, two of his sisters,

322

Marcus Vaughn, Winnie Dyke, and *four* from the family cellphone.

That one, he needed to return. "Hey, Mibs?"

"Hmmm?" She didn't even look up at him.

"Vannie called. I'm going to step out and see what she needed. Just in case it's important. Mom's there, but...."

This time her eyes rose and met his. His throat constricted, and his heart raced exactly as it had the day he'd realized that he'd fallen in love with her. For the first time in weeks, he saw genuine love for him in Aggie's eyes, her expression, the way she didn't want to look away. "Come right back," she whispered.

"I'll be back so fast you won't even miss me." Even as he spoke, Luke pleaded with her to come back with her usual retort.

A gleam entered Aggie's eye. She grinned. "Too late. Already do."

Aaah, some things never get old. Luke tore himself from the room before he chose self over family.

Vannie answered first ring. "Uncle Luke! You've got to send Gram home! She's going nuts trying to clean everything for Aunt Aggie, and the whole time you can hear her muttering lists of things not to forget for herself. She hasn't wrapped all her gifts, she hasn't shopped for Christmas dinner — all kinds of stuff. We're all going crazy."

"Okay...." His mind tried to race, but years of quiet, methodical thought processes overrode immediate need. "I've got it. I'll call. I also have a list of things Aggie needs. They're keeping her at least two more days."

"And Alanna?"

"She'll be here at *least* that long. It all depends on her breathing, if she gains some of her weight back, and something else. I can't remember what it was now."

Vannie's giggle — how long had it been since he'd heard her sound so carefree? — warmed his heart. "You probably looked at one of your girls and got distracted."

"Probably did. I'll call Mom. You guys be ready to visit at four o'clock, okay? If you come then, you'll have an hour before the dinner cart comes around. It'll keep the nurses from trying to kick you out early. And bring Mom or Murphy — even Mrs. Dyke. In case they want you to come in shifts." At that moment, Luke's mind exploded with all he'd asked of and expected of her in the last month. "Vannie?"

"Yeah?"

"You shouldn't have had to do so much recently, but I sure am glad you did—and that you did it with such a good attitude. I needed you more than I knew until just now. You hang on, okay? We'll find a way to get you some relief ASAP."

Silence from Vannie—a new concept. But when she did speak, his heart filled with gratitude all over again. "Uncle Luke, it's nice to be needed. I didn't mind—not usually. But being *appreciated?* That's even better. Thanks."

Alone in her room, Aggie tried to pray. Words refused to come. Heart heavy, she closed her eyes, tried to block out the machines, the sterile cabinets, and the wallpaper border—a nod at hominess that only served to make the room that much more unappealing. Instead, she painted a canvas in her mind—one with a verdant meadow, trees. A crystal clear creek bubbled over smooth stones and down into a valley. A man in long, homespun robes walked off in the distance, a lamb flung over His shoulders. Aggie's heart *willed* her to hear the sounds of the creek, the songs of birds in the trees, the bleating of the lamb. *"The Lord is my Shepherd...."*

She made it as far as "Even though I walk" and her mind went blank. The meadow—gone. Birds, shepherd, trees—all of it, gone. Only the darkness of a moonless valley at midnight remained.

The love and understanding Luke had shown her gave her impetus to try again. This time, she wandered back through the years, past difficult memories, around things that tempted her to stay and relive, and into Mrs. Beidermeyer's fifth-grade Sunday school classroom. Most classrooms boasted large posters purchased at the local Christian bookstore. Sunsets, oceans, and adorable animals with scriptures plastered across the images. Oh, and of course, every room had the obligatory poster with a "bookshelf" of the books of the Bible. From first through fourth grade, Aggie had been certain that somehow kids learned those books through osmosis or something. The teachers never commented on them—never even read through them.

But in Mrs. Beidermeyer's class, they'd learned those books by reciting them until they had each book down pat. They learned to do "sword drills." Most of the kids hated those. Aggie had loved the challenge of finding obscure passages quickly. By the end of the year, most of the class could even challenge the text. *"There is no Jude 3:16!"*

The door of her memory opened wider and beckoned her into the classroom. Enormous posters—hand drawn and lettered in Mrs. Beidermeyer's perfect penmanship, notes and all—of twelve faithful hymns decorated those walls. "Great Is Thy Faithfulness." "Angry Words." "Fairest Lord Jesus." The familiar posters filled her eyes, her heart. Blue-haired Mrs. Beidermeyer stood in front of the room and beat time with her chalk as the class sang, "In the Garden." Never one of Aggie's favorites, she "stood" there, eyes closed, and listened to the childish voices singing. *"...walks with me...tells me I am His own...."*

The words haunted her. *It's such a selfish song.* "...none other has ever known." *Really? I have such a special relationship with the Lord that I can sing that next to a hundred people all singing the same thing?*

But the words filled her heart again as the song looped through once more. *"...walks with me... tells me I am His own...."*

Of all the songs my memory would latch onto, why this one? Why the one song that I almost never sing?

Her eyes caught the piercing gaze of her beloved teacher. Aggie could almost hear the woman's words. *"Stop picking apart the imagery. It's a song of praise, rejoicing that the Lord makes time for each of His children. Focus on the purpose of the song."*

Aggie's eyes flew open. Heart racing, she shook herself and grabbed the cup of water she'd been ordered to drink before Nonni returned.

Sinking back against the pillow, her eyes closed once more, and the scent of black permanent markers and cinnamon candy swirled about her, drawing her back into a memory she no longer held any desire to relive. *Why would He "bid me go" with a woeful voice and then call back to me? It makes no sense. Why can't there be another song?*

325

Once more, Mrs. Beidermeyer's eyes bored into her heart and exposed ugliness there that Aggie didn't care to face. The words came—words that cut through to the heart and scrubbed at the contents. *"...tune my heart to sing Thy grace."*

A part of her, that corner of her soul not yet seared by her angst and bitterness, cried out for more. The words tried to form on her lips, but Aggie still couldn't sing them aloud. Instead, she entered the musical chamber of her heart and donned her best Anne Shirley shawl. *I'll just feel the song.*

"...streams of mercy, never ceasing...." Was it true? *Never ceasing?* She'd never allowed herself to wrestle the ideas of eternal security. Arguments from both camps, each backed by Scripture, left her mind hurting and her heart confused. *It always made sense just to keep myself so grateful for salvation that I'd never be tempted to reject the Lord. We see how well that worked out. Now where am I? I've come as close to rejecting Jesus as I ever have in my life. What does it even mean? I can't say I don't believe. I can say I believe other things I never wanted to now.*

Aggie choked back a sob. Her spirit warred against her heart as the next words from the song beat against it with the force and impetus of a battering ram. "Let that grace, Lord, like a fetter...." The words clawed their way through her lips in a broken whisper. She tried, with every fiber of her being she struggled, to sing the next words, but none came. *"...bind my wandering heart to Thee."*

Deep, ragged breaths wracked her body as Aggie fought off the next words. *I guess my heart is "prone to wander." And yeah, I "feel it." But am I truly going to leave the God I thought I loved?* The next line mocked and cajoled her in an unwelcome paradox. Her spirit ordered her to pray the words, even if she didn't feel them, and allow the Lord to make them true in her heart. Her heart nailed boards and shoved furniture against the door to block any hope of entry.

Luke stepped into the room, both relieving her and giving Aggie palpitations of a kind that he wouldn't find flattering. "How's my Mibs?"

"Struggling." The word flew from her lips before she could stop it. He didn't need to know more. He'd said he'd lean on the Lord for both of them. *Why did you just blurt it out like that? You could learn some lessons from him, Agathena Sullivan!*

"With...."

If she could have lied to him, Aggie would have. She tried—with surprising swiftness, the words flowed into her mind and tempted her—but she couldn't. "Trying to do what you said. Sing. Pray. Recite scripture."

"Which one are you stuck on?"

She swallowed and dropped her gaze. "Singing."

Luke seated himself beside her on the bed, pulled her close, laced his fingers in hers—everything but spoke. Enough time passed that, with the little sleep she knew he'd gotten, she almost wondered if he'd fallen asleep praying. But then he squeezed her hand and murmured his next question into her hair. "Which one?"

"'Come Thou Fount.'"

As if she wasn't ripping out his heart with her raw honesty, Luke asked the next obvious question. "All the verses, or just one?"

The answer exploded from her in a deep whisper. "Second half of verse three."

In his quiet baritone, Luke sang the verse. Telltale wavers at the beginning and end of each line—the only evidence of his emotional state as he sang.

> O to grace how great a debtor
> Daily I'm constrained to be!
> Let that grace now like a fetter,
> Bind my wandering heart to Thee.

Hesitation, squeezing, *love* poured through touch into her hurting heart. Aggie closed her eyes and waited for the next lines, aching to pray that they would be true for her, yet resisting even still.

> Prone to wander, Lord, I feel it,
> Prone to leave the God I love;
> Here's my heart, O take and seal it,
> Seal it for Thy courts above.

Luke's next words sent ripples of shock, confusion, hope,

and despair through her. "You know, Mibs. This distance you've created with the Lord? He can handle it. The question is, can you?"

Each time she tried to answer, the words rose up in her throat and stuck there, unmoving, unyielding. Luke's phone buzzed. "I think they're here." He kissed her cheek and whispered, "I'll be back in a few. Hang on. None of us are going anywhere. We love you too much."

"Fine thing to say when you're walking out the door." She'd meant it to be a joke. It came out as an accusation. Luke stood there torn as a tear slid down her cheek. Aggie wanted to assure him she was fine—silly, but fine. She couldn't speak.

After several long seconds and another buzz to his phone, Luke whispered, "Be right back."

Left alone in the room, Aggie stared at the ceiling, her eyes following a faint crack until it disappeared. She couldn't see where it began or ended. It just seemed to appear out of nowhere. *Kind of like the crack on my heart.*

Her bottom lip trembled at the raw emptiness that engulfed her. Singing—impossible. *Speaking*—equally impossible. But the words to one of her favorite—or it once *had* been—hymns welled up inside her, unbidden. Nearly two decades of habitual turning to the Lord in song won out over a heart bent on rebellion and resistance. She couldn't ask for them to be made true in her heart. Truth be told, in that moment, she didn't *want* to think about the words, much less their meaning. But they came, and as they did, another shower of God's goodness beat against the dry, crusty surface of her heart, soaking into her soul.

> All to Jesus, I surrender;
> Make me, Savior, wholly Thine;
> Let me feel the Holy Spirit,
> Truly know that Thou art mine.

Cari, Lorna, and Laird entered almost on tiptoe. Luke followed with a smirk and a heart hopeful that Aggie had at least *tried* to reconcile with the Lord. The anguish in her eyes could only mean she'd been unsuccessful. But peace washed over him as he watched her open her arms wide and welcome the girls.

"I missed you!"

Cari squeezed her and stood back, hands on her hips, and with characteristic honesty declared, "You look awful! You should come home. We take better care of you."

"Did you die?" Lorna looked up at Luke. "She looks like that girl in the movie who died and came back—with the machine, remember?"

The shock on Aggie's face could have been anything from amusement to horror. Luke shook his head. "Aggie's just fine. She needed a bit of extra help, but all mothers look a bit peaked after birth—except in movies or pictures. Somehow they always look great then."

Laird pulled something from his jacket—her journal. "Thought you might like this. Vannie wouldn't bring it. She said you didn't need anything to do but sit with the baby, but...."

A lump swelled in his throat as Aggie swung her legs over the edge of the bed and pulled the boy close. "I didn't even think of it, but yes. This is exactly what I need right now. Thank you." Laird's face flamed as she kissed his cheek and whispered, "I love you."

A glance his way—Luke predicted Laird's words with precise accuracy. "Are all new moms this emotional? I don't remember this from last time."

"We are!" Aggie bopped his arm with the journal and held out her arms to the girls. "I need better hugs, too. Then we'll walk down and you can see Lania through the window."

Cari's face screwed up in a disappointed scowl. "But we washed our hands just like the lady said! I thought we could see her!"

"I told you that only Aggie and I are allowed in the unit, Cari."

"But we washed our hands!" Cari glanced over at Lorna. "Did you think?"

The quieter twin's head bobbed. "Why would we have to wash our hands just to see Aunt Aggie, unless...." She frowned and focused on Luke. "Aunt Aggie *is* okay, isn't she?"

"She is. I promise."

329

Lorna hesitated and then pulled his ear down closer to her lips. "When can she come home? She *needs* to come home."

"Not for a couple of days. Maybe Friday."

This caught Cari's and Laird's attentions. Cari spoke first. "She'll miss *Christmas!*"

Laird's entire demeanor shifted. Disappointment cloaked every word, despite the bravery he tried to show. "We can wait. Christmas should be with everyone—you and Lania, too." He hugged Aggie once more, and Luke thought he heard the boy add, "Thank you for naming her for Mommy."

Tears sprang to his eyes as he gazed at Aggie and tried to smile as he mouthed, "*Smart decision.*"

They led the children down the corridor, around a curve, and to the great windows that led to the NICU. Luke stayed with them as Aggie went inside. "She'll have to get Julie—the one with the teddy bear scrubs is Julie—to help her. With the monitors and things, we can't just pick up the baby. But they know you're coming, so they're going to help." His eyes met Laird's, and he answered the unspoken question there. "Yeah, from what I gather, this is a little out of the ordinary. But they really do want to help us. That baby over there...." Luke pointed to the preemie that he felt sure would meet the Lord soon. "I think he's being transferred to Rockland later. They had to stabilize him before he could go. His name is Bronson. You should pray for him and his parents."

"He looks awfully little."

Luke nodded. "He is. His skin is so thin that they can't hold him very much." Aggie moved their way carrying Lania, while Julie followed pushing the incubator. "Oh, here she is."

Cari and Lorna gasped. Lorna burst into tears and buried her head in Luke's stomach, wailing something indiscernible. As Luke debated between allowing her to release pent up emotion and trying to wrestle the problem from her, Laird leaned forward, a goofy grin on his face. "She's pretty. I thought she'd be kind of ugly. You know how most newborns are. And she's so early...."

"She is pretty, isn't she? I thought it was just me—that proud papa thing." Luke gazed at his daughter's face. "I think she looks like Aggie from the nose up, but she has my mother's chin."

"Ears, too. Look how little they are. Aunt Aggie's are long.

Gram's are rounder—like that." Laird's hand pressed against the glass as if he could touch the baby.

Lorna still cried. Luke dropped to one knee and tried to wipe tears away. "What's wrong?"

"She's too little! My *dolls* are bigger than she is!" Her voice dropped to a whisper—agonized, tortured whisper. "Is she going to die? Does she have to stay here for a month until she's big enough? Is Aunt Aggie—"

"Shh.... Everything will be just fine. They'll both be home long before next month, unless something unexpected happens." Luke stood and sent Aggie a reassuring smile.

"Look at her little feet. They're tiny!" Cari sighed. "I think she's perfect."

As much as he hated to do it, Luke led them from the window. "We need to go. We're disrupting their schedule, so I need to bring up the others."

Cari pointed to a sign. "That says no children under age two. Why can't we go in?"

Oh, how he'd hoped they wouldn't notice. "Look, usually they'd let two of you come in at a time. But you can't. Legally you're not *siblings*. They have to go through a lot of hoops to get special permission." Luke pointed to Bronson's bed. "And he's so fragile, Cari. I couldn't ask them to risk that we'd bring something in. If we were going to be here for a long time, maybe...."

"C'mon, Cari. Let's go downstairs." Laird waggled the family cellphone. "I got a picture, and Gramby let me download Exploding Bananas."

Aggie waved. Luke sent her a silent promise to return immediately and led the children downstairs once more. Ellie, Ian, and Kenzie came next. He gave them the same speech—be quiet, scrub their hands, then sanitize. Ian didn't understand that one at all. "If we can't touch the baby, why do we have to wash *and* sanitize?"

"Because you're going to touch Aunt Aggie. And she might take something back to the baby."

"I think...." Ian's mind seemed to whirl at warp speed. "I think we should just be put in a decontamination chamber. You stand there, it sprays you with gas to clean you off—kind of like a giant can of Lysol—and then no germs. That would be better.

Because I'm going to get germs from my clothes on her."

"How do you know there are germs on your clothes?" Ellie dug under her fingernails with a thoroughness that would impress a surgeon.

"Because we watched that movie on germs, remember? They showed them under the glowing light and they were *everywhere*. A decontamination chamber is better."

As Ellie dried her hands and squirted sanitizer on them, she whispered, "Is it me, or is he four going on forty? He sounds *old* sometimes."

"There's something about him, isn't there?" Luke led the group over to the windows and sighed with utter contentment at the sight of Aggie rocking Lania. *Is she singing? Oh, Lord please let it be "Jesus Loves Me" or "All Through the Night." Please....*

Julie stopped at the entrance and waved. "Everyone here? I can get her. Without hesitation, Luke shoved his phone at her. "Would you record her for a minute, first? She seems oblivious to us." *And please forgive me for taking advantage of the situation.*

"Do you have to wash up every time you go in?" Ellie's voice jerked him from his thoughts.

"Yep. And we have to wipe down our phones if we bring them in. We have to keep them on vibrate, too." He flipped up the badge he wore. "I wipe this down, too. Have to have it, or they won't let me in—even though they know me now. I left it in the truck this morning, and she sent me back for it."

Their plan held a flaw—one Luke noticed as he watched Kenzie try to make faces at the baby—faces that a sleeping Lania didn't respond to at all. *What'll we do about them visiting with Aggie? I can't let Ronnie come up and go back down. He might protest, and the hospital isn't—*

That thought shook him to the core. *Lord, what have we done? I'm actually afraid of how my son will respond when he doesn't get his way. We were never afraid of Cari's reactions. Not surprised when they weren't appropriate, but we didn't dread them. And in public, she usually... oh boy.*

Aggie stared at him through the window, a question showing in the wrinkled forehead and uncertain expression. He held up one hand and finger-spelled the name. R-o-n-n-i-e. The fact that she understood immediately drove home just how serious their problem was. *I got him under control at Willow's. It can be done. Lord, we need it here. Just for this moment.*

Luke gave them a few more minutes to snap pictures and wave at the baby before he urged them back toward the elevators. "I'm going to take you guys back down and get the others. You'll come back up to the room once we're done with Vannie, Tavish, and Ronnie. I don't want Aggie to have to walk back and forth as much."

Everyone agreed — right up to the moment when the elevator doors shut behind them. Ellie pulled him into the corner and hissed, "What about Ronnie? I thought the idea was for him to go last so you could bolt out with him if he got loud."

"Well, I'm not making this hard on Aggie, and I'm not making you guys miss your visit with her, so this is how it'll have to be."

If he hadn't seen her swallow hard, Ellie's next words might have confused him. "Poor Ronnie."

Luke left a warning with his mother — a warning and a request for prayer. Libby shook her head as if she didn't understand. "Are you telling me you *expect* him to throw a tantrum?"

"I'm telling you that we've let it get to the point that I wouldn't be surprised."

"Oh, Luke, you should have told — never mind. It's not the time." Libby turned to Vannie, Tavish, and Ronnie. Her eyes lingered on Vannie and Tavish for a moment before she started speaking. "Listen to me. You need to be quiet up there. Mamas are working hard to have babies, and those babies need sleep. You need to use super quiet voices — whispers, even. Do you understand?"

The solemn nods — even from Tavish and Vannie — lent a hint of humor to an otherwise nerve-wracking moment. He led his children upstairs, ignoring shocked expressions from people he'd passed with the others, and to the NICU area. Ronnie scrubbed with excess exuberance. Tavish and Vannie with careful diligence. Vannie's eyes grew wide at the sight of Aggie at the end of Lania's little cot, rocking her as she stood there — rocking and singing.

"Aunt Aggie is singing!"

Luke couldn't hide his grin—didn't want to. "That she is. Julie... the one over there with teddy bears on her scrubs? She got a video of it for me." Phone out, video found, they all crowded around it to hear. As the faint sounds of "Brahms' Lullaby" reached his ears, Luke choked back his emotions and thanked the Lord for song. *It's a step. I need to remember that. She didn't sing at all for so long....*

"I thought she'd sing "Jesus Loves Me" or something." Vannie moved back behind him and whispered, "Is she mad at God for this?"

Oh, how he ached to say no. Every part of him screamed to deny it, but Luke gave a slight nod. "She is, but mothers sometimes aren't themselves when they're expecting. I just keep praying."

Aggie must have seen them, because she stepped closer to the window, Julie pushing the cot behind her. But Vannie didn't move. She caught his arm and stared up at him. "You could have told me. I could have been praying." The girl blinked back tears he couldn't see and sighed. "When did we stop talking as a family? Gramby didn't know Aunt Aggie was on bed rest. Aunt Marianne showed up with a ton of presents and apologized for not being there for us. You know what she said?"

I can only imagine. Luke just shrugged.

"She said, 'I would have been here if I'd known. Cheri's about ready to kill me for not telling her. But how could I? I didn't *know!*'"

"We weren't trying to hide anything, Vannie. We just—"

"Didn't talk. No one at the church knew." She frowned. "Then again, no one asked, either. They just heard she was resting and never offered to visit or—"

As much as Luke wanted to leave blame with the church, with the family—with *anyone*—he couldn't. "It's Christmas, Vannie. People are extra busy. And when you're extra busy, you don't see what you might otherwise. Don't blame anyone. We all made mistakes."

Ronnie's excited voice broke through their conversation. Luke hunkered down on his heels and caught his son's face in his hands. "Remember what Gramby told you about being quiet?" He stood and lifted his son. "See that baby—the one over there."

Once more, Luke explained about the baby's problems and how he had to be taken to a bigger hospital. "That's why you *must* be quieter. They'll make us leave if you aren't."

"You make them let us stay. Because you Lannie's daddy."

The showdown began. Luke prayed it would be quiet, swift, decisive. "It doesn't matter if I can or can't. I won't. You will be quiet so we can see Lania, and then we can walk Mommy back to her room."

Ronnie's eyes shifted to the window. "I see Mommy?"

"Just as soon as we get done looking at the baby."

"She's cute. Can we go?"

A snort from Vannie and a chuckle from Tavish nearly sent Luke over the edge. "Maybe Vannie and Tavish want to stay a bit longer…."

But with a lingering glance from Tavish, and a signed, "I love you" from Vannie, they backed away from the window — a signal for Aggie to join them. But even as they waited, as they walked the hall back to her room, as they waited for Aggie in the bathroom, Luke's mind whirled with thoughts.

Did I do this, Lord? If I had called for help, asked others to come — if I hadn't left her up there alone all the time, would this have changed, perhaps? Would it have been different?

MUST I SPEND THIS CHRISTMAS ALONE?

Chapter Twenty-Four

Wednesday, December 24th

The clock on her phone read 1:37. Somewhere down the hall, a woman screamed for an epidural. The quiet, soothing voices of the nurses hinted that, for whatever reason, the woman couldn't have one. Again, a scream ripped through the halls. Jerome peered in at her, gave her an apologetic smile, and unlatched the door stopper. "Do you want me to tell them down there that you're awake—just in case your little, fierce princess wants a drink?"

"Would you?"

"Happy to. Need anything?"

Saying her own bed wouldn't help any, so Aggie just shook her head. "I'm good."

A basket of goodies beside her drew her attention once more—the basket she'd forced herself to ignore for hours. Not for the first time since he'd left, Aggie regretted sending Luke home for the night. *I didn't know I'd be awake half of it.*

Aggie grabbed the basket and settled in for a "pamper fest", as Libby had called it. A book by her favorite author, a new pen and a box of note cards—the basket held a variety of things to keep her busy. She pulled out a can of mixed nuts, and a tiny wrapped package tumbled over onto the book. Aggie pulled it out and read the little tag tied to it.

I thought you'd like a countdown to Christmas calendar. Can't wait for you to get home. Love, Ellie.

The date on her phone mocked the idea. "You're a bit late for that." Still, Aggie unwrapped the little gift and grinned at the quarter-inch stack of sticky notes. The top one said, "3 days 'til Christmas." A lovely border of ivy and holly made it festive enough. Aggie tore it off and stared at the next. "Whaaa...." Again, the sticky note said, "3 days 'til Christmas."

She started to peel it off as well, but a giant three on the one beneath it stopped her. "What on earth?" A flip through the little stack showed a couple dozen green sticky notes—all saying three days until Christmas. But near the end, a yellow sticky note said one. She moved back and saw another yellow one—one that said two. Beneath those, one red sticky note stood out. A smile formed as Aggie's fingers slid over the green tree in the center, and in the middle of that tree, a giant number 1 made of ornament balls.

The bottom of the stack was the cardboard base. Ellie had colored it with a navy marker, painted a lovely white star in the middle, and on that star written, "Christmas is here!"

Phone out, she filmed a short video, showing each element, and turned the camera to herself at the end. "Why do you think she did that? All those 'three days' pages? I should be home in a couple of days—and not before Christmas."

Jerome stepped in the room as she set up the little calendar on her bedside tray. "What's that?"

"One of the kids made me a countdown to Christmas calendar."

He picked it up and frowned. "It's one day off. Can I take it off or...?"

"Go ahead."

Jerome tore off the top sticky note and laughed. "You knew it said three still, didn't you?"

"Check it out. I can't figure out why she did that!"

"Seems simple enough to me." Jerome set it back up and shook his head. "Clever."

As much as she hated to do it, Aggie had to ask. "Why do you say that?"

He helped her from bed—a silent testimony that she could see Lania—and asked about her pad. "Everything okay there?" Aggie nodded and waited. Once in the hall, he began talking. "Well, I don't know *your* kid, but I know when I was a kid, I would have done it like that because Christmas isn't Christmas if Mom's not there, right?"

"Okay… but why give it to *me* then? Wouldn't that be more for her?"

He shrugged. "Seems to me that a kid might think her mom would feel bad for missing Christmas."

Nothing sounded *more* like Ellie. As she settled into the chair for yet another ten minutes of ineffectual nursing, Aggie pondered the idea of a delayed Christmas. *Luke would be all for it, but what about the children. They shouldn't have to wait. I guess they could do stocking —* Her heart sank. *I didn't even make a shopping list for stocking stuffers. There's nothing in there. Nothing at all.*

All through the feeding that only served to agitate Lania, Aggie tried to think of who it would least inconvenience to send shopping. She needed ideas—fast ones. Fun ones. Fun *large* ones to fill the stockings quickly. The mental list grew as she allowed Lania to fall asleep while nursing.

Socks
Scarves for Ellie and Vannie
Gloves for the little kids.
Blocks of wood for Tavish?
Paints and brushes for Ellie? Maybe little bottles for ink?
Candy. Chocolate.
Fun T-shirts from the Christian Bookstore?
Books!
Coloring Books
Silly Putty for Laird. He'd be broken hearted if we didn't.

The list grew, long and detailed. Aggie only prayed it would stick in her mind until she could make it to her room again. "We're going to get this sorted out, little Lania. And you don't even *have* a stocking. You weren't supposed to be here, you know."

Mary, Lania's night nurse, interjected a protest. "I thought you and Luke were believers."

"We are." *Even if I don't exactly feel it much these days, it's still true. I believe.* James' ominous reminder that even the demons believe and have the good sense to tremble did little to reassure her.

"Then what do you think you're doing saying she's not supposed to be here. Does the Lord know what He's doing or not? She came exactly when she needed to—for whatever reason. Don't you doubt that for a minute."

Why… how… the questions filled her mind. Why did the baby have to come early? Why had she been on limited movement? Why had it been necessary to strip her of the dream of a beautiful home birth? How was she supposed to trust the Lord when He'd allowed her baby to be at risk?

I don't know. Everything I'd planned and wanted. All my goals and dreams – shot down because this little one…. Aggie gazed into the sleeping face of her daughter. *– because she wouldn't stay where she belonged without me confined to that room.* The alternative choked her. *What if I'd ignored it? I didn't think it was serious. I thought it was just everyone overreacting.*

"Wanna share?"

"I'm angry."

Mary's laughter, quiet but melodic, soothed rather than rankled. "Have you told Him?"

Aggie winced at the idea. At Mary's questioning glance, she added, "Because one doesn't tell Almighty God that one is ticked off at Him?"

"Why not? Don't you think He knows it?" Mary brought her a fresh bottle. Why don't you try to feed the little princess before you pump again?"

Lania woke the moment the bottle touched her lips. Aggie waited until Mary returned to her charts before she spoke again. "It just feels like we *shouldn't* get angry with God."

"Maybe we shouldn't, but I don't see how pretending it isn't true is any more spiritual. You admit it. Let it all out. Then shut your trap and let the Lord speak to *you*."

All the protests that welled up in her fizzled when they reached her lips. Instead, Aggie nodded. "Maybe I will. Maybe…."

If bad things happen in threes, then I want out of here. Laird stared at the puddle of cider that spread across the entryway, his mind refusing to tell him what he should do. Kenzie dashed through the door with a plastic shopping bag in each hand, and before he could stop her, slipped, fell and slid across the floor. Cans of tomatoes rolled out of one bag—onions and carrots out of another. *And that's three strikes. I'm out.*

Two seconds later, the resounding *crack* of her head on the floor or the wall, Laird didn't know which, registered. "Sorry, Kenz. The cider fell. Are you okay?"

She stood, dazed, and staggered forward. Laird leapt over the puddle and tried to steady her. Kenzie blinked up at him. "Huh?"

One look at her strange blinking sent Laird racing to the basement door. The sound of Tavish and Ellie coming up the steps—about-face and bolted to the door. "Watch the entry—big puddle. Kenzie's hurt." With that, he dashed to the mudroom, grabbed a few dirty towels, dashed back, and tossed them in the general direction of the puddle as he hurried back to the basement once more.

"Uncle Luke! Kenzie hit her head. She's acting funny!" At the first sound of feet on the stairs, Laird raced back to the entryway where Vannie, Tavish, and Ellie all skirted the odd pile of towels and puddle of cider on their way to check on Kenzie.

"It *smells* festive in here, anyway." Vannie grinned as she passed. "I knew that handle was going to break. I should have warned you."

The second Luke arrived, Laird gave Vannie a saucy grin and said, "It's Vannie's fault. She gave me the apple...." His voice dropped to a whisper. "*Cider*. But I didn't drink! I spilled that stuff. I resisted the temptation. Praise the Lord!"

Luke didn't respond at first. He watched Kenzie's eyes and assured her it was okay to cry. "Gonna call the clinic and see what they think." He turned to survey the mess. "Can someone actually finish wiping all that up?" His eyes rested on Vannie, and she moved toward it. "No, you...." Luke fumbled for his phone.

"Aggie sent me a text message—stockings. We forgot about them. She wants you guys to have stockings in the morning. Can you—"

As they spoke, Laird worked on the mess, carrying dripping towels back to the mudroom and returning with a mop. He wanted to go, but if Kenzie needed a trip to the clinic, then he'd have to stay to watch the little kids. *Sometimes being an older kid in a big family just isn't fair.*

A conversation he'd overheard between Gramby Libby and Luke rebuked him. *"I think she just let her disappointments pile up until they became personal demons. Instead of 'casting her cares' on Jesus, she clutched them to her heart."*

Laird shook off the feeling. *Gramby is right. It's like that Spiderman movie where the black stuff just clings to him the more he embraces his darker self. Gotta let it go. It's my fault anyway.*

"—Laird come with me? This is a lot of stuff, and he's better at the boy stuff."

Without hesitation, Luke agreed. "Great idea. And make sure you get stuff for Aggie's, too. I'll take it to her tonight. It'll make her smile."

Oh, how he ached just to agree and go. After all, it hadn't been his idea. But Laird, still filled with the idea of doing what is right, spoke up. "What if Kenzie needs to go in? Who's gonna watch the little kids?"

"I'll get Mrs. Dyke, Murphy, William—even Mom would come. You guys go." Laird barely reached his coat when Luke's voice stopped him. "But thanks for being prepared to do what we needed most. I appreciate it."

"I wasn't." Laird blurted out the words before his weaker side embraced the praise. "I wanted to keep quiet. I was feeling me—" He glanced around at a room full of questioning eyes and stopped himself. "I'll tell you about it later." He turned to Vannie. "Let me go get my wallet."

Inside half an hour, they inched their way through the over-packed garden department at Walmart. Vannie just wanted to get into the store, but the crowds were against her. As they waited, Laird saw a stocking—too small to hold much, but beautiful. "I want to get that for Lania."

Vannie's protest carried over the din of the chattering shoppers and the PA system. "It's too small. We'd have to buy another one next year."

"Or the next. But I don't care. It'll make Aunt Aggie smile."

"No.... I'm not wasting money on something we'll just give away."

Ignoring Vannie's objections, Laird set it in the front seat part of his cart and let the flap fall on it. "Well, I'm getting it. I'll pay for it. She should have a stocking, and Aunt Aggie should get to choose the 'real' one."

Her expected protest—Vannie never did handle dissention from her superior wisdom well—never surfaced. Instead, her eyes lit up. "That's what we should do for Christmas! When she gets home! We should have a *shower!* Can't you see it?"

He couldn't. Laird stared as she bubbled over with excitement about something he couldn't fathom and waited for a comprehensible explanation. Still, she waited for his response. "Sorry... lost."

The doorway cleared for half a second, and Vannie shot through it. "C'mon. Oh! Dog treats. They're not on the list, but Ian and Ronnie will be crushed if the dogs don't have *something* for Christmas." Laird just shoved his cart in the general direction of her retreating form and tried to keep up. As he rounded the corner, Laird could have sworn she added, "—get new flea collars, too. Aunt Aggie did that last year."

"Do we *need* to buy those *right now?* Don't you think we should *try* to be as frugal as possible?"

"Why?" Vannie stood beside giant bags of dog food and stared at him.

"Because this is going to be expensive—right on top of all those repairs? Did you *see* the electric bill for when we were gone? Trying to heat all of Brant's Corners for days isn't exactly cheap."

She gripped the cart and stared into it. "Oh...."

With that two-letter word, Laird's plans for *his* money changed. *The "shower" for Aunt Aggie. That's what I'll use it for.* He pulled out his wallet and counted. *So glad I didn't buy that robot....*

"Laird!"

His head shot up. "What?"

"I asked what you thought about the dog bones?"

Oh, brother. Why are girls so extreme? He reached across her and pulled two from the shelf. "That they can use now. I just

342

don't see why buying something they don't need right now makes sense when I know money has to be tight—or will be." He pocketed his wallet again. "I've got a hundred fifty dollars—almost. We can do a decent shower with that, right?"

She didn't even look at him. Vannie dug through her purse, pulled out her wallet, and counted her cash. "I only have seventy-nine. I bought Gramby—"

"It's okay to spend your money. If I had time, I'd go to the bank...."

Vannie's eyes widened. "That's it. Okay, you find a car seat that looks like it'll hold a tiny baby. Oh, and look for some toys—think *girl*. I'll go withdraw a bunch from my account. I have my debit card with me. Then I'll go buy a bunch of preemie stuff at that little store down the street—you know, the one Aunt Aggie was drooling over."

Relief—it had never felt so good. Vannie in a baby store—torture for anyone. *You're going to get married the day after you turn eighteen and be pregnant before you get home from your honeymoon if you have anything to say about it.*

"Send a text to Gram." At her questioning glance, Laird grinned. "About the shower. I bet Aunt Corinne and the others will want to do something, too."

She stared at him, eyes wide, and a huge grin on her face. "And to think I used to wish you were a sister."

"What does that have to do with anything?"

If possible, her grin grew even wider. "Because we totally would have fought over who got to go shopping for clothes and who had to stay and buy boring things like car seats and toys. You just taught me to be grateful for brothers."

Crackling logs and glowing embers provided the only light in the living room as Luke and the children gathered to read the story of Jesus' birth. He settled himself in the large, over-stuffed chair that he always used on Christmas Eve, and made room for Ronnie and Cari as had been tradition since the youngest Sullivan was born. Lorna settled in Laird's lap, just as she always did, and Ian curled up beside Vannie. The others scattered themselves—on the couch for Ellie, at Luke's feet for Kenzie, and as far under the tree as he could worm his way in for Tavish. Everything remained exactly as it always had—except for the heartbreaking absence of Aggie in the corner of the couch.

Luke pulled out his phone, slid his Bible app to the right place, and began reading. "'In the days of Herod, the king of Judea....'"

Ronnie fidgeted, but Luke knew that if he just kept reading, the boy would likely fall asleep. He did anytime they did a read-aloud at night. With that in mind, Luke kept the cadence of his voice as soothing and steady as he could—avoiding a monotone, but striving to keep it just a little less lively than he might otherwise have used.

As he read about Mary giving birth, Vannie sucked in air and Kenzie pressed her cheek against his knee. Luke did his best to keep his voice steady, but emotion broke it in several places. At the first mention of the angel, Tavish pushed the button that lit up angels perched on either end of the curtain rod over the windows.

Lorna's eyes twinkled as her mouth dropped open in wonder. "It's so beautiful!"

You say that every year. Luke's next thought nearly choked him. *It's Aggie's favorite part, and she's missing it.* He swallowed hard and kept reading. His finger slipped back and forth between Luke and Matthew to tell the whole story. At the mention of the magi and the star, Tavish flipped the toggle for the star at the top of the tree, and the moment Luke mentioned the gifts of gold, frankincense, and myrrh, Tavish flipped the final switch as he crawled from beneath the gift-laden tree.

She has a gift for making things both memorable and meaningful. And she's missing it. Lord, please don't let this harden her heart further.

"Uncle Luke?" Cari whispered her words into his ear.

"Hmmm?"

"Are you going to finish reading the story?" An arm stole around his neck. "I don't like the part about killing the babies, but I do want to hear about how he didn't stay with his mom."

You would.

"—would." Tavish grinned at her. "Do you think that's what the Bible means when it says He was tempted in every way that we are?"

344

Oh, boy. Luke decided to get them back on track. "We need to finish so I can take Aggie her stocking."

With those words, the entire tone of the room shifted. Cari buried her face in his neck. Ronnie glanced at the empty spot where Aggie usually sat, back up at Luke, and burst into tears, wailing for Mommy. Vannie tried to take him, but the boy clung to Luke and grew louder with every failed attempt. Luke shook his head and read louder—louder and much more rushed. "'...favor with God and man.'"

Whether he remembered previous years—years where, immediately after reading the story, he'd had to go to bed, or because the full impact of Aggie's absence had impressed itself on him, Ronnie took the moment as the equivalent of bedtime apocalypse and fought against it. Luke tried cajoling, praying, explaining—but sanity slapped him upside the head just as he almost resorted to bribery.

"Ronnie!"

The boy didn't even pause in his protests.

Luke stared down at him, took a deep breath, and swung him over one shoulder. One arm wrapped around his legs, while the other kept him steady as Luke marched up the stairs. "You guys stay down here for a few minutes. Ronnie and I need to have a little talk."

Ian and Ronnie shared a half-room at the end of the landing where most of their toys were stored. Luke set Ronnie on the bed and stood over him as the boy thrashed around. Indecision wracked him. Allowing his son to continue a tantrum seemed cruel. Then again, wasn't it just as cruel to chastise the boy for doing what he'd been half-trained to do? *Omission of good training is still training. It may be* bad *training, but it's still training.*

Before he could decide, Ronnie ramped up the noise, and this time there could be no doubt. It was all for show. Luke lowered his voice to a quiet rumble and ordered, "Ronnie, hush."

The boy didn't stop, but he did dial back the volume just a bit. The kicking, the flailing—just as exuberant as ever and likely an attempt to keep himself awake. *You didn't fall asleep in the reading this time. That's what I get for counting on that.*

Luke sat him up and held him steady. "Ronnie, you've already disobeyed once. I said to hush. Now I'm saying to sit still."

Ronnie's foot shot out and kicked Luke in the knee. That stopped the wails as the boy's eyes widened and his throat choked. Luke shook his head. "I said to sit still. Two times you disobeyed."

The boy swallowed hard and with wide, tear-filled eyes, choked out, "Two swats?"

"Yep."

"I stopped."

Man, this kid learned to negotiate before he learned to talk! How is that even possible? Now he's a master! But Luke couldn't take the time to ponder the mysteries of his son. "Yes—*after* you disobeyed. I should count throwing a tantrum in the first place a disobedience. You know better."

"Mommy lets me." The boy's bottom lip trembled. "I want Mommy."

Make it harder, son. Go ahead. Knife to the gut while you're at it?

"She needs come home."

"Lania needs her too, Ronnie. She's too little to be at the hospital alone. And Mo—"

The boy perked up and his eyes widened. "We give her to the pound? Like the kittens?"

Oh, brother. Kittens. What next? Luke shook his head as he seated himself next to his son on the bed. "Sorry, we're not giving away a baby. She's family. I sure am glad that Vannie and Cari and Ian didn't ask us to give *you* to the pound when *you* were born."

Ronnie crawled up in Luke's lap and buried his face in Luke's chest. "I not *really* want her to go. She's cute. Like puppies."

Someone's fixated on animals. If anyone even hinted *at a pet for Christmas, I'll shoot 'em.*

Ronnie yawned. "I sleepy." He crawled off Luke's lap and struggled to climb under the covers.

"Need help there, son?"

Inside two minutes, the boy was tucked in well, had prayed for Mommy and Lania, hinted that he wanted sleep to be over fast for stockings, and muttered something about Christmas for all the puppies in the world. *And that's a hint if I ever heard one. He's good*

346

at his age. Really good.

"Night, Daddy. I love you."

Luke kissed his forehead and whispered, "Love you, too, son. Sleep well."

His heart lighter than it had been in days, Luke jogged down the stairs and into the living room. Vannie and Laird looked up from their stuffing of Aggie's stocking with confused expression. "What?"

Laird shrugged and grabbed another bag. He rifled through it, pulled out a package of pens, and shoved it in the stocking. But Vannie, hand still stuck in a Walmart bag, just stared at him.

"You look upset." Luke stepped forward. "What is it? Did something happen?"

"I started to go upstairs a couple of minutes ago, but I heard you tell Ronnie he was getting swats, so I came back down."

Luke's groan filled the living room. "Man, that kid is good." He took the stairs two at a time, but as he neared Ronnie's bed, the boy's trademarked snore reached him. "Ronnie?"

Not a shuffle, not a change in breathing—nothing. The boy snoozed with what looked like blissful abandon. *Wait'll Mibs hears this one.*

That thought sparked a new idea. He hurried downstairs, found a pad of paper in the library, and while the kids finished stuffing Aggie's stocking, he wrote a letter. Three balled up pieces later, what he hoped to say filled the pages. Luke slipped them into an envelope and met the kids in the living room. "Okay, I'm going now. You guys go to bed. If you need me, just send a message."

"Are you staying all night?" Cari's voice held a note of forced bravery.

"Probably. I'll be home before you *should* get up."

Hugs, kisses, prayers, coat and keys. Out to the truck—back in again for Aggie's stocking. Slick roads sent his truck skidding—twice. He spun out in the parking lot, and only the lack of cars on Christmas Eve kept him from hitting anything. Luke fumbled for his badge, grabbed Aggie's stocking, and hurried into the building. Elevators, corridors, moaning women, crying babies—babies that had come just a little too early to be "the Christmas baby."

That thought twanged a sour note to his heartstrings. *She was relieved that we weren't going to have a Christmas baby.*

"Babies born at Christmastime get shortchanged around their birthdays. I'm glad it's January."

Lania's birthday was only three days before. *Please don't let her think of that.*

He found her bed empty but her journal open on the bedtable. One of Ellie's countdown sticky notes had been folded back and a note written on it. *Read it, Luke. This time, I want you to.*

Oh, how he wished he could refuse. His mind protested. His heart, as well. But ignoring a request—impossible. So, Luke read.

I've been thinking all day. Last night, Mary told me to tell the Lord how I feel. So, I'm doing it. I'm telling Him everything. She's right. It's not like He doesn't know. But maybe if I get it out, I'll know how to ask Him to take away this horrible anger I feel.

I thought it was just my birth plan. All that research was wasted, it seems. I blamed everyone for the disruption of my pregnancy — first the vandals, then Luke for making me go to the hospital, the kids for stressing me out, Luke for upsetting me by trying to be the guy I married. Just writing it down is disgusting. I hate this.

No, I'm mad at God. Furious. I've never felt more betrayed. I had no reason not to assume all would be well with the pregnancy. After all, my sister had <u>six</u> successful pregnancies, and I'd already had Ronnie. Of course, I expected to get what I wanted. And He gave me bed rest and a premature baby.

You know, nothing turned out like I expected. I should be teaching now — in Dad's old job. I should have a sister I get to visit with now and then. If I had any kids, it should be just the two I gave birth to — not because I don't <u>want</u> Allie's children, but because I want <u>Allie</u>.

It's probably full of myself to say it, but here goes. I feel like Job. God keeps stripping one dream after another from me.

Part of me says that's ridiculous. I have Luke. I wouldn't want any of those other things if I couldn't have him. But who says betrayal feels rational? And I totally feel betrayed.

I just want to go home and be done with it all. Start life again with the kids and little Lania. I'll have Luke. I'll have our home and our family. But for how long? Someone already tried to destroy our house. Will it burn down? Will someone take the kids from me? Geraldine? Is that what those gifts were? Trojan horses to lull us into false security? Is

348

He going to take that all away from me, too?

What does God want from me? Why? I'd say He wants me not to be angry anymore, but He <u>caused</u> *this anger. So then what?*

I need help. I can't live with this feeling. It's killing me. I'm going to leave this for Luke to read. I can't tell him this stuff, but he needs to know. He's probably the only one who can help me. I don't think the Lord wants to anymore.

I can't blame Him.

Breath constricting, eyes pooling, heart breaking, Luke stared at the last two paragraphs, begging the Lord for help. He pleaded for wisdom. *Lord, I knew she was struggling, but this…*

The memory of his aunt's rebukes and his mother's self-recriminations upon learning of their troubles prompted an immediate text message to both women as well as Marcus Vaughn. He hesitated as Vannie's face filled his thoughts, but chose to leave her out. The text message — short and simple. AGGIE STRUGGLING IN HER FAITH. PLEASE PRAY NOW.

A glance out the door and down the hall showed no sign of his wife returning, so Luke made his way down the elevator to the abandoned lobby. His finger hovered over one of his top contacts and tapped. The phone rang.

"Hey, there." The chipperness in Chad's voice grated on Luke's nerves. Grated and then filled him with guilt. "You guys ready for Christmas?"

Luke strained as he tried to swallow the lump threatening to choke him and coughed. "Not doing much for Christmas tomorrow — just stockings. With Aggie and Lania in the hospital and all."

"Sounds smart. Mom was put out at you, Luke."

"That's kind of why I'm calling." A glance around him — embarrassment sent his face flaming. *Am I honestly afraid of non-existent people overhearing? How ridiculous.*

"Luke?"

"Sorry. Okay. You know your ten thousand and one counseling sessions? Well, I'm calling in the debt. I need help."

Strained silence. Luke listened, concerned that perhaps he'd interrupted Chad at work. But before he could ask, the reason hit him. "You can laugh. I'm not going to be offended." When silence continued, Luke realized Chad hadn't even heard. He'd muffled the phone to hide it. "Anyway, I'll just keep saying it again and again until you return. I'm not offended. Laugh away. Go on. Laugh. I get it. Yep. Yes I do. Laugh, Chad. Just laugh."

"Sorry." A strained snicker followed. "I was trying... but *you* coming to *me*... that's rich."

If you only knew how I didn't even hesitate. His conscience ordered him to say it. "Um, Chad?"

"Yeah?"

He grinned at the mental image of Chad hearing what he planned to say. "I didn't even hesitate. I needed counsel and immediately dialed you."

"Wow."

He couldn't help it. Luke laughed. "No, we reserve that one for your wife. But yeah. Okay, here's the thing...." Though he'd planned to give the briefest of explanations, Luke found himself spilling everything—from her stress at arriving home to more vandalism to premature labor and bed rest. "She's taking it as an attack from the Lord. She's angry—feels betrayed."

"Aggie? Hymn-singing, Jesus-spouting, Aggie? No way. Seriously, Willow was ready to throttle her for all the hymns."

"She hasn't sang anything since we got home from your house—not that I can recall. She doesn't pray. She doesn't read her Bible. She seethes, Chad. She sits there and seethes."

The dead air between them spoke louder than any response Chad could have offered. "Are you sure, Luke? This doesn't sound like her."

"She left a journal entry for me—like Willow does for you. She said something like, 'I think God expects me to get rid of this anger, but I can't. God made me angry.'"

"Oh, man." Chad's voice muffled for a moment—not an unusual occurrence. He'd be back as soon as he slowed down a speeding car or sent a kid home who shouldn't be wandering the streets after ten o'clock. It rarely was anything more serious.

Three minutes passed before Chad returned. "Sorry. Guy going home drunk from his girlfriend's Christmas Eve party. Apparently there's a lot more nog than egg in their recipe."

"Did you know that Vannie didn't know egg nog was supposed to have alcohol? She was deeply offended."

"Whoa. You're trying to change the subject."

A protest welled up in him, but Luke couldn't deny it. "Maybe."

"Well, it's funny, anyway. Luke Sullivan changing the subject. I should mark the date."

It only took one word—a name—to bring Chad back to the topic. "Aggie...."

"Right. Okay. First, can I talk to Willow about it? She went through the loss of her mother. I remember the raw anger she hurled at me. If I hadn't been there, she might have turned it to the Lord and rejected Him."

As Luke pondered Chad's words, his spirit resisted. "But this is about the baby—the birth. How—"

Chad's interruption shouldn't have surprised him. Nothing characterized his cousin more than an eagerness to help. "I don't think so, Luke. Everyone has raved about how well Aggie dealt with all the changes thrown at her at once, but did she? Did she really? Or is it possible that she just *had* to keep going. To 'do the next thing' as Mom always says."

"Isn't that something Elisabeth Elliot said?"

"You're kind of missing the point. Aggie's whole life was turned upside down. And she was amazing. No one is saying she wasn't. She grieved for the loss of her sister. I mean, we all saw that. But—" Chad groaned. "Man, this sounds like a lot of psychobabble, but think about it. Did she grieve the loss of her plans—her dreams? I tell you those things were almost harder for Willow to deal with than the loss of her mom. As hard as that was, she'd see Mother again, but Willow can't get back those dreams."

Aggie's words struck his heart in strong, repeated blows until it bruised and bled. Luke choked. "She wrote that. It was in that journal entry. I just didn't *see* it." A glance at the time told him he should return to Aggie's room before she arrived, found the stocking, and found *him* gone. "Look, I have to get back up there, but thanks. I think you may have hit on something." Another thought strangled him for a moment before he whispered, "You don't think she regrets marrying me, do you?"

"Anyone who has ever seen her look at you knows. She thinks she's the luckiest woman on the planet. She probably is."

Praise usually left Luke squirming and miserable. This time he sighed and shook his head. "Thanks, Chad. Needed to hear that tonight."

The phone went dead just as he stepped into the elevator.

Their eyes met as they each rounded the corner. Disappointment filled her. *I hoped he'd read it before I came back. Now it'll be awkward. Great.*

A weak smile filled Aggie's heart with dread. *What's wrong now? So help me, I needed good news tonight. Something – anything – that says, "God doesn't hate you. You're not that farmer in the joke where God just says, 'There's something about you that chaps my hide.'" That's how I feel, Lo – God.* As much as she tried, acknowledging Him as Lord of her life didn't work. *I feel like You just don't like me, find me annoying, and delight in tormenting me.*

Luke reached Aggie just a couple of doors from her room and pulled her close, holding her with ferocity-laced tenderness. An inexplicable ache filled her – tormented her. "Luke?"

"I understand, Aggie. I do. Let's get you comfortable again. You look exhausted."

"I need more water, and they keep forgetting to refill my pitcher."

A stocking on her bed and the removed sticky note from her pillow explained the hug. "You *did* come in already. Why didn't you come to the NICU?"

"Had a call to make." Luke moved everything out of the way and helped her into bed. Then, without a word, he climbed up next to her, pulled her back to his chest, and wrapped an arm around her. "I read the journal. I hope you still wanted me to."

"I don't know how to talk about it. The more I try, the more it feels as if everything will be permanently awful if I say anything aloud."

Luke dropped his voice as deep as it could go and growled, "Do not speak that into existence!"

A giggle escaped. "Exactly."

How long has it been since I heard that giggle? It seems a century.

"Luke?"

"Hmmm?"

"Are you mad at me?"

His arms tightened around her. "No, Mibs."

"Disappointed in me?"

His breath blew hot over her ear. "More disappointed in *me*."

"Why?" Aggie rolled over—how many decades it took, she couldn't hope to calculate—and gazed into his troubled eyes. "I don't understand."

Seconds that stretched beyond the snapping point passed as Luke's jaw worked. He'd have something profound to say—or heart-wrenchingly tender. *I never can guess which it'll be.*

"When I first met you all, I watched for signs that you weren't allowing yourselves to grieve." When he paused to reflect, Aggie took slow, steadying breaths to avoid interrupting the trains of thought moving about the marshaling yard of his mind. Pain filled his eyes. His lips thinned as he tried to repress emotions. "I think I did okay with that, but...."

"You did great, Luke. Really. I missed so much with the kids—even with me. But you and Uncle Zeke. You both were so observant."

Luke hardly allowed her to finish—unusual at best. "But we didn't watch for *all* that you needed to grieve." Slight movement at the corner of his mouth told her he was chewing his inner lip. "I called Chad."

Her heart clenched and air whooshed from her lungs. As Aggie tried to control the unexpected rising panic within her, Luke's eyes pleaded with her to understand. Where and how she gathered the strength to smile and ask, "And?" she never knew.

Luke broke down. He pulled her close and sobbed into her hair. "I—fearful—resent me—just needed—counsel me."

"Oh, Luke, I'm sorry." Even as she said it, Aggie realized that for the first time in longer than she could remember, she truly *was* sorry.

It took minutes, several of them, for him to be able to talk again. First, his emotions held him hostage, then his thoughts attacked. Aggie saw it in every emotion flitting across his face. She saw it and wept for what they'd become.

"Chad was talking about Willow and how she handled her mother's death."

Words of protest welled up in her. It wasn't the same —couldn't be. Willow had lost her *mother*. The only other person in the world that she knew. Her entire world had been shaken to the core. *While I just lost my sister.*

"—said that losing her mom was hard, but she had confidence in seeing Kari again."

"Well, keeping that in her mind probably kept her focused on the Lord instead of growing bitter and angry at Him."

Luke cradled her cheek in his hand. Where the kiss came from, she couldn't say, but it had been longer than she liked to think of since they'd had a moment like that. *It used to be daily. I think the last time was when we embarrassed one of the kids in our room. A week ago? Two? I don't even know.*

"Mibs, she got angry. She lashed out. Chad was just in the way, so she took it out on him."

"I did that, too — some. I was furious at you for making me go into the doctor."

Something came over him. Aggie called it his "conscience's aura" when joking about it with others. He had something he wanted to share and felt it wasn't his place. *He'll do it, though. I wonder if he knows I can tell when he will and when he won't.*

"There were weeks — maybe even a couple of months — there when she wouldn't talk to him. She was bitter, angry, and took it all out on him. Remember the headstone he came to talk about that day? He did that *against* her wishes."

"But those are beautiful 'stones'. She oils them, you know. She went out once when we were there even. I asked her about it." Aggie swallowed hard at the memory. "She choked up a bit and said, 'Mother would be ashamed of me for being that attached to where her shell is resting, but those markers just make it special somehow.'"

"Those 'markers' as she called them...." Luke sighed. "Those were when I knew he'd fall in love with her. Sometimes I think he was already."

Aggie fought back emotions that she chalked up to plummeting hormones. "He said once that he fell in love with her when he became afraid she would say no to his proposal. Seems a bit backwards, but sweet."

"I disagree." Luke pulled covers over Aggie's shoulders and

smiled at her. "That's why he became afraid — because he already loved her. That's just when he realized it."

They lay there for the better part of an hour, not speaking, eyes meeting and fleeing at random moments. Twice, she thought he'd fallen asleep. Once, she nearly did herself. But the question she most wished to ask — to receive affirmation on — built inside her until Aggie broke the peace that had grown between them.

"She became angry? Bitter?" Aggie swallowed hard. "Unkind?"

"I remember his calls, Mibs. She was truly brutal toward him. Some of the things she said — the way she wouldn't acknowledge him. The way she tried to drive him away...." A low chuckle rumbled from his chest. "Then again, if I know Chad, he probably annoyed her — tried to mess up her plans. You know how she loves her plans."

"Yeah. I do, too. God obviously didn't. He kicked them out to the curb."

Aggie watched as his Adam's apple bobbed once, twice, and once more just for good measure, it seemed. He spoke with pain in his eyes and thickening his voice. "Just the birth one, Mibs. I don't know why. But everything isn't lost because you had the baby early and in a hospital. It's just geography and chronology. It's not a reflection of your worth as a person."

She wanted to protest. Such an idea sounded ludicrous. But the more she pondered Luke's words, the more they pierced her heart. "I...." She closed her eyes. "It's not just that. Christmas. School." Eyes flew open again. "And we won't even talk about my training plans for Ronnie. That boy...."

The last thing she expected was a chuckle at that. Luke hadn't been happy with the way she let their son walk all over her, and Aggie knew it. *He just does it before I can stop him sometimes. I turn around and* bam! *He's done it again.*

"Mibs, I've got a confession of my own."

"You? About what?"

"Ronnie." She watched in fascinated amazement as Luke struggled — not to find the right words, but to make himself say them. "I've blamed you for his behavior. I tried not to, but I doubt I hid it very well."

A small shake of her head — it's all Aggie could manage.

He kissed her again. Aggie fought against the growing cramping in her belly and jumped at the "Tsk-tsk" of the night nurse, but Luke didn't even pause. He let the kiss linger as long as he liked before turning to greet the man. "I don't think I know you. I'm—"

"I'm betting on Luke." The nurse stuck out his hand and flashed a grin at her. "She doesn't seem like the kind of woman to be making out with some other man just days after giving birth." His eyes dropped to Aggie again. "How are the contractions?"

"How—"

"Great way to get those after pains doing their job." He backed away. "I'll come back in a bit. You've got…." The man checked the clock. "Twenty minutes. Then I'm back to check your fundus again and do some vitals. Gotta make sure you can leave here on Friday."

The words choked her. Leave the hospital without her baby—inconceivable. As her mind whirled with possibilities, Luke laced his fingers in hers and pulled them close to her chest. "I tried to hide it. For what it's worth, I tried. But, um, it wasn't your fault."

Aggie listened in fascinated horror as he told of Ronnie's tantrum, the boy's insistence that "mommy would let him" do it, and then Luke walking away *without* following through on the promised spanking. "You didn't—"

"He just said he was tired, I tucked him in, and downstairs I went." A slow smile formed. "Of course, I was anxious to see someone, but…."

"Don't you keep blaming me, Ezekiel Lucas Stephen Sullivan."

Luke brushed his lips across her knuckles. "I wish you could have seen Laird and Vannie. They had to tell me what I'd done. I went back up, but the kid was out—no chance he was faking it—totally out."

"Will you give them to him tomorrow?" Aggie prayed he'd say no. It seemed wrong, but sometimes Luke had different ideas on these things.

"If he mentions it or acts like he remembers it if someone else does. Otherwise, no. It was my mistake. And well, we let him get this way. But it has to change. I think we need to make him our

356

papoose for a while—give him some good old-fashioned tethering."

Exhaustion washed over her just thinking of it, but Luke preempted her groan. "I'll probably start taking him to the house with me. Maybe him and one of the older kids for when I'm doing something I need extra eyes to help with."

"I thought you put the house on the market—maybe had a buyer." It galled him to tell her. She could see the answer in his eyes. The deal—if it had ever gone that far—had fallen through. "Well, there's one good thing about not selling."

"What's that?" Luke's eyes drifted closed as he spoke.

"We won't lose all the work you already did. We'll just pick it up and go. And Ronnie will get some Daddy time."

Without opening his eyes, Luke dropped the bomb she'd been waiting for. "Yeah, but instead of you getting a break when I get home, you're going to have to take over with him, or he'll learn to play you and obey me—not a wise combo."

"It'll only be for a few weeks." Aggie spoke with more confidence than she felt.

"Perhaps."

It killed her to say it. The words—she ripped them from her own heart and forced them through her lips before she could stop herself. "You should go home. The kids will be up at o'dark thirty for stockings."

"But this is the most natural we've felt in weeks. I need *this*, too."

Her heart cried out. *I do, too! You have no idea!* But despite the ache in her heart at the idea, she nudged him. "I know… but you'll be praying for me all the way home. I know you. And I *need* those prayers right now, Luke. I can't pray myself."

Luke kissed her cheek and stood. "I don't think you could have said anything else to make me go." He reached for her tote bag of journals and books. Pulling out her Bible, he laid it beside her. "Just open up to a Psalm and read it. I'll ask the Lord to turn it into a prayer from your heart."

She ached to protest. Every bit of her resisted, but Aggie nodded. "I'll do it for you."

Though he didn't say it, Aggie saw Luke's response in his eyes. *I'd rather you do it for the Lord.*

The moment he stepped through the door—after another five minutes of whispered assurances of his love and half a dozen more kisses, of course—Aggie closed her eyes and sighed. *I wish I could, Luke. Why is there such resistance?*

An hour later, after a shower and a few restless tosses and turns, Aggie pulled out the stocking, ignored the clock insisting that Christmas was still fifteen minutes away, and pulled out the first item—an envelope. On the front, her name. *Mibs.* Without hesitation, she unfolded the flap and slipped the letter from the envelope. Luke didn't write many notes, but when he did....

Mibs,

The name seems inadequate up there. It feels like there should be a salutation of endearment, but none fit. A man wants his wife to know how he feels about her, but sometimes the only way he can show her is in ways that no one else but her would understand.

Do you remember the night I told you about "mibs"? You were having a rough night and got upset with me. Did I ever tell you that I almost told you how I felt right then?

You didn't know about mibs being clay marbles—targets in a game. But you did draw the connection to the Lord being your Potter. Aggie, I love you enough to tell you that right now you are the clay telling the Potter what kind of marble you want to be.

Please try to "be still" before the Lord. He can work through this. It will take time, though. You didn't become weary overnight. Healing comes with rest. How better to rest in the Lord than to "be still" and trust that He can carry you through anything—even times of doubt. Thomas doubted. But Jesus just saw him and immediately said to prove to himself that Jesus was <u>his</u> Jesus. Only after Thomas' faith was restored, so to speak, did Jesus give him any kind of rebuke.

Allow yourself that time, Mibs. Allow the Lord to mold you where He wants you to go. In the meantime, we love you. All of us. The children, our parents, our extended family, our church family, me. I never can find the words to tell you how I love you. And the Lord— combine all our love and it's nothing compared to that of the Lord.

Hold fast to that for now. Be still. Let the Lord revive you.

All my love,
Luke

Aggie wept.

Chapter Twenty-Five

Wednesday, December 31ˢᵗ

Heart swelling with happiness and pride, Luke scrambled around to Aggie's door and opened it for her. He tried to get back to Lania's side to pull her out, but Laird had managed to bolt out the door, down the steps, and across the yard before he could help Aggie step from the vehicle. "I've got her, Uncle Luke."

"Thanks." Luke cleared his throat and tried again. "Sorry. Frog. Thank you — really."

The boy just gave him a strange smile and nodded. "Sure."

Aggie reached for her purse and the diaper bag, but Luke urged her forward. "I'll get them. You'd better go protect Lania from death by loving smothering."

Even as he spoke, Luke winced. "That came out wrong."

Then it happened. He hadn't felt it in over a month, but Aggie stepped close, kissed his cheek, and whispered, "I know what you mean. I told Vannie before we left to appropriate the baby the minute Laird got in."

You put me first — no…. Luke pulled her close and held her as his mind revised the thought. *You put us first. You haven't done that since we got back from the farm.*

"Mary told me to tell you."

Luke jerked his head up. "Mary? Nurse Mary? I haven't seen

359

her all week!"

"She was off for Christmas, but she came back this morning." Aggie shivered, but something in her eyes told him she wouldn't go inside until she'd spoken to him. Luke didn't bother trying to push her. "She told me to tell you that I prayed over Lania today as I dressed her. She knew you'd want to know. I didn't even think about it."

"Oh, Mibs."

Aggie shivered again. "Okay, I'm officially cold. C'mon."

They'd hardly made it inside when the first tears reached their ears. Kenzie started it. Cari and Lorna followed. Ian's lip quivered as his eyes roamed back and forth between the baby and the trio of weeping girls. Vannie—she just stood there, babe in arms, and rolled her eyes.

"They're convinced we have the wrong baby."

Cari found her voice first. "She's *yellow!*" She threw an accusatory look at Luke. "You *told* me that there are no yellow people! You *lied!*"

Aggie snickered. "What? Yellow people?"

Luke groaned and muttered, "They were having trouble with the lines from 'Jesus Loves the Little Children.' I tried to explain that it was exaggerated but...."

Aggie took baby Lania and carried her to the couch. Like a row of ducklings, the little girls followed. Ronnie and Ian crept close as well. The others just stood back a bit and watched with amused expressions on their faces. She stroked Lania's tiny hand and smiled up at the others. "Why did Lania have to stay in the hospital so long?"

Cari piped up first—shocker. "Because she drank stuff that went down the wrong way and messed up her liver."

Despite all efforts, Luke had to choke back a chortle. *She would get it exactly right and all wrong at the same time.*

"Well, that's mostly right. She did have stuff in her lungs, but that was fine in just a few days. No, she stayed this week because her liver couldn't work properly. She had something called jaundice."

This time, Lorna spoke up. "That was in Vannie's movie. Jaundice and Jaundice. It was important."

No one could keep their amusement quiet this time. Vannie

360

tried to explain. "That's *Jarn*dyce and Jarndyce. Not Jaundice. But yeah, I get how you mixed them up. They sound a lot alike."

Luke decided to step in before the conversation got any more derailed. *I can see the letters to Grandma Millie.* "*Lania was in a movie about a bad disease that took years to recover from. It's called Jaundice and Jaundice and people go broke waiting to heal from it.*"

"Okay. Well, the jaundice is what makes her look a little yellow. It's just the liver doing it. She's much better now, and in a week or two, she'll be her usual pink little self." The moment he said it, Luke regretted the choice of words. "I think using any color to describe skin should be banned. It never comes out right unless you have skin that matches chocolate or coffee!"

Fortunately, the children laughed. They laughed; Lania squirmed. And the baby's crying began. Ronnie took one look at the wailing infant and insisted she return to the hospital until they "fixed" her. "She still sick."

"Babies cry, Ronnie." Aggie pulled their son over to the couch where her pillow and a throw blanket waited to keep her warm and comfortable. "You know, when you were born, we thought you'd *never* stop crying. The doctor said, 'He has a healthy set of lungs!'"

"But healthy is good!"

"It is. And some people think that crying helps strengthen a baby's lungs…."

Luke's heart constricted—with the ache of love and utter contentedness—at the sight of his wife teaching their son as she always had. *That bit of normalcy is such a relief.*

Bleary-eyed and chest threatening to explode with excess milk, Aggie strained to see the face associated with the finger poking her arm. "Ian?"

"Vannie wants to know if you're awake."

She blinked, and her vision began to clear as she stared at him. "Um, you woke me up to find out if I'm awake?"

With a grin that half-blinded her groggy mind, Ian nodded. "Yep! I'll tell her."

Ian dashed for the door, but Aggie rolled over and

discovered Luke gone in time to stop him. "Hey, where's Luke?"

"He went somewhere."

A glance at the Moses basket showed a sleeping Lania—for the first time in hours. *And he woke me to find out if I'm awake. I think I get where postpartum psychosis begins.*

Thundering feet on the stairs—had to be Laird. But when Vannie peered around the door, Aggie mentally resigned from her fictional position as president of the non-existent Society of Prescient Mothers. "I give up. I've lost my touch."

"Huh? I wondered if you wanted breakfast while I'm making it—French toast and scrambled eggs?"

"Perfect. I'll take both." She hesitated, wondering if mentioning anything was cruel or not, but the idea of more sleep destroyed by inquisitive sons just trying to "help" decided for her. "Um, Vannie?"

"Yeah?" Vannie stepped into the room and stood on tiptoe to see Lania. "She sure looks better than the other day!"

Can't forget to lay her in the sun when she wakes. Distraction nearly killed her resolve. A yawn reignited it. "Next time? Send someone up who understands why you're asking if I'm awake or not, okay?"

"Wha— I don't get it."

"Ian did his job well. He poked my arm and asked me directly if I was awake." At Vannie's groan, she nodded. "Yeah. I was by then."

"I'm sorry, Aunt Aggie. Really...."

Time for some fast backtracking. "I'm not upset. I just know that I'll be exhausted if I can't sleep when she does. I don't need any more temptation to crankiness right now."

"If it helps at all, I have the prime rib ready to go in the oven at four, and the rolls are going in the second it comes out. Ellie is cutting up potatoes for mashed potatoes." Fingers ticked off items one by one. "I need to figure out if we're doing green beans or broccoli—got a preference?"

"Go for the green beans. Sometimes broccoli irritates babies." Aggie swallowed hard and tried to steady herself before asking, "Why the big meal?"

A wide grin flashed before Vannie disappeared. Her voice rang out across the hall and down the stairs. "Christmas dinner!

It's finally here."

Nooooo.... Guilt-poisoned knives stabbed her heart, but nothing sounded less appealing than *Christmas* when all she could think of was sleep. *At the hospital, I just wanted out of such a mind-numbing place. It's sounding pretty good right now.*

More guilt piled on as Ian appeared by her side a minute later. "I'm sorry I woke you up. I was misunderstood." With that, he bolted.

Aggie stared at the empty doorway and allowed herself the luxury of rolling her eyes. *Think you added an extraneous word there, bud. Still, you did use misunderstood correctly. Woo. Hoo.*

Food arrived before she'd had a chance to brush her hair or wash her face. Aggie tried to thank Vannie and send her on her way, but Vannie wouldn't hear of it. "You need to eat. Who cares about your hair? You got your man." She tossed Aggie a saucy grin before adding, "Now eat."

The words came as if she'd engaged auto-pilot before crawling from bed. "Someone once pointed out that 'getting' a man was the easy part. 'Keeping him' interested is harder—lasts longer, and he sees you at your worst instead of your best once you've 'got' him."

What Vannie said, Aggie never heard. The significance of her words struck home and bored into her heart. *Luke sure has gotten the worst of you lately.* Her heart ordered her to pray. Her mind refused. No matter what she did, resistance welled up and prevented any chance—any *hope*—of surrender. A new idea struck her, and in a moment of desperation, Aggie snatched up her phone.

"What are you doing?"

"Just sending Libby Mom a text message. You'd better get down there before the eggs get cold." Aggie gave Vannie the most genuine smile she could manufacture with her thoughts elsewhere, and tapped out her message.

It took less than three minutes for Libby to call. "I'm on my way."

"Mo—"

"No, Aggie. We need to talk. See you soon." The slightest pause filled the air with silence before Libby spoke again. "Do you need anything? Any after baby cravings? My Olivia had most of her cravings *after* birth."

With reassurances that she was fine, Aggie disconnected the call and jumped from bed. Lania still slept, something that should have proven to Aggie that miracles *do* still occur. Shower, clean hair, clean clothes—nothing smelling like sour milk—she emerged from the bathroom feeling almost as refreshed as she would have with adequate sleep. *It won't last, of course.*

Another thought hit her, and Aggie sucked in air to replace that which had been knocked from her. *It's like every single negative thought breeds twenty more.*

Lania wailed. *And there's proof. I'm exhausted just* thinking *about nursing her. Again. And going down for another bottle.* Again.

"C'mon, little girlie. Let's try to convince you to get your milk from me. This bottle thing is the pits."

A voice startled her just as the baby latched on—inadequately, of course. "I imagine it feels that way."

Aggie responded with a half-smothered cry and tears that infuriated and embarrassed her. "Oh, Lani...ah. You have to try."

"I think she needs not to have people startle her mommy." Libby offered an apologetic smile. "Sorry. I know better."

As much as part of her tried to snap about the pain she already endured at every feeding, Aggie's more rational side stopped—just in time. "I just wish she could latch properly. Going through all this pain just to give her half an ounce at best before switching to the bottle stinks."

"That's why you're still up here! It's much easier to get them to concentrate when they aren't overstimulated."

And because I wasn't sleeping down there when Ian decided to wake me up.

Libby's voice edged its way into her thoughts. "—got your text, I decided it was time to say something. Up here, we'll have some privacy."

Uuuuhhh oooohhhh.... How to answer that—no clue. Aggie fumbled and stumbled and finally just nodded. "Adult conversation is always a blessing."

"Your text, Aggie...."

"I thought you'd understand." Oh, how she regretted the defensive, almost petulant way she spat out the words.

Nothing could have prepared her for the way Libby laughed.

"Goodness! I was right. You are 'channeling your inner Jonah.'"

"What?" She blinked and gave up all pretense of trying to nurse a baby who refused even to attempt it again. Diaper, re-swaddling, hat adjusted. Aggie adjusted her shirt and started for the stairs, but Libby stopped her. "I'll get the bottle. We need to talk where the children won't hear."

That's kind of why I was going down there. I don't think I want to hear it. A crash downstairs gave her another excuse. "And I probably—"

"Should let me handle it? Yes, you should. Make that fierce little princess try again. I'll get the bottle." She pointed to the tray of food. "Do you want any of that reheated?"

"I'd love it, but it's a waste of time. I hardly ever get a hot meal anymore." A look in Libby's eye—how she guessed what it meant, she couldn't imagine—prompted her to add, "And I *am* grateful that I have food. Not every mother in the world does. I get that."

Libby came and took wailing Lania from her and tried to soothe the baby. "You need to eat. I'll go get the bottle."

Protests, a dozen or more, welled up in her, but Aggie took one look at the cooling food and nodded. "Thanks."

Just as she stepped through the door, Libby added, "You know, you're not alone in this, Aggie. We're all here for you. You just have to do what you did today—*ask*."

Because that doesn't feel ridiculous at my age. But Aggie only nodded. "I'm trying."

Her cellphone rang two minutes after she took her first bite—her mother. Several choice words—a couple bordering on the edge of inappropriate epithets—filled her mind, but the sound of her mother's voice is all it took to change the direction of Aggie's thoughts. "Mom! How are you?"

"Better for hearing your voice."

"Me, too! I just thought that myself! Wish you could be here. Vannie made the best French toast for breakfast. Man, she's getting good! Oh, and she is cooking our belated Christmas dinner. Vannie! It sounds like she's got everything under control!"

Martha sent her love, promised to call the next day, but refused to talk any longer. "You need your food. I just wanted to hear your voice before I take my walk."

"Walk?"

"I walk every day now. It's supposed to help strengthen me and my heart. Every day I walk one house further. I'm almost getting all the way around the block before I turn around." She giggled. "Do you know, I nearly had your father talked into a trip there? Ornery man remembered my doctor's appointment on Monday. A gal can try, right?"

Only her mother would call herself a girl at sixty-four. "Call back when you can. I want to talk, but every time I get a minute, I can't remember what I wanted to do."

"Well, you've had a rough month. Time for a fresh, new year." Martha sighed. "I'll keep praying for you, though. I remember those sleepless nights. It messed up my thinking and everything." Her voice dropped a little. "I shouldn't tell you this, but one night I handed you to your father and said, 'Take her. She's yours. I quit.'"

"Cried a lot, did I?" Aggie grinned at the mental image of her mother handing her over with unceremonious abandon.

Martha snickered. "Your father called it 'singing' whenever you girls cried as babies. He'd say, 'Oh, dear. Your mother doesn't enjoy your serenades, but you can sing to me anytime.'"

It sounded so like her father that Aggie's heart squeezed until she almost cried out. In an attempt to disguise the ever-increasing *need* to see her parents, Aggie opted for a weak joke. "Well, I think I take after you on this one. Lania, especially—she sounds pathetic when she cries. Ronnie just sounded mad and demanding. She breaks your heart."

"You know, I always thought it was why you had such a tendency to sing—even as a little thing. Do you remember 'Doggie in the Window'? You sang that until we heard it in our sleep. Sing to Lania. She'll remember it from the womb and it'll soothe her. You watch and see."

Aggie promised, but even as she tossed the phone on the bed, her conscience protested. "She won't recognize my singing, Mom. I didn't sing."

"Well, you can now."

For the second time in the space of half an hour, Libby startled her. "Oh! Hi."

"Mom was just saying...." Explaining didn't seem worth the

effort. "Anyway, she's doing better—taking walks around the block and everything."

As Lania drank in short, slow bursts, Libby listened to Aggie's disjointed rambles. Nothing made much sense, but Aggie didn't care. If she could only keep Libby talking.

"Aggie?"

She sighed out a disinterested, "Hmmm…?"

"You asked me to pray for you—for the Lord to soften your heart."

"Yeah."

Libby rotated Lania in her arms as if nursing the baby and kept feeding her as she continued. "I've heard and overheard just enough about where you are spiritually to say this with enough confidence, not to mention a lot of love."

"I can't take—"

"Another day without the Lord? Good. And if you were going to say anything else, just don't. You need to listen to me." Libby waited for Aggie's nod before she continued. "You're throwing a temper tantrum, Aggie. Every word I hear you, your children, or my son say about where you are spiritually screams 'Jonah!' to me." A weak smile began to form but morphed into a grimace instead. "Okay, you didn't get the birth you think you deserve. Jonah wanted the people of Nineveh to get what they deserved. And he pouted when it didn't happen. It ate away at him just as that worm ate the shade vine the Lord grew for him."

"I always kind of understood Jonah on the plant," Aggie admitted. "I mean, mercy to the Ninevites, of course, he should have been thrilled! I don't get his issues there. But, the plant… the Lord gives him this plant *to comfort him* and then just takes it away again. It seems cruel. I'm sure it means something, but I always just thought it was mean."

As much as Aggie expected Libby to blast her for blaspheming, it didn't happen. Libby sat there, fed the baby, and waited for Aggie to finish. Every word she spoke became more and more uncomfortable until Aggie began chewing her inner cheek to stop herself from lashing out. *What is wrong with you? Just leave me alone. I just wanted you to pray. I didn't ask for a lecture.*

"Aggie?"

Impatience welled up in her until Aggie lost all semblance of self-control. "Okay, just let me have it. I don't want to answer a bunch of questions. I'm *weary*." Her eyes widened as she heard her words reverberate around the room. "Oh, Ma. I'm sorry. I don't know what's wrong with me!"

Libby settled Lania's belly over her palm and began rubbing the baby's back. "I learned years ago that when I'm out of sorts with the Lord, I'm out of sorts with *everyone*."

"I can't imagine *you* ever out of sorts with God." Aggie stared at her plate of unappetizing, dry scrambled eggs.

"Well… let's see. Skipping all the times before I married, there was the miscarriage. I was bitter at the Lord over that one — until my husband reminded me that the Lord gives and takes away."

Well, if platitudes like that worked for me, I'd be set. It's all anyone ever says anymore.

"—then I became bitter at my husband, instead. Of course, when Stephen died, I was out of sorts with the Lord once the deep grief hit." Her smile faltered for a moment. "And I threw a whopper of a tantrum when my son came home from a job and couldn't stop talking about 'Aggie.' I suspected, right then, that this Aggie person had crushed my dreams of having a certain young lady at church for a daughter-in-law." Libby moved to her side. "In every case, the Lord knew best. Johanna would have been all wrong for Luke. I saw that the first time I met you."

"But losing your baby and your husband. How did you see those were best? They don't seem 'best' to me." Though she didn't say it, Aggie couldn't help but think, *I sure don't see how Allie's death was 'best' for anyone.*

Libby settled Lania in Aggie's arms before inching herself onto the bed beside them and putting her arms around Aggie. "I just learned that they were. I'll know why or how someday, perhaps. But I know they were now. And that's what matters."

"I'm glad that you're at peace with it, Libby. I am." Aggie closed her eyes. "But—"

"No, Aggie. No more buts. You know what's right. You just need to stop running from it. You need to pray."

Anger welled up and spewed from her lips in a matter of seconds. "No! No. I'm *done* being told that if I just pray or sing everything will be all right. No one understands that I *can't*.

Everyone acts like I haven't tried or something. Well I *have,* and it refuses to come. Maybe I'm like Pharaoh or something. Maybe the Lord hardened *my* heart. I don't know. But I *can't.*"

"I think," Libby said with a gentleness Aggie hadn't expected. "I think if you just keep trying—saying whatever comes to mind, instead of trying to have a 'prayer session', you'll discover that you eventually begin praying." She pulled Aggie's head to her shoulder and held her close. "When I couldn't pray, one of the prayers I prayed was just that. 'I can't pray, God. I just can't. I want to pray. I can't. I want to yell and scream. That I can do. But I can't pray.'" Libby's voice dropped to a whisper. "Aggie, I couldn't even address the Lord as 'Father' or 'Lord.' God was about all I could choke out. But those fumbled prayers eventually soaked through my dry, cracked heart. And then all the things I needed to say poured out."

Aggie had to remind herself not to squeeze Lania as she sat there, heart constricting, pain welling up until she didn't think she could take another moment. She had to ask—*ached* to do it. But Aggie could barely choke out a whispered, "Did it help?"

"Bit by bit, my Aggie. Bit by bit."

What had been a table loaded with the best food she'd ever cooked now resembled the carnage after battle. Vannie stared at the results and tried not to cry over the coming cleanup. *How does Aunt Aggie do it all? It's crazy.*

Ellie spoke up as the last fork hit the plate with a certain finality. "I can't believe Vannie cooked all that—and it was *good!*" A few snickers erupted as Ellie's face screwed up into a picture of embarrassed confusion. "That came out wrong."

"Thanks, Ellie. You helped."

"Chopping up potatoes and steaming green beans isn't exactly difficult. Ian could do it if necessary."

Luke choked on his bubbling cider. "Um, I don't care for minced phalanges in my potatoes, but otherwise, sure."

"I wouldn't put Angie in potatoes! Ew!" Ian shuddered and then grew pensive. He turned to Vannie and whispered in a half-hiss, "Who's Angie?"

Before Vannie could respond, Laird choked out, "Fingers, Ian. He was joking about you chopping off part of your fingers while cutting the potatoes." Laughter erupted around the table.

"Oh. Why would I do that?"

All hope of *not* laughing at Ian fizzled with that one question. Vannie tried to give him a reassuring smile, remembering similar moments with her parents as a young child, but she suspected it came off as more of a smirk. "Accident." The word exploded from her before she took a sip of her water.

Blank—his face couldn't have been more devoid of expression. With a shrug, he asked, "Does this mean presents?"

The clamor began. Vannie glanced at her aunt and uncle, and her heart constricted at the sight of Aggie's sigh. *Please don't say no. They've all worked so hard.*

"Sounds perfect to me." Aggie stood and shifted Lania to her other arm. "You know, for a baby at not quite five pounds, I can't imagine *how* she wears out my arms like she does."

Laird piped up with one of his cheerful, useful, ill-timed suggestions. "Next time, you should wear a five pound wrist weight for the last month." He swallowed at Vannie's glare and rushed to add, "Or two. Two might be better."

Who says there's going to be a next time? Did you think of that, Laird? Seriously? She doesn't need a reminder of how messed up this pregnancy was.

Aggie fled the table. Heart pounding and dread filling her, Vannie glanced at Luke. Despair—she'd never seen it in him, but it etched deep lines in his face. *I've heard of people aging overnight, but that was instantaneous. I swear he looks ten years older. Man, Lord, I don't know what's going on, but can You fix it?*

Before she could speak, Luke glanced around the room, and pointed to Laird, Tavish, and Kenzie. "You three clear the table and put the dishes in the dishwasher." He pointed to Cari, Lorna, and Ian. "You three wipe the table and benches and sweep the floor. We'll be right back."

"What I do?" Ronnie stared up at him—eagerness written in his eyes and dripping from his tongue.

When Luke hesitated, Vannie held out her hand. "Why don't you come help Ellie and me put away the leftov—?"

"They've got that, Vannie, but thank you. You two cooked a fine meal. You can just rest."

"We'll start the hot chocolate then." Her eyes pleaded with him. "That's always fun."

Luke's hesitation unnerved her, but he nodded just as he bolted from the room. Vannie grabbed Laird's arm and whispered, "Pray. I don't know how much more of this Uncle Luke can take. He's trying to be strong. I see it, but…."

"But we're all falling apart here!" Laird's lip quivered. He whirled in place and went to work. "It's like she died or something."

Oh, don't say that. She's just struggling. Right, Lord?

Before Vannie could pull out the cups, Luke appeared, almost beaming, and sent her to put her feet up. "I've got this." He turned to Ronnie. "Okay, how many cups do you think we need?"

"But—"

Aggie's voice behind her sent Vannie's heart on a sprint that her body couldn't keep up with. "Your uncle told you to rest. Now get out of here. Maybe you can hang the stocking for Lania that you keep trying to hide from me."

"Wha—?" She glanced at Luke, back to Aggie, and shrugged. *I don't know what happened, there, but I'm glad it did.*

Hanging the stocking—a twenty-second job. But as she turned around, Vannie found Luke watching her. "She went to write down the idea in her journal. She's joking about mommy brain and needing to be better prepared for whatever happens next time."

Vannie blinked. "Next time?" The grin came from out of nowhere. She hadn't liked the idea of *more* on her aunt's plate, but this… this sounded so blessedly *normal.* "Really?"

Luke disappeared through the doorway with only a grin and a finger pointing at his favorite chair. The silent order, obvious. *Rest.*

A hand on her shoulder just seconds later squeezed a screech from her lips. "Wha—oh!"

Aggie settled in her favorite spot, Lania fussing and squirming as she did. "Sorry. I just wanted to thank you for that. Luke said you hardly sat down all day."

"I was afraid I'd forget something." Admiration, awe, and a healthy dose of envy filled her voice as Vannie added, "I don't know how you do it!"

"If you'll remember, I *didn't* when I first moved in. We ate a lot of frozen burritos, pizza, and mac & cheese. Now I cook, but you guys do so much of the prep work for me." Aggie rubbed the baby's back, readjusted her even, but nothing worked. "I don't know how to make her content."

"I can hold her." Vannie held out eager arms to take the baby and almost squealed when Aggie nodded.

She waited until Vannie settled herself again before adding, "And thank you for my Christmas present. It is *exactly* what I needed."

A quick glance at the tree showed Vannie's present, front and center, as it had been for over a week. "I—"

"I don't know what you have under that tree, Vannie, but I couldn't have handled a meal like that today. And the family should have a 'real' Christmas. You made that happen."

Vannie's reply was drowned out in the flood of children. "Uncle Luke says it's good enough for tonight!" Cari grinned as she flung herself at Aggie. "Are you excited?"

"I am. For *you* especially."

The words—no one would doubt they were genuine. But in them Vannie heard weariness. *This is too much for her so soon. We should have waited.* Ellie flew past and bolted up the stairs. The faint sigh that Aggie struggled to suppress filled Vannie's ears and heart. *She's too tired for this. It'll just make everything worse. I wonder....*

Ronnie appeared with the first present—Vannie's for Aggie. "This one is yours." He pointed to the tag. "See? That letter is A. And Mommy starts with A."

When the others laughed and Ronnie began to pout, Vannie cried out to the Lord for a heavenly intervention. *If she gives in, he'll just be worse. If she stops him, it'll ruin everything.*

But Aggie shifted Cari over just enough to make room for Ronnie. She murmured something in the boy's ear. His protest filled the living room, just as Vannie had predicted, but Aggie's next word—a simple, "Stop!" spoken sharply but quietly— plunged the room into total silence. Eyes closed, heart full of prayers for intercession, Vannie waited. The other children stared. Ronnie buried his face in Aggie's neck. "Sorry."

Whoa, what happened there? She relived the days since Aggie had returned home—the first few without Lania—and something clicked. *She's kept him close — she and Uncle Luke. They did that with Cari, too, way back when. What did Gramby say? "Keep them close so you can stop them before they have the satisfaction of sinning." Guess it works.*

Luke seated himself beside Aggie and pulled Ronnie up on one knee. "I heard that, son. Well done." His eyes swept the room. "Who says we open *presents?!*"

The exhaustion that exuded from every pore on Aggie's face told Luke to wrap up the festivities as quickly as possible. Rest— imperative. But just as he opened his mouth to suggest it was time for bed, Aggie nudged him and rested her head on his shoulder. "Would you read Matthew and Luke? I missed it on Christmas Eve."

You want *me to read the Bible?* Heart swelling, thanksgiving forming on his lips, Luke nodded. "We missed you, too."

Ellie stood behind the chair, rocking a squirmy, fussy Lania in her arms in an attempt to quiet her, and with those delightful infant sounds as accompaniment, Luke began reading. With each section, from Zacharias in the temple to Jesus' trek to the temple as a boy, Aggie grew heavier against him, until he felt certain she'd fallen asleep. But as he read the final words, Aggie sighed. "Such an encouragement."

His heart jumped into his throat. "What is?"

"That even *Jesus* had to *grow* in wisdom—just like He grew in height and 'favor with God and man.' If God as a human had to *grow* in wisdom, then there's hope He'll grow it in me."

Throat constricting, tears threatening, Luke just held her fast—held her and prayed. "Lord, thank You for Jesus. We often pray our thanks for Your death and resurrection, but today we want to thank You for Your birth." A love-sized lump blocked his throat, making it impossible for him to continue. His heart prayed, but his mouth refused to join him.

Vannie's voice, a whisper that grew stronger with each word, slowly filled the room. "You left everything for us. Without Your birth, we couldn't have hope of eternal life. Thank You."

Laird picked up the prayer, followed by Tavish and Ellie. Kenzie's words let loose the floodgates of emotion that held Luke in its grip. "Thank You that our baby doesn't have to die for us. Sorry Your baby did. I am not just saying that. I'm *really* sor—" The child couldn't continue.

What Lorna and Cari prayed, he never knew. Luke strained to hear Ian, but Ronnie's voice cut in. "I wanna pray." He paused... waiting. "I can't pray. Sorry. But I wanted to."

And that means everything.

Ian just whispered an almost unintelligible, "Thank you, Jesus."

As voices, one by one, filled the room in prayer, Luke prayed for Aggie—hoping, pleading for her to at least attempt to join them. So when she shifted and a strangled sound came from her throat, Luke's hopes rose higher than they had in weeks. A sigh followed. Silence.

Oh, Lord....

But Aggie cleared her throat, and her voice, though not much more than a whisper, filled the room. "In Jesus' name, Amen."

It's something, Lord. I'll take it.

One by one, the children hugged them, thanked them again for gifts, and dragged themselves from the room. Luke watched as Laird and Vannie in particular glanced back two or three times before disappearing with arms full of gifts. Ronnie dashed back down, grabbed the sweatshirt Kenzie had made him, and flung himself into Luke's arms. "Can you help?"

"I'll take you guys up. C'mon." He gave Aggie a quick glance to see she was all right, but the sight of her rocking a sleeping Lania in the Moses basket told him he had a few minutes before she needed his help.

Prayers with each of the children—questions, answers, reassurances—they wore an already exhausted Luke to a frazzle. He ached to climb into bed and let the day dissolve into blissful oblivion. *How can such a wonderful day be so terrible? She's worn out. I'm worn out. I can't even remember what my gifts were—to the kids or* from *them. Our* kids *had to do Christmas for* us *instead of the other way around. That's just wrong. I'm with Mibs on that one, Lord.*

He found Aggie admiring her gifts—the carved book from Laird. Truly a work of art. Luke smiled as she ran her finger over the imperfection he'd pointed out to a disheartened Kenzie. "Would you have noticed the missing petal?"

Aggie yawned and shook her head. "Nope. I still say it's perfect, despite Kenzie's obsession with perfection." She pulled out the sweatshirt with an A—red, no less—painstakingly stitched onto the front. "And I can't see that it's off-center, either. I don't know what that girl's talking about."

Luke saw it, but he agreed that it wouldn't show when being worn. "I never knew she was such a perfectionist. I can't tell you how many times she restitched most of them. Weepy, fiercely determined."

"Sounds like our Lania came by her fierceness honestly." Aggie yawned again and stared at the pile of gifts for her and Lania. "A baby shower for Christmas. It was amazing." Her eyes reached his, and she smiled one of the first, truly genuine smiles she'd given him in weeks. "Thank you."

"I didn't do it, Mibs. That was all them."

They needed sleep, but she seemed inclined to talk. Nothing, not even the deep need for sleep, could tempt him to miss out on the chance to hold her and listen to her ramble about her hopes, dreams, ideas, plans. Those moments—sans the holding, of course—had first drawn his heart to her. *Still do.*

At that moment, Lania stilled. Aggie's grin grew wide. "She's out. *Finally,* she's out."

He snapped off the lights and left only the tree and the angels glowing. This time, he took her corner of the couch and beckoned her closer. "Come sit with me. It's too beautiful not to enjoy one more night."

"And disappear tomorrow." Aggie snuggled in beside him. "Promise me it goes away tomorrow. I need some semblance of normalcy."

"Before you come downstairs, it'll be down. I promise." A contented sigh escaped before he could stop it. At her questioning jab, he smiled down into her sleepy eyes and murmured, "You can't know how good it feels to say that you'll be coming downstairs. We missed you more than I ever imagined it possible to miss someone just twenty or so feet above us."

A creak on the stair interrupted Aggie's response. Vannie stepped out into the room but hung back. "Can I come in?"

"Sure, Vannie. Come sit with us." Aggie's voice, though tired, held a genuine note of welcome that filled him with joy and discouragement at the same time.

She settled in Luke's favorite chair, sitting close to the edge, as if ready to bolt. "I was just lying upstairs thinking about today, and you know what?"

"Hmmm?" Now Aggie sounded ready to fall asleep.

"This was the best Christmas ever. I mean, we didn't even do all the stuff we always do—like the snow nativity. I would have said we couldn't *have* Christmas without a snow Jesus, but we did." Luke's heart constricted as she gave Aggie a searching glance before adding, "You know, we had to rely on each other and Jesus in ways we've never had to do before." Her eyes dropped. "It was just so beautiful."

From the corner by the stairs, Ellie's voice rang out. "I was just thinking the same thing. This really is the best Christmas, because it's what Christmas is about—giving up yourself for others. That's what Jesus did, right?"

All of Luke's disappointment in the appearance of the girls disappeared with that line. He urged her to come sit with them. "I know exactly how you feel. We wouldn't have *had* a 'Christmas' without all that you guys did. Aggie could have had Lania much earlier if we hadn't been able to rely on you guys to help keep things like meals and laundry going."

Laird crept in a moment later with Tavish on his heels. "I'm sorry for not doing more, Uncle Luke. I kept trying to stay out of sight so I wouldn't have to do stuff." He ducked his head and muttered another apology.

"Well, I did that, too."

The entire group laughed, and Vannie spoke up first. "Tavish, you always stay hidden, but you *look* for things to do to help. Big difference."

Tavish grinned. "Am I the only one who thinks this was the best Christmas ever?"

Kenzie and the younger twins thundered down the stairs. As

though they didn't see the others, the girls rushed at Aggie and Luke, flinging arms around them. "Thank you for Christmas!" "We forgot!" "I'm sorry!"

Who said what, no one knew, but Kenzie stood and stared at the tree. "It's beautiful, isn't it? This is the best Christmas —"

The entire room erupted in laughter before adding in the worst attempt at unison in the history of mankind, "Ever!"

It took exactly six seconds for the two little guys to scramble downstairs. Ronnie spoke first. "It's morning?"

"Nope." Luke urged his son forward. "You might as well join us. We're having an impromptu gratitude fest."

Aggie stood. "I think this calls for hot chocolate. Who's with me?"

A half-crazed mass exodus stampeded for the kitchen. Luke stood but couldn't bring himself to move any farther. His heart listened to her joking, laughing, teasing. *She's almost back, Lord. Heal her heart. Please!*

"Can we use our new cups that Gramby got us?" Kenzie's voice reached Luke and the excitement in it prompted him to pull out his phone. NOTE TO GRAMBY: PERSONALIZED CUPS ARE A HIT.

Luke moved the Moses basket off the coffee table to make room for mugs of hot chocolate. Just as he started to set it on the dining table, a loud crash, followed by half a dozen indignant cries of, "Kenzie!" filled the downstairs. Aggie stepped from the kitchen, shoulder shaking with either repressed laughter or tears. Luke couldn't tell which.

Lania wailed.

Aggie lifted the baby from the bed, kissed the top of her head, passed her to Luke, and walked away. Around the stairs, down the hall — Luke heard the door to the guest room open and his heart plummeted to his feet. *Lord, no....*

A sniffle behind him. Luke turned to see their children clustered in the kitchen doorway — Laird and Tavish shell-shocked. The girls weeping. Vannie's face ripped a new hole in his heart. *She understands so much more than we give her credit for. She'll be suffering heartaches sooner than I'll be ready to handle.*

As he opened his mouth to reassure them that everything would be okay — how, he couldn't say — a sound reached them.

Eyes wide, everyone strained to listen. With each word, it grew stronger.

"—sing unto the Lord, for He has triumphed gloriously...."

With his infant daughter in his arms, and his children swinging from utter dejection to joy, Luke stood in the living room, tears pouring down his face, utter contentment in his heart. *Thank you, Lord.*

Author's Note

People have asked me, "Why did you make Aggie such a whiney, complaining character in this book?" To some, I ruined Aggie's character, taking her from a strong, faith-filled young woman to a teenager exploding with hormonal outbursts and negativity.

My answer probably doesn't satisfy, and it has certainly surprised some, but here it is. Aggie is exactly who she has been all along. Aggie has always whined and complained. She's always been temperamental and emotional. But in the past, her whining was dumped on the Lord and her complaining came through song. And this is why I wrote this book. This is why I showed the raw truth of who Aggie is. Because too often we delude ourselves into believing we've "got this." We think we know how to be a wife, a mother, a husband, a father. We're "solid" on this Christian living thing!

The Lord has a way of stripping those attitudes from us though, doesn't He? And when we're stripped of the things we use to hold us up, if we don't hold onto the One who really does "have this", we expose the real, raw, ugly self we've hidden — usually from ourselves as well. We see that, like Peter, without our eyes *always* fixed firmly on the Lord, we'll sink and drown.

I did not write this book to show how Christians *should* behave. I wrote this book to show what we often hide beneath the surface — to show that we often don't even realize it ourselves. I wrote this in the hopes that my readers would look inward and say, "Wait. Is this me? Am I like this? Am I only a loving, prayerful, praiseful son or daughter of the King when I feel in control, or can anything strip me of the true peace of the Lord?"

This right here is also why I didn't create a neat and tidy ending to this book. Such a complete swing to total repentance and renewal in such a short span of time would be unrealistic. Instead, I showed Aggie taking slow, deliberate steps back to fellowship with the Lord. Repentance is going to create a new, beautiful Aggie who is a richer person — to borrow from Scripture, she'll be a "new creature."

One of the most difficult things for me to write was Luke's realization that when forced to be quiet, when stripped of the busyness that characterized her, when unable to sing herself into a better place and keep going on, when she was alone and on her face before the Lord, she is just as flawed and messed up as the rest of us. You see, I don't think I and many of my readers are the only ones who saw Aggie as a strong young woman wholly dependent on the Lord. I think Luke and Aggie believed it too. He didn't know her anymore, because he'd never seen her *allow* herself to be in such a raw, vulnerable state.

In discussing this with advance readers, I know I left the impression (poor wording on my part) that Aggie was a fake all those years. That's not true. Her faith in the Lord was real. Her love of the Lord — unquestioning. Her dependence on Him and her natural turn to Him in times of trouble? Absolutely. She'd chosen to live her faith in a very real, open, transparent way. It just hadn't been tested. And when it truly was. When she couldn't mask the pain anymore and saw her life spinning out of control again, this time she couldn't hide in busyness and activity. She couldn't hide amidst the chaos of her family. This time she was forced to be "silent" before the Lord. She failed to embrace that. It was one of those refining moments that I think we all have from time to time. She resisted. I think most of us do, too. But poor Luke. I hated to put him through it with her. However, isn't that what our marriage vows are for? We have those reminders of "for better or worse" for a reason, don't we?

Aggie's past right actions were good — they were exercises in right behavior. She taught the children through them. She encouraged her friends. She encouraged my readers. And now her job is to encourage those same children, those same friends, and those same readers that sometimes you fool yourself into thinking that you have achieved some spiritual pedestal. But the Bible says, "Therefore let him who thinks he stands take heed that he does not fall" (I Corinthians 10:12).

Chautona Havig's Books

- <u>Front Window</u> (coming 2016)

<u>Noble Pursuits</u>
<u>Argosy Junction</u>
<u>Discovering Hope</u>
<u>Not a Word</u>
<u>Speak Now</u>
<u>A Bird Died</u>
<u>Thirty Days Hath…</u>
<u>Confessions of a De-cluttering Junkie</u>
<u>Corner Booth</u>
<u>Rockland Chronicles Collection One</u>
(Available only on Kindle: Contains *Noble Pursuits*, *Argosy Junction*, and *Discovering Hope*)

The Agency Files

- <u>Justified Means</u>
- <u>Mismatched</u>
- <u>Effective Immediately</u>
- <u>A Forgotten Truth</u>

The Vintage Wren (A serial novel beginning 2016)

- January (Vol 1.)

Sight Unseen Series

- <u>None So Blind</u>

Christmas Fiction

- <u>Advent</u>
- <u>31 Kisses</u>
- <u>Tarnished Silver</u>
- <u>The Matchmakers of Holly Circle</u>
- <u>Carol and the Belles</u>

* * *

Meddlin' Madeline Mysteries

- Sweet on You (Book1)

* * *

Ballads from the Hearth

- Jack

* * *

Legacy of the Vines

- Deepest Roots of the Heart

* * *

Journey of Dreams Series

- Prairie
- Highlands

* * *

Heart of Warwickshire Series

- Allerednic

* * *

The Annals of Wynnewood

- Shadows & Secrets
- Cloaked in Secrets
- Beneath the Cloak

* * *

Not-So-Fairy Tales

- Princess Paisley
- Everard

* * *

384

Legends of the Vengeance

The First Adventure

Made in the USA
Coppell, TX
07 September 2023

21342564R00213